Arcadia

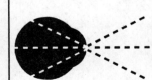

ARCADIA

LAUREN GROFF

THORNDIKE PRESS
A part of Gale, Cengage Learning

GALE
CENGAGE Learning

Detroit • New York • San Francisco • New Haven, Conn • Waterville, Maine • London

GALE
CENGAGE Learning

Thorndike Press® Large Print Basic.
The text of this Large Print edition is unabridged.
Other aspects of the book may vary from the original edition.
Set in 16 pt. Plantin.

LIBRARY OF CONGRESS CATALOGING-IN-PUBLICATION DATA

Groff, Lauren.
Arcadia / by Lauren Groff.
pages ; cm. — (Thorndike Press large print basic)
ISBN 978-1-4104-4861-3 (hardcover) — ISBN 1-4104-4861-4 (hardcover)
1. Communal living—Fiction. 2. Nineteen sixties—Fiction. 3. Coming of age—Fiction. 4. New York (State)—Fiction. 5. Domestic fiction. 6. Large type books. I. Title.
PS3607.R6344A73 2012b
813'.6—dc22 2012005149

Published in 2012 by arrangement with Voice, an imprint of Hyperion, a division of Buena Vista Books, Inc.

Printed in the United States of America
1 2 3 4 5 6 7 16 15 14 13 12

For Beckett

The women in the river, singing.

This is Bit's first memory, although he hadn't been born when it happened. Still, the road winding through the mountains is clear to him, the rest stop with the yellow flowers that closed under the children's touch. It was dusk when the Caravan saw the river greening around the bend and stopped there for the night. It was a blue spring evening, and cold.

On the bank, trucks and buses and vans circled like bison against the wind, the double-decker Pink Piper at the heart. Handy, their leader, was on the Piper's roof doing sun salutations to the dying day. Naked children darted on the fringes of camp, their skin rough with goosebumps. The men built a bonfire, tuned guitars, started suppers of vegetable stews and pancakes. The women washed clothes and linens in the frigid river, beating wet fabric against the rocks. In the last light, shadows grew from their knees and the current sparked with suds.

Bit's mother, Hannah, unbent to peel a sheet like a membrane from the water's surface. She was all round: cheek, limb, hair in a golden loop of braids. The denim of her overalls was taut at the belly, where Bit was inside, building cell by cell. On the bank, his father, Abe, paused to watch Hannah, her head cocked as she listened to the other women singing, a smile just under her lips.

Later, the smells of supper died beneath the woodsmoke and the fire blazed against the cold. More music: "Froggy Went A-Courtin" in Handy's famous rasp, "Michael, Row the Boat Ashore," "The Sounds of Silence." The laundry dried on the bushes, specters at the edge of sight.

It is impossible that Bit could remember all this: weeks before his birth, three years before Arcadia, 1968 all over the radio, Khe Sanh and the Grenoble Olympics, the Caravan in the middle of a hopscotch across the country, that evening with its blue light and bonfire and sheets ghosting in the dark. But he does. The memory clings to him, told by Arcadia until it became communal, told again and again until the story grew inside him to become Bit's own. Night, fire, music, Abe's back keeping out the cold, Hannah leaning against Abe's toasted front, Bit himself curled within his parents, wrapped in their happiness, happy.

City of the Sun

Bit is already moving when he wakes. It is February, still dark. He is five years old. His father is zipping Bit within his own jacket where it is warmest, and Abe's heart beats a drum against Bit's ear. The boy drowses as they climb down from the Bread Truck, where they live, and over the frosted ground of Ersatz Arcadia. The trucks and buses and lean-tos are black heaps against the night, their home until they can finish Arcadia House in the vague someday.

The gong is calling them to Sunday Morning Meeting, somewhere. A river of people flows in the dark. He smells the bread of his mother, feels the wind carrying the cold from the Great Lake to the north, hears the rustling as the forest wakes. In the air there is excitement and low, loving greetings; there is small snow, the smoke from someone's joint, a woman's voice, indistinct.

When Bit's eyes open again, the world is

softened with first light. The tufts of the hayfield push up from under trampled snow. They are in the Sheep's Meadow and he feels the bodies closer now, massing. Handy's voice rises from behind Bit and up toward all of Arcadia, the seven dozen true believers in the winter morning. Bit twists to see Handy sitting among the maroon curls of the early skunk cabbage at the lip of the forest. He turns back, pressing his cheek against the pulse in his father's neck.

Bit is tiny, a mote of a boy. He is often scooped up, carried. He doesn't mind. From against the comforting strength of adults, he is undetected. He can watch from there, he can listen.

Over Abe's shoulder, far atop the hill, the heaped brick shadow of Arcadia House looms. In the wind, the tarps over the rotted roof suck against the beams and blow out, a beast's panting belly. The half-glassed windows are open mouths, the full-glassed are eyes fixed on Bit. He looks away. Behind Abe sits the old man in his wheelchair, Midge's father, who likes to rocket down the hill at the children, scattering them. The terror washes over Bit again, the loom and creak, the flash of a toothless mouth and the hammer-and-sickle flag as it flaps in passing. The Dartful Codger, Hannah calls the old man, with a twist to her mouth. The Zionist, others call him, because this is what he shouts for after sundown: Zion, milk and honey, land of plenty, a place for his people to rest. One night, listening, Bit said, Doesn't the Dartful Codger know where he is? and Abe looked down at Bit among his wooden toys, bemused, saying, Where *is* he? and Bit said, *Arcadia,* meaning the word the way Handy always said it, with his round Buddha face, building the community with smooth sentences until the others can also see the fields bursting with fruits and grains, the sunshine and music, the people taking care of one another in love.

In the cold morning, though, the Dartful Codger is too small and crabbed for terror. He is almost asleep under a plaid blanket Midge has tucked around him. He wears a hunter's cap, the earflaps down. His nose whistles, and steam spurts from it, and Bit thinks of the kettle on the hob. Handy's voice washes over him: *. . . work, as in pleasure, variety is evidently the desire of nature . . .* words too heavy for the soft feet of this morning. As the dawn light sharpens, the Dartful Codger becomes distinct. Veins branch across his nose, shadows gouge his face. He rouses himself, frowns at Bit, shuffles his hands on his lap.

. . . *God,* says Handy, *or the Eternal Spark, is in every human heart, in every piece of this earth. In this rock, in this ice, in this plant, this bird. All deserve our gentleness.*

The old man's face is changing. Astonishment steals over the hoary features. Startled, Bit can't look away. The eyes blink but come to a stop, open. Bit waits for the next puff of smoke from the cragged nose. When it doesn't come, a knot builds in his chest. He lifts his head from Abe's shoulder. A slow purple spreads over the old man's lips; a fog, an ice, grows over his eyeballs. Stillness threads itself through the old man.

At Bit's back, Handy talks of the music tour he is going on in a few days, to spread the word of Arcadia. . . . *be gone for a couple of months, but I have faith in you Free People. I'm your guru, your Teacher, but not your Leader. Because when you've got a good enough Teacher, you're all your own Leaders . . .* and the people around Bit laugh a little, and somewhere little Pooh screams, and Hannah's hand comes from Bit's side and smoothes down his cap, which has come half off, his one ear cold.

Handy says, *Remember the foundations of our community. Say them with me.* The voices rise: *Equality, Love, Work, Openness to the*

Needs of Everyone.

A song boils up, *Sing a song full of the faith that the dark past has taught us,* they sing. Abe shifts under Bit to the rhythm. *Sing a song full of hope that the present has brought us; Facing the rising sun of our new day begun . . .* the song ends.

A silence. An inhale. In the great *Om* that rises from the mass of Free People, startled crows speckle up from Arcadia House roof. The sunrise blooms all over them.

In such perfect dawn, even the old man is beautiful, the blue of his beard under the newly luminous skin of his cheek, the softness in his jaw, the tufts in his ears touched golden. He has been gentled in living light. He has been made good.

When the last voice falls silent, just before Handy's *Thank you, my friends,* Midge puts her hand on her father's shoulder. Then she takes off her glove and presses her bare palm against the old man's cheek. And when Arcadia moves, soul-shakes, hugs, shares its good energy, Midge's voice cuts through the din. Father? she calls out, low. Louder, then: Father?

It is not in the speed with which Hannah grabs Bit and rushes him back home to the Bread Truck, or the fact that Abe stays behind to help Midge. It is not in the special treat, the dried blueberries in the porridge, or Hannah standing, wordless at the window, blowing on her green tea. It is not even what Abe says when he comes in: Karmic energy rejoining the ether, or Natural, the cycle of life, or Everybody dies, Ridley, honey. Abe does his best, but Bit still doesn't understand. He saw the old man turn beautiful. He wonders at the worry on his parents' faces.

The sadness they feel begins to crack open only when Hannah drops the dirty breakfast dishes on the table and bursts into tears. She rushes out over the Quad to the Pink Piper, to the comfort of Marilyn and Astrid, the midwives.

Abe gives Bit a tight smile. He says, Your mama's okay, Little Bit. It's just, this morning struck a deep chord with her because her own papa's not doing so hot right now.

In this Bit smells the small sulfur of a lie. Hannah has not been herself for a while. Bit lets the untruth slowly dissolve away.

Hannah's dad who lives in Louisville? he says. In the fall, the grandparents had visited, a fat man in a porkpie hat, a nervous puff of a woman in all pink. Bit had been squeezed, remarked upon: So tiny, the woman had trilled, I would have said under three, not five years old! There were sideways looks at him, and Hannah saying through gritted teeth: He's not *retarded,* he's *fine,* he's just really *small,* God, Mom. There was a meal that the pink lady wouldn't touch, a handkerchief lifted to the corners of her eyes every few seconds. There was a bad argument, then the fat and the puff went away.

As her parents drove off, Hannah'd had angry tears in her eyes. She'd said, May they rot in their bourgeois capitalist hell. Abe had laughed gently at her, and after a minute, the fierceness fell from Hannah's face. Grudgingly, she had laughed, too.

Abe says now, Yeah, your Louisville granddaddy. He has a wasting disease. Your grandma wants your mother down there, but Hannah won't go. Anyways, we can't spare her.

Because of the Secret, Bit says. Everyone has been whispering about the Secret for a month, since Handy announced his music tour. While Handy is gone, they will finish Arcadia House so they can all move out of Ersatz Arcadia, that loose mishmash of buses and lean-tos, and, at last, live together. They had meant to these three years, ever since they bought the land and found the house, but they were distracted by hunger and hard work. Arcadia House is to be a gift to Handy when he returns.

Abe's eyes crinkle and his lips split to show his strong teeth in the red of his beard. I guess it isn't a secret if even the little guys know, he says.

They play a game of Go Fish until Hannah returns, her face raw but calmer. She tells them that Astrid and Marilyn have been called to the Amish neighbors' for a birthing. For a hello, Hannah rests her cheek in the crook of Abe's neck for a moment and kisses Bit gently on the forehead. Like a sigh into breath, life releases into life. Hannah turns to stoke the woodstove. Abe fixes the drafty chink where he had built the lean-to against the Bread Truck. They eat dinner and Abe plays a tune on the harmonica and when night falls all three curl on the pallet together, and Bit sleeps, a hickory nut within the shell of his parents.

The forest is dark and deep and pushes so heavily on Bit that he must run away from the gnarled trunks, from the groans of the wind in the branches. His mother calls for him to stay in sight, but he doesn't slow. When he comes into the clearing by the Gatehouse, his face smarts with cold.

Titus, pocked and immense, heaves up the

gate. He seems old, older even than Handy, because he was damaged in Vietnam. Bit adores Titus. Titus calls Bit Hop o'My Thumb and can lift him with one palm and will sometimes even smuggle Bit a few goodies from the Outside — pink coconut cake in cellophane or peppermints like bloodshot eyes — despite the ban on sugar and the harm surely done to animals in making the goodies. Bit believes the treats' chemical afterburn is what the world beyond Arcadia must taste like. Titus slips him a throat-thickening butterscotch in a crinkle of yellow paper and winks, and Bit buries his face in his friend's greasy jeans for a moment before he hurries on.

All Arcadia has gathered on the frozen road to say goodbye. Handy sits in lotus on the nose of the Blue Bus with his four blond children: Erik and Leif and Helle and Ike. His main wife, Astrid, tall and white-haired, gazes up at them. She unknots a hemp necklace from her throat and ties it around Handy's neck, kissing him over his third eye. Even above the roar of the engine, the radio belts out a jiggly country song. Handy's other wife, Lila, who wears feathers in her black hair, sits with skinny little Hiero, her other husband. The band hugs those they are leaving behind and lugs their stuff up into the bus, then Handy passes the children down: Ike, inches taller than Bit though a year younger; Helle, froggy as her father; Leif, who is always angry; chubby Erik, who slides to the ground by himself and lands on his knees and tries not to cry.

On the Gatehouse porch, Wells and Caroline argue with flushed faces. Bit's friend Jincy peers from parent to parent. Though the wind makes her curly hair spring in ten directions, her face is pale and still.

From the path comes a sweetness of bells, of voices. Out of nowhere, great broad heads of giants bob in the branches. Bit's gut swirls with loveliness. Onto the road come the Circenses Singers, Hans and Fritz and Summer and Billy-goat, in their white robes, carrying the Adam and Eve puppets. These are new-made creatures, naked and huge with flushed genitals. The Circenses Singers go off on the weekends to protests and rallies, staging dances at concerts, sometimes busking for change. Now the robed people bend and sing under the vast and eerie bodies above them. When they finish, everyone cheers and they pack the great bulbous beasts into the back of a Volkswagen van.

Bye-bye-bye-bye, shouts brown little Dylan from Sweetie Fox's arms. Bit runs to his friend Coltrane, who is poking at an icy puddle with a stick. Cole gives Bit the stick, and Bit pokes, too, then hands the stick to Cole's brother, Dylan, and Dylan waves it around.

Gingery Eden, her pregnant belly enormous, cracks a bottle of pop over the hood of the Blue Bus and rubs her back when she stands. The dazzle of her white teeth under her copper hair makes Bit want to dance.

Handy shouts about how they'll be back before Spring Planting, and the Free People huzzah, and Tarzan hands up a cooler of beer the Motor Pool sold an engine to pay for, and Astrid lays a long kiss on Lila's pretty lips, and Hiero does, too, and slides to the ground, and there are other kisses, the band's chicks and wives smooching up into the windows, and then the engine gets louder and the bus starts to move off toward the County Road. Everyone cheers and some people cry. In Arcadia, people cry all the time. Others do funny dances, laughing.

Helle stumbles after the bus, sobbing for her father. She is always in tears, the big-headed, strange-looking little girl, always screaming. Astrid scoops Helle up, and the girl wails into her mother's chest. The bus's sound softens and filters away. The noises they are left with seem doubly loud in the quiet: the ice that cracks in the branches, the wind like sandpaper across the surface of the snow, the flap of the prayer flags strung across the Gatehouse porch, the squeak of rubber boots on frozen mud.

When Bit turns, everyone is looking at his father.

Abe grins at them, the ones who can't play music, the four dozen left behind. They seem so few. Abe calls loudly, All righty, everybody. Are you ready to work your bones to sawdust and shards?

Yes, they shout. Bit wanders back to Hannah, and rests his head against her hip. She blocks the wind and warms his face with her heat.

Motor Pool, you ready to go out into the wilds of New York and salvage and steal and sell your sperm and blood to buy what we need to do this?

Hells, yes! shouts Peanut, and behind him, Wonder Bill and Tarzan pump their fists.

Womenfolk, are you ready to clean and polish and varnish and scrape and sand and take care of the kidlets and operate the Bakery and Soy Dairy and Laundry and cook and clean and chop wood and do the everyday stuff we need done to keep we

Free People going strong while all this work's happening?

The women cheer, and way above Bit's head, Astrid mutters to Hannah in her strange lilt, As if it is not what we already do, already. Bit looks away. When Astrid speaks, she shows her teeth, and they are so yellow and crooked he feels he's looking at something private.

All you Pregnant Ladies from the Henhouse, you ready to sew those curtains and braid those rugs and make the rooms all cozy and homey? Scattered yeses, the Hens surprised into acquiescence. A baby begins to squall.

Abe shouts: All you men, ready to work in the cold and stink of that old house to get her up and ready, with plumbing and a roof and everything? The men yell and yodel.

Abe's face goes solemn; he raises a hand. One thing, my cats and chicks. I know we're a nonhierarchical society and all, but since I've got my degree in engineering and Hiero has all those years under his belt as a construction foreman, we were thinking we'd be the ones to report to, yeah? We're just the straw bosses here, so if you got a better idea to do something, just let us know. But run things by us before you go off on your own initiative to do new stuff and we have to waste our time and dough to undo it. Anyways, serious talk over. We got about four more good hours of daylight today and only three months to totally refinish a fallen-apart nineteenth-century mansion. Or orphanage or whatever it was. So let's get our beautiful beatnik asses cracking.

A shout, a rush, and the group steams forward, up the mile-long drive scabbed with ice. They laugh, they are warm, they are ready. The last time Bit was in Arcadia House, he saw a sapling growing in a clawfoot tub and the roof caved in to show the clouds and sun. How wonderful it will be to have the house finished, tight and warm. If sleeping in a nest with two parents is happiness, imagine sleeping with eighty! Children dart around the legs of the adults until Sweetie Fox rounds them up and takes them down the shortcut to the Pink Piper to play.

Bit falls behind, feeling something gone wrong. He turns back.

Hannah stands alone at the gate. The ground is muddy around her. Bit hears a bird's low call. He begins to walk back toward his mother. When he is almost the whole way to her and she still seems small, he runs. She is hunched in an old sweater of Abe's, shivering. Her face is folded in on itself, and though he knows she is twenty-four, she seems younger than Erik, younger than Jincy, as young as Bit himself. He takes off his mitten to put his hand in hers. Her fingers are ice.

When she feels his hand, she smiles down from so high, and he can see his mother again within this shrunken woman. She says, All right, Bit. All right.

A snowstorm blows in. Bit dreams of hulking, hungry wolves with red eyes circling the Bread Truck. They howl, scrabble at the door. He startles awake. He wants his mother, but it is Abe who rises and shows Bit, through the window, the clean white sheets blowing down, the trackless heaps of snow. Abe heats up soymilk, and burritos Bit in the softest blanket. In the hope of lulling him to sleep, Abe tells him the story of his birth, which Bit knows the innards of. The legend of Bit Stone, the first Arcadian ever, is another story so retold that everyone owns it. The bigger girls play it in the Pink Piper, substituting the newest babies for the role of Bit.

You were born on the Caravan, Abe says softly, when we were a bunch of groupies, following Handy around for spiritual food.

Two dozen, max. Going to the concerts, staying for the meetings after. Everywhere we went, we saw communes, some that worked, others that didn't. Yurts and geodesic domes and sweat lodges and squatted-in mansions in the inner cities, and we started having an idea that even though everybody else was doing something along these lines, what we wanted to do was unusual. Pure. Live with the land, not on it. Live outside the evil of commerce and make our own lives from scratch. Let our love be a beacon to light up the world.

Anyways, those days, Handy was the only one with any medical training from being a medic in Korea, and he thought Hannah was five months along, because she wasn't huge. So here we are, driving through the mountains, trying to get from Oregon to Boulder, when a sudden snowstorm comes up, flakes huge as plates on the windshield, and wouldn't you know it, Hannah chooses this time to pop. We were in that little Volkswagen Camper the Motor Pool uses for trips into town. I'd fitted it out with a stove and all, pretty nifty, but we were in one of the smaller vehicles, so we were stuck at the back of the line, in these narrow mountain passes. I knew I had to get up to where Handy was because I sure as hell didn't know how to deliver any baby, undercooked or not. So up we go, fartleking past everyone in the left lane, and we'd all be dead if anyone came the opposite direction. Finally we pass the Pink Piper, and I slow the whole zoo down. Turn at a sign that says Ridley WY, pop. five thousand something, and I think there's got to be a hospital there, but there's snow on the sign, and of course, I turn the wrong way. On and on and on, mile after mile, and it's black out and finally we see lights and stop, and the Caravan folds itself around us and the Pink Piper to keep out the wind, and the door opens and some snowy person bursts in. I was expecting Handy, but who was it? Astrid.

Handy is seeing faces in the bus ceiling, she said (Abe says this in Astrid's Norwegian lilt; Bit giggles). He just ate three tabs of mescaline. But I have a Ph.D. in Victorian literature and I have three babies myself. I am well used to parturition.

She may have been thinking leeches as far as I know, but I know less than her, so I say, Okay, sure. So we all get naked because that is natural, and Astrid orders me around, Boil this water! Boil these knives! Get clean towels! But as soon as I have the hot water on, Hannah faints, and just like that, out you come, all bloody, with a plop. Well, I had no hope. You were so little, an apple, and barely moving. You couldn't even cry. Your poor lungs were too tiny. But Astrid cleaned you up and put you on your mother's boob and you had this ferocity for life, little man, you just started sucking her nipple like this huge sugartit as big as your own tiny mouth. Astrid gave out a cry and moved back down to Hannah's yoni because, guess what, there was another thing coming out, an afterbirth.

Abe pauses, strokes Bit's head absently.

Astrid wraps it all up in a batik and sends me out with a shovel and I struggle on through the snow to the black lake and dig through the frozen pebbles and into the ground and finally get it all covered and say a few words of gratitude and trudge my way back.

Then it was morning, and the sun came up, and I'll tell you, it was beautiful. It lit up that frozen lake so it was shining from within and the ice looked like hot lead at the base of these gorgeous purple mountains, and the churchbell rang up in town to celebrate you, our miracle baby. Then the townspeople came out, all shy, with food and bread, and deposited it on the hood of our Camper. That morning Astrid knew she'd found her calling. Her hands were meant to coax babies into the world. You were a gift, she said. She wrapped you around and around with a thick wool scarf and went to the grocer's and weighed you. You were three pounds, exactly. The size of an itty-bitty butternut squash.

The old grocer lady was this crusty German hag, cussing out all we longhairs among her twisted potatoes, her cabbages, but she took one look at you and her face cracked wide open, suddenly stunning, I mean a beam of light blasted out of her mouth. And she said, Oh, well if that ain't the littlest bit of a hippie ever made!

So this is how you came to be, Ridley Sorrel Stone, named for a town we never did see. Our Littlest Bit of a Hippie. Oldest soul in Arcadia. Our heir with no spare, Abe says, and his eyes pinch, then go clear again, and he nuzzles Bit around the neck, which tickles and makes Bit laugh, healing the invisible soreness in the Bread Truck, making them both forget the red-eyed wolves and the storm and the weariness of Hannah and the morning full of hard work now bearing down on them.

The first few days without Handy, the world feels off balance. He's not there for the weepers or the bad trips, for his daily cheery wanders around each work unit to urge them on. No scraggly gray beard, no quick-blinking eyes, no constant tinkle of his guitar or ukulele or banjo. For a few days, the ones left behind tread too softly on the ground, and every other word that falls from their lips is *Handy.* Then, one morning goes by and Bit doesn't think of Handy at all, until he trips over little Pooh, who throws herself in Bit's path, and he skins his hands, and waits for Handy to come down from the Pink Piper to lift him, to look deep into his eyes and gather cosmic energy, and say, *Oh, Littlest Bit, you're A-OK, man, don't have a freak-out. Pain is your body telling you to be more careful.* Instead lovely Sweetie Fox kisses his palms and rinses them with cold water and puts a bandage on them. Abe organizes the work crews. Astrid smoothes over conflicts, assigning the hug therapy or work yogas to dissolve the tension. Two of the guys from the Singleton Tent are so mad at each other that in their yoga they rip down almost all the rotten plaster in the upstairs of Arcadia House in one day, a miraculous feat, and now are best friends, hanging on one another's shoulders. The music isn't as good but there still is music: recorders and guitars and harmonicas. It is as if all of their edges have bled a little into the space where Handy had been, the way separate stews eke across the plate to mingle when the rice in the middle has been eaten.

In his half sleep, late, Bit hears Hannah murmur: It's nothing. I'm just tired.

You sure? Need a break? I'm sure we can scrape together the Greyhound . . .

No, baby.

Fabric sounds, something against his foot.

Speaking of which.

Hey. Wait. I'm sorry. Babe, I'm sorry, no.

Will we ever? Do you think? Ever again?

It's just. I would prefer not to.

Okay, Bartleby.

His parents laugh quietly, and when they stop there is a different kind of silence. Bit listens until his hearing fades and he carries only the sound of the kiss with him into his sleep.

Like the tractor that leaps forward with a nudge of the throttle, Arcadia jumps into high gear. Someone is always breathless, someone is always running. People have long conversations about wood rot and epoxy. There are knocks on the Bread Truck door in the middle of the night, the Scavengers home from Syracuse, Rochester, Albany, Utica, from the abandoned mansions they rip into for parts. In the morning, Abe whistles while he fondles the intricate carved mantels or soapstone sinks that have magically appeared on the Quad in the Octagonal Barn. He is a whirlwind of plans, sudden private laughs, and his energy spreads into the others, makes even Bit want to dance.

Bit makes up a song and sings it to himself all the time: *Renovelation, renovelation, renovelation, fix and patch and clean and paint . . . renovelation.*

At night, making soy cheese and onion quesadillas, Abe beams at him, saying, Renovation, honey. But Hannah squeezes Bit and whispers, I think your word is apt. Re-novelization. Reimagining our story. She touches under his chin with her soft fingers, his mother, and he laughs for the happiness of pleasing her.

It is morning. Hannah has put hot coffee into Abe's thermos. She has made them scrambled yeggs, soft, fresh tofu yellowed with nutritional yeast. When Abe marches up the hill to fix Arcadia House, his toolbelt jingling, Hannah goes to work in the Bakery.

Bit is building a castle out of woodblocks with Leif and Cole when he sees Hannah trudge back across the Quad and go up into the Bread Truck. He waits all day, but she doesn't come to get him. Twilight spreads over the windows. All around the Quad the cold air sounds with the voices and boot-steps of the menfolk and ladies who are coming home. The Family Quonsets are abuzz, the Pink Piper spills kids into the dusk, the scents of fried onions and tempeh rise from the Singleton Tent, the tinny wail of baby Felipe is answered by the echo of a smaller baby, Norah or Tzivi, startled awake. Doors open, doors slam, voices call out in the raggedy homecomings of Ersatz Arcadia. At last, he gets Sweetie to suit him up and walks home alone.

Hannah sits up from the bedclothes, stretches, and gives Bit a piggyback outside for a pee, hopping barefoot over the frozen ground. Inside the loo, it smells like wet muskrat, though it is warm out of the wind. Hannah curses when she eyes the wipe-nail, filled with glossy squares cut from a *Life* magazine. Glossy means sharp and cold against your crack, itching later.

When they come in, the damp chill of the Bread Truck seems somehow colder than the outdoors, and Regina is standing at the kitchen table, a loaf of bread before her. She turns and gives a small wave. Hey, she says.

Hey, Hannah says, setting Bit down. He runs to the bread and tears off a hunk to gnaw. Bit hid when Hannah didn't pick him up for lunch, and hasn't eaten since breakfast. He's starved. Hannah crouches to start a fire in the white ashes of the woodstove, the pinecones a fragrant kindling.

So we missed you this afternoon in the Bakery, says Regina. I looked up to ask you to make the granola, and you were gone. She has flour in her black crown of braids and a smear of something shiny on her cheekbones. Her eyes are tiny and set deeply in her head, her eyebrows are crows' wings.

I got sick, Hannah says. Her voice is taut, but when she touches the match to the kerosene lamp, her face looks normal in the glow. I didn't want to get anyone else sick, so I thought I'd go home.

Oh. Uh-huh, says Regina. Okay. It's just that what with the Arcadia House project, it's just me and Ollie up at the Bakery when you do that. Which is okay on the days you tell me, but when we're relying on you, it's a real pinch.

Sorry, Hannah says. I'll be there all day tomorrow.

Is this about what happened in the fall . . . begins Regina, but Hannah makes a shushing sound. Bit looks up to find Regina peering at him.

Really? Regina says. I mean, it's not really our style to hide, you know? It's a matter of life —

He's so little still, Hannah says. We'll tell him when it's time. It's our choice.

Handy says that kids don't *belong* to individ—

My kid, says Hannah, more forcefully. I don't care what Handy says. If you had one, you'd know.

The women turn away from one another and pick up things to examine: Hannah a match, Regina the coffee percolator. The air is rich with the silent adult language that Bit can never understand. All right, says Regina. She sets the percolator down with a bang. She picks Bit up, squints at him. Little Bit, make sure your momma pulls her weight, okay? she says. No slackers allowed in Arcadia.

Okay, whispers Bit.

When the door clicks behind Regina, Hannah says, Nosy bitch.

Bit waits for the sourness in his stomach to pass, then says, What's bitch?

A girl dog, Hannah says, and bites her lip and puffs out her cheeks with air.

Oh, Bit says. Pets are not allowed in Arcadia. Bit doesn't ask what he knows in theory from picture books but longs to understand better: what, exactly, a dog is, or why people want to keep them. Jincy once nursed a baby bunny with soymilk for three days until her mother, Caroline, found it and made her leave it in the woods. When Jincy cried and cried, Caroline said with a shrug, Come on, Jin. You know personal property's not allowed. Besides, you really want to enslave a fellow creature?

Petey wasn't my slave, Jincy sniffled. I *loved* Petey.

Petey will grow up to be a big strong bunny hopping through the meadows, the way he's supposed to, Caroline said firmly. The next day the squirmy pink thing was gone from the little pallet of leaves where Jincy had left it. Now the children make a game of scanning the underbrush for their tiny friend. Often someone runs shouting back to the Kid Herd, sure that they've seen Petey from the corner of an eye, rosy as a lump of flesh, swift in the brambles, a creature miraculous and tender, their shared secret.

Hannah has brought Bit in the predawn to the squat stone Bakery, and he wakes on the flour sacks in the corner. It is hot; loaves plumpen on the shelf. The flesh of the dough makes Bit hungry, makes something warm rise up in his sleep-swimmy head, and he creeps to where Hannah stands, hip against the mixer, talking to Regina and Ollie. Bit tugs Hannah down, and she bends absently, and he lifts her teeshirt, and latches his mouth to her breast.

Hannah slides her nipple away, pulls the shirt over her body, hugs it to her, pushes his cheek gently with her hand.

You're too old for that, baby, she says, and stands.

The room trembles in Bit's eyes. Ollie murmurs something about Astrid nursing Leif until he was eight, Regina says something and hands Bit a soft pretzel. Hannah says *Something-something-can't,* but Bit doesn't hear her words exactly, his sorrow a too-loud wind in his ears.

When it's too dark to work, Abe comes home. His coat and overalls and workshirt shed sawdust. When his gloves come off, his hands are nicked and chapped. During dinner, Hannah yawns. Bit and Abe can see the tiny man bobbing in the cavern of her throat. She says, I'm bushed. Sometimes she washes her face and brushes her teeth with baking soda before she falls asleep, sometimes she doesn't. The nights are long.

Abe picks Bit up and reads aloud whatever he's studying at the time (*New Politics, Anarchy and Organization, Mad* magazine). Bit can pick out sentences, can follow along the swoops of emotion in Abe's voice, can sound out headlines to himself. Parts of the world click into shape, like pieces in a jigsaw puzzle. But the puzzle is alive; it grows; new pieces appear for him to fit together faster than he can gather them in his mind.

He fights sleep to think about it all. His father washes dishes and fetches water from the stream so they don't have to in the morning, and when he unbuttons his shirt with heavy hands, he falls, already sleeping, into bed.

There is, Bit knows, what happens on the surface, and there is what pulls beneath. He thinks of standing in a river current, the wind strong in the opposite direction. Even in the happiest times — Cockaigne Day in the middle of summer, Blessing Day at the end of the year, the Harvest Festival, the spontaneous gigs — even during all that dancing and happy arguing, the Slap-Apple, the banquets, in the corners there always sit a few muscled young men with a badness in their eyes. There are murmurs when they come to Arcadia, *dodger, four-eff, rather . . .*

jungles . . . bayonet babies? There is old Harriet, whose braless breasts waggle at her navel, who hoards food under her bed (*Poor thing,* he overheard someone once say, *watched her parents starve to death in the siege of Leningrad*). There is Ollie, one of the original Caravaners, who worked alone for the first two years to reinforce the secret tunnel between the Octagonal Barn and Arcadia House with sheets of metal, stocking it with barrels of water, canned goods, matches, tarps, iodine salt. Ollie has the pale softness of a salamander down by the stream; sometimes, he jerks and blinks and goes silent in the middle of a sentence.

The badness even spreads, at times, to the kidlets. Bit won't go into the fruit room in the Free Store, despite all those delicious wrinkling apples in their barrels. Someone put up an enormous black-and-white poster with a glowering man in moustachios. There are words Bit is far too frightened to piece out beyond *Big Brother;* and even when adults go in, they look at the poster and come out fast.

Hannah and Abe share the same nightmare from their childhood: a dim room with a fat woman who stands before them, a siren overhead, a scramble under the desks, a white flash. These dreams have been catching at Hannah often recently, spiderwebs tightening the more she tries to escape. Most days, when the first sun melts itself across the Bread Truck linoleum, the panic from the dream slowly vanishes, leaving an oily taste behind to taint the air.

But this morning, Bit wakes alone, heart racing. The icicles in the window are shot with such red light of dawn that Bit goes barefoot over the snow to pull one with his hand. Inside again, he licks it down to nothing, eating winter itself, the captured woodsmoke and sleepy hush and aching cleanness of ice. His parents sleep on. All day, the secret icicle sits inside him, his own thing, a blade of cold, and it makes Bit feel brave to think of it.

He watches his parents kiss goodbye. Their lips slide from each other's cheeks, and as they turn, Abe pats the level on his belt with a hand and Hannah frowns at something Astrid calls out, waiting on the other side of the Quad with heaps of laundry in her hands. A shock; Bit hasn't understood until now; his parents are vastly different from one another. There is only one Abe, beamy and talky and gathering his energy from *things,* Arcadia House made solid; but there are two Hannahs. Summer Hannah is going away, the one who loved people, who gathered the children's boots while they slept to paint the snouts of animals upon them, pigs and horses and birds and frogs, according to their wearers. His laughing mother, the loud one: in a place where all bodily functions are matter-of-fact, where even in solemn moments there are whole brass sections of flatulence, her gas is legendary for its thunder. La Pétomane, she nicknamed herself, with a flushed half-pride. That Hannah is as strong as the men. When someone yells "Monkeypower!" to get help with a mud-stuck truck or with digging sand from the creek for the Showerhouse concrete, she shows up first, works the longest, her back under the sleeveless shirt as taut and muscled as any of the men's. That is the Hannah who cracks jokes under her breath until the ladies around her snortle; the one who shuts the curtains on the Bread Truck some days and opens her small, secret trunk that she isn't supposed to keep, all possessions in Arcadia held in common. Then she pulls a delicate tablecloth out, her great-grandmother's Belgian lace. She pulls teacups out, porcelain tender as skin, ten oil miniatures and a mahogany case of silver with five different kinds of forks, all vined with tiny lilies. She sets it up and makes a mint tea and orange-peel cookies with smuggled white sugar, and Bit and she have a tea party together all afternoon long.

Ridley Sorrel Stone, one chews with one's mouth closed! Summer Hannah says in the acid voice of her childhood deportment teacher. One puts one's napkin on one's lap! She and Bit clink teacups solemnly, accomplices.

But this Hannah is burrowing inside a new one who has let the winter in. She has begun to stare at the walls and allows her braids to unravel. She forgets to start supper. Her golden skin fades to a pallor, blue bruises press under her eyes. This Hannah looks at Bit as if she is trying to see him from a very great distance.

Bit is chopping wood with Titus Thrasher up by the Gatehouse. He gathers the chips that spurt off the ax and puts them in a bucket for kindling.

You want to talk about what's bothering you? says Titus, and Bit says a low No.

They watch Kaptain Amerika tool by in a croaky station wagon he has taken from the Motor Pool. The Trippie is going into Summerton for his psychotherapy, which the state pays for. Many in Arcadia are on food stamps or disability. When there's been a long spell without new people to put money in the pot, welfare keeps them going. Kaptain Amerika was an English professor, but turned on too many times and messed up his brain. Now he sharpens his long beard into two points and wears a sarong made of an American flag. Bit had once heard Astrid defend him: Yeah, he is a creepo, this is so, she'd said. But he has his moments of lucidity. Bit supposes she'd meant the moments when Kaptain Amerika will shout: Uncle Sam wants *me.* Or, *Nixon* is the albatross!

How come he's called Kaptain Amerika? Bit says, watching the blue exhaust from the station wagon curl and fade. Not Professor Merton?

Titus leans on the ax handle. He is steaming with sweat, his undershirt the color of a teastained mug. No woman lives with Titus to wash his things, so they never get clean, unless Hannah or another woman steals them when he is out. He smells like a turnip gone bad. He says, People get to choose who they want to be here. Part of the deal. Near everybody's got a nickname they gave to themselves. People come here to become what they want to be. Tarzan. Wonder Bill. Saucy Sally. He flushes when he says the last name, and Bit studies his friend in silent wonder.

A car pulls up the long dirt road. Titus steps to the gate, mopping his face with a bandanna. Four young men with fringed leather jackets and cameras in their hands pour out, slamming the car doors behind them. Hey, man, says one, and Titus says, No, no, no. You're welcome if you're serious about living here, man, but you've got to respect our privacy if not.

Oh. Well, we're on the paper at the college in Rochester? says one of the boys. And you don't have a phone. We thought we might interview Handy?

I dig his music, says a pipsqueak with red ears. He's the American Original.

The four grin, sure that admiration is their ticket inside.

Sorry, says Titus.

Come on, man. We're hip, says another. He hefts a thirty-pound sack from the trunk. We brought some yams for the Free Store. Just let us poke around? We'll be gone after dinner.

A hardness comes over Titus's face. We're not zoo animals, he says. You can't bribe us with peanuts.

Yams, the boy says.

Titus swings the ax to his shoulder and strides closer to the boys. They falter, break apart, only one holding his ground. At times, Titus has to be violent to keep the gawkers out. Bit is afraid to see his gentle friend turn into the ugly stranger he sometimes needs to be. He runs away. All afternoon, Bit stays in the woods, poking at icicles and frozen puddles until he is too cold to hold off going home to the Bread Truck any longer. When he comes in and puts his fingers on the back of her neck, Hannah shudders awake.

Abe comes home shouting, the Children's Wing is roofed! It's plumbed. It's insulated and airtight. The babies'll have a place to live!

Bit dances, and Hannah stretches to her full height, releasing her warm smell from her sweater and murmuring, That's lovely.

In the morning, sweet with snow, a train of women with mops and buckets walks up to Arcadia House. They will scrub and polish and paint it all, redo floors, re-plaster. Hannah goes with them. She is shaky on her feet, a cage of bones.

Bit, honey, Hannah had urged, Go play with the Kid Herd in the Pink Piper, but he said No, no, no, no, no. He hadn't seen the house since the big push on the day that Handy went off on his concert tour. At last, Hannah lets Bit come along. He sits in the little Red Wagon with the vinegar and rags, a box of sponges on his lap. Hannah pulls him over the sludgy ground, falling behind the others. The women call to each other in the sharp air; they laugh. The men on the Arcadia House roof stand up like woodchucks in a field to watch the women come through the terraced apple orchards. They wolf-whistle. Abe makes great arcs with his arms above his head.

But when the women march through the courtyard and into the Schoolroom, they go silent. There are vast begrimed windows; a curious, squat old woodstove; coat hooks that range from tall to tiny. The heaps of desks are scalloped with rainbow fungi. The walls shudder with cobwebs disturbed by their entry. Someone long before had camped in the middle of the floor and burnt a great black pit into the planks. The plaster of the ceiling has come off in spurts and chunks, baring the raw lath and, over the ghosts of antique calligraphy on the slate board, someone has scraped a huge *Fuck* with a knife. Bit spells it out in his head, says the word under his breath. The women are still, wide-eyed.

Then plain Dorotka with her granny glasses puts down her bucket and rolls up her sleeves. She ties her long gray braids around her head, crowning herself. Ladies, she calls out, disturbing the fur on the wall so that it shifts and floats, loose as hair under water. We have us a job, don't we, now.

Don't we now, don't we, the women softly echo.

Bit is given a rag, sat at a desk, told to scrub, but he watches the women sweep the walls with their brooms until wigs of cobweb fall slowly.

He can, he finds, walk out unnoticed.

In the hall, he hears the pounding of the men somewhere. There is music, something familiar, Hendrix on a radio but warped by the distance and the walls and the beats of the hammers until, all together, the music and the cleaning and building sounds blend into a snowstorm, all winds and rattles.

At the end of the hall, a built-in seat cowers below a small window. He tries to climb, but the cushion collapses when he touches it. He flees the upswell of dust, a snow of mold and dead spiders, goes down a darker place, turns to where the wall goes jagged with stairs. He climbs them. Some treads are missing; he leaps these, and when he does, something moves in the gap below him, and he scrambles, up, away, the terror bitter in his throat, his heart jigging in his chest, onto the next floor. It smells of pine and sawdust, the fresh beams of the new roof above, but he must skirt great jagged holes in the floor. He creeps along, rounds a bend. One door opens as he passes and he looks inside. It is a vast and dark room, the Proscenium, he remembers someone calling it. A tarp stretches over the ceiling where there once had been full sky.

Hannah has told him it's not possible that he remembers the day they came to Arcadia. He was only three, she says; no three-year-old could remember *any* single day. But he does. The Caravan had been on the road for too long and had grown too large. Wherever they went, people joined them, bringing more trucks and buses. At last, all fifty of the Free People were weary. When they picked Titus Thrasher up in an army-navy store, he told them about his father, who had inherited six hundred acres in upstate New York from an uncle. Titus had been with them only a week when he walked out of a drugstore phone booth and said, simply, It's done.

They drove all night into deep countryside, and arrived on a rainy spring morning. Barton Thrasher was a roly-poly man who came weeping out of the stone Gatehouse, extending his arms to his long-lost son. They went into the Pink Piper, and Harold, once a lawyer, checked the papers. The state needed a name on the deed, and they agreed it would be Handy's, though it belonged to all, equally. Only when the papers were signed could Titus say to his father, Bad blood between us, Pop, but now I reckon everything is even. In response, Barton Thrasher leaned against his son's broad chest, and Titus stood still, bearing the affection.

Then, someone let off a Roman candle and everyone cheered.

The leftover rain fell on them from the trees above as the Free People took their first quiet hike through the woods to see their land. The men beat down the overgrown trail with machetes and the women held the kids and picked over the path behind them. They came into the Sheep's Meadow, and gasped. There were enormous structures on top of the hill, which nobody had expected: Barton Thrasher said he thought it had all been farmland and hadn't known that the buildings existed. Arcadia House reared above them in a blush of brick, a tangle of briars overgrown upon it, the huge gray ship of the Octagonal Barn behind, the stone outbuildings swallowed in grass. Up the Terraces they went, their feet wearing through the mud and weeds to the hidden flagstone steps. The apple trees were stark and ancient, heaped goblins, and the raspberries were wild between the trunks. Last autumn's windfall stuck, a too-sweet mud, on their soles. They came out onto the slate porch and gathered before the huge front door.

In Arcadia Ego, someone said. They looked to the lintel, where the words were hastily chiseled.

Astrid said: Arcadia. It means, *Even in Arcadia am I.* Poussin made a painting. Quote comes from Virgil —

But Handy interrupted loudly, No egos in this Arcadia! and they shouted for joy. Astrid muttered, No, not ego, it's not what that means, it's . . . But she trailed off. Nobody heard her but Bit.

Arcadia, Hannah whispered into Bit's hair, and he'd felt her smile in his scalp.

The entryway: a chandelier fallen, crystals underfoot mixed with filth, animal spoor, leaf litter; stairways that curved to sky, the roof ripped off. The Free People separated, searched, discovered. Hannah carried Bit through the mess, the tumbleweeds of dust, the antique graffiti, the doors unopened for a century. Arcadia House was an endless building shaped like a horseshoe, embracing a courtyard where a vast fifty-foot oak tree presided. The wings of the house were filthy, broken, went on forever. Out a window, Bit saw the glimmer of the Pond, and outbuildings like ships in a sea of weeds. There were holes everywhere: in roofs, in walls, in floors. He was frightened. At last, they all met up in the Proscenium, a grand hall with benches, a stage, ratted curtains faded the color of dirt, a deep red velvet in the hearts of their folds. The Free People were filthy and starved and craving a party. After the long years they'd debated their community, shared readings, talked about the kibbutzim and Drop Cities and ashrams that some among them had lived in, they had come home. They longed to celebrate with music and pot and maybe something stronger, but Handy wouldn't let them. If we don't do the work now, my beatniks, he said, when will we do it? And so they stayed in the Proscenium as the afternoon faded and became midnight, they argued it all out, the rules of their Homeplace.

There was a hole in the floor where the Entryway grew black beneath, until all that remained were a few gleams of the crystals in the dirt; there was a hole in the roof where the night turned inky and soon went up in a blaze of stars.

All things would be held in common, all possessions — bank accounts, trust funds — would go into the pot, everyone who joins must give everything they have. Bills and taxes would be paid with this money. When they made dough, it would be by midwifery or by hiring out Monkeypower to work in the fields, until in the end they ate only what they harvested themselves, and sold their surplus. Within Arcadia, filthy lucre would be forbidden.

All people would be welcome to join, as long as they promised to work; those who were too damaged or weak or pregnant or old to work would be cared for. Nobody was beyond help. But no fugitives; they didn't need the authorities on their heads.

They would live pure and truthful lives; no illegal activities. Well, they amended, when the familiar skunky smoke rose up, nothing that *should* be illegal.

Punishment would be unnecessary; all must subject themselves to Creative Critiques when they erred or didn't pull their weight, where they had to undergo the community telling them off, a ritual cleansing.

Whoever you fuck, you're married to, said Handy; and thus rose the four-, five-, six-, eight-part marriages of the beginning, most of which soon splintered apart into singles and couples.

They would treat all living creatures with respect; they'd be vegan, animal goods and pets forbidden.

Until the day came when they could renovate this great, strange ship called Arcadia House and live together in love and kindness, they would make an Ersatz Arcadia.

By the time their rules had been laid out, agreed upon, named, it was almost morning. Many had fallen asleep. The few who were awake saw Handy's broad face kindling in the dawn through the filthy windows. He made a grand gesture toward the heap around them, saying, This land, these structures we found here today are gifts of love from the Universe.

Then the years of transience broke in him and Handy cried.

Three years passed full of hard work, some failed crops, some good. They borrowed oxen from their Amish neighbors to plow the fields. Later, the silent, hardworking Amish men came — a surprise — to help reap the sorghum, barley, soy. There was enough only to eat and none to sell. The midwives went into the towns beyond, into

Ilium and Summerton to deliver babies for money. The Motor Pool was founded to drive trucks for pay, and to find abandoned vehicles to salvage for parts. Every autumn, they rented Monkeypower to the fields or apple orchards to make as much cash as possible. They made alcoholic Slap-Apple and sauce and pies from their own apples, they canned just enough wild strawberries and raspberries and goods from the garden to make it through the winter. But even the previous winter in Arcadia, there was a week of hunger that would have been worse had Hannah not succeeded in wrestling her trust fund from her parents' lawyers. Together, they survived.

One night in December after the Solstice celebration, when Handy was in a Vision Quest in the sweat lodge they'd built off the Showerhouse, Abe called a secret meeting for the Arcadia House Renovation Project. He had chosen a few people to join him, the straw bosses of the work units: Fields, Gardens, Sanitation, Free Store, Bakery, Soy Dairy, Cannery, Midwifery, Biz Unit, Motor Pool, Kid Herd. Hannah had brought Bit along under her poncho, because she had been the straw boss of the Bakery then and didn't want to leave him in the Bread Truck alone. They met between Arcadia

House and the Octagonal Barn, in the tunnel that Ollie had reinforced against nuclear strike.

Listen, said Abe. I've been thinking, and we've reached a kind of turning point. We've got to move into Arcadia House soon, or we may stall out on putting all our big ideas into action. Just get comfortable in Ersatz Arcadia and let our dream of Arcadia House fritter off and *never* move in.

There was a protest, something about money, but Abe held up a hand. Give me a minute. It's pretty clear we're working too hard, too inefficiently, doing redundant stuff just to live. It's all about division of labor. If we had centralized child care and cooking and didn't have to worry about carting our own water up from the Pond or getting the stuff from the Free Store for our suppers or making sure we chopped plenty of wood to be warm this week, we could actually get enough work done to support ourselves and make money. I've done the math, he said and held up a paper covered in his tiny script. If we fix up Arcadia House and all live there together, we can do this. We can make it work. Maybe even make a profit this year.

Abe's beard split, his smile so big Bit feared for his father's cheeks.

There was a silence, the sound of someone in the Octagonal Barn above dragging something heavy across the floor. The straw bosses all began talking over one another, pacing up and down the tunnel as they dreamed aloud, building their vision detail by detail.

The deeper Bit pushes into Arcadia House, now, the more he is bitten by a wretched clammy cold. The men haven't touched these rooms yet: they are moldy and dark. He pushes at a latch, and a door swings open with a foul exhalation. Between the darkness of the hall he is in and the light above the stairwell, he takes the light and goes up, though the dust is to his ankles. He finds himself on a catwalk that skirts a deep room, an intact couch, a grand brick fireplace, a sea of filth that moves ten feet below from the air he displaces. From this spot in the house, he can no longer hear the men on the roof, their music, or the women far away in the Children's Wing as they sing and talk.

There is a black spill beneath the first door, an evil that spreads from the crack. He skips it, creeps on. From behind the second he hears a sound, a sigh, a whisper, and feels a cold in the metal of the knob, so he skips it, too. The third opens when he pushes hard, and he enters.

The room is furred with dust, inches deep. It grows off the walls, over the floor, spreads itself across lumps that are furniture, Bit discovers, when he inserts his hand and feels wood beneath. He touches a filminess under one, cloth, and finds it a bed.

In the middle of the floor, a delicious lump, and Bit plunges in both hands. There are hard things deep down. He brings out his fist and peers at a series of tiny bones, a mouse's skull and skeleton. Then, a handful of buttons in a strange, dense material, creamy white and shimmering. At last, an object, hard and soft at the same time. He blows on it until the book reveals itself.

On the leather cover, there are embossed flowers, a boy who peers from behind a tree, and letters in gold. Bit traces four — G-R-I-M — then grows impatient and opens the pages.

At first he sees an illustration. It is the most vivid thing in all of Arcadia House; it sucks the daylight into it. A girl with a squinched face seems to be using her cut-off finger for a key. On another page, there is a tiny man who splits himself in two while blood spills in gouts from his wounds. On another, a girl in a long dress walks beside lions, her mouth open, her hair up in a furry acorn hat.

He finds the smallest story. His finger runs under each word as he puzzles it out. It is about a mother with many children in a time of famine, something Bit knows: the terror in the belly, winterberry and soybeans all they have left in the mason jars. The mother wants to eat her children. They are angelic and choose to die for her. But she is so ashamed with their sacrifice that she doesn't eat them. Instead, she runs away.

Horror is heaped within horror: the mother eating her children, the children dying, the mother disappearing forever into the dark behind the story.

He drops the book back in its heap of dust, clamps his hands over his eyes. The world moves in tight and squeezes him. He holds his face until the terror scuttles off and he can breathe again.

From afar, Hannah's voice, high, frantic: Bit! Come here, right now! Before he leaves, he snatches the book, shoves it down his pants, and runs down over his own treadmarks in the dust, runs and runs, turns the wrong way, loses Hannah's voice, bursts into a familiar hall, hears her voice closer now, goes down the stairs, leaping the gaps in the treads, stumbles into the Entryway, goes down a corridor, loses her voice, goes another way and at last finds himself in a glassy room with half-collapsed long tables, where Hannah's back is turned to him, where she is shouting for him. She is so happy to see Bit she snatches him up under the arms and hugs him to her so tightly he can't breathe, and puts him down, and wipes her wet face on her shoulder and says, Don't *ever* wander off here, Bit. You can get hurt. This place is very, very dangerous.

She holds him away by the arms. God, she says. You're black with filth.

Then her mouth shifts as she feels the book in his pants. She looks at him, and Bit watches her, and is almost disappointed when she lets the book go. She has been letting everything go, these days.

Midge comes from a back room. Since her father turned to ice during the February Morning Meeting, Midge's face has gone sour, as if she is constantly sucking a gooseberry. She snaps, This is no place for a kid, Hannah. Take him home.

Midge has no neck, Bit notices. Her head swivels on her shoulders like a ratchet.

Away they go again, rattling down over the hill in the Red Wagon. Bit leaves the book under his shoes and pants when he and his mother go into the cement-block

Showerhouse together, though their day to bathe isn't until Sunday. Most days, they do what Hannah calls a KACA Bath: dip a washcloth in hot water, soap it up, hit the Kisser-Armpit-Crotch-Ass. Today the Showerhouse echoes, empty. Everyone else is working. There's a dangerous luxury to the steam, the rosy softnesses of his mother under the hot water, the faces of sleeping babies that live in Hannah's knees, in his own layers of darkness that fall as she rubs at him with her chapped hands until she has scrubbed him raw and red as an infant again.

Clean in the quiet of the middle of day, Hannah makes herself a cup of tea. She sits at the window, Edith Piaf on the record player. *Non,* the invisible singer warbles, *je ne regrette rien.* Bit hears: *No, Gina rug-wet again.* He thinks, *Poor Gina,* heartstruck for her shame.

Hannah's so deep in her thoughts that Bit is invisible. He waves his hands before her eyes, but she doesn't blink. He takes the book he stole from Arcadia House from his pants and sidles down the steps from the main Bread Truck into the chilly lean-to, and puts it into his Stash tin, where it just barely fits if he takes everything else out:

the snakeskin and glass eye with a green iris and arrowhead and sparrow with working wings that Abe had once carved for him.

Daring, he goes out into the afternoon and carries his treasures to the Free Store, where he puts them on the shelf where all of the other unused things live. He touches the hemp necklaces that Sylvia braids, the single rollerskate, the musty paperbacks, the neat stacks of patched and folded jeans, the flannel shirts. Cheryl is weighing dried cranberries in the corner and putting them into paper bags for the cook of each homestead to pick up, and when her back is turned, he plunges his hands into the flour barrel and squeezes the powder deliciously through his fingers. Muffin looks up from where she's funneling cooking oil into mason jars, and the spatters of oil on her glasses refract her eyes into many tiny blinking eyes. But she doesn't tell on him. He takes a piece of dried apple from the snack bin and runs home through the cold. When he comes in, his mother cocks her head and says, Where'd you go, Little Man?, but doesn't even listen for his answer.

He makes a plan. Tomorrow, he will sneak home from the Kid Herd and spend hours in his new book happily, piecing together the terrible, sharp stories until the world is stuffed full of them and nothing else can get in.

The snow melts under a freezing rain and the sky is the color of lint. Jincy comes over. Her face is red with tears. She is eight and her head is a wild screw of white curls. She is much older, but Bit's best friend. They zip themselves into his sleeping bag, and in the closeness there, she whispers: My parents are fighting.

There is so much for Bit to say that he doesn't say anything.

They play Babysitter and Baby, they play Boycott, they play Handy and Lila. They play Nixon, Jincy making her face loose, veeing her fingers, saying *I am not a crook.* They play Midwife, in which Jincy is Astrid, and Bit pushes a porcelain babydoll out of his pretend yoni, until Hannah sees and blanches and says, Hey, kids! Let's make cookies! Then they stir and mix and bake, oatmeal cookies with almonds and raisins and molasses, while Hannah gives them directions from the kitchen table.

A good bubble rises in Bit, and he moves lightly to keep it whole.

Abe comes home while it is still bright out, and cooks dinner for them all: crepes with tempeh and preserved mushrooms and soy cheese. At nine, the parents have to go to a Creative Critique of Tarzan up in the Octagonal Barn because he has been making unwanted sexual advances on a number of chicks, even the Pregnant Ladies, which is really spreading some bad vibes. Hannah huddles in her overlarge sweater, looking like a snake about to shed.

Abe says, frowning, I don't know if the kids should stay here alone . . .

Jincy says, We'll be good! We won't touch the woodstove or go outside! If we're scared, we'll run to the Pink Piper! Reluctantly, Hannah and Abe go into the dusk.

In the sleeping bag again, Jincy hugs Bit too tight. When he complains, she lets go and starts to whisper stories.

Under the footbridge over the river, she says, there's a troll who needs a sacrifice before you can go across. A nice leaf is fine, or a bolt taken from the Motor Pool, or a piece of fruit, but only a little one, so as not to waste.

What about a booger? Bit says.

A booger will do, Jincy says, and they laugh.

Her voice goes lower. Jeannise had sex with both Hank and Horse, and now the twins aren't talking to one another. Which is bad because they're the Sanitation Crew and pump out the loos.

Wes and Haven are going to have a baby, and Wes and Flannery are, too, she says, and Haven and Flannery got into a chick-fight and their faces are all scratched up.

Jincy heard a mouse conversation last week. They were squeaking that they were so so so so so so hungry in their little tiny voices.

When Peanut and Clay light one cigarette off an already lit one, it's called a Dutch fuck, though they don't do the regular fuck, because they dig chicks.

A witch lives in the woods. Last summer, at the Cockaigne Fest, when all the adults were drunk on Slap-Apple, Jincy went to the Sugarbush because her parents were yelling, and she saw a huge old hunched lady in black just stop and look at her and go away. She had long white hair and a terrible bad face. She floated in the air.

Bit drifts to sleep with Jincy's voice still murmuring on. He sees the shadows full of creatures, trolls like so many green and stunted Handys. He sees the Sugarbush, sinister with gloom. He sees the Pond glistening with moonlight. There, a witch with Astrid's bad teeth and Hannah's winter-stringy hair and Midge's sour yellow face looms up, again and again, out of the shadows, until the witch is so familiar that he begins to wait for her, then long for her to arrive, until he tells himself within the dream that he is no longer afraid. And he is not.

An uproar in the middle of the night; men come for Abe, talking over each other. When Hannah rises and makes coffee, Hiero says, Oh, hey there, Hannah-baby. Fred Major claps his great hand upon her shoulder. But none of the men are there to drink the coffee by the time it has finished percolating. Hannah sits at the table. Her eyes glint in the shadows.

Bit's pajamas are too small for him; the hems ride his calves, his forearms, his belly is cold in the air. He goes over to Hannah and climbs up into her lap, and lays his head upon her chest to hear the slow slosh of her heart.

She says, In the morning, my friend, someone you love will be gone.

Bit says nothing, but he thinks *Abe?* and something begins to collapse in him. Hannah must know what he's thinking because she says, No, no, no, no. Wonder Bill. He had a different name before he came here. He's done some bad things that we didn't know about until yesterday and has to go.

Monkey Wonder Bill? Wonder Bill who can go hand to hand from branch to branch in the Sugarbush? Wonder Bill who makes animal sounds better than the animals, his turkey gobble in the fall (oh, so long ago, the jewel-bright leaves, the golden silver smell of autumn), the noise that made a turkey as tall as Bit sprint lusty from the bush toward them?

In the morning, the Pigs come to look for Wonder Bill. Arcadia gathers on the Quad as the Pigs rustle through the dwellings, searching for him. Nobody speaks. Bit sits on Hannah's feet to insulate his bum from the frozen ground.

He is confused. He was imagining pinkness, snouts, curly tails, the pictures in the Kid Herd storybooks. These are black-suited men with reflective sunglasses. They *are* pink: that, at least, is true. Perhaps their tails are hidden under the creased pants they wear. They trail strange smells behind them: *Cologne,* Hannah whispers, making a face.

The Pigs go into the first Family Quonset, then into the second. The ones who ring the woods hold guns, and with a startle, Bit sees green under their feet. Garlic mustard, hummock sedge, Dorotka tells him when he asks. Spring is coming. He is tired of the men who murmur into radios. He wants them to go home.

Bit hears Leif ask Astrid, Are they gonna shoot us? Astrid shakes her head no although her eyes are hard, and she presses her son's face against her belly.

Crashes from the Singleton Tent. The Pigs go into the Pink Piper, they go out, they go into the Bread Truck, they go out, they go into Franz and Hans's lean-to, with the half-made puppet head hanging from the rafter like an oversize piñata though the Circenses Singers are all out on the road. They go out, they go into the Henhouse, and stay in there for a while. The Pregnant Ladies run out, huge and indignant, in their men's boots and sweaters, squawking.

Up on the hill, Arcadia House crawls with Pigs. Bit peers at the roof, but Abe is not working up there today. There are no Arcadia men there at all. They must be waiting to start work until the Pigs in black leave.

At last, a Pig comes over with an angry, fat face. The sheriff from Ilium is beside him, a man in a khaki shirt whom Bit has seen drinking coffee up at the Gatehouse with Titus: his sandy hair lifts and falls like a mudflap over his bald spot. He winks briefly at Titus then looks away.

The three talk together. The angry head Pig begins to shout. The sheriff makes soothing sounds. Titus says very little.

At last, the men troop over the snow back up to Arcadia House. The Free People move behind them. From the top of the Hill on the slate porch they watch as the Pigs get into cars and trucks that flash with red and blue lights when they drive away.

When the last pulls out, a cheer goes up around Bit, so loud and unexpected that he startles and turns his face into the closest legs, Eden's swollen thighs, to hide. Her forehead is a moon over her pregnant belly when she laughs down at him.

Abe returns in the afternoon in a Volkswagen with a case of maple spouts and pails for their first sugar season this year; the Sugarbush is huge and ancient, the syrup one more thing they can sell. They had lived near it for three years without suspecting what the copse of trees really was until Dorotka stood up one Sunday Morning Meeting in the Octagonal Barn and nervously suggested making sugar this year. With what? said Handy, our cane didn't do so hot. She looked confused, then said, Oh. The Sugarbush? It's a mature old stand, we can get gallons and gallons out of it. And

Handy said, What Sugarbush? And Dorotka threw back her head in astonishment and led them down to the Sugarbush, the miraculous woods on the other side of the Pond, and they all couldn't believe the new bounty; they threw the snow that was too soft that day to make snowballs, the entire community dusted in sunbright powder.

Handy had wanted to call the product Free People Sugar, Titus wanted to call it Sinzibuckwud; Abe prevailed quietly but persistently as he does sometimes, and they are calling it Arcadia Pure.

Hannah and Bit come out to the Quad to meet him and help him unload. Abe pulls up to the Bread Truck, the radio spits out a whine, "Tiptoe Through the Tulips."

How was Vermont? Hannah says.

Abe envelops Hannah in his arms and whispers in her ear. He is tall, she is tall, and between them Bit is pressed as if by the warm trunks of old trees. He doesn't want the hug to end, but after a minute it does. Their bodies fall apart. His parents turn away.

On top of everything else, the women must do the sugaring: the men work up in Arcadia House from sunrise to sunset and often beyond. They scrape and hammer, put in pipes and plaster, roll on the oopsie paint they got from a store in Ilium in exchange for Sweetie Fox and Kitty posing provocatively with rollerbrushes in the store's advertisements.

The Kid Herd follows the sugaring ladies out one day to learn. The huge maples are hung with icicles, roots so intertwined they form a mat above the ground. There is no wind here, and when the sun finally touches the copse, it glows softly as a kerosene lamp.

Like a church, breathes Maria and turns away to privately make a four-pointed sign from head to belly to shoulder to shoulder, which Bit mimics again and again behind a tree, loving the gesture's solemnity. He doesn't want the others to see. Superstition, snorts Hannah when the others talk about God. Though people here have private rituals, Muhammad kneeling on a bit of carpet during the day, Jewish Seders and Christmas trees, religion here is seen much like hygiene: a personal concern best kept in check so as to not bully the others.

Mikele drills holes into trunk after trunk, and Eden screws in the spouts. The trees bleed clear blood into the buckets. The ping-ping-ping on metal is a sound like warm rain on the Bread Truck roof. But this sound feels different; sweetness will come of it.

Language has begun to shift in Bit. There are small explosions of comprehension every day. He remembers last August, when he lay in the sun-warmed shallows of the Pond while under the water he was nibbled by things unseen. With his Grimm book, it is as if he has his eyes below the surface and can at last see the tiny fish there. Speech splinters into words, each phrase with its own order: Scuseme becomes Excuse me, Pawurduthpepel becomes Power to the People, all words he understands both alone and combined.

Separate drawers emerge in his mind, now, to sort people into. Handy is a frog king. Titus is a lonely ogre in the Gatehouse, keeping out the Pigs and gawkers. Tall Abe, with his tools, his ax, his beard, is a woodsman. Eden, with her bright coppery hair and pale skin, eating the succulent greens raised in the south window of the Henhouse for the Pregnant Ladies, is a queen. He hopes she is not the good mother who must die to make way for the wicked stepmother. He hopes she is not the bad mother who sells her baby for the herbs. Wonder Bill, with his mobile face, with his monkey clambers, had been a fool. Astrid is difficult:

her hair shines like a princess's, but her face is old and her teeth terrible like a witch's; she delivers babies and gives people medicines like a witch, but she's married to the Frog King, like a queen. He will decide on her later.

Most clearly, though: Hannah. In her bed as the day rises and falls around her, she is a sleeping princess, under a spell.

Bit puts the book back in its place and feeds another log to the woodstove. If he didn't, his nose would drip and Abe would come home from a terrible long day on the cold roof to frown at Hannah on her pallet. She would close her eyes and let his disapproving silence wash over her. Bit closes the stove and eats a piece of dried pineapple and watches the lump of Hannah for a long time.

Will she wake on her own? The day begins to go shadowy. The wind picks up within the forest, and Bit can hear its dark rush toward them.

At last, Bit washes his hands carefully and brushes his teeth three times with baking soda. He kneels behind his mother's pillow. He cups her cheeks. Slowly, he lowers his mouth to hers, kissing with all he has within him, pressing his lips hard against hers until he can feel the shape of her teeth behind her lips and taste the bad tang of her breath.

She doesn't awaken when he lifts his head away. He takes his hands back sadly. This is what he'd feared. Bit is not the one. He is not her prince.

The women boil down the sap in a water heater Tarzan welded into a huge double boiler, and the air all over Arcadia smells sweet and a little burnt at the edges. Bit can almost taste the sugar when he puts out his tongue. One morning, when Sweetie brings the Kid Herd over the fresh drifts of snow to the Sugarshack, Mikele and Suzie, who have boiled all night long, are giddy, and paint the soft snow with streaks of syrup. The syrup sinks as it cools, and when they fish it out, it has hardened into candy.

Don't tell Astrid, says Suzie. She hacks the syrup taffy into pieces and hands them out to the kids. His piece is so sweet that Bit gags, but to not hurt their feelings he swallows it anyway and pretends to want more.

Abe's clothes stink with sweat and sawdust; the men are finished with the entire roof. Tomorrow, the joints of Abe's hands won't have ice in them all the time, and Bit won't startle when he accidentally brushes them in his sleep. Tomorrow, Abe will start to put in bathrooms and plumbing to the Eatery, and the huge heap of salvaged copper pipes down at the Motor Pool will shrink to nothing.

When we're in Arcadia House, people say all the time now, longing writ on their faces. Always, the dream of *when.* Things will be better, we will be warmer, people won't argue, we will send extra aid into the world, we will start the publishing company, nobody will have vitamin D deficiencies, the kidlets will go to school, the midwives will be on hand, the bears won't come out of the woods and ransack the garbage pails and scatter the unwashed diapers or Menstrufleeces all across the Quad, there will be no loos.

Muffin, who once lived with her mothers in an apartment in Albany, tries to describe toilets to the kids: You turn a knob, she says, and water gushes out and swallows up your poop.

Helle begins to cry. Like a monster, she sobs. It eats your shit!

The others sigh and shift away, as they usually do when Helle cries. But Bit goes to her and hugs her to him, this squishy hard girl, all elbows and pudge. At first she pulls back, but when he lets go of her, she sinks against him. She is bigger than he is, but sometimes he thinks she's younger, even, than the toddlers. She is strange. She smells like a vanilla bean. Bit always feels a little sick for her.

Not like a monster, says Muffin with disdain. It's like the loos. But it doesn't stink and isn't cold and there aren't spiders and the Sanitation Crew doesn't have to pump them, and you don't have to spread lye. You just turn the knob and it goes away.

Where's away? says Leif.

I don't know, says Muffin.

They look at one another, thinking. At last, Erik, who is eleven, says, I think the ocean. Yes, they all agree, away must be the ocean, which Bit pictures as the Pond on a windy day, people in strange outfits waiting on the opposite side: women in kimonos and wooden shoes, men in paddy hats and dashikis like Muhammad's, little flotillas of shit rushing over the surface toward them, scrap-paper sails and all.

As they sleep, a cloud dumps snow upon them. Ersatz Arcadia has become a smooth pretty village of white, poked with playful, smoking chimneys, like the old-timey picture in Hannah's book on Russian serfs. Today, again, Hannah doesn't get up. Every part of her is filmy with oils. She murmurs and grabs Bit and pulls him in gently under the blankets, against her warmth. When he is very still and breathes with her and drifts off to sleep in her wake, he sees pieces of her dreams: a gray street that Bit has never seen, a tree with coppery bark, a fountain under oaks draped in dusk, a huge black bird with its beak cracked to a red tongue. Deeper, and he is in the belly of a closet and something soft brushes his temple and voices are raised outside. There is a dinner table with many forks and spoons laid out in rows and a tiny silver bowl into which a white hand dabbles. There is a return to something private, slippery, that tips and spills. When he wakes, he is drenched with sweat but shivering.

Midmorning is blindingly bright. His friends are rolling yarn balls from unwearable sweaters, and the Pink Piper smells like sweaty oatmeal. When Bit passes the Free Store with the Kid Herd, out for what Sweetie calls their Afternoon Constitutional, he sees Kaptain Amerika on the porch. The stars in the Trippie's sarong flap in the wind. He beckons Bit close with a bony finger. *Inside my ear a bed she laid. And there she slept. And all became her sleep,* he murmurs with his sour breath. Rilke. My translation, of course, he says. Bit doesn't understand. The Kid Herd has moved past the Store, and Bit runs to catch up and, safe again, looks back to see the old Trippie gazing at him. The Kaptain's words tumble over one another in his head all afternoon, like a small room packed with toddlers.

Jincy's mother, Caroline, is gone. She has left her things and run away. And though Jincy weeps and her father, Wells, spits about abandonment and puts Caroline's clothes in the Free Store, Bit knows what happened.

This morning, when there was pewter frost on the grass, Bit came out for a pee and saw a huge white bird on the roof of Jincy's bus, bright in the predawn. He saw it spread its wings and turn, once. It flapped. Then Jincy's mother heaved herself up into the air and flew away.

Jincy comes over to stay at Bit's, to sleep in his sleeping bag with him, to squeeze him until she feels better. He goes limp and bears it.

At night: Sweetness. Hey. Hey, sweet girl, wake up.

Umph. What.

I'm worried about you. Regina tells me

you haven't been going to the Bakery these past few days. Dorotka says you're not going up to Arcadia House with the women in the afternoon.

I'm just tired. You know how winter always gets me down.

Yeah. Yeah. But this seems worse than usual. Are there days you're not getting out of bed?

Hannah says nothing.

It's just. I know with your dad and the other thing you're pretty sad. But, I mean, I'm working my ass off. It's already March and the plumbing still has another week and then we'll start in on the rest, and we're already behind, and in that last letter of Handy's he was talking about cutting out Oregon so they all could get back here the week before we have to plow, and we can use all the Monkeypower we can get so that we're all done before they get back.

Nothing. Bit's own heartbeat in his ears.

Sweet girl? Don't want to talk?

Only the trees shaking outside.

Okay. You take your time. Take a week or so, sleep it off. But I'd like you up and at 'em next week. Okay?

His mother's even breath.

An emergency. The Showerhouse water

heater is dead. Abe takes Bit with him. When they get down to the low hut by the Pond, there is no hot water left and the Thursday bathers look on, miserable, soap in their chilled hair.

Abe must examine the hookups under the tank, and Titus and Hiero and Tarzan help move it. Someone gasps, someone screams: mounded under where it had stood, they find a coil, a ball of snakes, hibernating rattlers.

Abe's muscles are quick, and with the heavy heels of his boots, he smashes until blood splatters, a great deal of it, bits of snake everywhere. Bit wants to bend down and touch one of the rattles that sticks above the gore, delicate as a mushroom. But Abe picks him up and thrusts him at Titus. Just as someone begins to shout in horror, Titus goes back into the night with Bit, his long-legged giant's stride impossibly fast over the ground. Hannah doesn't awaken when Bit crawls into bed with her. In his sleep, the wind blowing through the forest becomes Hannah's breath, becomes the embers falling in the woodstove, becomes a distant roar.

Sweetie outfits the kids in their anoraks and boots and takes them to the Pond, which has finally, this late, frozen solid. They wait for Bit, shaking the Bread Truck on its axles until he reluctantly comes out. It is a tearing in him to leave Hannah behind. But when he is in the fresh cold air, he feels scrubbed. All morning, they slip and slide across the ice in their boots. They scream. Hysteria smacks them in the gullet. They form whiplash lines, where one of the bigger kids, Leif or Erik or Muffin or Molly or Fiona, is the pivot, the little kids at the end. Bit, one of the littlest, littler even than Pooh, who is only three and a girl, is released and flies, over and over and over across the ice on his feet, then his knees, and into the pillowy snowbanks at the edges.

The sun peeps out sporadically, and when it does the ice glows green. The trees that rim the Pond dazzle with icicles that clatter together when wind blows, that make a sound like chimes when they fall.

Helle forms fat snow angels connected like paper dolls around the Pond. It takes her hours. Jincy and Muffin spin until they're dizzy. Leif finds a great fish frozen with his snout to the surface, and talks to it in a low voice. The babies who can walk, Felipe and Ali and Sy and Franklin, dabble their mittens in the snow, toddle and fall in the drifts. The boys knock each other down.

Astrid and the pregnant teenagers Saucy Sally and Flannery bring grilled soy-cheese sandwiches and thermoses of chamomile tea down for the kidlets, and take the babies home. The bigger kids are refueled for another hour when, one by one, they drop.

Bit can feel the ice cold and hard through his snow clothes. He feels his body washed clean by the winter, by the hard good work of playing. When he enters the Bread Truck, his mother is at the table with Abe.

Abe's eyes are red-rimmed, and he gives Bit a kiss on the head before he takes off Bit's jacket and snow pants and hat and gloves. I'm sorry for what happened last night, Little Man, he says. I'm sorry you had to see it. It was instinct, that's all. I never, ever meant to kill anything, even snakes. You know it's wrong to kill. It's really bad Karma.

Bit pats his father's face, forgiving him. He is shy near his mother, scans the air around her head. Hey, baby, she says, and pulls him onto her lap. He gives a little hiss of pain through his teeth, and she sets him down again, takes off his jeans. Oh, my God, she says. Oh, my God, baby, what happened to your legs?

He doesn't recognize them at first, they're so purple with bruises. His knees are also raw, skinned bloody. He shrugs, and she kisses each one gently, and Abe swings back out and up to Arcadia House, as if chased.

That feel better, Bit? Hannah says, rubbing Bag Balm into his skin.

Bit's tongue is frozen. As he struggles and fails to speak, he understands that he hasn't said much for some time. He tries to count the days but loses track. Words have buried into him, gone to sleep, a frozen ball under the earth of him, coiled and waiting for the thaw.

You're so quiet these days, baby, Hannah says, pausing as she dreamily combs out her waist-long hair. She gives up when she meets the matted knots. She pulls him to her. It feels too sharp inside Bit to look at her, and so he turns and sits on her bony lap and lets her comb his hair. The teeth of the comb are so gentle on his scalp, it feels like crying. He had forgotten this small pleasure. She says, pressing her lips into the top of his head, My strong, silent boy. Let's sing. She begins, her voice scratchy, but he won't sing along to the lullaby, and when he doesn't, she also stops.

He wakes to see Abe watching Hannah as she sleeps. Oh, Bit thinks. He waits, but Abe lies down. And it is Bit who touches his mother, who pats her face, hands, belly, again and again and again.

In the afternoon, he hides behind the toy-box in the Pink Piper while all the other kids pull on their winter things to play outside. He is left alone in the quiet bus. The shouts of the others are muffled by the snowy world outside, and the babies are downstairs with Maria, having a snack or a bottle. He hugs his chest and tells himself the story of the girl and her swan brothers, holds it in his mind and looks at it this way, that way, to find out what it means to him.

Once upon a time, he tells himself, there was a princess. She lived with her six brothers out in the deep forest, hidden from her father's mean new wife. The stepmother found out where they lived and knitted silk shirts out of magic and threw the magical shirts over the boys and turned them into swans. The princess became sad when her brothers flew away and went into the woods to try to find them. She walked and walked, until she found a little cabin. At dark, she heard the sound of wings and six swans fluttered in the windows. They took off their wings and turned into her brothers, but the boys could be human for only a short time before the robbers who lived in the cottage came home with their booty. She asked her brothers how to reverse the spell, and they said she had to go six years without laughing, singing, or speaking and she must make six shirts out of starflowers.

But remember, they said, if you say even one word, the spell will be broken and we'll be swans forever.

So the girl went away to collect starflowers and sew. She was quiet as a mouse. One day, some men were walking along and they saw the girl up in her tree where she lived. They called for her to come down and she shook her head and she kept throwing down clothes, trying to get them to leave, until she was naked. Then they dragged her to the king of a faraway place who married her, even though she couldn't say a word. But when the girl gave birth, the king's mother stole the baby and told the king that his wife had eaten it. This happened three times until the king believed his wife ate their babies and he said to kill her. The day she was supposed to die was the last day of the girl's six years of quiet, and she'd sewed everything but one sleeve of one shirt. The brothers flew down to her and she threw the starflower shirts over them and they turned back into people, except that the brother who got an unfinished shirt had a swan's wing instead of one arm. Then the girl could speak, and she explained what had happened and the babies were brought back and the king's mother got the electric chair. And the girl and her brothers were happy forever after. The end.

A vision rises before Bit, a celebration: a keg of Slap-Apple under the stars, one boy winging in spirals toward the moon, the girl golden and round as Hannah had been in the summer, the old Hannah, who had stood on a picnic bench and shouted about freedom, love, community. He imagines those babies who lived for so many years without their mother, what it would feel like to be hugged by her for the first time, her warmth at last against their bodies. How they would clutch her to them and never let her go. He imagines not talking for six years, until he is almost twelve, so many years, more than he has been alive. The days stretch out before him. He tries not to cry, but the world he can see from where he is hidden (the loft of the Pink Piper, the heap of hammocks where they're stored during the day, a baby's shoe on its side) goes wavery in his eyes.

Last, he thinks of Hannah, her face drawn to something he can't recognize. This thought fills him with an electric pulse; it thrashes, fishlike, in his gut. He must do something. He must.

He concentrates. He pushes back the words that were already sickly until they die on the bitter part of his tongue. They send bad tendrils into his chest. They heap, a toad, in the cave of his throat. When he walks and eats and plays, he can imagine the slimy thing there, waiting angrily for a word to slip past, for a chance to curse them all.

Tonight, all is peaceful on the surface in the Bread Truck. Hannah has cooked dinner, and the three of them listen to some scratchy voice singing "Your Eyes Have Told Me What I Did Not Know" on a crank Victor that the Motor Pool picked up from a trash heap in Buffalo. Bit is on Abe's lap, following along as his father reads the newspaper aloud. Bit once points to a caption that says "Goose bites baby" and does his new, silent laugh, and when he looks up at Abe, his father is studying Bit, his lips sucked in at the corners.

Hannah puts down her book and sniffs once, loudly.

Bit sniffs, too. Something somewhere is burning.

Abe flicks his paper down. Bit's parents

gaze at one another. They leap up and in their slippers and bathrobes run out the door.

The cold air roils with smoke. Shadows pour from the doorway; the gong bangs and bangs and bangs. Family Quonset One is on fire.

Abe is running with Bit to the Pink Piper, and he thrusts Bit inside, and the kids who live in the Family Quonsets are being shoved inside, too: Jincy and Sy and Franklin and Ali and Pooh and Molly and Fiona and Cole and Dyllie. The midwives have disappeared. The kids who already live in the Pink Piper run downstairs, and the Pregnant Ladies come over from the Henhouse, shaking muddy snow off their boots, shivering. Flannery and Eden and Saucy Sally pick up the littlest ones and comfort them. Someone thinks Bit is one of the littlest ones and presses him against her taut warmth, and Bit is grateful again for his smallness, to have these soft arms around him.

Where's Felipe? whispers Flannery, and Imogene, who lives in Family Quonset One, makes big eyes.

Leif and Erik hold Bit up to the window so he can see, though there is not much there: the world across the Quad swirls with yellow and gray, the last of the snow on the ground reflects the fire, the shadows of people dart with buckets.

Dylan sidles over. He is younger than Bit but taller.

It went boom, he says softly. Back where Ricky and Felipe and Maria live. And then Maria had the fire wings.

Shut up, Dylan, says Coltrane, who pushes his little brother and runs up the spiral staircase to where the hammocks are strung.

Dylan's eyes well up. He comes even closer to Bit.

She did too have the fire wings, he whispers, his voice full of sleep. Also she had hair of fire, Bit. And also a head full of fire, too.

Bit stares so long at the burning Quonset that the world blotches in his eyes. The other kids have gone to sleep. The Pregnant Ladies are at the kitchen table, trying to swallow their sobs with glasses of water or cups of chamomile tea.

Outside, he sees people going slowly back to where they live. Some of the people who lived in the burnt-up Quonset go into Hans and Fritz's lean-to because those two men are away with Handy; the Pregnant Ladies go back to the Henhouse. Only a few Arcadians remain outside, watching the twisted metal and the embers within. In the dully gleaming dark, Bit recognizes his parents leaning into one another, tall Hannah, tall Abe, her braids on his shoulder, his arm around her waist. Bit shuts his eyes and blindly feels his way into Jincy's sleeping bag, to keep his parents standing there together.

In the morning, Ricky and Maria and Felipe are gone.

Bit overhears Astrid telling the older kids that the baby had died. She cries, pursing her mouth up over her terrible yellow teeth, the way the horse the Amish bring for harvest draws his lips over a carrot.

Burnt up? says Molly, who cries and cries. Her sister, Fiona, begins to wail into her hands so that only her vast white forehead is visible.

A burnt baby. Bit pictures one of the marshmallows from before Astrid's war against sugar, crumpled and black on the edge of the bonfire.

No, Astrid says. From smoke. In his sleep. Small blessings. Maria is burnt, but she will be home soon. Ricky is with her in the hospital.

Leif says, angrily, Handy should know about this. If Handy knows, he'll come home and make it better. My dad can fix it.

Astrid does her funny in-breath that means a yes. Assent on the intake, Hannah calls it. I called Handy in Austin, Astrid says, kissing Leif. In Texas. He told me to tell you he loves us all and he is sending vibes into the ether. He wanted to come home, but Maria and Ricky said no, don't return early, we need the cash from the concerts. Besides, they're not ready yet to have the memorial. We'll have a service for Felipe in the spring.

I want my dad, says Leif; and his big boy's face crumples and he begins to cry.

Astrid pulls him to her, pulls all of her children, Erik and Leif, froggy Helle, hyper Ike, to her, and says into their matching white-blond hair, Well, that's another story, indeed.

In the morning, Bit runs to the stream trickling in the woods. Yellow jags of ice edge the water. Bit kneels on the ice and puts his head in the stream, and the cold is enough to rip the breath from him, a relief.

Handy sends a letter, express. Astrid calls a meeting in the Octagonal Barn, and they gather in the late afternoon to hear Hiero read it aloud. Handy says greetings to all his beautiful beatniks. He is devastated by the news, and feels profoundly for the Free People keeping the faith at the Homeplace. He urges them to remember that suffering is what tempers the steel in the human soul, and when one suffers in community, the community grows stronger.

Hiero's voice shakes when he reads: *Pain, when given its proper place in the human heart, can be a door that leads to a feeling of oneness with the Universe. This is a path to deeper empathy.*

Soon enough, Handy tells them, they will all be together. Try to be strong and we will bear the impossible weight of our sorrow in communion. Namaste.

Namaste, they say, and the women cry, holding one another. The babies goggle at their mothers and pat their faces.

After one week, Maria returns from the hospital, her head and arms wrapped like gifts in white bandages. Ricky and she seem to be carrying one another wherever they walk.

Bit sits under the table as Marilyn and Hannah drink St.-John's-wort tea. They talk about the oil embargo, about Marilyn's webbed feet, about thalidomide babies, born with flippers. Bit thinks of a wee newborn flapping underwater, like the beaver that lived in the stream behind the Family Quonsets and gave them all giardia one spring.

He goes back to his book, the story of the fisherman and his wife. The women forget about him. They begin to murmur.

I don't know how much longer I can handle it, Hannah says. This isn't what I signed up for, this isn't a better life, this isn't anything but poverty and hard work and not enough money to buy the kids winter boots.

I know, says Marilyn.

Hannah's voice goes muffled when she says, . . . *want . . . out.* She makes a sound that doesn't seem human. Bit watches her legs worriedly, afraid she is sick.

Marilyn's voice, softer than ever. Hang in there. We move into Arcadia House in less than a month. We'll all live together, and everything will be better. You can make it.

I can't, Hannah says. Fucking Handy . . .

You can, says Marilyn, and her voice sounds like a door closing, and Bit knows that there exist things even outspoken Hannah isn't allowed to say.

A taste of Saucy Sally's poppyseed cake, the way Leif can swing Bit by the legs so the world spins deliriously past, the feel of running on the last crust of snow when the others fall through, that softness at the end of a branch that is the whisper of a bud. He adds to the list in his head. Raspberry jam on just-baked bread. The smell of the pocket of Titus's waxed coat, pipe tobacco and lint and cedar. The four blond heads of Handy's kids around a letter. The feel of fresh plaster. He sits by his mother and comes up with these fragments and tries to beam them into her head. Once or twice, he is sure he succeeds. She sighs sweetly in her sleep when he remembers the smell of a newborn's crown or the downy feel of her own soft cheek upon his.

The Kid Herd is at the stream. The footbridge is not safe: it wobbles, its ends dunked in the wild runoff. White suckers churn upstream, their many bluish bellies transformed into a single pulsing one. Bit stares down, the stick gone heavy in his hand. Toothwort bobs on the bank.

Do it! shouts Leif, who has turned into a dancing goblin. He is hysterical with violence.

Bit, calls Jincy over the roar, and Bit looks up at her. Her curls are wilder than usual. There has been a charcoal smear on her cheek for a week. It's wrong to kill, she shouts, close to tears.

The others stand, a mass, uncertain, waiting to see what he will do. Helle has begun to wail, though her eyes bulge with anticipation. Bit looks at his friends. Cole and Dylan, side by side, make the same face Sweetie makes when one of the kids hurts another. Jincy covers her mouth with a hand.

He thinks of a fish body wriggling on the stick, of a mass of blood.

Bit grips the stick that Leif whittled with Abe's pearl-handled blade. He pulls it behind his head and hurls it into the stream. It bounces back at him and smacks him above the eye. The pain is terrible, like swallowing a brick of ice. Leif and Erik and Ike and Fiona shriek and dance, Helle wails, Jincy says, No, no, no, no, no. Molly, who thinks she's a horse, who has made them call her Secretariat since last summer, even though Secretariat is a boy, whinnies and throws her mane and stomps her foot. In fury, Bit grabs the stick and chucks it as hard as he can toward the bank, where it grazes Muffin's knee.

Muffin's face goes red behind her glasses, and she screams. She claws up the muddy bank and runs off through the forest, over the fields.

Now you're in trouble, says Fiona, her voice humid with excitement. Her bangs are slicked with sweat and her forehead gleams. She runs off. The others follow, the boys whooping like Indians through the afternoon dapple. Helle stays for a second to scream IhateyouIhateyouIhateyouBitStone, then she, too, scurries off. Her round little body falls behind her brothers', and she ruins a patch of early spring beauty flowers as she goes. She pumps her arms and tiny corncob legs to catch them but they move off without her, as ever.

Alone, Bit is seized with grief. He comes down tentatively to the edge of the brook and tries to leap to the shore, but his boot fills with water. His shocked foot inside the boot feels the way his stomach feels inside his body.

He crouches for a while on the side of the brook, watching the frantic push of fish. He sends out mute apologies, waits for the great King Fish to surface, its stern face leathery and terrible, to open its vast mouth and curse him. Or eat him. Or maybe, he thinks with a pulse, to send him off on his search to find the thing that will save his mother. He holds his breath until he feels faint and, when nothing happens, moves up the bank to sit among the fiddleheads, their bald skulls rearing shyly from the dirt. The wind blows cold from the top of the trees, brushing down, and the parched leaves chatter under it. In the hollows to the north of some trunks, he dips his fist into small pockets of snow.

He sits long enough for a squirrel to emerge and almost run over his foot. A hawk swoops over the stream and snatches at something and rises again as if riding a pendulum.

For a few breaths he forgets himself in the swim of nature around him. Its rhythm is so different from Bit's human own, both more nervous and more patient. He sees a bug that is smaller than a period on a page. He sees the sky, bigger than all that's in his head. An overwhelm from two directions, vast and tiny, together.

From behind him, footsteps. He hears them when they are still far away. They thunder the ground. He knows from his Grimm that it is probably a giant come to eat him, but he can't find the energy to fight. Bit bends his head and waits for the great hand, the teeth. Instead, he smells something fleshy and feminine, blood and pus and sweat and rose soap. Astrid. She sits beside him and he waits for her to yell.

She doesn't. She just sits. When he dares, he lifts his head to look at her. She studies her feet, unshod and luxuriating in the cold mud. She smiles down at him. I love spring mud in the toes, she says. Makes me think of home. Norway, you know.

He takes off his own shoes and wallows his toes in the mud.

After some time, Astrid claps him on a thigh and stands. She scoops him up. So light, little Bit, she says. You are maybe twenty pounds? I'm sure I have delivered a new baby almost as heavy as you. You are a marvel.

They come out of the forest onto the Sugarbush path, then up into the Sheep's Meadow. Already, flowers spread on the ground like small open mouths, purple bells, white stars with golden hearts.

He rests his head on her shoulder, and she says, Not to worry. You will grow. And one day things will not be so confusing. This I can promise you.

When they come into Ersatz Arcadia, she says one last thing into his ear. She says, Don't think that nobody knows you are not talking, that nobody worries about the words that are stuck in you. But you take your time. When you can, you will tell me the story of everything you feel and I will do everything to make it better. This I also promise you, she says, and Astrid's face is kind as a field of dandelions.

Astrid carries him into the Henhouse, and only now, in its warmth, does he know how cold he has been. It smells like chamomile and yarrow and lavender, other herbs that hang from the rafters in the kitchen. Someone moans above, and Flannery lopes downstairs naked, with a basin in her arms, her belly vast, her face panicky. She is one of the teenagers who have been showing up every few weeks, petrified but knowing, as they somehow do, that the midwives take care of the Pregnant Ladies who come to them.

Oh, thank God you're back, she breathes. Marilyn was called off to Amos the Amish's daughter, and Midge had to go take a nail out of D'Angelo's foot.

Astrid looks down, and touches Bit's head, and says, You'll stay here, in the kitchen, with Flan? We can have our talk after Eden's baby is born, yes? And Bit nods, though he knows he won't say a word. Astrid strips off all her clothing and washes herself for a long time with soap and water so hot it steams. When she goes upstairs, she is nude, also.

Flannery puts on a bathrobe and makes a face at Bit. So what's your story, she says. You're the retarded one, right? He shakes his head, but she snorts, and gives him a piece of apple cake, and goes off to lie down on the couch. Jesus, she says. I'm *definitely* not looking to get this little bastard out of me if it's gonna be like that. She points, finger trembling, skyward.

In a moment, she is asleep and breathing heavily. Bit goes upstairs.

The room is murky where Eden is lying on her back. At first, he can see only the gleam of her coppery hair, then a lady's swollen bottom and a great upswell of flesh. Astrid is astride her and rubs her belly with something glossy, breathing with her. You must remember, she says, it is a rush, it is good energy, it is the energy it takes to get this baby into the world. There is no pain here. Do not push. All in its own time.

Eden grimaces and gives a low whine, and seems to release something, and Astrid says, Good, good.

Astrid puts two long white fingers into Eden's folds and feels around. They are bloody when she takes them out. She nods and grunts.

The coil begins to wind again in Eden. Her feet clench. In the middle of the grip, she opens her eyes and sees Bit there at the door and locks her eyes into him, and Bit locks back, pushing the way she pushes at him. Then she relaxes again, and lolls her head back, and Astrid coos, and Eden picks up her head and winks at Bit. Hey, she says. Thanks for that one, Monkey.

Astrid turns. You! she says, Ridley Sorrel Stone! But before she can shoo Bit away, Eden says, No, no. He was helpful, Astrid. I want him here, okay? He's good at this.

Astrid goes to the doorway and calls to Flannery, who takes Bit downstairs, grumbling, and scrubs him until he hurts. He is naked when he climbs back up, and shivers in the chill. He burrows into the bed with Eden and rests his head against her shoulder. She smells like chicory and fatigue and onions; she is vast and hot. He puts his hands on her forehead and smoothes out the wrinkles there.

The light dies in the windows. People come in and out, among them Abe, worried. He tries to talk to Bit. But Bit is concentrating. People leave. Astrid changes the sheets by rolling both of them over. Someone gives Bit a piece of warm bread with applebutter, but he doesn't care to eat. He stays with Eden. He sleeps when she naps between waves, and wakens when she surfaces in pain.

Something suddenly shifts in Astrid: she becomes quick, efficient. Flannery rubs Eden's shoulders. New light kindles in the panes of glass and grows. It is somehow day. Astrid makes coaxing noises, and Eden gives high moans, which Astrid tries to make her lower. Marilyn comes in, fresh and smiling and bearing two quilts and a mince pie, her voice spinning over the miracle of the Amish baby she just delivered, fat and blue-eyed and rosy as a piglet. Eden shouts, and Marilyn screws up her lips and goes away.

Eden manages to eat some porridge, which comes up. She drinks some tea. She grips Bit's tiny arms, and he won't feel the steel in her hands until later, when Hannah will take him to the Showerhouse and cry at the purple on his skin, touching the bruises gently with her fingers, as if to brush them away.

Eden's body is a fist as she pushes. Bit hears voices saying, Good, sweetheart, so good, the head is here, it's wonderful, one more, Eden. But Eden gazes into Bit's face, her canines catch on her lower lip; and in sudden overwhelm, the smell of shit. Then there's a breaking, a slippage, and in Astrid's hands there's a bloody, waxy, frantic beauty, a creature that wags its tiny arms and begins to squawk like a seagull. Eden and Bit rest against one another and watch through half-closed eyes.

Eden lifts her arms up for the baby, which Marilyn has already washed and wrapped in a blanket. Astrid guides the tiny mouth to Eden's fist-size nipple, and shows the baby how to latch on. It grunts and snorts, the most urgent thing Bit has ever seen.

Bathed in the dim early morning light, in sweat, in exhaustion, Eden swims in the last thrashes of pain. She holds her baby and looks down into the ancient face. Bit takes everything he feels now and buries it deep in him, a secret shining place to visit in his quietness, the best place he has ever known.

The women come for Hannah. They come into the Bread Truck while Abe is still there, before the sun has risen. They bring the spring cold in the pockets of their clothing. Their breath steams in the warmth of the Bread Truck. Up, up, they say, and Hannah stands. Magnificent women, the women of Arcadia, all legs and thin hands, bandannas, white throats, cracks at the edges of their eyes where the sun has creased their skin. They seat Hannah at the table, brush out her hair, braid it up again tightly. They warm water and strip her. Bit's mother's body is thin, her bones show, and they wipe her down with hot cloths. Slowly, her smell is thinned with Astrid's rose soap. Her skin, her hair, her sleep, is watered until, at last, what is her own disappears.

The women take her away.

Abe is distracted during supper, oat groats with soy-sauce, fresh bean curd. Hannah hasn't been back since the women took her. Bit is free to think his thoughts, and he thinks of how he will go into the forest, soon, to help his mother. He wishes for someone to tell him what to look for, and he hopes that it won't be someone too frightening or ugly. He listens to the wind in the pines, but it doesn't talk to him the way it talks to boys in his stories.

When all is cleared and clean in the Bread Truck, Abe deposits Bit at the Pink Piper to sleep in Cole's hammock. He kisses him gravely and leaves.

The metal roof clicks with tiny icy snow. Astrid's children breathe lightly. Sweetie's boys snore and shift, Cole jabs at Bit with his heels. The pile of Family Quonset kids tangle together under the blankets.

Bit turns and sees Helle's eyes are open, yellow, in the dim. Tadpole of Handy, he thinks, bulby and strange. She looks at Bit, her mouth swelling with information. She is nosy, a listener at doors, a tattletale.

She whispers, They're making a Critique tonight. Of Hannah. Of your mom.

Bit hears Marilyn downstairs talking to someone, Saucy Sally it sounds like. He gets out of his hammock and creeps down the stairs. They're smoking funny stuff out the window, even though Sally is pregnant. They gab, are not watchful. He goes out the door.

Ice glazes on the grass and his feet are bare, his legs cold under the thin pajamas. His soles burn until he can't feel them anymore, and he must pump his arms to be sure he is still running. The wind smacks his face with a cold hand. When he longs to lie down in the sinister rows of the apple orchard, he thinks of Hannah and goes on.

Up the slate stairs to Arcadia House, up the stone porch. He can't reach the doorknob, but he pushes and the vast door swings open.

A powerful stench: varnish and polyurethane and paint, beeswax and vinegar and sweat, sawdust and copper and cold nails. The stairs are finished but dark because there is no sky above them, only plaster and ceiling. The grand chandelier has been pieced together, and it hulks overhead in half shadow.

Over the still-tacky floorboards, to the stairs, curving up. Halfway there, he hears voices. Another corridor, paint sticky under his hand. Another stairway. The voices are louder. When he reaches the doorway to the back of the Proscenium, the voices are very loud.

He crouches and puts his eye to the crack. His feet come alive again, and he would cry with the pain if he didn't first bite the inside of his cheek to blood.

From there he sees the silhouettes of bodies, some shiftings, the shadow of a hand that rises to a face, heads that move together then apart. Beyond, elevated on the stage, uplit by three kerosene lamps, there is Hannah.

She is tiny, shriveled, so distant from him. She is alone. Her hands are folded in her lap, and she looks down and nods. Someone, a man, says: . . . *mean, Hannah baby, we love you and want you to feel better, man, but it's just such a drag, you're like bringing down all our energy and we've got a shitload more work to do before Handy and them get back and we need all the energy we can get for the planting, you dig?*

Hannah nods, nods, nods.

Now, someone else says in a calm cold

voice, . . . *Mahayana, big boat, caring for everyone, but you're manifesting pure Hinayana, small boat, taking care of yourself . . .* Hannah nods.

And someone, a woman, says, *Listen . . . when you're good, there's nobody better . . . in the fall know you had that accident . . . sad to lose a baby . . . over it by now?*

And Hannah's hands clench at her skirt and her face contracts, then smoothes out, and still she nods.

Now a familiar voice, Titus's. He roars. He says, . . . *fucking nuts, man, it's like taking someone whose leg is broken and jumping on the fucking leg, we're not doing anybody any favors here, I've been there, Hannah, I've been where you are, I've been down so low the black dog is at my neck, man, I know what it's like so don't listen to these hypocritical assholes . . .*

An uproar, voices shouting over Titus's. Hannah looks out into the audience, finds a face to fix on, and stares at it. In this moment the whole of her is present. His mother, so wispy, so far away.

Bit can't hold himself: he leaps up from where he is crouched and begins to run. Down the endless aisle, down past the people who sit on the benches, down past the folks sprawled on the floor, to the stairs, up. Out of the shadow and into the shallow pool of kerosene light, with Hannah alone in the center. He thrusts himself onto his mother's lap and cradles her head in his arms. He can feel all the others' eyes heavy on his back. For a long moment, nothing, silence.

Briefly, a wet warmth on his belly, his mother's face pressing into him.

Briefly, her mouth moving against him, kissing him through his shirt.

Now, Abe is on the stage and lifting Bit, and Bit floats halfway down the aisle in Abe's steely hands. Abe is whispering fiercely into his ear; Bit twists and fights to return to Hannah. In silence, Bit struggles, desperate, and when they go down the third-floor steps, down the curved entry stairs and out into the night, he hears what Abe is saying, . . . *I know, little one, I know you're in pain, I know you're holding it in, monkey . . .* Abe presses Bit against him and Bit hangs on to his father, his warmth, his one solid ground in the spinning awful world, his gravity. He presses against Abe and tries to push him away, tries to fly back toward Hannah, clutches his father; pushes him, clutches. Abe is saying . . . *don't have to let it out yet . . .* It is only when they are halfway home, as Abe begins to trot over the hard ground, that Bit's internal scream lurches and burbles and emerges in a sour rush of vomit.

In the night, he hears: Now or never, baby. I left a Bug outside, keys in the ignition.

A silence so long Bit almost sleeps. Then a whispered No.

Then you have to try. You have to begin to try. You have to. You have to.

His father's voice is thick and shuddery, and it makes Bit go thick and shuddery inside.

A very long silence. Bit is almost asleep. Then it comes, soft, soft: I'll try.

He wakes, gnawed. He breathes with Hannah until Abe gets up, feeds them, drops Bit off at the Pink Piper. Before he goes, Abe kneels before Bit and brushes the hair out of his eyes, and says, Whenever you want, you talk to me, okay?

All day long, Bit is being eaten inside. The nameless bad pushes in his legs, makes his shoulders ache. He longs to rip up the pillows and send the hammocks a-scattering over the Quad.

His silence isn't working alone. He will need a Quest. And if he doesn't go on his Quest soon to find the thing to save Hannah, he is afraid what he might do.

Sweetie tries to talk softly to him, but he runs away. The Kid Herd is quiet today. Dorotka takes time from starting the seeds in the solarium and now leads the kidlets into the forest to tell them about trees. He trails the other kids, stomps his boots. He must *do.* What? His longing twists and flicks in him.

The Kid Herd moves across the meadow and into the bitter woods. Bit lags five steps, ten steps behind.

Mud has dried into pocks and pits here. Pussy willows velvet the banks; other willows are awash with gold buds. Sweetie and Maria take the babies back to the Pink Piper with the wagons. Jincy and Muffin and Fiona roll down the tender-grassed slope. The boys stop smacking things with sticks to listen to Dorotka: Look, she urges them, Ulmaceae, elm. It has simple alternate leaves that are just coming out, look! It comes from Asia, originally. It seeds with a kind of samara, let's see aha, aha, here's one from last year.

She lifts a seed and it flutters down, a propeller.

She beams. They beam. Springtime, she says, a letter from a loved one.

Dorotka hugs the trunk, and one by one,

the children do, too. They move deeper into the shadows. Dutchman's-breeches! she calls. Look, miterwort. Look, hobblebush.

There is a crack in the gray sky and the sun sifts through, falls over the ground, powders the new buds. This is it, Bit understands with a great pulse in his throat where his words used to live. This is where his Quest begins. Bit crouches behind a rotten log where a fern grows in a bed of moss. He watches the others go. Soon, he cannot hear them at all.

Below the log, a cold spot, snow. Up through the snow push tiny wild strawberries that he eats and lets the bright sweet juice stain his hands. This is good, a sign to go deeper, to find what he needs to find.

He pushes off the path and into the woods. He is alone and everything is sharp, full of hungry life. Two chipmunks chase each other from branch to branch, and one falls, bounces on the ground, runs off again. The thickets grasp at him and only reluctantly let go. A stream sings in the distance: he turns a corner and almost stumbles into it. He goes onto his belly and leans over, and with a smooth stick he has found, he can almost touch the surface. His head is a splotch in the white sky, rimmed by the black reflected trees; his clothes are full of burrs. He knows he has a gash in his face only when he sees a drop of blood fall and be sucked down into the water and fade like smoke.

Now it will come, he thinks. Out of the water, probably. He hopes for a golden swan or a water nymph, but he would take a troll, an ugly little man Bit's size, a monster. He waits. Nothing happens.

In time, he moves on. His bones are weary. The day has gone cold and the sky above the greening branches is a deeper blue. Out of nowhere a doll's-eyes plant, googly with great white eyeballs, watches him. Through the hole in the trunk of one tree he sees a whole and early moon, and it reminds him of a pie. But when he looks closer, he sees the face embedded there. Why has nobody ever told him that the man in the moon is shouting in alarm?

He is so very little. And the woods are so black and deep.

His feet have gone numb when he finds the hiccup in the woods, the clearing. He feels an airlessness here. Stones stick out of the snow-burned grass, and Bit thinks of Astrid's teeth, the way they are haphazard and yellow.

He sits to gather himself, and finds his fingers tracing words carved in the stones.

Minerva, one says. *Whose Name Is Writ In Air.*

1857, another says.

A tiny one, a milk tooth, says simply, *Breathed once, then lost.*

He doesn't know how long he sits. The trees whisper among themselves. Dusk falls, and the stone under him grows chill. There is a sense of gathering, a hand that clenches the center of a stretched cloth and lifts.

From the corner of his eye, he sees a white movement. He watches it obliquely for ten breaths, then turns his head to look. He expects to see one of the stones crawling off into the darkness, but it is not a stone.

An animal stands there, pointy and white and tall, fringed. It is graceful as a white deer, but it is not a deer.

The beast fixes Bit with its yellow eye and sniffs. At its side, the shadows thicken. The texture flows vertical and becomes fabric. Bit holds himself tiny and still, and looks up the dress to find a face. A woman stares at him, a very old woman. It is the witch, the one he has dreamed of. But she is not ugly: her hair is a soft white with a black streak, and she has roses in her cheeks. Though her lips are set in deep wrinkles, the lips themselves are plush. The way she looks at him, Bit feels pinned.

They gaze at one another, the woman and Bit.

This is it, the nut of the Quest, what he was meant to find, the moment where everything will turn. He waits for her to speak or give him a sack of gold, to give him the curse or the antidote, a vial, an apple, an acorn to crack and spill, a silken dress, a horseshoe, a feather, a word. She will tell him, give him, help him. He feels his body, so tiny in the great, twilit world, but he knows he will do what she asks of him. Even if he has to live with her forever and ever in a small stone tower in the woods and never get to see Arcadia again, he will do it.

He thinks of Hannah, a shape in her bed. He thinks, Please.

He wishes he could shout but fears the old curse that may befall Hannah if his lips split and his longing pours out.

He waits, but the woman only steps backward and becomes the woods again. Then the beast lifts its thin front leg and, with a snort of steam from its nostrils, it, too, trots away. Their sounds fade. He is sitting in the blue dusk alone. His hands are as empty as ever.

His heart settles again into its rhythm, and he trusts himself to move. His jeans are wet in the seat and down the insides of his thighs. The forest pushes down so hard on him he can hardly breathe. He cannot cry, not now.

Bit begins to run, crashing over the sticks, stumbling in the sudden gouges in the ground. Trees loom like dreams in the dim before him, and it is all he can do to swerve around them. Something scatters the dry leaves behind him, something catches up, something will grasp him with its bony fingers. He runs harder, and it runs harder, pressing on him, and he can smell its terrible breath, and at last he hears the lap of water and bursts out onto the stony edge of the Pond. It seems vast tonight, and he realizes he is on the side opposite where they usually swim. Up the long black lawn, he sees the outbuildings hunched, the Soy Dairy, the Bakery, the Octagonal Barn; he sees Arcadia House, lit in some windows by the new generator the Motor Pool liberated from somewhere. Even from the lonely side of the Pond, he can hear the roar.

A glow warms a window upstairs where Bit imagines his father, good bearded Abe, rehanging a door. It calms Bit to imagine Abe in the lantern light, fixing, building, making better. This is what Abe does: he is steady, calming. There is a golden warmth also in the arched windows of the Eatery. Tonight, he remembers, is their first collective supper in Arcadia House, cooked in the stainless-steel kitchen ripped from an abandoned restaurant in Ithaca. He hopes his mother has been drawn to the light and warmth and food. It hurts him to think of the others, laughing, in the Eatery while she is alone in bed.

The ice along the border of the lake is thin as a glass ornament. He crunches it as he runs. When he reaches the path where the snapdragons will grow in the summertime, he begins to sprint. In the distance, people move in a line lit by lanterns and flashlights up the path from Ersatz Arcadia.

He bursts inside, into the overwhelming warmth. Here, too, is a thicket of legs like birch trunks, and he almost runs into one. Hey, there, man, someone says. Whoa, where's the emergency, someone else says. What the hey was that? someone asks, and someone else says, Oh, just your average forest elf, and there is laughter and he screws his fists and pushes harder.

The kitchen blasts with heat, hurts him. It smells so good he wants to cry. It is something fried, vegetable stew. He finds Hannah stirring vinegar into the roasted beets in a huge steel bowl, and clutches her knees. She smiles down at him. She lifts him and washes his face with warm water at one of the sinks. She says Brr, when she touches his hands, and picks the leaves and twigs out of his hair and lifts him to sniff at his rear end, and makes a little face, shrugging. We all have accidents, she whispers. It's okay once in a while to piss yourself, I'd say.

He puts his face close to his mother's warm mouth, and like that, the chasing thing in the woods draws away and dissolves back into the night.

Out in the Eatery, under the exposed beams, they sit at newly varnished tables for a moment of thanks. Someone says, *Itadakimasu,* I take this nourishment in gratitude to all beings; then they pile up their plates. Hannah pulls Bit up onto her lap and cuddles him there. She feeds him from her fork, small bits of bread and stew, and his day comes over him in a great wash. The words that others are saying go meaningless in his ears. With a bit of seitan still in his mouth, he closes his eyes and falls asleep.

He has done it, though he is confused, though he doesn't know what he's done.

There was no key he was handed, no word that he said.

Hannah is not out entirely, but she is emerging. She rises every day. She brushes her hair. She bakes at the Bakery. Only sometimes when Abe isn't looking does Hannah close her eyes for a long time, and Bit holds his breath. But with an effort that seems to wrench her, she always opens them again.

Though Abe frets at first, Astrid commands the afternoon off. They will play, she says, and dares anyone to protest. They do not. The afternoon is bright and warm. The men go onto the tender green lawn between the porch and outbuildings, carrying the lacrosse sticks that Billy-goat, a real Onondaga Indian, had made one winter out of ash sticks and reclaimed raincoats. The women braid the hair of the men into plaits like their own, and then the men strip down all the way to their cotton shorts, torsos glowing winter-pale. Bit sits with the laughing women, who smoke wackystuff and chat among themselves and drink iced tea from pitchers, who pass around babies and blow tubas on the bellies of the wee ones. The other kids are playing somewhere, but he sits on Hannah's thin lap, he watches the heaving mass of men chasing down the little ball, colliding and breaking apart, singing and arguing, falling to the ground, sweating. He watches his father drop a ball out of the basket of his stick and blush all down his neck and chest, how Titus's fat-tire flops at his waistband, how Hiero is so nimble he doesn't even seem to run, just appears where he needs to be. And Bit realizes as Tarzan shoots an easy goal and his team leaps and shouts and pats and squeezes that none of these big adult men, despite their smells and strength, are much more than boys, not so different from Bit himself. The world contracts in a friendly way around him.

Time comes to him one morning, stealing in. One moment he is looking at the lion puppet on his hand that he's flapping about to amuse Eden's russet potato of a baby, and the next he understands something he never knew to question. He sees it clearly, now, how time is flexible, a rubber band. It can stretch long and be clumped tight, can be knotted and folded over itself, and all the while it is endless, a loop. There will be night and then morning, and then night again. The year will end, another one will begin, will end. An old man dies, a baby is born.

Summer Hannah will take over from Winter Hannah with a slowly crisping voice and a new pair of dungarees. Not completely yet. But soon.

Sweetie passes, and puts her cold hands under his chin. What's the matter, baby? she says, wiping his cheeks. Are you hurt?

His secret swells in him, almost bursts; it is good, it is wonderful. But he must be silent, he remembers almost too late, and shakes his head. She carefully dries his cheeks with a clean bit of her sleeve and gives him a cookie she tells him to keep secret from Astrid, whom she calls the Sugar Nazi. Then she kisses him. He would like to stay like this, Sweetie's soft lips on his skin, but with a long breath he reluctantly lets time flow again.

The dawn of the day that Handy is to return from the concerts, the clouds break their bellies overhead and a surprise snow sweeps down in layers upon them. The forest hushes under the unexpected weight, the green buds startled inward, the birds huddled together in suffering. Late in the night Abe had fallen into bed in his work clothes, supervising the last of the woodwork, the last of the painting, the last varnish and sconces and what curtains they have, thrift-store finds, bedsheets sewn into curtains, curtains made from old Indian bedspreads still smelling of sandalwood. Loosely braided rag rugs, even stenciled oilcloths pretending to be rugs, are scattered everywhere. The house is ragtag, Bit overheard Midge complain; but it is complete, paint and plaster, woodwork and glass. Bit, who has never lived in a house, thinks it's breathtaking, the most amazing thing he's seen: the space alone threatens to drown him. Abe's sweat on the pallet last night, though, stank of anxious incompletion. He tossed, fretted: he sleep-talked of broken window weights, unmatched molding, unpainted doors.

Against the sharp bones of his mother's ribcage, Bit slept. When Hannah dreamed, the dream was so vivid it entered him; he saw a giant in a charcoal suit, as big as Arcadia House, half the size of the sky. He felt his hand, Hannah's hand, extend to touch the swollen damp flesh. A nail nicked the giant's skin, and air began to hiss out like a punctured tire. The man slowly deflated, flabby, shrinking. He was the size of the oak in the courtyard, then the Pink Piper, then the Showerhouse, then the Bread Truck. He was the size of Abe, then Hannah. The face was blank, like those of the Amish dolls Astrid once brought back in repayment for midwifing a baby. The suit the man wore became a pond. He shrank to the size of Bit, then smaller. He became a baby, then a nubbin of a baby, a fleshy balloon in a small red pool.

At last, the balloon popped. The man was gone.

Bit opened his eyes to find Hannah looking at him.

My dad's dead, she whispered.

Bit put his hand to the pulse of his mother's throat, and she fell back into sleep.

The sun is shy on the white fields now. Before the coffee is finished, the spring warmth melts the snow on the new Arcadia House roof until it is fragile as lace.

From the window, Bit watches Titus Thrasher come over the Quad with a sad face. A telegram flutters in his hand.

Hannah is red and puffy. But the invisible straps that kept her arms at her sides have dissolved, and her hands now seem to float. Even her breath seems less labored. Her eyes are enormous in her face.

I'm okay, she insists to Abe when he clutches her to him. I'm really okay. He kisses her on the temple, but his face is pale, disbelieving.

They stand again at the Gatehouse, eager for Handy, under sun so hot the snow has vanished. A dozen Newbies wait on the porch, a shoal of Germans unpacked from a hearse painted with passion-flowers; two pregnant girls hugging themselves; a matted-haired Trippie muttering angrily to his shoelaces. The Newbie tent is full. Handy will know what to do with all these people.

It seems to circle, this wash of relief, above and through the crowd: *Handy is returning, Handy will know what to do.*

The day is splendid, and as they wait, the men toss a Frisbee on the long road. The women stand in loose clumps, touching one another on the shoulder, on the waist. Eden's baby is the newest and is passed around. They gaze into her walnut face, each in turn sent on the cosmic energy trip of meeting a new soul. Kitty is so keyed up she takes off her teeshirt, and a man somewhere says in a thick voice, Far out, and Kitty shakes her stuff with a little grin, and it strikes Bit with a sudden force that she is beautiful. With her brown bob and pointed chin, she is a chestnut come alive.

It seems like forever ago that Handy and

the Free People Band left, three months. Bit was a very tiny boy then. He can see himself that day, half a head shorter, his brain a blank, nothing at all to fill it but snippets of images. He sees his mother alone in the winter mud, her stare down the road.

Now the sound of a motor, and someone's trumpet blares, and in the far distance around the bend, there it is, the Blue Bus, with Lila in a crocheted bikini and handkerchief posing like a pinup girl on the hood. On the driver's side, Handy leans out the window, pulsing the horn, a shout braying out of his Confucius beard. Other heads hang out all the windows now. The engine dies and the bus coasts in and people pour off in a fug of smoke, and everyone embraces and Handy shouts. The Circenses Singers are in a goldfinch-colored bus that rumbles to a stop behind the Blue Bus. They pour out. They take out their now-dirtied Adam and Eve puppets, and then two new puppets they've made, an ancient man with muttonchops and a gaunt woman with a psychedelic dress. Four new puppeteers have joined; they sing and ring bells, and their song now is even stranger, trembling and breaking in air, making even the spring-fevered birds hush to listen. They finish their tune, and a roar goes up.

Bit sees new people who clamber out of other vehicles, stretch their limbs, grin; two dozen Newbies that Handy picked up on the road. One of the Newbies says, . . . were *going* to go to the World's Fair, but, man, this place is way better . . . One begins to clap her hands and breaks into song, and the old, familiar Arcadians catch on and they all sing now: *'Mid pleasures and palaces though we may roam, be it ever so humble, there's no place like home;* and at the end everyone hoots and hollers, and Handy leaps up onto the nose of the Blue Bus with little froggy Helle on his shoulders; she clutches her father's head and kisses and kisses his thinning crown. With a hat made of little girl, with glasses filled with sunlight, Handy starts one of his raps. *My good people, my friends, my Free People,* he says. *How blessed we are by the Great Goodness in the world to find ourselves together again, at last . . .* Bit is in Hannah's arms, his hand on her hand, and though everyone else watches Handy, Bit watches the old flowers begin to bloom again in his mother's cheeks, and he can hardly bear it, it is so good.

When Handy finishes, Abe lifts Bit from Hannah's arms and puts him on his shoulders, and steps up onto the Blue Bus bumper and shouts: Those of us who stayed behind have made you quite a present. Brace yourselves, all ye who went on tour!

Now Peanut and Tarzan roll out the wheelbarrow they decorated in garlands of spring flowers and apple boughs, and they hustle Handy into it and set off at a dead run, and everyone runs beside and behind, and they take turns jostling Handy over the ground to the circular gravel drive at the base of Arcadia House Hill.

Such billows of laughter! Such long-legged joy! Bit clutches at Abe's hair as his father gallops beneath him.

Then someone puts a blue bandanna over Handy's eyes, and they chair-carry him up the steps while he chortles. Abe throws open the great door and whips off the bandanna and scoops up Bit so that Bit can feel the heat and pulse of his father's body, and Abe turns to everyone massed on the Terraces.

We've done it, he shouts. We worked ourselves until we were worn out. But we finished Arcadia House, and there's room enough for a hundred fifty, maybe more, what with the kids' dorms and the itty-bitty bedrooms, and we even got ourselves a Library and Eatery and toilets and even a generator for a few hours of light and music in the evenings.

The cheer is the loudest thing that Bit has

ever known. A stunned expression grows over Handy's face. His eyes blink fast. This is . . . neat, Handy says, slowly and quietly, to Abe alone.

Under Bit, Abe seems to deflate, his shoulders loosening, his head lowering. The people mass behind them and push them into the Entryway, under the great chandelier. Everyone goes quiet because the room is grand and full of sun, and all the Old Arcadians, the original true believers, remember the holes and the spoor and the darkness, the house splintering around them. This, the contrast, the vastness of the space here that they will never be able to fill, eighty tiny bedrooms, a children's dormitory; all of this magnificence steals their breath from their lungs.

They scatter. Some find their names on cards on the doors, in Harriet's calligraphic hand. Others run from room to room to find a place to trade. This new couple wants to be together, these Newbies would like a nicer room, this married couple separated on the road and needs space apart.

Someone shouts from upstairs, They've enameled the toilets in gold! In the hilarity that rises and echoes in the house, something in Handy's face relaxes.

That's funny, he murmurs. I get it. Diamonds and carbuncles, silver baubles for the kidlets. I read that book, too. Which was it?

More's *Utopia,* Abe says, a little sullen.

Yeah, Handy says, and he considers Abe. Then, miracles, Handy breaks into that famous smile of his, that dimpled Buddha beam; it turns plain old Handy into something charming. He puts his hand on Abe's shoulder, and they lean toward one another for a moment. Handy says, Well, all right, then. All right. It's a good thing. You've done good to keep us together, this is a good thing. A great gift. I thank you, Abraham Stone, with my full heart.

Under the older man's words, Abe flushes with pleasure and ducks his head like a child.

That afternoon, before the kegs of Oly beer and jugs of red wine, before the Slap-Apple and pies, before Handy and the Free People start to play their music out on the grass during the wild reunion party that will stretch, thanks to the generator, deep through the night and into the quiet parts of the morning, before the kids heap together to sleep like baby chicks in a nest, before all this uproar, they bring up from Ersatz Arcadia everything that they need for the night, the mattresses and sheets and toothbrushes and soap. Everything else will be carried up the next day.

Then someone sets off a Roman candle, and in the after-stink of sulfur, the party begins.

Deep past midnight, Handy stands on a table. How small Handy is, but how he seems to fill all of Arcadia. People are sleeping in the grass. Bit is on a blanket with the other children, their faces smeared with jam and juice, the night turning cold on their limbs. Handy begins to sing, his voice whetted to a knife edge by the Tour. It cuts Bit to wakening when he hears *Ole, oleanna, ole, oleanna ole, ole, ole, ole, ole, oleanna.* The Norwegian lyrics stretch toward something fleeting, the perfection Handy talks about all the time, dreams about, weaves his seductive words around until it rises, whole and beautiful, before the rest of them. He sings as if today, the day of homecoming, he can reach out to touch what he sees, as if mixed in the victory there is still nostalgia, but for the good present that will soon be the past. Bit looks beyond Handy, to a blanket on the ground where Hannah and Abe are clenched so tight together that it is hard to tell his skin from hers. Yet Bit sees it clearly when he looks at them: even in the darkness, the empty space that keeps the one from the other, the thing the size of a fist, a heart, a loaf, a rose; the size of his sister he'll never see. Something rips in Bit, and he begins to cry. He cries his overfull heart out, pours it into the dazzled sky. He does so silently. Not yet, noise. It's still not time.

It is the day after Handy returned, the day before May planting, and the sun is hot and good. The grass is bristling with green. The women move the last of the stuff up from Ersatz Arcadia, and the children nap in the Dormitory. It feels too strange to sleep without his parents' smell in the sheets, and Bit watches in the window where a lazy fly buzzes on the glass.

Like ants that bear bits of leaf and bread, the women go up the hill with their armfuls of goods. Bit's breath stops: under the green and welcome arms of the oak, he sees Hannah.

His mother pauses in the courtyard and puts down her pillows. She unfurls her fists. She lifts her arms up and closes her eyes and cants her chin toward the sky.

Hannah, hands full of sun.

■ ■ ■ ■

A soft dawn, under the copper beech that Felipe loved. Maria sings, her voice broken: *Gracias a la vida.* Ricky's hands are clumsy on the guitar. Under the leaves, the skin of Maria's burnt arms shines, slightly wrinkled, like the bark of the tree above her. Her face looks like Hannah's does when she is in her thickest sleep. The song ends, and someone gulps, and here are the long soft waves of people crying. A minute of silence to remember.

All that Bit can bring back, though, is one moment of Felipe, a coo of delight, the baby's face wide with glee, three awkward steps. Then a tumble, and the baby beams up at him from the ground. Even this will fade. Soon, Bit knows, Felipe will no longer be inside Bit but will become a story they all remember together, and better, this way.

Bit thinks: We are a hive. Get up when we hear other people waking up. Do yoga in the Proscenium together. Warrior pose, corpse pose. Good food smells from the Eatery, breakfast, lunch, dinner. Cookies all day long. No more cold loo on my thighs, warm toilet. No more spiders and wind in the Bread Truck. Now radiators that hunch under the window and clink and hiss on cold nights like wheezing monsters. Now when parents come home in the evening from their work units, they have time to talk. Hannah in a book club, *White Niggers of America,* her voice flaming bright in the Library; Abe in a political theory group, ten beards leaning into the circle, the soft cheeks of the ladies in the shadows. They build societies of air, then carefully tear them down. The adults have grown softer. They squeeze each other's arms when they pass, give happy hugs. In the Dormitory, the children lie next to one another for nap-time. The warm pile of children, the smell of crayons and clay and paste. Handy's voice booming and joyous everywhere.

Bit thinks: Oh, we love each other better now.

He sleeps one week in the Dormitory, on the squeaking cots, far from the bodies of the others. Leif snores. Jincy sleepwalks. The Dormitory is so vast the shadows thicken and move in the corners. He wakes three times per night, desolate for his mother. At last, he writes a note to Sweetie. He labors over it with a red pencil.

Im to little, it says. *I have to sleep with Abe and Hannah.*

When he hands it to Sweetie, she goes speechless. You can read? she says.

Sweetie gives the note to Hannah, whose lips form an O.

Oh, Bit, you can write? she says. She kneels to his height and kisses him.

He moves into their tiny room on the second floor of the Main House, and sleeps on the old pallet on the ground beside their small iron bed.

As he sleeps, a fast wind descends on the world and rain slants horizontal. He wakes to the forest thrashing outside in a strange green glow.

There is lightning, a blue snap, and the world goes jagged. In the flash he sees Hannah midmotion, hair spun over her mouth, sheet peeled to her waist. One breast is in the open. A hairy arm buckles her shoulders.

In the swallow of black after the flash, he understands what was in the shadow above her crown: Abe's face, eyes closed, mouth a deeper darkness in the dark of his beard, straining toward something, it seems, he can just about grasp.

Bit crouches under the cherry tree on the lawn. Wet petals fall on his head and the sun is gentle. The adults are in the fields, planting, save Abe, who must fix the place on the roof where the oak branch fell during the storm. Bit can see the pale blue sweater of his father as he works, reflected upside down in a puddle. From here, his father's head points into the center of the earth.

When Bit closes his eyes, he can see what Abe can see, how Arcadia spreads below him: the garden where the other children push corn and bean seeds into the rows, the Pond. The fresh-plowed corduroy fields, workers like burdocks stuck to them. Amos the Amish's red barn, tiny in the distance. The roll of the forest tucked up under the hills. And whatever is beyond: cities of glass, of steel.

There would be a strong wind up where his father is. It would be hot, because it's closer to the sun.

Bit sees the pink petals skim the surface of the water, passing like ghosts through his father's body. It is wonderful, absurd. He laughs with sudden lightness, and the sound emerges whole from his mouth before he can clamp it in, a needling sound like an old hinge. He presses his hands to his mouth, and his skin tastes like grass, like dirt.

For a moment after Bit's sound, there is nothing. The wind ruffles the water. A bird passes overhead, a brief cold shadow over the sun.

But now, reflected in the puddle, Abe. Rolling off the roof; a marble, a pebble. For one bright moment, Bit's father hangs in the air. He is stuck, hovering; some string must be holding him. But there isn't a string. Abe flies down the surface of the puddle.

Bit lifts his eyes from the water and into the world. He blinks. Things are dim, like looking into the night from a lit room. On the courtyard grass Bit sees a tiny blue crumple. Somewhere, an engine roars to life and a crow hisses from a branch above and Bit's foot breaks the puddle and he begins to run.

Heliopolis

So lovely, the goosefleshed girls in suits gone flabby, the girls with lips rimmed in blue. Queen of all is Helle. She has been away with Astrid since winter began, returning a week ago to dazzle. She sits, bone white, on the boulder by the edge of the Pond. She is dreadlocked, nose-studded, her elbows puckered with cold. She is so pale Bit can hardly look at her.

The Pond roars with voices; it hurts Bit's ears. An early day in May, and freezing, but the kidlets and Ados of Arcadia have come here to soak up the chill sun. What had once seemed to Bit an impossible stretch of water has shrunk with two hundred thrashing bodies in it. He swims to the center of the Pond and goes under. The boys whiten the surface; the girls' feet dangle off the boulders, small, skimming things. He goes deeper, to the bottom, where the young weeds are nubbins under his feet and the cold clutches at him.

There is peace in this deep. He is free from the layered tensions of Arcadia, the overcrowding, the hunger. But up where the surface meets the sky, a speck becomes an open hand, becomes a star slowly falling toward him. A pulse in his gut when he sees that it is Helle, her eyes open to search for him. Her feet, landing, send shivers of mud to his knees. She reaches toward Bit, touches his side. Bad Helle, she tickles him.

He has to race the silvery swim of his lost air to the surface. There, he gasps and chokes, tears starting to his eyes. Helle comes up, laughing. Her dreadlocks float around her head, weeds themselves.

You're avoiding me, Bit, she says, her mouth half underwater.

No, he says but can't look her full in the face. He isn't avoiding her; he just can't see the old Helle under the new gloss and glamour of the Outside in her.

She says, no longer laughing, Look at me. It's just *me,* Bit.

The other girls are swimming toward them, their heads like a flock of pale ducks over the water. Before they reach Helle, he does look at her. For this one moment, he sees the old Helle, that vulnerable girl more lost, more watchful than even he had been.

At last, the kidlets have turned blue and fled, and only the toughest remain, twelve adolescents — Ados — every one of them Old Arcadia. His best friends shiver in the drizzle next to Bit. Ike, lanky and shining with the same white light as his sister; Cole and Dyllie, with Sweetie's beautiful face, in shades of pink and brown. They sit together, feigning ease, listening to Helle, who was never known for grand storytelling, fill them in about the Outside: *Everyone's fat and smells like chemicals. They wear stupid buttons all over their jackets and all they talk about is the World's Fair.*

All at once, it seems, his friends are straining to listen. Then he hears, too, and knows that he has been hearing the beat for some time, under the birds, under the wind, under the leaves moving in the trees. Helicopters. Bursting over the treetops, glossy black and taloned, flying low. Bit can see the pilots in earmuffs and the grim men in the doors holding machine guns.

The wind from the blades tosses water in their eyes, sends rocks against their skin. The choppers pass, and the Pond sloshes against the shore. Bit leaps up and races his friends toward Arcadia House, easily outstripping the rest over the mud paths worn into the lawn, though Cole, too, is fast.

People clump in the doorways of the Soy Dairy, the Bakery, the Eatery; heads mushroom from the windows and shyly withdraw. A herd of Trippies scatters, leaving their Minders behind. People pour around the Terraces, massing in the circular drive, and Bit hurtles through the sunburnt bodies, pitchforks and shovels, mudded feet and bodily stink and screaming kidlets, the babies wailing from their slings, practically the whole crowded nine hundred Arcadians having left their scattered pursuits to gather here. Bit scans, panicking, for Hannah. When he finds her — hair in twinned crowns around her head, plumper now because of the pills, frowning up at the sky — he is washed with relief. Her apron is smeared with soy; he takes her hand and puts himself between her and the machines. But she is shouting *Abe* in his ear, and here it is again, the sharp stone in Bit, his guilt; Abe always an afterthought. Bit scans until he sees his father in his wheelchair, on the Arcadia House porch. The thin pale legs in the shorts, the streaky beard. Abe is trapped up on the rain-slick hill. Without Hannah, he would have stayed there. Bit sprints up the Terraces. His father pats his shoulder, says, Good boy, steer me down.

Bit can barely hang on to the wheelchair

as they slide on the thin path beside the stairs, his puny hundred pounds no match for Abe's mass and acceleration, chill mud splattering over Bit's bare chest and face.

The helicopters vanish over the forest to the north, though they are still loud. Above the noise, Handy is roaring. He has gone half bald since the troubles began and hides his vaster forehead behind a folded bandanna. He stands like an orator on the terrace to address them.

. . . they're looking for a reason to shut us down, he's shouting, and we're so stupid we're giving it to them. Old bastard Reagan and his war on drugs are fucking *here,* guys. So what we're going to do is, we're going to go pull up that fucking weed and burn it. Now, now, now.

Peaceful Handy, Buddha Handy, furious, his face purple. The charge to the air is electric. Bit finds that he has stepped behind his father's chair.

But Abe's shoulder is knotted and shaking under Bit's hand. His voice rises, and as it does, the world seems to constrict. Fuck, Handy, no consensus? he shouts. No Council of Nine? Just handing out the diktats, yeah?

Handy searches out Abe, and when he finds him, he takes off his glasses and carefully polishes them on the hem of his teeshirt. His movements are slow and deliberate, and in the space he opens with his silence, people begin to murmur, to call to one another. But when Handy puts his glasses on again, it is as if he has miraculously peeled the anger from his skin. His body has softened, his hands have unclenched, his face spreads out in its old magnetic smile, only a gray eyetooth these days to mar it. The change in the bodies around Bit is swift. He can feel the crowd relaxing, the energy unknotting, shifting out toward Handy.

Fine, old buddy, Handy says in his concert-loud voice. You're right. Soon as the Council of Nine was voted in, I got left to do the more spiritual guiding. But, listen, I got a personal stake in all this. When Titus's dad sold us this place for a buck, it was my name they put on the deed. Martin "Handy" Friis, that gorgeous Norwegian surname Astrid gave me when we were hitched. Deed's in the Library, go look it up. So, you know, they're not going to arrest all nine hundred beatniks, they'll be arresting *me*. And, if you'll remember, I've already done time for you all.

He looks from one face to the next. When his glance falls on Abe again, measuring how his words are going over, Bit feels hollow with collective guilt. Five years earlier, the Feds had found a cottage industry of shrooms out of Arcadia and arrested Handy. It was only Harold with his Harvard Law degree who had gotten Handy out.

Let me tell you, Handy says. Even seven months in the hooch is no cakewalk. And so, I respectfully beg of you, beautiful Free People, to do me a solid and go out with me into the woods, and pull up all the hemp that we got growing out there, though it may hurt your souls to see all that good stuff go to waste. Consider it a way to save your old spiritual teacher a shiv in the ribs.

He has won them all over again. It is always so easy for Handy; there is a switch inside him that he can flick on and off. Arcadia laughs. Loudest of all are the Newbies, thrilled to get a glimpse of the legendary Handy, so rarely seen these days. Surrounding him are the old stalwarts, still in love with him, and, closer still, his family. Lila and Hiero chuckle beside Fiona, a woman now, her head against Handy's legs. Ike is puffed with pride. Leif, alien-blank, stands with the Circenses Singers, Erik is away at college. Only Helle sits gravely on the stone terrace wall, looking up at her father, her face still, her long pale mouth a line.

Wrapped again in Arcadia's adoration, Handy begins to organize the pull and burn.

Abe spins a wheel to face Bit and Hannah. In a tight voice he says, Stone Family meeting. Now.

In Abe and Hannah's room on the first floor of Arcadia House, Hannah shuts the window. The Tutorials have resumed in the courtyard: little Peter is repeating something in Hebrew to his tutor, Theo, five feet away. Theo seems harmless, but it is hard to know these days who is on whose side. In the swelter of the close, dim room, the stink of Arcadia House rises to them: sweat, onion, jizz, cheap incense.

Oh, dear, Hannah says. Eau de three hundred bodies.

Bit laughs, but Abe says, We don't have time for jokes. Hannah raises an eyebrow and opens an orange from the nightstand, a treat saved from dinner a few days ago. The spritz from the skin is immediate relief.

What's going on? Bit says. He bites a hangnail, calming with the taste of blood.

His parents look at him. Handsome Abe, Hannah golden with her early tan. We should keep him out of it, Abe, she says.

He's still a kid, he just turned fourteen last week. She takes Bit's hand from his mouth, kisses it, and holds it to keep him from chewing. Her fingers have acid from the orange still on them, and he is glad for the sting.

We need him, Hannah, Abe says. And it's not as if I haven't smelled it already on his breath.

Hannah sighs and her hand tightens around Bit's, and it is all he can do to prevent himself from crawling into her lap.

Please, Bit says, just tell me.

Abe says, Sorry to have to bring you into all of this, but Handy's minions are out there destroying our next year of groceries. Back in the winter, some of us in the Biz Unit decided to invest in some high-grade marijuana seeds, ready for Cockaigne Day in July. Arcadians who left have agreed to sell to the Outside for us. The Great Pot Plot, we call it.

Bit says nothing, but his disappointment in his parents wings itself, a trapped bird, around the room.

Listen, Hannah says. We know it's wrong.

Well, Abe says. Debatable. It's just not legal.

We had to weigh evils, Hannah says. We would never do it if we weren't so poor. We owe for seed for two years. And there are all the new fucking projects that Handy greenlighted, Astrid's Midwifery School down at the satellite in Tennessee, the stupid Circenses tour. I mean, Jesus, Handy, put your own house in order first. We owe too much. We'll *starve* if we don't do this, she says, and Hannah's callused hands clutch the sheet she's sitting on.

Bit frowns. What about the Motor Pool? The ceramics? What about Monkeypower? All the food we produce? There has to be some other way.

None of those make nearly enough, Hannah says. Plus with the Trippies and the Hens and all those fucking runaways, we have too many mouths to feed. We had no choice. I'd rather risk jail time than let our babies starve.

Amen to that, Abe says, and there is a look between his parents that makes Bit thrill with embarrassment. Sex is a tornado that suddenly smashed him a year ago. It is a whistle too high for human ears, and he awoke one morning a dog. He finds it everywhere, especially where it dismays him: in the bulging, dripping cheesecloths in the Soy Dairy, enormous mammaries; in the slide of a pitchfork through compost like the half-nasty mechanism of intercourse. It is here, in his father's flush as he looks at Hannah, her own face lit up with certainty.

We need you right now, Little Bit, Abe says. Your mom and I decided to keep the biggest crop a secret from Titus and Saucy Sally and Hank and Horse. For exactly what happened today.

Even fucking Titus, Hannah says bitterly, and Bit remembers, just after the helicopters, Titus's face cracking open in its old hopeful beam as he watched Handy speaking.

But, Bit says, I'm just a kid.

You're a kid who can run, Abe says. Bit tries not to look at his father's legs and fails; the familiar guilt, sickly, greasy, is heaped on guilt. But Abe is still speaking: . . . get there first and do anything to keep them from finding the plot. Pretend to be coming back from there, saying that you looked and there was nothing. Make a wild moose call or something. Smack them over the head with a rock.

No violence, Hannah says.

There is a shuffling in the hallway, and they stop to listen until whoever it is moves on. Honey, Bit, I can't force you to do anything you're uncomfortable with, she whispers. If you say no, I'll get out there as fast as I can, but I don't know the secret paths through the woods like you. You're so fast and quiet. But you have to know about the consequences of getting involved. We could go to jail or get shamed out of Arcadia if we're caught. It's your choice. We'll always love you, no matter what you decide. We respect what your conscience tells you to do.

Her voice, though: the tightness in it. It just kills him. All right, he says.

Abe exhales. All right, he says. It's the little island in the stream north of Verda's. She knows all about the Pot Plot, she sympathizes. Go as fast as you can off the path, and when Hannah can hike out there, she'll take over the watch from you. Ready?

Bit thinks, No.

He says, Ready.

Run, Abe says.

Bit runs. The smoke of the bonfire in the Sheep's Meadow is already strong. They must have pulled up a patch already. He is beyond the tents that have spread in the past year into the woods, for the people who can't find cots in the separate encampments; he is beyond the smell of the fields, the loos, the compost heaps. He can hear people crashing through the forest, clumsy ogres. Bit knows the deer paths. He goes, invisibly, beyond where they are. Past the noise, the old watchful silence of the woods presses in on him: he settles into his legs and lets the trees whip by. He startles a crane from a pool, sends the white tails of deer bounding over logs. Miles later he slows and sees the island turtling out of the stream. Only when he has waded through the hip-deep water and has come a few steps in does he see the plot, cleverly hidden on the eastern side of the trees. The helicopters, Hannah had known, would come from the navy base in the west or the army base to the south.

When Bit's heart has stopped its pounding, he washes the dried mud from his chest and shoulders, finds a bucket tied to a tree, and makes himself useful, watering.

He hides again in a cold pit in the willows and looks back toward Arcadia. He sees nothing, hears nothing but the ordinary sounds of the woods settling after his disturbance. A contrail puffs fat overhead. A muskrat draws two slender lines in the water. After some time he swivels his head and looks toward Verda's cottage sending up its thin stream of smoke.

He has known Verda forever, since he was six. Before he knew these miles of woods like his own small body, he would get lost on his wanders. He met the old woman one night when he was in a snowstorm and dark was falling fast. He had lost a red mitten, and he put both his hands in the remaining one and held it in front of him as if it were a lantern to light his way. But the forest was avid: it wanted, that night, to eat him. Through spindrift he had trudged, through black. At last, he had smelled salvation in woodsmoke and followed it to a stone cottage squatting at the edge of a field. He knocked and knocked. The door fell open to the witch he'd first seen in the dark woods the spring before, the strange dog at her side that Bit had thought was a tamed white doe. Bit had been too tired and too cold to feel fear, until his wet clothes were off and there was a blanket on him, smelling of sun and lavender. Then the witch leaned into her woodstove and the light caught and underlined her sharp nose, her wrinkles, her lank hair, and some spark of a story alit in his head and Bit began to scream. From the hearth, the white beastie watched him, panting in the heat. The witch let Bit scream until he lost his voice, and when he did, she handed him a bowl of soup. It was venison, the first meat he had ever eaten. It tasted like death. He threw it up. He found himself in a truck, and Titus came to the Gatehouse door, Saucy Sally and the baby in the lanternlight behind him. Titus began to cry with relief: Oh, Bit, you're found, he said, gathering him up in his great heavy arms. We thought you were froze to death. Bit looked back into the night, and the witch put her thumb on his chin. Little Ridley, she said softly. Come back and see your Verda sometime; and she disappeared from the dream he'd thought he was in.

Now he tries to send Verda brainwaves to bring a handful of shortbread and a blanket, but she doesn't hear or heed his silent calls. He tries not to think of what would happen to him in a jail-type situation. He is so small still; he looks far younger than he is. He has heard bad stories of juvenile hall, filtered up from the runaways, and his mind shies away from ideas of violence and nasty food and never seeing his parents again. In the sky blazes Venus, a calm blue, and Bit thinks of last year's syzygy, the alignment of planets, how Ollie was so convinced of apocalypse that he spent March in the reinforced tunnel between Arcadia House and the Octagonal Barn. When the anxiety gets to Bit, he rolls a green leaf into a little cigarette and lights it with the matches all Old Arcadia kids keep in plastic bags in their pockets, with Swiss Army knives and some gorp. When he's calmer, he laughs quietly to himself and startles a chipmunk into a tree.

In the shadows of the trees, it grows cold. Bit's cutoff jeans have dried on his legs, and he has to clutch his limbs to his torso to keep from shivering. Dusk thickens. The forest breathes in a way he can't hear when he is amid the clamor of Arcadia. On the path a few hundred yards away there is a rustling, the distinct sound of human steps, and he stands, a rock absurdly heavy in his fist. But it is Hannah. She's wearing the same ripped-sleeve flannel shirt and cutoff shorts as before but now has a knapsack on her back and her work boots on her feet, as if she were off for an innocent hike.

She presses a finger to her lips and wades across the stream. When she hugs Bit, she must feel how cold his skin is, and she takes off her shirt, baring her bra to the air. She drapes the shirt on him. It holds the warmth of her body in the weave, her bready smell. You're the best, Little Bit, she whispers. Lila and Hiero weren't too far away from me on the path, so be careful.

He carries the weight of her hug, a ghost of Hannah, on the run back home. He comes out into the Sheep's Meadow in the pale twilight just as the gong begins to ring, calling the first shift of Arcadians, the most fragile, the Hens and Trippies and kidlets, to their supper.

Bit wakes, pulsing with dread. From his top bunk, Cole's hand reaches out and pats him on the chest. Just sheep, Bit's friend mutters, you're okay.

Baa baa, murmurs Ike, still asleep in his own bunk.

Bit concentrates on ujjayi breath to calm himself, imagining the windmill in the back of his throat. The same nightmare has circled in Bit since he was little and Handy put actual sheep in the Sheep's Meadow: not to exploit, he explained, they're not *pets* and they won't be *eaten,* but for their wool, which they gladly gave and which the Arcadians could sell. The kidlets loved the sheep; the women dreamed of woolen sweaters, lanolin on their chapped hands. Then Tarzan, who appointed himself shepherd, came down dizzy, with great open sores, and Astrid came speeding back from the hospital in Syracuse where the AmbUnit had rushed him, her hair wild, her face frantic. For hours, Abe and Handy and the midwives and Titus, the people who wore power in Arcadia then, conferred. That night, Bit woke to an unfamiliar stink. He crept out of the Children's Dormitory to follow the acrid smoke. He found a grim group of three in the meadow around a bonfire. When he came closer the fire turned gruesome, the bodies of the sheep in a ziggurat within the flames. Bit watched a lamb's eyeballs explode. He sat in the darkness, struck frozen until Astrid, who stood apart from Hank and Horse, brought a hand up to push her hair from her face, and her arms were blackened to the elbows with blood.

When a certain pressure builds in Arcadia — overcrowding, not enough food, the strange hidden undercurrents that make the adults' faces pinch — the sheep come back to Bit's dreams; sheep springing through the dark like live torches, the stench of burning fat. Over and over they leap until, at once, the creatures turn toward Bit. They crowd him, open their muzzles, almost say something. He knows it is something he couldn't bear to hear, and he wakes almost screaming.

For hours, he waits for sleep. Shortly before dawn, he gives up. When he rises, he listens for his friends' breath to stir. They sleep on. He opens the window to air out the room, the awful dead creatures that are Ike's feet, the mixed adolescent body stink. He carefully dresses in his shirt and jeans.

His broken sneakers mouth open when he walks, toes lapping the air like tongues.

Through the Ado Unit Common Room, through the hallways, plaster gapping and lath exposed, down the smooth polished banister for silence. Through the Library, heaped with *Whole Earth Catalogs,* old *New Yorkers,* silverfished books dug up from the basement where the first inhabitants had stashed them: *American Eclectic, Walden, News from Nowhere.* Also Carlos Castaneda, Julia Kristeva, Herman Wouk, paperbacks scavenged from Dumpsters or bought for a nickel. He slips through the Eatery, redolent of last night's enchiladas. It is early for the Breakfast Shift, who will soon clang pans and stir yeast and soy into scrambled yegg and wash the apples, wormy but good. All is still and nobody is awake but Bit.

Out in the black, he runs down the slate steps by touch alone. The encampments across Arcadia are dark, only a few bobbing lights from afar, the flashlights of people rising for the loo. From the Bakery, a rich bread smell rises. His skin prickles with cold; dew flings from his heels to his back. There is a sharp edge to the sky, pine tanging the air, stones scattering like live creatures under his step. He runs as fast as his legs can take him, very fast for a body small as his, then slows to enjoy the darkness softening in the woods.

A cardinal flushes from a bush, but he has forgotten his new camera that his grandmother has sent him. He thinks of returning, but the run back is so far, and daybreak won't wait for him.

One breath before dawn, he climbs the hill.

At the top, in a cluster of sweet William above the pines, he sits to watch day begin to hatch its yellow. A hawk stretches its wings and swirls as it rises. The fog rolls from the ground like a blanket and swiftly covers the distant mountains, the fields, the Pond, the streams; covers Amos the Amish's far-off barn, the thin lace that is Verda's smoke. A hungry creature, the fog; it gobbles. It climbs up the Terraces with the crooked apple trees. At last, only Bit and Arcadia House sit turned toward each other, each alone on a hill, above the fog's milky sea. Two islands, they are, brightening in the dawn.

The world is sometimes too much for Bit, too full of terror and beauty. Every day he finds himself squeezed under a new astonishment. The universe pulses outward at impossible speeds. Bit feels its spin into nothing. Beyond Arcadia hulk the things he has dreamed of: museums, steel towers, pools, zoos, theaters, oceans full of strange creatures.

He knows that his understanding of the Outside is imprecise, both gleaned and muted. It is whatever makes its way to his ears, the stories people bring with them, what he has read. He has never been away from Arcadia since the Free People arrived when he was a toddler, not unless he counts Verda's cottage at the edge of the forest, a tiny atoll of one. There have been times he's been offered a ride to Summerton by the Motor Pool, or the chance to go with Hannah to visit the university library in Syracuse, but every time he has said no thank you. He is frightened of the Outside: either that it will be all that he imagines or that it won't be.

Claus, a Circenses Singer, delights in asking Bit questions fit for babies: *How big is an elephant? What does a subway look like? How many people can Yankee Stadium hold?* Bit can understand only vaguely why Claus laughs until tears roll down his cheeks when Bit answers: *An elephant is as big as the Octagonal Barn? A subway is like a train of Volkswagen Beetles in a big steel tube? Yankee Stadium can hold . . . two thousand people?,* twice the size of Arcadia, and the limit of how large he can picture a crowd.

You kids, Claus says, sighing back into his chair, wiping his face. You're like some crazy jungle tribe with bones in your noses. A sociologist would have a field day with you.

Bit knows this isn't true. They're not ignorant or innocent. From the Tutorials he chooses after the State Lessons in the morning, he knows local botany, the classics of English literature, geometry, physics, human physiology. He has assisted with over six birthings down at the Henhouse. He and the other Old Arcadia kids know how to play a guitar, bake and chop wood, pull pots and spin flax, knit their own socks and cultivate grains and vegetables, structure a good story, brew Slap-Apple out of windfall apples, and make anything at all from soy.

He feels no lack. If he concentrates, he can imagine the world in its many forms: the humid density of the jungle; the desert's clean rasp of sand; the cold clarity of the Arctic. He imagines cities as larger Arcadias, but harder, meaner, people walking around thrusting cash at each other. He has seen the coins like embossed washers, the bits of green paper. Humans out there are grotesque: Scrooges and Jellybys and filthy orphans in the caverns of blacking factories, in lonely depopulated homes, a blight called television like tiny Plato's caves in every room. It is grimmer in the Outside. There is a war in the Falkland Islands, there are Sandinistas and Contras, there are muggings and rapes, terrible things he has heard the adults talking about, has read about himself when he can find an old wrinkled paper in the Free Store. The president is an actor, placed in power to smoothly deliver the corporations' lies. There are bombs among the stars and murders in the inner cities, red rain over London, there are kidnappers and slaves even now, even in America.

He has decided that he will leave for college when he is eighteen to study, to learn the magic of pulling images from the darkroom bath. He thinks of Erik at the send-off party, his flabby face radiant with the anticipated glamour of the Outside. Bit will borrow that same glamour for a few years, then come back to Arcadia forever. It will take him every day from now until he leaves to ready himself for what awaits him. He knows his only weapons against the threat of the Outside are knowledge and words: when anxiety bubbles up under his thoughts, he has to say Hannah's name a hundred times or recite "Desiderata" until the words lose their meanings. If his thoughts skirt close to the forbidden, or he dreams stickily of little Pooh, who is only twelve but with a sweet body and full lips, or if, after his German lessons with Marlene, he runs to the darkroom to relieve the pressure in his pants, he makes amends to Helle in his head. He memorizes poems, and tells them in her direction: *She walks in beauty,* he thinks. *One man loved the pilgrim soul in you, and loved the sorrows of your changing face,* he thinks. And even with knowledge and words, he feels sometimes the dark news from Outside could crush him. He keeps his deepest belief tight to him: that people are good and want to be good, if only you give them a chance. This is the most magnificent thing about Arcadia, he knows. It is the shell that protects them.

The wind rises. A rock presses against his sitz bone, and the tide of fog draws off the hill. The first Breakfast Shift will be swarming up to Arcadia House. His face has dried, and the skin pulls taut. He can tamp down the nameless longing that arises in him only by running from the mountain as swiftly as his legs can go.

Bit returns to Arcadia in the full light of morning. He is wrung out. The woods seem deeper in the new light, less benign, like the dark forests in the Grimm book that peopled his childhood with nightmarish creatures. He finds a bush heavy with serviceberries and fills the belly of his teeshirt until he has to take it off and tie it into a sack so he can carry them all.

He can smell Arcadia before he sees or hears it: the loos are being pumped today. The Agri Unit will compost the shit, mix it with straw, and spread it on the fields for manure. The Sanitation Crew is already at work.

In the distance, he hears people shouting, the daily Trippie meeting where all the freaked-out, strung-out, acid-wracked gather to tell their dreams. The hope is that they can be returned to themselves by community and love, though only a few have succeeded. The Trippies arrive every week, an endless stream of the damaged. Each one is given two adult Minders, who keep him safe. Though his conscience pings, Bit is glad he is still too young to work full shifts. He hates minding Trippies, their anger and fear so raw it seems to infect him as well.

Bit walks into the Sheep's Meadow, the grass verdigris with dew. He puts down his berries and pulls a clump of new clover from the ground and scrubs and scrubs at his face until it feels fresh and the traces of his tears are gone. Goldfinches dart like flying fish from the grass, into the sun, back into the grass troughing and cresting in the wind. At last he feels strong enough to brave the Eatery, the jostle of breakfast. The women will pet him for the berries, he knows. Maybe, even, they will let him take seconds of bread. He cradles the fruit against his bare chest and begins to run again.

He has to go water the Pot Plot. Hannah, busy in the Bakery, had asked him; but before he knows it, he is swept into a work unit. Cole and Ike go off together to the gardens and, with a fluttery feeling in his chest, he wants to tell his best friends to stop, to wait up for him, knowing he can slip out of weeding easily. But Helle has partnered herself with Bit somehow. She is already talking.

. . . can't work outside, she's saying, and she slides the neck of her teeshirt over her shoulder; he sees her sun-blistered skin. He wants to lay a hand on it, to feel its feverish heat, but just the pressure of the thin shirt is enough to make her wince. She is not wearing a bra. Let's do a Newbie shift, yeah? she says. In a lower voice, she says, See if I can score some downers.

Oh, he says. He looks at her slantwise, wondering about the drugs. She sees and says, Why do you hate me now, Bit?

I don't, he says. I mean, I really like you.

I really like you, too, she says, squeezing his forearm. Her bitten fingernails, her cold hands. You're the only guy here except for my brothers who isn't always hitting on me.

There is so much he can say to this that he goes quiet. They walk together in silence toward the Gatehouse and Newbieville, that sprawl of canvas out by the County Road. He thinks of the pot plants on their little island drooping, curling at the edges of the leaves, and has to concentrate on the next step on the soft ground, then the next to keep from breaking into a run.

Because, beyond the oppression of his duty, something under his lungs hums with happiness to be walking beside lovely Helle. His attention has sharpened. Every leaf is in clear focus, the weave of the birdsong both intricate and glassy. In the distance, people are bent over the garden. A man carrying water in a bucket to workers is one of the dozen mutton-chopped cats in Arcadia these days who call themselves Wolf. Wolves come and go: Bears and Foxes and Hawks and Falcons and Jackals roam. The women are Rainbows, Sunshines, Summers, Rains,

Meadows, Stars. Every day there are new Crows, new Autumns. It is hard to know everybody. At the movies projected some nights on the Octagonal Barn, vivid underwater explorations narrated by a Frenchman or strange, sad black-and-white flicks (piles of bodies in Auschwitz; an eyeball sliced open), Bit will sometimes look up and see clumps of strangers. He will peer around, panicked, to find some familiar face. There are good Newbies who believe in work and poverty and simple food. And there are others, freeloaders, Trippies and Runaways, people hiding out here, diluting the pure beliefs of the Old Arcadians.

Helle says, So many new people. I wish we had some way to weed them. Constructive criticism doesn't work if you don't give a shit about the people around you.

In his surprise, Bit dares to look Helle full in the face. She beams at him, Handy's magnetic smile, and with her tongue clicks the new retainer she finagled from her time in the Outside. It's a flesh-colored crab in the cavern of her mouth, endlessly fascinating.

How did you know what I was thinking? he says. He hopes she can't read minds.

We're alike, she says. You and me. We notice. What you're thinking is written all over you. Like, yesterday, at the Photography Tutorial, you were looking really hard at this trail of ants. I could see you start to imagine yourself as one of them. Thinking about dismembering a grasshopper, how huge it was to your tiny size, how you would drag it underground, and then about the darkness down below, all the trails and little caverns and halls, and then what it smells like, what it's like to live in full-body armor. It seems like everybody is so busy that nobody else notices things like that. Except for you.

There is a swimming feeling in Bit, to be read as casually as a paragraph.

They have arrived at Newbieville. Lisa holds a clipboard while Scott takes down the names of the people who have shown up this morning. They are the usual suspects: Trippies with their leathery faces and wild auras, a pregnant mother with two hungry-looking children, a young couple necking on an orange towel. Lisa's face looks weary; there are blue marks under her eyes.

Here you are, she calls to Bit and Helle, and turns and calls out two names from the board: Armand Hammer and Penelope Connor. One is young, a beefy Runaway with a nail through his infected septum.

Every few seconds, he sniffs in what's oozing from the sore and winces. The other is a Naturist, a sixty-year-old woman with firm breasts and gray streaks in her bush.

Lisa says cheerfully, Congratulations. You have proved to us that you are willing and able to do the work we ask of you and have spent the required month in Newbieville. Now you are welcome to join our Community.

There is sparse applause from the tents and cots. The jittery boy and the old woman stand. They carry their things in cardboard boxes, some clothes, books, a few letters, not much.

Job's easy today, kids, Lisa says to Bit and Helle. You know what to do.

Welcome to Arcadia, Bit says. Helle repeats it, absentmindedly, scanning the Newbies. She chews the tail of one of her dreadlocks, disappointed with what she sees. Bit takes Penelope's box from her, and the old woman ruffles his hair. Sweet little guy, she says. When she stretches, he tries very hard not to look at her strangely beautiful chest.

They walk in silence down the hill toward the stream behind Ersatz Arcadia, and Bit has to tell Penelope to watch out for a poison sumac she's just about to brush: he has a bad image of the tender skin of her buttocks breaking out into white blisters. The closer they come to the Naturist encampment, the more flesh they see, pink and tan and white lines everywhere. By the middle of the lima bean patch, all the bodies bending over to weed are nude.

Two women, very large and pink, very small and grayish, run out of the Quonset and hug Penelope. They take the box from Bit and escort the newest Arcadian inside. Toodles! she calls back at Bit. He wonders how long she'll last. The Naturists have the highest turnover rate: the winter wind snakes through their Quonset, and its metal is very cold. He thinks maybe he'll see her again, then doubts it.

On the way back up the hill, Helle says, How come the Naturists are never the people you *want* to see naked? Bit and Armand Hammer laugh.

The laugh burns away Armand's shyness, and he says to Helle, I know it's trite and all, but it's awesome to be here. I was in a squat in Portland and I saw this one-hour special on Arcadia? And it was, like, heaven. All singing and working in the fields and people free to do what they want, and Handy so eloquent. And the mansion! My parents have a shitty duplex in Pittsburgh. When do you ever get to live in a mansion?

Plus, the prettiest girls I've ever seen.

He's ogling Helle openly now, the acne-scarred boy. Bit is surprised how much he wants to punch him in the throat; Bit, who would be broken with a flick of Armand's wrist.

They stop outside the Runaway Quonset. On a brown-stained mattress three Runaways sit, a fat girl braiding the hair of a boy with the triangular face of a fox, a topless girl with delicate wrists. The topless girl smiles to see Armand gawking at her, and it startles Bit, as it always does, to see perfect teeth in the mouth of a person his age. Many Runaways, mostly suburban kids, had orthodontia, while the kids of the Old Arcadians often have twisted teeth, sometimes set two deep.

Helle says, flatly, Here's your new home, Armand Hammer. Then she laughs, feeling his ridiculous name leave her mouth.

What's this? Armand says.

It's where you stay, Bit says, trying to not enjoy the crumpling of the other boy's face. I know you were looking forward to Arcadia House, but we're too crowded. You can try to get a cot in one of the other camps. Singleton Tents, Swingers' Tents if that's your thing, Naturists. If you get enough people for a family unit, you can apply for a bus or van from the Motor Pool and park it in Ersatz Arcadia. Then, if the Council approves of you, you can move up to the House when there's a place.

Yeah, right, says the topless girl. I've been here two months and nobody even lets us go anywhere up there but the Eatery.

That's a lie, Helle says flatly. The topless girl looks her up and down and mutters something that sounds like *skinny cunt.*

Bit sees Helle expanding the way Astrid expands when she's angry, and he takes her loosely by the wrist. He says, as calmly as he can, You can use the Library, and you're supposed to be going up in the mornings for the State Lessons. And you can go to all the lectures and slide shows and concerts you want in the Proscenium or the Octagonal Barn.

But the topless girl rolls onto her belly and says into the mattress, If I wanted to learn things, I'd still be in school.

Whatever, says the fox-faced boy, it's all bullshit. Handy goes on about equality and subverting the hegemony, but Arcadia's no different from anywhere else. You all are up on your hill. We're down here in the mud. I've been here for a year and a half. If that's nonhierarchical, or even fucking respectful, I'll eat my own ass.

I don't see you working, you little shit, Helle says. Try *working* once in a while and maybe you'll deserve respect.

The boy slowly stands up, and Armand drops his junk on the ground, folding his arms, stepping before him.

But all the fox-boy says is, All right. Okay. Make you a deal. First time I see Handy out busting his ass like the rest of y'all, I'll be glad to work myself. Until then, I do what he does.

The boy settles back between the plump legs of the girl on the mattress and touches the bare back of the other girl with a long, slow stroke. Both girls giggle.

Helle blanches and strides away.

Bit would like to explain more to Armand, but the other boy is savagely kicking his box of shit into the Runaway Quonset, muttering, I want to live in the mansion, I fucking came here for the mansion. Bit escapes under a volley of catcalls and sneers from the mattress, and catches up to Helle in Ersatz Arcadia.

She is crying, and Bit says, aching for her, Helle. Oh, don't. They're not worth it. That guy was an idiot.

Helle passes a forearm over her eyes. She gives a shaky laugh, and the new, harder Helle slides over the old one again. In the face of this complicated girl, Bit feels the straightforward pull of the Pot Plot: there, at least, he knows what he has gotten into, and why.

Yeah, she says. I know. But, she says, a new sour look on her face; what sucks is that he's also a little *right,* Bit.

It is hot for a June midafternoon. The scent of Verda's rosehip tea fills the air; her anise cookies are sweet in his mouth. Beside him, on the rug faded into ashy roses, Eustace, the white dog, snaps at his own privates and looks a question at Bit. Bit rubs Eustace's head, and the dog sighs back to sleep. Bit frames his mother and Verda in the viewfinder of his camera, their heads on opposite sides of the table, loose wisps sparking with light from the window. Hannah is intent on Verda, who has gone distant, the recorder spinning at her elbow.

They were deeply strange people, she says in her anchorite's rasp. They called themselves Divinists, because they believed that people could become perfect, therefore divine. They believed that intercourse was a gift from God and had great quantities of it with everyone in the community. To avoid the consequences, namely babies and love, they had a rotational schedule: every night, a new woman with a new man, and the men had to release themselves into their handkerchiefs.

Bit shrivels inside himself a little. Verda looks at him. You will forgive me, Ridley, for my bluntness, she says in her grand and distant way.

She says, But then their leader, John Noland, my great-grandfather, decided it was time to reproduce. He had gone to a Shaker community and saw that they were in danger of dying out, and didn't wish that upon his people. And so they instituted a program called Eugeniculture. The most spiritual men and the most spiritual young women were allowed to mate, after a very thorough matching. Of course because the most spiritual men were old men, and nobody was more spiritual than John Noland, out of forty-eight babies born, twenty-three were his. One of them was my grandmother Martha Sutton. Her mother, Minerva, was, at the time, a bare thirteen years old.

Verda smiles wearily. One finds that when children are involved in these things, she says, the cracks in the system become clear. Babies that belonged to individual mothers, the claim on the fathers. There was some romantic love going on, verboten of course, and the breeding program interfered with the heart. And, of course, the parents had to watch as their twelve- and thirteen-year-old daughters slept with old men. Word spread to the outside, newspapers had fiery editorials, and John Noland was chased out of Summerton by the townspeople. He fled to Canada. There was nothing binding the community. The center could not hold.

Hannah's face is shining. Bit clicks another photo of her, and then one of Verda, reflected again and again in the tarnished silver tea set on the table. Verda says, My dear Hannah. I have to stop. I am very tired, and I need to be alone.

Thank you, Hannah says. Her hands are shaking when she lifts her teacup to her lips. Do you have any primary sources, by any chance? Papers, things like that?

Verda says, Loads. She stands and pulls down a hatbox, and when she releases the top, there pours out the smell of sage and tobacco. I'll give you my great-grandmother's diary, she says. But that is all for this visit, at least. I'd like for you to return for something, even if it's just a dusty old book.

She sees Bit gaping into the box and lifts out the dull gleaming thing he is trying to see.

Scrimshaw, she says, putting it in his hands. Walrus tusk. One of John Noland's sons went out on the high seas and carved the face of his wife over and over again. After a year away, he came back to port and learned that she'd died of yellow fever the day after he'd left.

In wonder, Bit traces the woman's face, echoed in the bone. It is Helle, to the life.

Please, Verda says now, taking back the scrimshaw and closing up the hatbox. I have a headache bearing down on me. But do return and bring some of your bread. And those leaves to smoke. It helps with my arthritis. Also bring young Master Ridley, who was so bored he took a nap today.

I wasn't bored, he says. I'm relaxed in your presence.

They grin at one another, and she almost touches him, her claw hovering over his shoulder. You give me hope for the next generation, she says. Not that I believe humankind will last another century. She gives a gruff laugh.

He says, Doom and Gloom Verda.

She says, Off you go to your delinquency. Off you go, Hannah, to write your book.

Something peculiar flits across Hannah's face, a daring, a desire, and then she tamps it down and says, softly, It's just a lecture.

Nonsense, Verda says, closing her eyes. And my migraine has arrived. With bassoons and timpanis. Let Eustace out to fend for himself.

They tiptoe out and close the door. Again in the bright expanse of the day, Bit wants to break into a run. But Hannah mutters out of the side of her mouth, Let's go tend our plot, and Bit is returned to the world of worry. In Verda's little cottage, the plants out on the island had simmered at the back of his mind, a shadow thought that only sometimes overwhelmed him.

They find the plants huge, almost overgrown: all females, the males plucked out early, all almost twelve feet tall. Bit crouches on the bank, skipping stones until Hannah is finished, and they wade back through the stream to the path. Two more weeks, she says. Then pick and dry and we are on our way. She touches his arm, smiles crookedly. Then you can be a kid again.

He tries to sink himself into identifying the plants at his feet, the jimsonweed someone sowed long ago, the painted trillium, the jack-in-the-pulpit. But when they are halfway home Hannah sees Bit's face. Oh, kiddo, what's wrong? she says.

He says, It's just. I mean, if someone gets in trouble, it may be us, but it may be

Handy. It's not right.

Handy schmandy, Hannah says. None of this would be necessary if Handy didn't make those decisions he made and get us into a bind and then back out of the Council of Nine. He abandoned us. Got us into a mess and left us to fend for ourselves.

He didn't abandon us, Bit says. He's still our spiritual leader.

Hannah snorts, says, Right. All-Arcadia Yogas? Remember the time he made us all have an Eyesight Yoga? No corrective lenses because they separate you from the spiritual world? Remember what happened?

Muffin fell in the well, Bit says.

And the Weeklong Silence Yoga?

The kidlets freaked out and had bad nightmares, Bit says.

And the Poverty Yoga? When we weren't supposed to have medications or extra food for three months and send all that money we saved to Mount St. Helens victims?

Bit shivers, remembering: Hannah, off the pills she'd been taking religiously, had returned to the dark creature in the bed whom he'd had to slowly draw into the light so many times over the years. I remember, he says. Okay.

When they come into the sunflower field, Hannah shields her eyes from the glare and laughs to see Simon welding away at his sculpture. Bit was near Hannah when Simon sidled up to her in the Eatery the other day; he was close enough to overhear their conversation. Simon had been famous in the Outside, an artist. He was handsome, with hard blue eyes and a tight frowning face. He'd muttered to Hannah that he was building her a sculpture out in the sunflowers. She was his Muse, he said. For a moment, through Simon's gaze on Hannah, her motherness fell away, and Bit saw her as lush and attractive as she must be to men, with her long golden braids and roundness and the warmth in her large eyes. Oh, she'd cried out happily, that's so lovely of you, Simon, and Bit felt the beginning of the old anxiety moving through him, that she would break the fragile bond of family and find a new allegiance away from him.

When Bit says to Hannah, jostling her back onto the path, Are you really going to write a book? he knows he's really saying, Please don't change and leave me.

And when she touches his cheek with her callused hand and says, Maybe yes, maybe no, he knows she's really saying, You don't have to worry about me.

Helle comes up to Bit. Cole and Dyllie and

Ike have pushed their dinner plates to the side, and they are playing kick hockey with a bottle cap they found in the Motor Pool.

Hey, she whispers, Bit, I need you.

Ike looks up, his face contorted with disgust; he *hates* his sister, he says, but he watches and mimics her. Cole looks up, too, confused. Dylan does not even see Helle; he has the gift of focus and is kicking the bottle cap across the table with his fingertips.

Gimme a second, guys, Bit says. He crosses the Eatery with Helle, feeling tall for the first time in his life. They go down the hallway where the Tuesday night bathers are waiting for their three weekly inches of warm bathwater, and into the Library. In the far corner, there is a raging book discussion of *The Mismeasure of Man.* Abe is there, face full of joyous argument. He sees Bit and lights up further, and waves, blowing a huge kiss. Bit pretends to be embarrassed.

Helle turns to Bit. I need you, she says again, so low only he can hear it, and she twists the hem of her teeshirt in her hands. She is jittery, darting. You're the perfect accomplice, nobody ever gets mad at you. Please, please, please, she says.

There is magic in *perfect,* in *accomplice,* and he says, without thinking, All right.

They go up the grand Entryway stairs,

hearing the noises of a house overfull with people: someone plays on a common room piano (stuck D-flat), the recorder group trills its way through a madrigal, voices are raised, shouting or just discussing, babies shriek and are hushed with breasts or murmurs, the kidlets in the Dormitory across the courtyard are singing the good night song: *The Dream passes by the window. And Sleep by the Fence* . . . He follows Helle into the brightest, biggest common area. Arcadia House is arranged around six central common rooms, each area separating into anywhere from twelve to fifteen bedrooms big enough for two adults or three tightly packed Ados. This common room they are in is the grandest: the two-story windows hold the dying sunset, the people pouring across the lawn, the lights coming on down in Ersatz Arcadia. There's a catwalk with another floor of bedrooms up a curved staircase that Bit can never look at without a sense of foreboding.

Helle puts her hand on Bit's lips and pushes open Handy's doorknob. Before Bit can protest, they're in. Handy and Astrid have the largest bedroom in Arcadia House, two smaller rooms knocked into one, from a time so long ago when there was more space than Arcadians to fill it. Ludicrous thought! In the wall, there is a door built leading to Lila and Hiero's bedroom.

Why are we here? Bit whispers, something curdling in his throat. When the community grew beyond Arcadia House, four years ago, they established the Council of Nine, an elected board, and although he and Astrid were given permanent seats, Handy protested: *let it all grow organically,* he said. But the rest were afraid that the needs of people down in Ersatz Arcadia, the Hens and Singletons and Newbies and Nudists, would be ignored for those of the privileged up in the House. In a pique, Handy withdrew, mostly to his room. Although all bedrooms in Arcadia are ostensibly open to everyone, Handy's alone feels sacrosanct. Bit has never heard of anyone just walking in.

Helle is on her knees digging through Handy's cardboard chest of drawers. Bit runs his hand over the instruments mounted on the wall: guitar, ukulele, banjo, sitar, fiddle. He peers into the closet. Astrid's side is severe, the long sack dresses, the clogs, the folded shawls. Handy's overflows with Hawaiian shirts and army jackets, corduroys, luxurious heaps of newish socks.

When Bit turns to Helle, she is draped across the bed. He remembers the Indian spread from the Pink Piper long ago, but in the wedge of late, sickly sunset, the pinks and golds seem alive. Helle's threadbare teeshirt goes transparent, and he can trace the slopes of her ribcage, the warm nestle of her belly button, the pointy bra that all women of Arcadia wear, a Dumpster full of them found outside a lingerie factory in Binghamton. The bow between the cups seems as delicate as a petal to Bit, as if it would fall off if touched.

She sees him looking. Come here, she says. He goes and lies in the dying light beside her. You have a girlfriend, Bit? she says. She smells like the vanilla the girls beg off the Bakery and dab at their wrists, napes, behind their ears.

No, he says. He is careful not to touch any part of her, even the fabric of her shirt. In profile, there are hollows under her cheekbones. She looks like the feral cat that haunts the Octagonal Barn: angular, hungry.

I had a boyfriend Outside, she says. He was forty. A bartender. Her smile is a private one. She says, He took care of me. She turns her head, and he can feel her breath against his cheek.

Did he know you're only fifteen? Bit says.

She closes her eyes, turns her head away. Didn't matter, she says.

He would lie like this forever. It doesn't

matter that they're not touching. Her weight bends the mattress, her warmth radiates the length of his arm. She palms something and puts it in her mouth and swallows it. When she turns to him, she holds another pill in her hand, something red and white, and puts it gently between his lips.

Swallow, she whispers.

He holds the pill there between his lips for a long while, debating. When the first line appears between her eyebrows, he swallows the pill. She closes her eyes. Good Bit, she says, petting his arm.

He doesn't know how long he is there with Helle; the window goes black. He watches her as she rests. Then her eyelids spring up when the door opens and the light goes on overhead. He feels a bad sickness stir at the roots of him.

What the? says the old familiar raspy voice; Handy is home. Oh. Helle, he says.

Handy puts down his guitar case in the closet and sits on the ladder-backed chair on the side of the room.

Heya, Little Bit, Handy says, nodding to him. May I ask what you two are doing in my room?

Helle struggles up, pulling at the hem of her teeshirt, her movements exaggeratedly slow. Handy, she says. Just relaxing.

You couldn't find any other place in this big old barracks to relax, huh? he says. Like a common area? Like your own room?

He's smiling, but his cheeks look too taut. If only Bit could find his tongue, he would be glad to tell Handy all about it.

Astrid let me come into your room whenever I wanted to, Helle says.

Astrid's not here, Handy says. Did you ever imagine, Helle, that I might have had a visitor tonight?

We *are* your visitors, Helle says.

You know what I mean, Handy says.

I know what you mean, Helle says, and whatever drug had tarred her voice is gone: it is now the crispest thing in the world. She says, Fiona, right, Handy? I think that's just sick. She's like three years older than I am. You knew her when she was four.

She's of age, Handy says. Not that it's any of your business.

Oh, no, Helle says. It's none of my business, even though you're my dad. And Astrid is none of my business either, even though she's my mom. Why she chose to open up the school all the way down in Tennessee way far away from you isn't my business, clearly. Never, no, not at all. We don't get involved in each other's lives in the Friis family.

My private life is my own, Handy says, his voice gone steely. Just as yours is your own.

Right, Helle says. Exactly. I can fuck whoever I want and you wouldn't care.

Feel free, Handy says. Just do it somewhere else.

Okay, Helle says. Maybe I will. How about Kaptain Amerika? He's old and ugly and fried as hell. Our kids would have gills or something. Maybe I'll go seduce, oh, I don't know, Hiero. What would you think about that?

I would think it would be awfully strange if Hiero would succumb to your oh so evident charm, Handy says.

I get my charm from my dad, Helle says. Hiero will love it. Or, what about, let's see. Bit right here. Little Bit. Sweet and gentle little Bit, the kid who you always liked more than all the other kids in Arcadia, or so you said over and over again in front of us when we were little. Over and over and over, That Bit Stone is plugged in to the Universe, man, she says in Handy's voice, then turns, furiously, toward Bit. So, what do you think? Want to do the nasty?

Helle, come on, Handy says. That's enough.

Helle? Bit says so quietly that he may have only said it inside his own mouth.

What's enough, Handy? What's enough? What's wrong with Bit?

There's nothing wrong with Bit, and you know it, Handy says. You just leave Little Bit alone and don't get him all mixed up with your dramas, okay?

Yeah, Helle says. Great. I get it. Bit, who is no blood relation to you, sparks your protective fatherly gene. Magnificent.

She turns to Bit, snarling, and he doesn't understand what is going on, or why she hates him so much right now. Helle? he says. She's running headlong from the room. Handy leaps up and bars her way. They struggle in the doorway, and Handy jams his hand down into Helle's right pocket, and pulls out a plastic bag. You little idiot, he says, releasing her into the common room, where she rubs her upper arm. Already, a bruise is forming on her white skin. Handy says, You thought you could steal from me. She backs out the door of the common room, keeping her eyes on her father's face, and when she reaches the hallway door, she pulls another bag out of her left pocket.

Thanks for the treats, Daddy dearest, she says, shaking it like a bell. Then she's gone.

Bit finds himself standing in the middle of Handy's room, his whole world swimming up around him. Handy turns to Bit, his face red. They look at one another across the expanse, and Handy says, Listen, Little Bit. I know your pops and me aren't getting along right now, though we used to be best friends, and that grieves me. But I like you for you. Some kids just have goodness deep down in them, gentle little souls. So you do me a favor and stay as far away from my daughter as you can. That girl is fucked in the head, I'm telling you. You hear me?

Yes, sir, Bit says; and now he is irrationally afraid that Handy is going to ask him about the plot of weed on the little island in the woods, that it is all going to spill out of his mouth and then Hannah and Abe and he will be thrown from Arcadia into the cold night. He steps around Handy, and when he comes back down to the Eatery to his friends, they are still playing with the bottle cap, waiting for him. They scan his face. He can see each one coming to the decision not to ask him what happened. In the long draw of last light across the Eatery, as the tables around them are scrubbed with white vinegar and only they are left in their island of four, flicking the bottle cap from one to another in silence, he is grateful, again, for the infinite generosity of boys.

At the midafternoon field break under the wild cherrywood trees, Bit sits listening to two of the Circenses Singers who went to the rally against nuclear armaments in Central Park. They are talking about how Springsteen was both electric and a throwback, how the taste of a hot dog with yellow mustard brought them close to tears. Bit feels ill at the thought of meat in his mouth. Someone is saying: . . . *the countries were like little boys standing in a pool of kerosene, bragging about how many matches they have in their hands . . .*

Bit stops listening: Helle is nearing, under a huge sombrero, clutching a bouquet of cornflowers. She sits beside him and gives him the flowers. He holds out for ten seconds. Then he touches her thin ankle, forgiving her. She touches his knee, grateful to be forgiven.

After the discomfort passes — blazing sun forgotten, hotspots numbed to blisters, shoulders' rise and dip overcoming the ache by sheer repetition — the future sharpens before him, the way every blade of grass on a clear summer morning seems etched by a pin. He is in Arcadia still. He feels himself older, his body tighter in the joints, the muscles softer. He can feel his parents nearby. And Helle is there, older, too, and smiling, and she loves him.

He feels his hope breathing and stretching, a living creature.

He closes his eyes to keep the daydream in. Fervently, he bargains. It doesn't have to be as perfect as it had been in the brief pulse of a vision. He knows that a longing for perfection is the hole in the dam that can let everything pour out. He doesn't have to be as elevated as Handy when he's older, or even Abe, or even Titus; he can be a normal person, a worker bee, a Wolf. Helle doesn't have to be so beautiful; she could lose her looks tomorrow, it wouldn't matter. If he had to give up the quiet, good dreams he has started to have about himself, a life of making photographs, for Helle loving him, for living the rest of his life in Arcadia, he would.

He focuses again. Cole is at the end of the row looking at Bit, lines between his eyebrows. You okay, man? Cole says.

Language fails Bit. No words could possibly contain all he has to say. He manages to utter, at last, I'm okay, and this is enough for now.

The gang is in its hideaway in the basement,

finishing the prank. Helle's music blares on the deck, cassettes she'd shoplifted in the Outside. Cole nods to the driving beat, Dylan winces, Ike thrashes. Bit tries to listen, to love it, but unlike the friendly folk of his youth, this music is furious, full of rusted nails and bile, the darkness in the world beyond. It feels like private anarchy. Bit hopes nobody in the rooms above can hear.

Punk, Ike had said in his jittery way the first time he put it on. Sex Pistols. Fuck, yeah! Now he lies on a broken settee and spins out names for their own band.

The Pissers, the Fockups, Badmass Mothafathas, he says.

Dylan says, Spade and the Whities.

The rest are careful not to look at one another. Two months ago, Dylan discovered he was black, though everyone else, it seems, had known for years. Now Dylan teases his hair into a short Afro and hangs out at the Motor Pool with Peanut. Now he axes, digs, finnas to do. It is embarrassing to peachy white Cole how unnatural this language sounds in his little brother's mouth, how hard he seems to be trying.

Hearts of Darkness, Biohazards, the Bloody Mayhem. Shrimp and the Shrimptones. No, no, no! Bit Sinister and the Kidney Stones, says Ike.

Bit puts down the toadstool on which he has glued a Monopoly house, liberated from a half-dead game at the Store. He is weary of his friends. Under his several pressures — the crop in the woods, Helle screaming at him the other night, sweet to him this afternoon — the boys seem childish, stuck in their innocence. Helle had invited Bit to a party at the Runaway Quonset tonight, *Break down the invisible barriers between the Old and the New!* she'd said. *End the apartheid!* but Bit had refused out of a sense of duty to his friends. Now he has a pang of regret. He would like to be near Helle, if just to insulate her from people like Armand Hammer.

He says, How about Antonine Plague and the Buboes?

Cole whistles. The other two go quiet. Then Dyllie nods and says, If that in't just like Bit Sinister. Don't say much, but when he do, it's right on.

Right on, echoes Ike. Antonine Plague and the Buboes. Lead singer Isaac Vomit.

Excuse me? Cole says. Your voice is shit.

It's *punk.* It's *supposed* to be shit, says Ike, and Bit relaxes into their squabble.

Their hideaway is behind a heap of furniture that the Free People salvaged when they renovated Arcadia House so long ago: it is all broken, but not impossibly, waiting eight years for somebody to have free time to patch it up and put it back into commission. The boys have strung the marijuana plants they gleaned from the woods on the rafters, where they hang like sleeping bats. Cole rolls a spliff and passes it around. When Bit breathes the smoke out, the world relaxes the close of its fist on him.

He is grateful for marijuana. He's sure it'll stunt his growth, but he's resigned to being five foot three. His friends have all beanpoled over six foot, even Dyllie, who is younger than Bit, thirteen in a month.

Bit shakes the gold paint he took from the Motor Pool and sprays the whole project.

Finished, he says. The others stand to look at his handiwork. Cole gives a low whistle. Bit Sinister, he says, you're a fucking artist, man.

On a board, there is a tiny golden village of toadstools and windmills and even an octagonal barn Bit made of an oatmeal cylinder.

Time check, Bit says, and Dyllie looks at the clock he liberated from the Biz Unit, the only people who have a timepiece in Arcadia. He says, 4:30 A.M.

Showtime, Bit says. Ike gives a giggle.

They put the balaclavas Peanut bought for them at Kmart over their faces. Now they are complete, transformed into their own dark side. A hippie gang, utopian goons; they call themselves the Sowers of Destruction.

They creep out into the night. Ike and Cole carry the diorama between them, Dyllie a bag of moss, Bit the box of accoutrements. Beyond the Tool Corner, the Pottery wheels, up the root cellar steps, into the courtyard. They hear a sound and pause to listen, but it is only the tap of oak branches against windows. They can still hear the party raging down at the Runaway Quonset, and Bit has to hold his breath to banish the thought of Helle high, Helle kissing someone else, Helle passed out on the floor.

Into the Children's Wing they go, into the Schoolroom, up the stairs in their bare feet.

The breath of the sleeping children fills the Dormitory with sweetness. Maria and Phyllis sleep on cots in the corner; Sweetie sits in the overstuffed chair in the play area, snoring. The boys lower the miniature Arcadia carefully to the ground, and Bit takes out the sphagnum moss. Silently, they cover the board and its edges and place other bits of moss and wee ferns throughout the room.

Ike sprinkles glitter on the pillows of the kidlets. Cole puts the teacups made of acorns on the windowsills. Dyllie scatters the pieces of birch bark with tiny cuneiform scratched on them. Bit presses footprints over every surface with a clothespin and baby powder.

Just before they leave, Bit motions the other three out. This is the trickiest moment, and if someone is to be caught, it should be him. He can contort himself out of punishment like a small Houdini. He closes a window and it comes down softly. Into the sill crack, he places two dozen butterfly wings: blue-dazzled, green, yellow, luna pale, moth brown with furry startled eyes.

Now he joins his friends out under the oak, leans against its warmth. It is near dawn. The cooks move in the Eatery.

Soon from the window they hear a little voice say a dazzled Ooooooh. Then it calls out, Wake up, wake up, wake up, the fairies have been here! Everyone, wake up!

Ike snorts into his hands. Cole bites his smile into his knees. Dyllie laughs.

Upstairs, the children shout, gleeful, voices pitched high. Sweetie laughs, delighted. And then a voice screams: Oh, my God! and begins to wail, and now Bit pictures a little girl finding the wings in the sill. He can see the delight fall off her face, her stricken expression when she understands that the fairies were smashed when the window fell.

No, a boy cries. No, no, no!

Bit's heart is wrenched. He stands, agitated, would take it all away if he could.

Sweetie cries out, Nonsense. She lifts the window. Look! There're no fairy bodies here! They just put their wings down to rest and we woke up before they could put them on again and fly away. I bet they're hiding somewhere in this room, hoping we don't look for them too carefully or else we'll see them.

She leans out the window, and there's a touch of menace to her voice when she says, In fact, I bet if we all go to breakfast really fast, they'll be gone by the time we get back.

A torrent of little bodies passes through the courtyard in nightgowns and pajamas, into the Eatery. When they're gone, Sweetie says to the air, I'd say the fairies have fifteen minutes to do their business. Then she, too, goes in. Cole whispers, Aw, don't listen to my mom, she's lame. But there is a flush on his perfect skin, tooth marks in his lips. Even Dylan looks ill.

This is awful, Bit says, near tears.

Ike says, Come on, Bit, man, it's like the whole *point* of the Sowers of Destruction, to be mean. The little kids are ripe peaches of disillusionment, ready to be plucked. He laughs, awkward, his Adam's apple dancing in his throat. Bit has to force himself to see the Helle in Ike so that he doesn't hate his friend. He is alone when he slips in and gathers up the wings in his hands. He puts them into his pockets, where they burn during breakfast, then runs out to bury them in a hole deep in the forest, saying the loveliest words he can find to make it all better again.

Even this, he knows, may not be enough. Childhood is such a delicate tissue; what they had done this morning could snag somewhere in the little ones, make a dull, small pain that will circle back again and again, and hurt them in small ways for the rest of their lives.

Late June and the world bursts with greenery. Abe is throned in his chair, the center of a circle of boys on the ground under the oak in the courtyard. The other kids and Ados are scattered across the grass: Kaptain Amerika reading Chaucer with the older girls, Marlene leading four-year-olds through German numbers, Peter and Theo conversing like sages in Hebrew. It is Bit's second meeting of the History of Revolutions Tutorial. State Lessons are over for the summer, and the Tutorial was Bit's idea so that he could see his father every day, but to his surprise, eight other boys signed up on the bulletin board in the Eatery and are listening intently as Abe talks. Today, the theme is Satan. *The mind is its own place,* Abe says, *and in itself can make a Heav'n of Hell, a Hell of Heav'n.* The apostate angel said that, *Paradise Lost.* The ur-rebel. Ike, what do you think?

Ike tries to answer, but his mind jitters off like a lizard when he thinks, and he is left with a handful of tail-thought. He says, Like, isn't Satan just then building the big old palaces of Hades? Building his own place?

He is, Abe says. But that's not what he means. Bit, go ahead.

Bit says, We make our own heavens and hells. He's saying that things look bad but we can transform what they are by applying thought to our situations. When we are in hell, it's our own fault. It seems like a kind of radical idea for the time Milton was writing because instead of putting faith in a God who predetermines everything, Satan is implying that we can be our own gods in a way. It's privileging self-creation over being fated creatures who have no say in our destinies.

His heart pounds: he wants to follow his idea farther as it escapes through the grass, but Abe says, Good, good, and makes a motion with his fingers to slow Bit down for the others.

Cole says, face taut with confusion, Wait, but. Like, Satan says this and he's bad? But *we* believe it, right? That people can create themselves. So what's wrong with that?

Go on, Abe says.

For example, the Trippies, Cole says. I mean, we have to believe that they can make themselves better, or else we wouldn't waste all the Minders' time on them, right? And the whole idea of Arcadia. That civilization can be better if we just believe. Like the way Handy always says that we're emanating light, and that light will touch the dark corners of the world and make them light, too. I mean, that George Eliot guy's quote.

Go ahead, Abe says to Bit, eyes crinkling over his red beard.

Bit says, *I have a belief of my own, and it comforts me . . . That by desiring what is perfectly good, even when we don't quite know what it is and can not do what we would, we are part of the divine power against evil — widening the skirts of light and making the struggle with darkness narrower.* And Eliot was a girl, he says. Cole flushes, then lobs an acorn at Bit that nails him in the temple, and they laugh, friends again.

Great, Abe says, and Bit feels a burst of pride. Then he finds a handful of humility and covers it over.

Abe says, Both Satan and Eliot are backing up the same sort of idea, that desiring change is a powerful way of making change; that change unfolds from this desire. Harrison, tell us what you think about what Satan says, in the light of our everyday lives.

That we are doing good by trying to do good? says Harrison. That our intention is what matters?

Intention matters, says Abe. But if you listen closely to both quotes, it's not the only thing. In Eliot and in Milton's *Paradise Lost,* there's the idea of struggle, the attempt to *act* in order to make your heaven come to fruition. So push your thinking. Let's use Arcadia as a case study. Think about how things are these days. Think about what you most desire to do differently, what doesn't make sense, how we should act on our good intentions in the way we're not right now. We're not in hell, but we're getting there. And this is from someone who used to head up the Sanitation Crew in the middle of summer before I broke my neck. Believe me, I do know hell.

The boys laugh, but there is a new tension between them, and when the laugh dies, they are suddenly shy. The wind picks up among the oak branches and waggles spots of light all over them. Okay, says Harrison, at last. He is the oldest boy in the Ado Unit, used to speaking up. I guess one thing is that we're all supposed to be equal, and yet Handy is still our leader, making commands and things. It just doesn't square to me. Why do we need a leader *and* the Council of Nine? Shouldn't we all just democratically make up our own rules?

Yeah, says Dylan. Plus, he never works like everyone else. It's like he's the head Trippie or something.

Hey, says Ike so softly that only Bit hears him. Abe smiles. He says, Down with the king!

Abe's blasphemy takes a moment to set in. When it does, things go still. Kaptain Amerika's head stops, mid-swivel, mid-Chaucer. Caro unbends mid-stand from her French lesson, a bird is caught in a net made of air.

Ike says, You mean, my dad is, like, getting in the way of democracy?

Time snaps back. Three stories above,

Handy's head comes poking from his bedroom window. His jowls hang; his beard forks; he is uplit yellow by the sun reflected off the hard dirt below. Abe sees the boys looking and peers upward, his lips parting in a smile.

I'll be right down, Handy calls out, and withdraws his head.

Oh, goody, Abe says, looking at his ring of boys.

They wait. A sour wave rises in Bit's gut. Handy lopes out of the Eatery with his banjo in his arms, twiddling a mindless little tune, and when he comes to their group, he seems relaxed. He leans up against the tree, towering over them all. He finishes his song and puts the banjo on the ground. Abraham Stone, he says, in a voice that almost seems admiring. Fomenting discord. So openly, too. Nobody ever said you weren't ballsy.

It's a Tutorial, Handy, Abe says. I'm not fomenting anything.

Yes. You're pure of purpose in all things, Handy says.

Perhaps I am, Abe says. Perhaps our purposes have diverged.

Perhaps you're the one who has diverged, Handy says.

Perhaps, Abe says. But the converse is equally valid. That I have stayed anchored in our original aims and it's Arcadia that has drifted.

Pretty, pretty, Handy says. Oh, you talk so pretty, Abe.

Yes, ad hominem, the defense of petty minds, Abe says.

Handy is pink around the nostrils. He smiles down at Abe, his gray eyetooth winking. He takes a few breaths and says in an exaggerated country accent, shaking his head sorrowfully, It is a sad sight, kids, the day a true believer loses his belief. Like a snake with his spine ripped out; all a sudden, he ain't nothing but a worm.

Abe goes pale, and clutches at his useless knees. Bit stands and puts himself between Handy and Abe. He can feel Handy's breath on his face. They look at one another for a while. Bit's heart is so loud it overwhelms the day.

I meant, of course, the worm in the age-old apple, Handy says, beaming into Bit's face so intensely that Bit has to fight the smile echoing behind his lips.

We're taking this inside, Abe says and turns his wheelchair and slowly squeaks into the Schoolroom. Handy, playing the same cheery tune on the banjo, follows him in. What just happened? says Ike, and Bit presses his friend's arm. I don't know, he says. A few moments later, Hannah runs up from the Soy Dairy, her legs embarrassingly long under too-short cutoffs, and then a few other adults pour in, Lila and Titus, Horse and Midge. When the adults' voices again begin to rise, the little children scatter from the Schoolroom, a handful of seeds.

Helle, lolling on the flat stone by the Pond on a hot, gray day, her pupils swallowing her golden irises. Helle, in the common area, playing rummy with the other Ados, boneless, leaning up against Harrison, rubbing her heel against Arnold's thigh, smiling through her eyelashes at Bit, none of the three boys looking at one another. Helle, asleep in the sunflowers when Bit runs back from watering the Pot Plot, awakening only when he slaps her. Helle, coming up from the Runaway Quonset at dawn, nearing Bit, who stands in knee-deep Queen Anne's lace, waiting for her. Helle, close to Bit and he can smell the marijuana on her, the sweat, the vanilla, the kerosene from the lamps, and she puts her head on his shoulder, and holds him closely to her, and he can feel her ribs against his, her knees hard on his knees, and he wants to be angry but can only put his arms around her. Pulling away her head, eyes full of tears, Helle says:

You're my only friend, Bit, and holds his hand as he walks her back to her room. With every step, something goes wobbly in him.

He takes photograph after photograph of Helle, and she vamps for him, blushing under his attention, flaring her fingers like gills, moueing like a model. Every photo takes him a hairsbreadth closer to her, to the essential core of Helle, a purified Helle that he will one day hand back to her on a sheet of photographic paper.

Here, he imagines himself saying. This is you.

She will look at the print and know herself, at last, and she will wonder how she missed herself all along. Helle, seeing Helle as clearly as she sees the rest of the world: this is something to be dreamed of.

It is a week until Cockaigne Day. The third-grade kidlets have put an enormous kraft-paper calendar on the Eatery walls, and the days are filling up with beaming, big-maned suns. Time is slippery in Arcadia; the gong rules the days, the seasons rule the rest. The calendar feels to Bit, unused to such order, like an imposition. Arcadia seems strangely hushed since the great fight during the Tutorial, which has taken on epic tones as the rumor of it has passed from person to person. There is a sickness in the air.

At dinner one night, they flee the tension, Hannah and Abe and Bit. In three mornings, Hannah and Bit will go to harvest the crop, and spend the next few nights in the Sugarshack to cure it. Every subtle changing tone in the daylight brings them closer to the end point. They are thrilled, they can hardly sit still, even Abe, who has no choice. Now they are together on a blanket spread under the copper beech, in the cool summer evening, and Bit feels the old happiness circling him, watches his mother's hands flying like swallows to portion out the food, sees the way Abe looks at Hannah with his heart in his face. If he weren't undone by gratitude for this old companionship returned to him, he wouldn't say the silly thing he says. Which is: What if the Pigs find the Plot before we can pick it?

How odd that this deep, murmuring fear would choose now to emerge. Between Hannah and Abe, a line tightens, a subtle disappointment in Bit.

Unbearably, his parents ignore Bit's question. They talk about the fireworks Clay and Peanut bought for Cockaigne Day, the shameful waste of funds. They talk about Hannah's lecture, how the slides have come out beautifully, thanks to Bit's new photography skills. They talk and talk, and Bit is alone in the chilly shadow, food in his hands, as he watches his parents move off into conversation without him, leaving him to sit alone in his clammy worry.

Verda is the best thing Bit can think of to give Helle. She is the biggest unknown piece of him; her wisdom, her calmness can give Helle an anchor, the way the old woman anchors Bit. Until they can slip away today, though, they are with the rest of the Ado Herd, weeding the corn. Bit loves the breeds: Blue Baby, Reid's Yellow Dent, Bloody Butcher. Dorotka has been collecting seeds for a decade, and people send her the strangest ones they can find as gifts. He loves the carrots: Dragon, Scarlet Nantes, St. Valery, Paris Market. The potatoes: Caribe, Desiree, Yellow Finn, Purple Viking. The peppers he skirts because he once touched the leaf of a Fatalii and rubbed his eyes and could see nothing but a shifting red light for two weeks, which he spent in bed in the Henhouse. Blind, a birth was a horrible event to overhear.

Leif curses the weeds as he pulls them, ever more inventive. Bloodyballed codpiece, he says. Funkadilic dildo, he says. He hates any time spent away from his art. That boy loves puppets more than people, Bit heard Hannah whisper in the spring, watching Leif at a Circenses Singer performance. Takes after his father, Abe muttered out of the side of his mouth, and both his parents snorted, then flushed when Midge turned around and hushed them furiously.

Helle comes to him at the end of a row, and they steal off together into the woods. The air is cool, brushing past his skin like water.

Helle says, with a catch in her throat, I saw something today. A girl out in the garden. It was really early. She was super little, like five or something and naked, and she was crouched there under a cucumber, chewing on an ear of corn. Like a wild child, like one of those feral children you read about. And I got so upset, looking at her, that I wanted to throw up. I mean, this *little* girl. So hungry she'd run out in the morning to eat unripe vegetables. With all these people showing up every single day, these strangers. I mean, what if one of them was a bad person? What if a Trippie saw her and flipped out and hurt her? Who was there to protect her? I'm sorry, I don't get what's going on anymore, I just don't get it. I don't. Helle's voice has a tremble in it, but her face is pale and blank.

I don't either, Bit says.

It's so weird, says Helle. Nothing's *right.* Remember when we were little, Bit, and no matter how bad it was, we were always this tight little unit? I keep thinking of felt, the fabric, you know? I mean when you take a sweater or a piece of knitting and you soap it up and rub until all of the threads and rows blend together in this one inextricable mass. But now we have like a million insane knitters all doing their thing in their own little directions, and this guy's making a belt, and this chick thinks she's making a pot holder or something, and we've got the biggest, ugliest, dumbest blanket of all times that can't even cover us and keep us warm. She stops and laughs and says, low to herself, Holy fucking metaphor, Helle.

It's dead on, says Bit. Listen, he says, and then, feeling as if he is pushing against a current that is just about to dash him over a waterfall, he tells her about Hannah and Abe's project, the Great Pot Plot, the cash, the relief that will be sure to come.

It'll be all right, he says. After Cockaigne Day. Don't worry. We'll have enough then.

She looks at him, biting her thumbnail, and says nothing at all.

They come into Verda's yard, the stone cottage, the cherry. Verda is out in the garden, tossing corn to her chickens. She frowns when she sees Helle and looks at Bit narrowly, her meaning clear: *Another visitor? Don't you know I choose to be alone?*

He looks at her with hope in his face, and she sighs and says, Might as well come in.

They do. Helle and Verda sit stiffly across the table, sipping tea, studying each other through their eyelashes. The conversation is surface-bright: weather, Cockaigne Day, Bit. If he didn't know Verda so well, he would say the visit was going swimmingly, but her nostrils have flared as if they smell something off, and her answers have become increasingly curt.

They stand to go, and Helle bends to pet Eustace on the floor, and Verda, uncharacteristically, reaches and pulls Bit to her. She smells good, like sun-dried clothes and Amish soap. She says in his ear, fast and low, Careful, Ridley. Most powerful people in the world are young, beautiful girls.

Then she releases him and shows them to the door.

Out in the day, Helle looks unsatisfied. They are halfway home when she says, I know she's your friend, but . . . , and she trails off. Later, she shivers and says, That whole time? I was imagining how I'd feel to be so old and so alone like her. I think I'd kill myself.

Oh, Helle, Bit says, choked.

She looks at him, and says, I'm just kidding, Bit. But her voice is heavy, and when she goes up to her room to take a nap, he can hardly bear to let the door close between them.

In the middle of the Photography Tutorial, Bit has a moment: there is the evening sun and the heft of the Leica in his hands, so right, so *his,* to him the most valuable thing in Arcadia. There are the other Tutorials in the courtyards, the young heads alongside older ones, and he feels, with a gathering of wonder, how this is *exactly* what makes Arcadia great: this attention to potential, this patience for the individual, the necessary space for the expansion of the soul; and he sees the way Helle darts glances at the glorious warm sky, the chipmunks chittering on the eaves of Arcadia House, her own dirt-crusted feet, how she sees Bit looking and smiles her rubber-band smile, and it fills him to overflowing. And when, at last, the children in the Kid Herd launch into a spirited version of "Tea for the Tillerman" with bongos and tambourines, it is all he can do to be cool, to not get up and dance like a holy fool filled with the ecstatic light of god, like the print Hiero showed them last week by his namesake Hieronymus Bosch, a garden where nude people gathered in mussel shells and fruit, spilled from organlike pink huts, rode joyously in a rodeo of pigs and leopards, let finches drop berries into their mouths, every person on the canvas filled with a quiet, green joy. Bit has to hold himself in and breathe in and out until the happiness returns to a safer distance, until it becomes a blanket of sun, of children, of calm, of Arcadia, and Bit is once again only one thread within the greater whole.

At supper, Bit watches Simon sidle up to Hannah and whisper. A bolt in the gut when Hannah flushes. She says, loudly enough to carry to Bit: All right, then. Dawn.

All night, he imagines Hannah vanishing. He imagines waking up to a world empty of her forever, that old fear from deepest childhood. Bit is at the front door when Hannah comes out, her step soft, her feet bare under her overalls. She sees him and murmurs, My knight in shining armor, and ruffles his hair.

The nitid knight of nighttime delight, he says to make her laugh, but she doesn't.

Together they walk to the field. Simon meets them, pacing anxiously, where the sunflowers pour from the throat of the woods. Aztec Sun, Irish Eyes, Velvet Queen. His hair is wet and parted down the middle; he is wearing jeans so new they creak when he walks. He frowns when he sees Bit and looks at Hannah meaningfully, but she is examining a mosquito bite on her arm. Simon says, Oh, come on, and turns his back and strides off through the plants. They follow. Hannah's hand grazes Bit's, and Bit lets her hold it. The day is only a new shine on the furry leaves. In the center of the field, Simon's work stands, a fist covered in tarps. The flowers are at shoulder level and shush as they walk through, and by the time they wend their way to the center, the sky has already flushed with light.

They stand before the sculpture for minutes, in silence. When Simon judges the light to be perfect, he goes around the back, and they hear a hatchet strike twice. The rope releases, the tarp falls like a skirt.

Bit laughs, but Hannah pinches his upper arm, quick and searing. She says, Simon, it's wonderful. Simon looks at her, his eyes pools with stony bottoms.

What seemed to be a humble windmill,

beginning to spin in the slight wind, reveals its parts to be more. The spokes are rifles, the heart the nose of a bomb. When Bit goes to touch the legs of the structure, they are sharp.

Swords to plowshares, Hannah says. Her cheeks are flushed.

Bit says in his manliest voice, Really? Did it have to be so literal?

Don't be a teenager, Hannah hisses, and Bit is stung.

Simon ignores Bit, explains. On one of the Motor Pool's scavenging missions up near Canada, Simon had found an abandoned automobile with a cache of rifles in the trunk. Old bootlegger, he thought, lost in the woods. That's where the idea came from. Then in an army-navy store, he found the bomb nose, mounted like the head of a deer. The swords he'd made himself on the forge. It was supposed to be an embodiment of all that was great about Arcadia. The peace, the work, the simplicity.

It's magnificent, Hannah says. It works?

It works, says Simon and flips a small lever, and the windmill spins and hums. There is a bitter tone to his voice when he says, In this blasted place, there is no use making something that doesn't function. Even I know that.

Bit thinks of giving a gift of art, something he'd put his whole being into, and having it fall so terribly flat. For a brief spasm, his empathy for Simon floods the irritation, glazes the strange-looking windmill with a beauty born of Simon's love.

Thank you, Hannah says, and Simon nods. He seems crestfallen. They walk back together. Hannah gives Simon a hug, and Bit finds himself gauging the length of the embrace, its force, the way Hannah doesn't look Simon in the face when she pulls away. He thinks of Abe still sleeping, his legs shrunken under the sheets. Because of this, he escorts Hannah back to her small room. He waits until she knocks and Abe's voice answers and she goes in, and only when she is safely back with Abe does the eel thrashing in his stomach swim away.

Bit and Hannah were awake long before dawn to cut and load the hemp into a pickup truck; now their hands are raw, their clothes steam with sweat in the chilly morning. In the deep blue minutes before sunrise, they hustle the flour sacks of bud and leaf into the Sugarshack and park the pickup they used back in its spot in the Motor Pool. When the Eatery doors open, they beg entrance, though it isn't their shift, and sit, exhausted, over coffee. Eden stops by, pregnant for the eighth time, and whispers that there is an Emergency Council of Nine called for tonight in the Octagonal Barn. Bit watches her waddle away and, with a terrible sense of sorrow, sees the old, zaftig Eden superimposed over the one whose body has been flattened by the eight tiny steamrollers of her babies.

All day, a sense of panic taints the air: someone, somewhere, advertised Cockaigne Day, although nobody knows who, or nobody will admit to knowing. But here it is in *High Times, Whole Earth Catalog, Henderson's.* A tiny write-up in the *Voice.* Arrivals have picked up this week, thirty on Monday. Today, the Thursday before Saturday's Cockaigne Day, Bit walks to the Gatehouse and finds a zoo: two hundred visitors. Though Titus has emergency backup to keep people from crashing, his method worked only in the beginning of the week. The visitors have begun to find their way in through the woods. Now they pitch tents in the forest, sleep in the cars, mass up at the Eatery for grub. They grumble when the food runs out. They go into Ilium and come back swinging greasy bags of burgers, and even though Titus pitches a fit that roars all the way up to Arcadia House, they persist.

At dusk, it is so crowded in the Octagonal Barn for the Emergency Meeting that there is no place to sit. People stand, and some climb the lofts and rafters and sit in the dark up there. The Council is at the fold-out table, Abe on one end, Handy at the other. On hot humid nights like this, the ghost scents of ancient animals rise from the floors and fill the air. Hannah rushes in. She leans over Abe, whispering, and runs back out.

Bit watches his father go paper white. Steady Abe loses his composure so entirely that the debate is well on its way before he seems to snap to. Titus is roaring, reading out a list: *What if we're harboring a murderer? A pedophile? What if one of our people gets killed? Raped? What if some of the Runaways' parents are trying to find them? What if the girls lie about their age in the Swingers' Tents and they're underage? What if we're hiding a terrorist?*

For three pages, he goes on, and in these words, Bit can hear Abe. Something relaxes in Bit, now that Titus is firmly on his parents' side.

Then Handy opens his hands on the table. He says, First of all, it's only going to be for Cockaigne Day, and then they will all have to either go or live in Newbieville for the month, as per our rules. And secondly, he says, going very stern, Titus, I resent your bigotry. Even murderers, he says, deserve a second chance.

There is a whoop and holler, voices all over the Octagonal Barn rising in agreement.

When it calms, Abe says, What about food? We have no money to feed anyone, Handy, especially with the dough we're sending to Astrid's Midwifery School, and the other stuff that's happening. Even our own Trippies and the medicine for the Hens strain us. You know this. You of all people know this, Abe says.

Handy says, I stand, as always, humble in the knowledge that the Universe will provide.

On and on they debate for an hour, until Regina with her black brows claps the mallet. We're not getting anywhere. Vote time, she says. Lanternlight glimmers on her cheekbones.

The vote passes to the Council of Nine; five yea to allow the gatecrashers to stay, four nay to drive them out. Down the stretch of the table, Abe and Handy look at each other, fury against gloat. Bit thinks of a high front meeting a low, the storm that ensues.

Abe is tongue-tied, scarlet: he would kick something, if he could. The meeting moves on.

It is too much tension for Bit, and his stomach goes sour. He leaves and runs across the twilit lawn down to the Sugar-bush, to see why Hannah was so agitated. He gives a long knock, three short; two short; one long, *Bit* in Morse code. Hannah opens for him.

It is a swelter in here, a hundred twenty degrees. The stove is being fed with wood, and Hannah is in her knickers, soaked through with sweat. She has drawn the curtains and is reading by flashlight in the corner. Heaped on the screens are quantities of drying herb. But it doesn't seem like very much to Bit. Not enough, certainly, to finance all of Arcadia for a year.

Bit says, Weird. Seemed like a lot more this morning.

Hannah says, That's because it was. Now he sees what he'd missed in the gloom: Hannah is livid, her face trembling. I went out for a pee, she says. I didn't bother to lock up. Ran back in a minute later and three fourths of the junk was gone. Gone. Like that. One pee, and thousands and thousands of dollars' worth of the best of our bud, gone.

Bit thinks of Helle looking at him from the corners of her eyes in the woods, biting her nails, just after he told her about the Pot Plot. He wants to shrivel into nothing. This is his fault. Something must cross his face, because Hannah says, Bit? Did you tell anyone about this?

The sudden divide, the seesaw, and he has only a moment to choose.

No, he says.

His mother turns away, nodding. Sweat trickles in the dark hollow between her shoulder blades. When Bit offers to stay up all night with the drying weed, Hannah says, thoughtfully, No. I don't think so.

Bit waits outside her door, reading, but Helle doesn't come back that night. When she staggers in at dawn, rum fumes precede her into the Ado Unit Common Room, and she is inarticulate. Bit helps Jincy and Molly put her to bed. He stands, watching her sleep, and Jincy squeezes Bit to her chest. Good, sweet Jincy, his first friend.

She doesn't deserve someone like you, she says in his ear.

We're just friends, Bit says.

Right, Jincy says gently. I'm kicking you out, friend Bit. It's time for you to go to sleep.

■ ■ ■ ■

Midmorning, Bit passes the open window of the Cannery, where a work crew is putting up raspberries. He overhears a woman saying . . . *Helle. Acting out since she's been back.*

Another woman says, . . . *a Trippie, if she isn't . . .*

Someone says, *Georgia!* then laughs.

I saw . . . a murmur.

Louder again, . . . *like her father.*

Too much, says someone, emphatically.

Bit looks in. The women wear men's undershirts soaked through, identical blue bandannas on their heads. With the dimness, the distance, the uniforms, he can't tell who they are. They could be the same anonymous woman. To Bit, right now, they are.

Bit rises, unable to sleep. Outside, the hundreds of extra people in Arcadia make a roar like what he imagines an ocean sounds like. Ike is snoring through his nose. There is a light under the door from the Common Room, and when he goes out into it, he finds Helle with a kerosene lamp. She's sitting on the spavined couch, staring at a book. She looks up when she sees Bit and claps the book shut.

Hey, she whispers. Hey, he says. In his throat, his sorrow, thickening. He wants to ask her why she stole from them; why she wants Arcadia to starve. He wants to tell her that he knows. But she looks so sad that he can't, not yet. She must be coming down from some high: her pupils are still huge, and the long rubber band of her mouth ends at the corners in bitter knots.

He sits next to her, and she puts her head in his lap. He can feel her breath warming his thigh, her eyelashes as they slide across his skin. He thinks of his hands washing dishes in the Eatery, sliding gunk off plates, scraping compost, the steam so hot on his fingers they feel like they're blistering, anything to keep himself in control. He scratches her scalp, moving between the dreadlocks, her oils collecting in his nails. His hands move to her long neck, kneading the knots out of it, and he sees how small her ears are, tiny mouse ears, so delicate under her haystack of hair that he wants to gnaw them. With this thought, his penis gives an involuntary jerk. She must feel it. She sits up. The skin of her face looks loose, and there are shiny dark places under her eyes. She studies Bit for a moment. She clicks out her retainer, trailing silvery filaments of spit, and leans forward, and puts her mouth on his.

It's a shock, this kiss. It is his first. To taste her breath, pungent with the anise seed some Arcadians chew after dinner. How rubbery her lips are, the strange slabby tongue in his mouth, their teeth clinking. He is shaking. He thinks about the Common Room door opening, someone seeing them on the couch. She takes his hand and slides it up her shirt to one of the dough lumps there. She takes her hand and unbuttons his jeans, her cold knuckles on his lower belly. It is too much for him. He gasps, there's a great, woolly spasm, and his shorts have a hot wet spot in them.

He wants, badly, to cry.

She pulls away, and now her hand is under his chin. She brings his face up until he looks at her, pale, serious, determined. Let's try again, she says and moves her mouth close. Her hands in the waistband of his jeans. Her hands against his skin, warming him. Bit lets himself go, sink into this strangeness. This is it, he thinks. This, Helle's softness against his, her weight, the hard tailbone against his thigh, her legs lifting, and the sudden welcome, this, this, is the culmination of all good things he has ever known. There is a hunger in him to stay here forever, suspended.

And then the worry returns as she bites his lips to keep him from groaning: entering him as if from the depth of her mouth come the warring feelings, a ghost in either ear, that what she is doing to him just now is either a deep kindness or a deeper curse.

Midsummer, a tongue of heat in the air. Cockaigne Day is here.

Music squeals and bashes against other music: someone has plugged in an electric guitar down at the parking lot on the County Road, a ring of chanting men in saffron robes beside the Bakery. Three dueling transistors play at the Pond: Led Zeppelin, Black Sabbath, Cat Stevens.

Let me wander if it seems to be real switch on summer in your garden it's an illusion from a slot machine . . . A chimera of song.

Someone has rented a huge white-and-red-striped tent, where they're staging a love-in for peace. Anyone can go in who has proof of age, but Cole sneaks in to see what's going on, and when he comes out, his cheeks are blown up like a puffer fish's with hilarity. The smell of shit intensifies, people pooping everywhere, neglecting to bury their spoor: Bit can almost taste it when he eats his porridge.

Astrid, down in Tennessee, has sensed something, or someone has told her there is trouble brewing. She drove all night from the Midwifery School and arrived this morning to see what she can do. At breakfast she stands, her hands on Hannah's shoulders, the two tall women speaking softly to each other. They could be sisters, though their blondes are honey and white: the Twin Towers, everybody called them when Bit was growing up. But as he watches, Astrid's face closes down and Hannah turns abruptly, walks away. When Bit asks what happened, Hannah, who hasn't spoken to him since the Sugarbush incident, only shakes her head.

Later in the morning, Bit passes a bush jostling wildly, someone fucking someone within. He wants to take a stick and beat them out of there like birds from a tussock. Instead he shouts, There are *kids* here!, and his voice is so high, so childlike itself, it must shame them into pausing because the bush stops shaking until he is past.

He walks up to Arcadia House with hot eyes. Someone built a badminton court among the lettuces, and the tender leaves are trampled. Dorotka is on her knees, sobbing in them (Forellenschluss, Red Leprechaun, Lollo Rossa, Amish Deer Tongue, Merveille des Quatre Saisons). He can hardly look at her, the granny glasses speckled with tears, the loop of her peppery braids, just as he can hardly look at the mangled ground when he puts his hand on her back, and pats and pats until she calms.

He is rolling vegegristle meatballs in the sweltering Eatery kitchen before lunch when he sees Helle go by the window. He is just in time to call out, Helle, wait, I need to talk to you, when she turns and flushes when she sees him, and gives a wave of her hand, and disappears into the thronging masses, some already drunk and dancing to music that Bit can't, quite, hear.

They are gathered, at last, for Hannah's Cockaigne Day address. The Proscenium blazes with light, the curtains are sodden with heat. A bead of sweat gathers on Hannah's cheek and slowly trickles down her chin, although she has given only a few welcoming remarks. She has to shout her words over the noise rising up from the lawn outside.

In the past, people waited until after the address before they began the party.

In the past, of course, there was no flood

of strangers to trample Arcadia's etiquette; there were the stories that kept them in line. Cockaigne Day was just the twilight in midsummer and the Sheep's Meadow mown so the rich green smell stirs them and the music and the love.

Still, something is going on that isn't just the interlopers' rudeness: tonight, the audience is pitiful. A stranger, wandering in, would never believe that Hannah had been here from the beginning, that to be invited to give the Cockaigne Day address is the greatest honor in Arcadia, that Hannah has been preparing for months. Bit writes the names carefully in his head: Abe, beaming with love; Titus and Saucy Sally and their many children; Sweetie and Maria and Ricky; Regina and Ollie; Astrid, looking especially grim. Marilyn and Midge, who fans herself, farting a little. Tarzan and Kaptain Amerika, Cole and Dyllie and Ike, Jincy, Fiona, Muffin. Helle sits beside Ike, smiling everywhere but at Bit. Late, in walk D'Angelo and Scott and Lisa. But that is it, that is it, that is it. No Dorotka. No Eden. Nobody else. No Handy, especially.

Behind Hannah, who speaks of the nineteenth-century Divinist cult that created Arcadia House, the lawns are roiling, masses busy with bongos or pot or bunched around a great trash barrel, which Bit suspects is Slap-Apple liberated from the Storeroom and laced with LSD. The Circenses Singers come white-robed over the lawn in slow-moving procession, the puppets doing their limber-jointed dances. Bit recognizes Leif's blaze of white hair; he is operating the Fool puppet's head. Adam and Eve waltz together, refreshed with a coat of peach paint. Even through the glass of the Proscenium windows, the song can be heard, the discordant tune, the drums, the hundreds of bells. A thick circle forms around the puppeteers, gawkers caught by their spell.

Bit imagines a great hand descending from the sky and smashing the revelers like a bad boy smashing a trail of ants. Ashamed, he tunes back in to Hannah. But the heat is brutal; even Bit is sickened and can't listen as deeply as he'd like to her story. He notes that there are his slides and Verda's voice unreeling into the dim from a recorder.

Hannah looks out, sees how her audience, though brave, has wilted. She says a little sadly, And here we are. Not unlike the Divinists, idealistic, hardworking, spiritual. Unlike them, she says, we know enough to learn from history and change before it's too late.

She pauses to gather herself, and in the pause something explodes outside, a green firecracker snaking up into the dimming midsummer sky and bursting into red sparks. She turns to look behind her. Her golden hair is full of glints. And when she turns back, Bit can read on her face that she has decided to end it there.

Thank you, she says. Now let us all enjoy Cockaigne Day. And though they applaud her as greatly as they can in the echoing empty Proscenium, his mother's shoulders slump as she walks down the stairs.

Outside, the air is cooling a little, the grass sweet-smelling, crushed. A wallpaper of people has spread across Arcadia House lawn, a shifting mirror game of hippies in their gauzy white dresses and halter tops and full-body denim. A long line from the kitchen moves the food out to the fold-out tables. There is lemonade for the kidlets. There is a great barrel of popcorn with nutritional yeast topping, mangled lettuce salad, tomato salad, tempeh salad. Bulgur wheat and bean salad. Spicy tofu salad. Yegg salad. Pasta salad. There are heaps of bread rapidly depleting. Rice and beans. Salsa. A vat of yam stew. So many pies that they will have no more preserves until harvest. Soy cream in pistachio, vanilla, chocolate, strawberry. Some of the day visitors are not so bad: some have come back from various towns laden with grapes and bananas, crates of oranges, celery sticks, great cans of peanut butter, industrial bread, which tastes like paper to Bit. Huge bags of crinkled things someone calls chips that are so salty they make him gasp. Cookies from huge boxes that taste the way batteries do when licked.

As usual, the kids and Pregnant Ladies and Trippies go first, even though some of the new men are high enough to crash the line. When everyone has gone through, there is still some food left over. For a day, everyone eats their fill, then beyond until they can eat no more. Even Bit, who resists the excitement with the solid moral core of himself, relaxes when he is full and lets the summer night in.

Music begins in the Sheep's Meadow amphitheater. Handy's voice rises into the air, scratchy and magnificent, the Free People Band in fine form, banjo and fiddle and accordion each taking long, luxuriant solos. Tarzan, the drummer, is eloquent in this, his only language. The day darkens, and the joints and cigarettes outshine the fireflies. The kidlets are high on unaccustomed sugar and chase one another. Bit's lungs burn with running, with laughing, scooping up the wee ones and throwing them in the air, catching them, wrestling his friends. Cole and Ike and Helle and he sneak to the vat of acid-spiked Slap-Apple and dip out four hurried mason jars. They take them behind the Octagonal Barn. Helle bites the rim of her jar with her smile and closes her eyes to down it. Bit watches her; he wants to smash it into her face, then, maybe, lick it off her chin. She looks at him and says, daring him, Scared?

He is. He likes his brain. He does not want to end up like Kaptain Amerika, forever tweaked. There are over sixty walking cautionary tales in Arcadia, burnt-out Trippies, their psyches gone rogue.

No, he says, and tosses it back, the alcohol burning his throat. Helle takes Bit's hand as they come out from behind the barn to wait for the acid's slow seeping in. Her fingers are cool in his, and though he wants to pull away, he doesn't. As they walk, she squeezes.

Down at the concert, Handy is leading the whole bunch in "Goodnight, Irene." In the little side area of Christmas lights, Astrid and Lila lean against one another, their eyes closed, swaying. Saucy Sally is tiny, clutched to Titus's chest. Somebody whispers about a party at the Runaway Quonset, and the Ado Unit begins to trickle down that way. Bit and Helle pass the Pond, where puddles of clothes await the splashers who have gone in, naked. It is as full as the Pond generally is during a summer afternoon, but with adults, in the moonlight. Bit and Helle and Ike and Cole pass a group of four little kids who look up fearfully at the Ados going by, then go back to portioning out what Bit at first thinks are pebbles. He looks closer, sees blue pills. He tries to say something, but he has lost his words somewhere, and so he scoops up the pills and shoves them into his pocket. Some little kid kicks Bit's ankle; he is showered with gravel as he walks away. The Runaway Quonset blazes with kerosene light, blasts with someone's radio. Beside the crooked woodstove, there is another barrel of liberated Slap-Apple. There are so many people moving here that they become one shouting mass, a many-armed monster.

Helle whispers in his ear, and Bit doesn't catch what she says. When he turns his face to her, his anger with her must be suddenly apparent. She jerks backward and disappears.

Now people sharpen into individuals. Little Pooh is dancing, throwing her arms up in the air. One stranger with teardrops tattooed on his face leans back on his arms and watches her; his friend, also in a black leather jacket, is pressed up against some Runaway chick on the wall. Bit looks at the jacket and sees a dead pig, and almost throws up when he passes by and smells an animal musk. Strange, he thinks, to find men here when most in this place are kids.

He loses this thought with a shock: on a cot, Jincy makes out with one of the Runaways, a chiseled black-haired boy with a vulture feather in his hair.

Hey, Jincy, Bit says, shaking her shoulder, and she looks up, smiling, says, Hey, Bit, and goes back to kissing. Let her get bird lice, who cares.

Ike puts in a tape, and new louder sounds roar into life. Misfits! he screams and bashes his head against the sound. He is sweating so much he has hoops under his arms. Bit's own shirt is stuck to him.

Helle reappears, dreamy, confused. Hey, she says so softly only Bit can hear. That's my tape? He wants to bite her lips. His body would like to melt into hers. He reaches up to her face, but when his hands get there they have turned into someone else's and Helle is no longer before him, she is gone.

The acid has begun its work. Inside the

universe he can feel something white and warm, pulsing. Time slows, stretches, becomes a spiral. The Runaway Quonset is full of beauty and it is terrible and Bit knows he is weeping: he knows what everyone is thinking because he has thought it himself, how Cole can feel the earth throbbing beneath his feet, how Helle's body is warmed against Harrison's as they press together, dancing, how Armand Hammer can feel Helle's ribs as he, too, presses close from behind. How generous, he thinks, the boys are to not look at one another, how gracious it all seems to him. The faces around Bit begin to make such grotesque shapes that he can hardly believe a thing. No! he thinks, watching Cole's eyeballs grow as big as his ears, No!, Pooh's lips swing to her knees, No!, Helle's face whittles away to a pinprick, to nothing. Everything is rich with the incredible.

The music splinters into fragments of light that he can catch with his mouth. It is so much, too much, overwhelming. He crawls to one corner and closes his eyes and whispers his own name, over and over and over, until someone picks him up and carries him away.

Somehow, he is outside, and the metal of the Runaway Quonset is cold on his back.

Ike is beside him, and they are passing a joint back and forth. The earth burbles underfoot, he can hear the roots of the trees rubbing sexily against the dirt like legs rubbing against legs. Cole is against the Quonset, his lips locked onto the face of a pretty, tiny girl, his hand under her skirt. Bit peers and peers until he can make out Pooh. When Bit can winch his head around, Ike is blinking very fast and hard a few inches from Bit's face.

I think — Ike's breath is humid in Bit's ear — I'm gonna get lucky tonight, and he laughs and staggers back inside.

Bit only wants to be alone. He pushes off into the dark of the forest to find a warm spot of dirt under a tree to curl up in. He wants the hold of the woods on him, the animals to crawl over him, he wants to sink into the roots of the trees and become the earth.

In this little hole at the base of the hill, the old stories fill him up again, the forest thick with magic, witches sitting in the cruxes of trees. This happens whenever he's not protecting himself; the dark bad fairies are dancing endlessly below him in halls filled with rush light, in fur coats made of squirrel tails, in little shoes whittled from bear claws. They are planning their tricks, the beasties. If they saw him, they would blow poison nettles at him and make him fall asleep there, to awaken a century later, Bit van Winkle, his life gone by in sleep. He is so terrified he starts to cry, then forgets his fear in the beauty of his fingernails shining in the moonlight.

He walks. He touches the bark as he passes each hulking dark tree, and each bulges and sucks itself in. When the sound of the Quonset dims and blends into the more distant sound of the concert and there rises the rushing of the stream somewhere ahead, he realizes he must piss.

It has to be the right place: he touches tree after tree, and none gives him permission.

A new sound arises out of the forest, a low groan that, at first, he thinks is the music of the spheres, the great cold stars singing, not at all as lovely as he'd imagined. But it is too close, and Bit freezes, waits to see where the sound is coming from.

There, he sees a pool of darkness, an oil slick that grows upward, becomes a black lump on the ground, lit in some places by unshadowed moon. Even in his off-kilter brain, he knows it is a couple of people having fun. Something isn't quite right, though, with the way the bodies are. Bit squints through the pulsing fog in his eyes. There is a person on top of another, yet the head of the second is in the wrong place, yards away, as if the body is both enormous and bent. A quickening, a rattle in the chest, a raw bear growl, and then a belt buckle tingles, the fucker stands over the fuckee's legs.

Thanks, baby, comes a man's voice quietly. You were amazing.

A voice rises, a girl's. Sure, she says, it was fun.

Now the man says, Hey, you think you have a little sugar for my buddy here? What do you think? Share a little? If not, it's totally cool, but he really digs you. Be a favor for me.

You're just a gorgeous thing, says another voice, higher-pitched, male. Prettiest thing I've seen in a long, long time.

There is a long pause, then the girl says, hesitant, I don't . . .

Come on, says the first man. It's no big deal. He kneels and begins to whisper, and at last, the girl's voice emerges from the darkness. Okay, she says, with bravado.

The second man rises, belt jingles, crouches down, merges with the girl's body on the ground.

Bit can't move. He can't breathe. The man

finishes, and both men stand up, looking at the lump on the ground, struggling to sit. Let's take her back, one says, and they pick the girl up between them and dust her off. One of them, it seems, picks something tenderly out of her hair.

Bit shrinks behind the tree beside him as they crash past over the sticks and leaves. They come straight at him, so close he can smell the musk of sex, clove cigarettes, blood, alcohol. Even closer, and he wills himself into the tree. They pass, and Bit sees a sprinkle of black under one man's eye, the shimmer off a leather jacket, and Helle's face gleaming like its own moon, a comet tail of white in the air where she'd been.

When he can no longer hear them, Bit returns to his body. The stars are still out, the sky endlessly black. The stream gurgles. On the wind, there is the distant sound of cheering from the Sheep's Meadow, the end of a song. He doesn't think he saw what he saw. There is no way. It was, like everything else tonight, an alchemical reaction: desire poured from a great height into a beaker of fear.

And yet, he begins to run. He doesn't believe; but he still has to find Hannah or Abe or Titus, someone who can do something, Handy, Astrid, a midwife, an adult, someone. Branches rake his cheeks. He trips and feels rips in his palms, warm blood spilling out of the bag of his skin. At last, out to the Pond, Arcadia House still very far. He has a stitch in his side, has to stop to breathe out his lungs.

When he stands, he is so tired that his limbs are made of stone. It is all he can do to keep trudging, step after step. He tries to focus, but he can't remember now what he was afraid of. There were woods and people fucking, or the woods fucking itself. Stars and fucking and woods. He can't quite figure it out. There was Helle, possibly. Or Pooh. Helle and the trees, Pooh and men? There was a yes? He wants to weep for the overwhelm that sucks him in, a quicksand. The word *rape* surfaces in his brain, hot and glowing, and he pushes it down again. It wasn't. Still: not right. There is something wrong, and if he could ask Hannah, she would make it clear for him, make him understand what he doesn't understand; he doesn't believe his own nose, here, his hands, the hunger a purple spike in his belly. It vagues in and out, and he knows only that he has to find Hannah somewhere, Helle somewhere, Hannah, Helle, Hannah.

Bit passes an ember burning in the dark, which develops as he nears into Kaptain

Amerika. The old Trippie singsongs as Bit passes,

> Children born of fairy stock
> Never need for shirt or frock,
> Never want for food or fire,
> Always get their heart's desire.

The ember vanishes. Kaptain Amerika is moored in the shadows eddying behind Bit.

Almost to Arcadia House. Bit's blood is weary. The air seems so heavy upon him. He is almost to his own bed. What if he dealt with everything tomorrow? His legs buckle, and he crawls through the apple terraces. The moon silvering the branches soothes him, and he lies and sleeps. He wakes to a hard green apple banging his temple, a misty dawn, and sits up, wracked with pain. The dew has crept into his joints. Somewhere he hears a strange sound, a clip-clop, and thinks of the choppers and stands to warn the rest of Arcadia, then falls again, dizzied. But there is nothing on the horizon save the sinking moon, and when he looks down he finds the source of the sound: an Amish buggy clipping around the gravel drive. He ekes his tender way down and stands where the horse comes to a halt. The beast's sensitive nostrils dilate and prod at the air, smelling something strange in it: the bonfire, the wasted bodies, the chemicals coursing through thousands of bloodstreams, Bit's own confusion.

Amos the Amish slides off the bench, face blank. Bit looks for irritation, but the man gives nothing away. He opens the buggy's door, and out spill three Trippies: a man who wears a wedding dress; a plump woman whose brain has snailed into itself; Henry, who tried once to yank Midge's tongue from her mouth because he believed it had turned into a rattlesnake. Of the fried ones, the man in the wedding dress is clearest.

What happened? Bit asks him, and the man shrugs. We tried to go, he says and shuffles off, his hem gliding gray in the dirt.

Where were you trying to go? he asks the woman, and she grunts and twists her face this way and that and says Kalamazoooooooooooo, ending up with a hoot like an owl.

Henry says to his knees, No, no, no, no! Xanadu. And when Bit doesn't understand, he says, Honeydew! Paradise of milk. Of paradise!

Bit says, Were you hungry? and both Trippies nod and look at him hopefully.

Where are your Minders? Bit says, and Henry shrugs.

Amos climbs back onto the bench and takes up the reins.

Thank you for bringing them back, sir, Bit says. I'm sorry if they bothered you.

But he will get nothing from the Amish man. Amos only clicks his tongue against his teeth, and the horse moves off. The plump woman strokes Bit's cheek. Honey, she croons, stroking, smiling her brown teeth at him. Little little little little little honeydew.

Bit wakes, groggy, in the morning, to the sound of yelling and fast footsteps all over Arcadia House. His brain is very slow. He shuffles into the bright day, then cringes across the lawn and into the shadow of the Octagonal Barn. Ten thousand people, it seems, are milling about, shouting. Bit stumbles toward Sweetie, who is sobbing so hard Bit can barely make out what she's telling Abe. Apparently, Bit gathers, an hour ago, when the Kid Herd went to the tomato patch to pluck tomatoes for dinner, one girl stepped on a hand. It seemed to be growing from the mud, a zombie claw. She touched it with a finger and called to Saucy Sally. Sally tracked the arm through the mud until she found a shoulder, a face, a pair of eyes, unblinking. She sent the kidlets screaming toward Arcadia House. When the AmbUnit went to collect the young man (corduroy jacket, hair shagged into his face, tanzanite class ring, purple lips), their attempts to revive him were hopeless. As soon as the ambulance reached the hospital, the police descended on Arcadia.

Abe puts his arms around Sweetie, and though she has to bend awkwardly, she sinks her face into his neck and blubbers there.

Bit looks out into the hubbub, a new panic surging in him. He sees the police beyond, so thick that, even with his muzzy head, Bit understands they had been waiting all weekend for exactly this. Some are state troopers. Most are town police. But there are so many. Some must have been borrowed from the bigger cities, Syracuse and Rochester, and maybe even Buffalo. He sees glee in their fleshy faces. They are a tornado, a mob. They tear down tents where people are sleeping, cut down hammocks, turn over everything in Ersatz Arcadia, looking for drugs. Men and women are shoved to the ground, cuffed. The six midwives have locked arms and so far have been successful at keeping the Pigs out of the Henhouse but are now being arrested for resisting arrest. The men go in, drag some of the pregnant girls out. Astrid stands alone, a rigid statue, daring them to look her in the face. None do.

The Pigs go into Arcadia House and come out with Harrison, bellowing, icy Midge. They come out with Hank and Horse, who are clean-living, who don't do drugs.

Planted, someone mutters nearby.

Bit spins, squinting for Hannah; in a wave of despair, he remembers the pounds of weed she'd been holding. He closes his eyes and prays that she had given it all to the others to sell last night, that she is somewhere calm, on a hike in the woods. That, at the very least, Bit and his parents can find some way to escape together. There is a pressure on his shoulders, Helle grabbing him from behind, her arms around his neck and her smell of vanilla, her dreadlocks slithering over his shoulder. He sees Hannah beside the Bakery, shouting in the face of a boy-cop. He dissolves with relief and feels Helle's warm breath in his ear, saying, *Oh, God, Oh, God.*

He is glad Helle can't see his face. He is crying. Not because of the police, not for the dead boy, not for all the people he loves being yanked, bewildered, away. For Helle, for her thievery of Arcadia's future, for what he remembers of the night before, the men in the leather jackets.

He can't stand for her to touch him; he can't shrug her off. He stands suffering her arms around him, unable, just yet, to comfort her. He watches Cole and Dylan holding hands, until he can bear to look at the scene again.

The rest of the Pregnant Ladies are running as fast as they can up to the Octagonal Barn. All together, shouting, they strip themselves naked, veiny and rashy and swollen, silvery with stretchmarks, each one with the most gorgeous breasts he has ever seen. Now everyone is shedding clothes. Helle's arms cross as she lifts the hem of her shirt. Bit looks away, sick to death of it all.

Come on, Bit, Helle says, removing her arms from the buds on her chest, and he takes off his clothes, slowly, covering himself, afraid both of smallness and of sudden expansion. Ike runs up, grinning, and swings his dick so it flap-flap-flaps against his thighs.

None of this bothers the police at all. The ones who usually take photos of bodies are now snapping photos of the naked hippies. From afar, Bit can see the police in the Circenses Singers shed take out the papier-mâché puppets and slit them, looking for a stash, and Leif falls on his knees and rips at his white hair.

The crowd hushes: the police emerge from the Eatery with Handy, in a holey army shirt. His face is pillow-creased, drowsy as a koala's, his hands are bunched at the wrist and cuffed. He is murmuring instructions to Fiona, who is walking beside him, her chestnut hair so filled with light it seems like it's on fire.

Bit looks at Ike and Helle, frozen in the naked moil. Dad, screams Helle, and when Handy doesn't look up, she screams, Handy!, and Handy hears and searches for her. When he sees them, he gives both of his younger children a broad smile, that poor gray eyetooth flashing. I'll be back, kids, don't worry, he shouts. Handy is barefoot, in boxer shorts. The officer hits his head hard on the edge of the doorframe when he pushes him into the squad car.

One last pale wave in the window. Then the lead car pulls off, followed by the vans and buses they brought in to cart the people away. All that is left is a ring of yellow tape in the tomato patch, detectives still stomping the plants, Saucy Sally leaning against Titus, telling her story again, her newest baby as wide-eyed as a lemur in her sling.

Bit touches Helle's thin arm, but now she shies away.

■ ■ ■ ■

One hundred fifty-three were arrested for drug charges. Five for outstanding warrants. Twenty-six for resisting arrest. Fifteen minors, all runaways, sent back to their parents or juvenile court. Handy charged with fifteen counts of unlawfully harboring a minor. Twenty-four counts of aiding and abetting drug transactions. Five counts of possession. For the boy's death, a count of criminally negligent manslaughter: Handy, at least nominally, owns Arcadia's land. He allowed a party to happen at which drugs were freely available. Astrid goes to the courthouse and comes back at night, her face raw. She heads to the Biz Unit and makes a call on their telephone, and when she comes down to the Eatery, Leif and Helle and Ike are waiting for her. Around them, a protective shield has gathered: Hannah and Abe, Midge and Marilyn and Eden, Lila and Hiero, Sweetie and Cole and Dylan. Fiona, far from Astrid. Bit, of course.

Well, Astrid says. I have money for the bail. Handy's, that's all I could get. My mother, Margrete, in Norway. Old witch.

Helle says, Conditions?

There are always conditions with Margrete, Astrid sighs. One, I must divorce Handy, as she has always wished. And, two, you children go to her in Trondheim.

I'm not going, says Leif, his strange elfin face tight against its bones. I'd kill myself.

You are eighteen. You are not a child. It is your choice, Astrid snaps.

Me neither, Helle says, and Ike repeats.

Oh, yes, you are, Astrid says. Margrete always gets her way.

But what about Handy? says Ike, trying not to cry. It's not fair.

Astrid strokes Ike's fuzzy cropped head. She touches Helle's face with both cupped hands. Handy wouldn't want you to see the trial, all that. Norway will be good for you. There will be nobody to care for you here when Handy goes to jail.

The Eatery seems to grow so small it presses against their skin. In the weak light, every single one of them looks wan.

The visitors ebb away. Some of the Runaways leave with them, some of the Newbies. A number of Wolfs have encountered a number of Meadows and vanish into the sunset. Dorotka shocks them all. She finds a mate among the revelers at the concert, the dead boy in her garden proves the tipping point, and she packs a bag and, weeping in Polish, goes. As soon as she does, the aphids move in and coat the soy yellow.

Some of the charges are dropped. Most people make bail from outside Arcadia, but many are furious that the community to which they'd dedicated their lives wouldn't bail them out. Whole families disappear into the night. There are beds open in the Ado Unit. Among the Old Arcadians who leave are Pooh and her mother, who vanish in the early morning after Cockaigne Day. Cole and Ike both look guilty when they hear the girl is gone.

Bit comes in from his Photography Tutorial with Mikele. He finds Hannah alone at a table in the Eatery, head in her hands. Hannah? Bit says. What's wrong?

She stands, wordless, and leads him by the hand to the pantry. The shelves, which are usually stocked full, now shine, mostly bare. There is vegetable oil, white sugar, some spice.

We have no more food, Hannah says. We have tofu. And bread. And a few preserves from last season. We're going to starve to death unless we come up with something. Nobody has sent back money from the Plot, and I don't even know how much of it was confiscated.

Her voice, serrated, hits Bit in the gut. What about the Motor Pool? Bit says. Can't they sell an extra car or something?

Extra? Hannah says. Have we ever had extra anything?

Pregnant Ladies and Trippies and mud, Bit says to make her laugh. He can't help it: he thinks of Hannah's secret cache, the miniatures in their frames, the Belgian lace, the tea set. As if she knows what he's about to say, she says, There is only so much you can sell before you start to sell yourself.

What about sending Monkeypower out? he says, and she says, Bit, take a look at the fields. This morning we sent out a hundred of our best workers. That will feed all six hundred of us for a few days. Then, nothing.

Even when she walks back up to her room, Bit wants to call after her, Let me talk to Helle. Let me get back whatever weed she has left, or the money she made.

But he can't: he can't approach Helle without seeing the men in the trees, Helle's face cometing off into the dark. He can't go near. Helle first looks wounded at his coldness, then she too stays away.

Handy comes home on bail. Bit watches with Abe and Hannah from their bedroom window as he steps from the Chevrolet. He seems shrunken, and when Helle and Leif and Ike run to him at the bottom of the hill, they are all taller than their father.

Why is nobody else down there welcoming Handy back? Bit says.

We're all fed up with Handy's shit, Hannah says. I'm not the leader, but my word is your command. Everyone must work, but freeloaders are welcome in Arcadia. Fucking Cockaigne Day. A community based on work, but I get to spend all day up in my fancy room, high as a kite, sticking my dick into any of the chicks who will lay down in front of me.

Hannah, Abe says.

Hannah snaps, What? I know you think the same thing.

Yes, he says. I've never heard you say the word *dick* before. Cussing becomes you.

She says, Ha! and kisses him, very slowly, on the forehead.

Now she sits on the bed and says, Stone family meeting. Item one and only. Do we stay or do we go?

For an hour, they debate. Carefully, cautiously. With Handy out of the picture, they can change Arcadia; if they stay, they will have to shoulder the crippling debt. If everyone works their asses off, they can survive the winter; how can they work with so few people left? They love Arcadia with all their hearts; their hearts are so very tired.

They decide to not decide. They will stay, and if staying becomes unbearable, they will go.

Bit tries to wait for Helle at night. They have to talk, but she doesn't come back from wherever she is disappearing to. In the mornings, he sits outside the room she shares with Jincy and Muffin, but she doesn't emerge. She is a smooth white fish, darting away from him. He wakes at midnight shaking from another nightmare, and rises. The moon is full and cold. He tries to run but gives up, the rock in his stomach too heavy. He finds his way into the thick, watchful woods. There is the familiar press upon him, the eyes from the dark. The menace could kill him. He walks until he finds himself at Verda's and knocks on her door. She is up sleepless also, making cornbread muffins. He sits at the woodstove in her blanket, Eustace curled around his feet. Verda reads him and says nothing. At last, after he has picked apart his muffin and held the tea until it is lukewarm, she says, Even when you think you can't bear it, you can bear it.

He doesn't say anything.

Sometimes you have to let time carry you past your troubles, she says. Believe me. I have been where you are. This is something I do know.

In the morning, the Pink Piper roars to life. Peanut and Clay have spent all night getting it into working shape. Astrid is going back to the Midwifery School in Tennessee with all the Pregnant Ladies, the midwives. She and Handy have one last kiss on the porch. He says, I hate that this whole thing is over.

Still, there is — what? the release of losing? the hope in devastation? — in his face.

The lawyer will be in touch, you know, Astrid says.

She kisses her children. When Helle says, Take me with you, Astrid says, You must have your year in Norway. It will be grand for you. Margrete is very tough and will help you mend your ways, my girl. You are too wild.

Ike, unabashed, weeps, and Bit can do nothing but pat his shoulder until he calms.

When Astrid boards the bus, Lila goes with her. Hiero stays. Arcadia feels like a book with the pages ripped out, the cover loose in Bit's hands.

Titus and his family drive off before lunch, cramped in a Volkswagen van that had been such a beater even the Motor Pool had left it for dead at one corner of the lot. It may be, Bit thinks, the van he was born in. Jincy and Wells hitch into Syracuse, but not before Jincy bends to hug Bit. I love you, she says. I'll find you. At a loss, he kisses her hands again and again, his wild-haired sister. Muffin goes with her mothers, screaming. The Free Store is unmonitored for two days until Abe presses people into shifts there, and in that time, things are taken from the shelves with nothing to replace them. Good things: knives and pouches of tobacco, candy bars and handkerchiefs, handmade pillows and afghans, gone. They wake to find more people missing. Tarzan. Peanut. Clay. Harrison, whose charges are dropped. More and more, faster and faster. The Ado Unit echoes, rooms empty. Only two hundred people eat supper that night.

Handy disappears the afternoon he is supposed to return for his trial. For hours, Cole and Bit and Dylan talk over Handy's flight through Vermont, up into Canada, growing breathless at the thought of his being an outlaw. But Helle and Ike trail back into the

Common Room at midnight, limp. With a weary air, Helle says, I drove us. And we went all the way to Niagara Falls after we dropped him off, just to see the waterfall.

They stare at her. You took Handy to Canada? Cole says.

I wanted to keep going to Canada, says Ike. But he insisted on going to the jail.

And you know what he said? Helle says. Right as he got out of the car? He said, Be good, kiddos, that's what he said.

There was no *Stay strong, and brave, my beautiful children.* No *I love you,* Ike says, trying to make a joke of it.

Helle looks at her brother with Astrid's cold eyes. That's because he doesn't, she says.

Bit grabs Helle's hand as she stands to go to bed with the other girls. She sits back down beside him and watches the doors close. You're mad at me, she says when they are alone.

I am, he says. He means, he thinks, stealing the marijuana; but when he says it, he sees the pool of darkness, the bodies silvered with moonlight.

She opens her mouth, she closes it again. When she speaks, she seems unstuffed, a pillow that has lost its feathers. I thought you knew who I was. I'm so sorry, Bit, she whispers. I didn't know you thought we were together like that.

Together? he says.

She frowns. Isn't that what you mean? Me with other boys.

No, he says, though his heart mutters, Liar.

What, then? she says.

The pot, he says. That you stole. That we couldn't fucking sell, Helle, and now we're as poor as ever. You're the only one I told.

She hunches her thin shoulders up until her neck is gone. She closes her eyes and seems to shrink. When she pulls herself to standing, she says, Does it really even matter? I mean, she says, gesturing out at Arcadia with both hands, does it? In the end?

Bit is on the rock in the Pond as the other Ados dabble in the too-warm water. He feels old. The spores of milkweed gust in on the wind and fold themselves flat when they touch the surface. On boulders a hundred feet away, Armand Hammer sits, king of the Runaways. His buddies strip off, dive into the pond. Alone, he pulls from a knapsack at his feet the biggest plastic bag of marijuana Bit has ever seen. Armand sees Bit looking and grins, his upper lip touching the nail that sticks through his nose.

Want some? Armand calls out. Ten bucks for the whole bag. I got a shitload more in the woods.

Where did you get that? Bit says.

Armand shrugs and says, Someone told me some asshole was using the Sugarshack to cure it. And so I helped myself.

It's not yours, Bit says.

Armand says, What's your deal, man? It's a fucking commune, it's everyone's.

Bit doesn't know how he gets from his rock to Armand's so fast. He doesn't know how hard a face can feel against a hand, how teeth can split a fist, how fury can make even Bit, a half a head smaller than Armand and forty pounds lighter, the stronger boy. He hits until something goes loose in his head, and he flies backward, a trickle forming in his eyes, and he sees Cole and Ike and Dylan and Harrison and Fiona come sealing wetly up out of the water, hopeless skinny hippie kids about to get knocked off their blocks. From where he lies in the cool space between two boulders, Bit sees Helle standing, white and apart, not even looking at the fracas. She is looking only at Bit. She bends as if from a great height, and he closes his eyes to feel her fingers on his face.

■ ■ ■ ■

Bit takes a trash bag of weed to Hannah and Abe's room. His mother is sitting on her bed, hands between her legs, looking heavy. He puts the bag on the bed beside her, and when she looks up, she takes in his split knuckles, his bloody head, the eyes squeezing shut under their bruises. She kisses his hurt hands. Thank you, she says, but she's not smiling.

Now we can sell it, Hannah, he says. We can pay our debt.

For a long while she says nothing, and when she speaks, it's in a whisper that he has to lean closely to hear. Too little, she says. Too late.

In the night there is the sound of breaking glass on the first floor. In the morning, they find the windows of the Eatery smashed out and down the hill the Runaway Quonset kicked down. It looks like a tornado went through it, Cole reports. Sheets and cots and mattresses all split and twisted and wet. All of the Runaways are gone. Soon, the Trippies vanish, most of the Newbies go home, or to other communes, hitching to cities, rejoining the world.

▪ ▪ ▪ ▪

Ike is not in their room. Cole and Bit search the Pond, the Bakery with its few loaves of golden bread, the Soy Dairy, the Octagonal Barn, the Showerhouse. They walk the fields for him, check the Gatehouse, where Titus's old badger smell still hangs in the air.

At last, Cole says, Waterfall, and he and Bit check the sun. If they start now and trot, they can make it there and back before dark. Bit has matches in his pocket. Cole has a little gorp in a paper bag.

They go through the forests, through the afternoon. They stop once for wild blackberries that stain their teeth and hands, and keep on. At last, they hear the tremendous pour. The air goes clammy, plants grow up the length of trees, rocks they're jogging over turn slippery. Around the bend and there it is, the tallest thing Bit has seen, forty feet of falling water. It surprises him every time, its power and spin and foam, the deafening crash and split of the water on the rocks. The lick of the ferns in the misted air. The strange, kind softness of the very atmosphere. A pulse of pleasure goes through Bit that ends with tears shivering in his eyes and a hurried swipe with his sleeve.

Cole and Bit scale the cliff, clutching at roots and ferns, and heave themselves over the edge. Ike is sitting in his jeans in the shallow water, five feet from the drop. They pick their way to him carefully: the current is strong enough to carry them over the edge. In more carefree times, when they jumped into the pool, they had to aim with precision or their bodies would smash into the rocks below. They sit on either side of Ike, who says nothing. The skin of his arms is bluish and pocked with goosebumps. Bit wonders how long he has been sitting here.

Above the treetops, the sky turns woolly, a slick dark silver. Sun pokes through holes in the cloud cover and fingers the distant ground. Bit feels prickles behind his ears, as if he's being watched. A bobolink calls. A doe steps to the pool below, and after a moment, so do her fawns.

Ike says, They don't want me. None of them. My parents.

This is not the time to lie, and the boys say nothing. For a long time they sit like this, together, in the rush of the stream and watch the water anneal at the edge, hear it break upon itself below.

They come out when Ike is shuddering with cold, and Bit makes as grand a fire as he can. Ike clutches his bare legs to his chest, his pants steaming in the heat. He pulls a little bag of weed from his shirt pocket, and Cole gets busy with it.

The daylight emerges for one last breath, syruping the valley. There is a movement in the trees, and they look up with alarm, thinking bears, when two boys step out onto the bank. They aren't Arcadians: they're wearing overalls and linen blouses, and are as tall as Cole and broad in the shoulders. One throws the stick he's been peeling into the fire with a shy underhanded toss. The other crouches down. Bit is alert, wary, waiting for a sudden move.

But the first boy just says Hi? and Cole lets out a snoutful of smoke and says, Heya.

Heya, the other one repeats. He is dark-haired and younger than his brother.

No English, the first says, the one with a gap between his teeth. Amos boys? Amos Two, John, he says, pointing at himself, his brother.

Oh, dig, yeah, Cole says. We know Amos. He's cool. You're his sons.

The crouching boy looks at the roach going to Bit's mouth. Bit inhales, considers, offers it to him.

The boy takes a big lungful and begins to hack it out. Cole grins at him, and Bit hides his laugh in a fist, and then the young one steps forward and takes a big inhale, and lets it out, coughing only a little.

Bit watches the sturdy boys with their square faces and knuckles. The Oldest Utopianists, Hannah said once, watching the Amish men who came to help with the harvest: for generations, they've lived the most perfect lives they can believe in. Bit imagines meals of animal flesh and hard chores and a huge family and girl cousins in demure frocks. What a relief it would be to live always among family. To be among people who all look like you, think like you, behave like you, have the same God to love and fear, a God angry enough to smite and loving enough to give, a God with an ear big enough to hold the secrets you whisper into it, who lets you empty yourself and walk back into your life, infinitely lighter. He feels loss for something he's never known.

They sit, companionably, passing the joint. The world darkens more. At some signal, the Amish boys stand and nod at the Arcadians and disappear into the woods, back toward their safe, solid houses, back to their families.

Ike puts on his dryish pants, Cole kicks dirt over the embers of the fire. They begin to walk fast, homeward. Bit holds his words in for as long as Ike needs him to. They are halfway home before Ike looks at his friends. His face is baggy; for miles, his stomach has been audibly rumbling.

Those Amish dopes were so fucking weird, Ike says and begins to laugh.

Cole gives his little whinny. Bit finds himself laughing, too, laughing and laughing until tears spring to his eyes and he has to lean against a tree to stop it, or he will piss. When they're quiet, the boys look helplessly at one another. They feel tired in their very bones.

Those mofos, Cole says. They're even weirder than we're going to be out in the real world.

Bit begins to shiver, though they are going quickly enough to warm themselves. He feels sick, wants to break into a trot, a gallop, a sprint. He cannot imagine himself in the Outside. Because, he can admit it now, no matter how he strains his brain, he cannot imagine the greater world at all. He is not ready.

Night has fallen when they come up into the Eatery. They have missed their dinner. The kitchen is dark and empty. But they find a note on the stainless-steel counter: Hannah had saved plates in the oven and a whole loaf of bread, just for them. Bit hides the note in his pocket so Ike won't see how his mother wrote *I love you* at the bottom and feel his own lack.

They are just finished when Helle comes into the kitchen, her cheeks glassy. Ike, she whispers, Margrete's here.

In blows an old woman, straight and white, Astrid but smaller, the air around her dense. There is a power to her. A witchiness. Her mouth telegraphs rules, hard chairs, cold-water showers, feline familiars with bladder troubles. You come now, Isaac, she says in Astrid's accent, comically exaggerated.

Ike stands and towers over his grandmother. She pats his cheek and goes out. Air returns to the room.

Ike says, I'm not saying goodbye. Goodbye means never again, and I'll see you in weeks. Months, at most. He turns his back on his friends and rushes out.

Helle hugs Cole for a long time, too long, Bit thinks. When she comes to hug Bit, he drowns in her vanilla, her dreads making a tent around his face. Her retainer is a flash on her tongue. He has grown, he sees with a startle: he can almost see level into her golden eyes.

Don't forget, she says, leaning her forehead against his. Me.

I couldn't, he says.

If you do, it'll be like I've never existed at all.

He's all knotted up. She kisses him, sharp of teeth, touch of tongue, hands cold on the back of his neck. He wants to tell her so much that he can't say anything; if he does, he will spill out onto the ground. She holds his hand and Cole's as they go down the slate steps to the car waiting on the gravel. Before she turns, he pulls out the photograph he's been carrying in a plastic bag, pinned to the inside of his shorts. He puts it in her hand. It is Helle at the Pond, so early in the morning she thought she was alone, standing naked on the rock, reflected in the glassy water. A taper with a shock of blond dreadlocks at each end, so beautiful, *beauty* was no longer the word for it. She looks at the picture and winces; she braves a look at his face, and with a terrifying swoop in the chest, he knows she understands. Ike has a pillow over his eyes and won't look when they knock on the glass.

Helle gets in, the car gentles off. Out of the darkness at the edge of the wood there steps a giant, which is caught now in the headlights and shines. It is an old man, comically bug-eyed, fork-bearded, with bendy spaghetti arms. It waves and bows in graceful, almost human movements. When the car passes beyond and the darkness steals back out from where it had hidden at the edge of the woods, Bit sees Leif under the puppet, still dancing in the dark.

They are one hundred. Regina and Ollie bought a truck in Ilium, a beautiful, sleek Ford with a huge bed. They go to the Bakery in the middle of the night and take the industrial mixers and one of the ovens before anyone has time to stop them. The next day, two old people in a Jaguar show up for Scott and Lisa, and before they are allowed in the car, they must take off their Arcadia clothes and put on new ones, khakis and a button-up shirt and blazer for Scott, a dress and panty hose for Lisa. Bit watches, heartstruck, as Scott and Lisa climb into the backseat and hold hands, and smile uncomfortably at their knees as the driver in his boat shoes and golf pants roars at them, choleric, speeding off.

Hannah says, I always suspected they were secret Republicans.

They were your friends, Bit says.

Friends, Hannah says. What a word.

There are sixty left. The tomatoes rot on

the vine.

The toilets back up in Arcadia House, and there is no Horse or Hank to fix them. The smell drives out thirty Arcadians. Hannah makes dinner by herself, out of what they have: tempeh from the freezer, a few cans of beans, some boiled cabbage.

The next day, Sweetie comes to the Ado Unit, trailing Dyllie. His little face is electric with nerves. He is pale, almost as pale as his brother. Sweetie seems heavy with her sorrow and runs her hands over Cole's head, the hair sparking with static electricity under her palms. We're going, Cole, she says. A girlfriend of mine's going to take us to the city.

Down at the car, Cole and Dylan hug Bit wordlessly and get in. The car moves off. After his friends have gone, the sound of a woodpecker in the forest redoubles, festive as castanets. There is a puncture in the world, and everything Bit knew about himself is escaping.

Hannah wakes him in the night. Baby, she murmurs in his ear. Grab your things.

He has kept a brown bag under his bunk for a week now and takes it out, and climbs out of bed, full-clothed. When he stands up, Hannah is already gone. He catches her on the spiral staircase and sees something hard shimmering on her face.

Out into the cool. Down the slate steps. He cannot look back; he knows what happens when one does. There is a car coughing on the drive, a junky Pinto. Abe already sits in the front seat, his wheelchair strapped to the trunk. The family's few effects are on the backseat, in a box. Bit knows that the faceless cloth babydoll on top, an Amish gift, is stuffed with high-grade bud.

Hannah closes the door and puts the car in gear. The forest is hunched as they slide past, the Gatehouse is dark. The County Road curves to the path that pushes out to Verda lonely in her stone cottage. There, Hannah turns off the engine, and Bit and she climb out (the cherries in full fruit over the night-darkened door making all slick underfoot). Eustace gives a desultory woof, and Verda emerges in a white nightgown, holding her rifle on her shoulder. Slowly, she lowers it.

Oh, she says. The day is come.

I'm sorry, Hannah says in a whisper.

Verda disappears inside. She comes back out with a bundle she places into Bit's hand. I won't see you again, Ridley, she says. He hugs her fragile bones. Hannah steps up and hugs her too, and Verda says, Go along then.

Her hair blazes in the headlights, but her eyes are only sockets as they pull away.

Bit unwraps the bundle. In it is a bag of rosehip tea, a four-inch thickness of papers bound with a ribbon, the scrimshaw, a wad of cash as soft as mouse fur. He hands the papers to Hannah, who pats them and returns her hand to the wheel, and the money to Abe, who gives a whistle. Bit holds the scrimshaw, feeling the fine carvings with the pads of his fingers until he has memorized the shape of the face repeated in the bone.

He leans his head against the cool window. The same moon hovers. A line flaps with sheets, a mailbox shines. The road passes beyond everything he knows of it. They go around a bend he has never been around, a house he has never seen; all is doubly new, sick with newness. A bridge made of steel; an ice cream parlor; cows, much larger than what he'd imagined cows to be. A sidewalk, a flag on a pole. A brick school. A Ferris wheel. The endless hills, heaped and sleeping.

The sun rises. In the window, it reflects him back to himself. There is so little to Bit: a fine hem of gold hair, the filthy neck of a teeshirt. Fragile, pale flesh over a sharpness of bone, and eyes so vast in his face they threaten to swallow the world just now spinning past, threaten to be swallowed by it.

Isles of the Blest

It is early October. Outside, the city rests between the winding down of day and the winding up of night. The fish-shaped nightlight shines a creamy cup on the wall and Grete is curled against Bit. From where he sits against her headboard, she is all eyelash, forehead, tiny slope of nose, his beautiful daughter.

Sleepy yet? he says, and she says, No.

He doesn't mind. He could stay here forever against his daughter's small warmth. He looks at the mural he's painting on the wall across from her bed, the only thing he can do to fill the restless hour between when he comes home from the university and when Grete is walked back from daycare by Sharon, the mother who lives in the apartment downstairs. Sharon is a small, quick, dark-haired woman. Her name is about all he knows of her; yet Bit feels close to her. He once said, on a morning that he was picking up Frankie, We're a good team: solidarity of the abandoned! But this was a mistake, and Sharon didn't smile.

The painting on Grete's wall is Arcadia, the apple trees twisting up toward Arcadia House, the Octagonal Barn, outhouses, Ersatz Arcadia, Pond. He has spent months detailing the landscape, and now has begun to populate it. The only people in the painting, yet, are essential: Hannah in the garden, Abe in his wheelchair under the courtyard oak, Astrid holding a newborn baby to the sun, Handy on the roof of the Pink Piper. There is Verda and her dog, Eustace, at the edge of the forest, only a dapple of sun if you don't know to look for them. Cole and Dyllie play cards; Jincy stands in the door of a lean-to, a white bird on her roof; Leif dances under a puppet; Erik sits, a blob; Ike is frozen in a swan dive into the Pond. Bit himself is tiny, studying Helle. She is long and white, on the rock with her feet in the water, a naiad.

None of it is as beautiful as the place that lives in his head, of course. Though the vast gulf between imagination and execution is familiar, it still always comes as a sharp surprise. It is a relief, though, from his photography: all his art, these days, seems to die under the pressure of his teaching. It doesn't matter that the mural is not how Arcadia looks anymore, taken over by Leif's computer animation business, Erewhon Illuminations. Leif has gutted, sleeked, chromed, and glassed the entire second floor of Arcadia House for his own private quarters; one man now lives where, once upon a time, over two hundred had slept. The Octagonal Barn has become office space and conference rooms. There are tennis courts in the soy patch, a parking lot where Dorotka's garden had luxuriated.

Leif always did hate weeding, Helle had said when they first toured the new Arcadia, and they had laughed, the laughter catching in their throats. He nuzzles Grete's shoulder, popcorn and warm milk, to banish the thought.

Sleepy yet? he says, and Grete says, No. Story.

He searches for one he hasn't told her, and feels it rise in him when he looks at the white bend of Helle on the rock. Okay, he says. This story is about the very first Helle. The one your mom was named after. In Greece, a long, long time ago — But Grete interrupts.

No. Once upon a time, she says.

Once upon a time in Greece, Bit says, there was a beautiful girl named Helle and her brother, Phrixus. Their father had divorced their mother, and the new stepmother, Ino, was wicked, wicked, wicked, and jealous of the children. She plotted and planned and decided to make Helle and Phrixus into scapegoats. She baked all the seeds in the land so they wouldn't sprout, and when the plants didn't grow, the farmers panicked. What do we do? they cried. Who is responsible for this famine? They went to the oracle that Ino had bribed, and the oracle pointed her knobby little finger at the children and shouted, *They* are! Those horrible children! And the farmers hustled the little ones away to kill them, to get rid of the curse.

But their real mother went to the god Hermes and pleaded for her children. Please, she said, I love them, please help them. Hermes was moved by the mother's sorrow and sent a flying golden ram that picked up the children to carry them to safety over a body of water called the Dardanelles.

Bit pauses. Funny fact, he says. Lord Byron once swam the Dardanelles.

Who? Grete says. She is three.

Never mind, Bit says. Anyway, the ram flew so high that Helle grew dizzy and fell off its back, down, down, down into the water.

Now Bit has to scramble to change the story. He hadn't thought it through to the terrible end, the drowned body in the waves, the very first poor dead Helle. How Grete would think of her own Helle, her mother, and conflate the two lost women.

So he says, And everyone laughed and pulled her out and gave her a crown and made her a queen. She lived happily ever after. And they found another, better, name for the water she fell into: the Hellespont.

The Helle spot, whispers Grete and carries her smile with her into her sleep.

All is dark in the window. A passing car's headlights draw an arm of light across the room. He closes the curtain and shuts the door. Bit feels the coolness of the wood on his fingers as he moves through the dark apartment alone.

Bit's grief changes shape nightly. His head is already with the Greeks; he thinks of Proteus, old man of the sea, the truth teller who hated truth and would shape-shift to avoid it. Bit reaches out his hands to grasp his sorrow, and it slides through, becomes water, a snake, a mouse, a knife, a dumbbell so heavy he has to drop it. It has been over nine months since Helle went for a walk and didn't come back.

He wonders at himself, sitting in the window with his wine, watching the night-club across the street begin to glow. He is tenderhearted Bit Stone; he cries when he reads Russian novels; he cries when he sees the hands of the woman who comes to clean his apartment, gnarled with callus and arthritis. He hasn't cried for Helle. He keeps thinking it will all be explained to him, that he will wake up one morning to hear the key in the lock and Helle will come in, weary; that he will cross a sunlit park, and look up, and there she will be moving toward him, her shy smile on her face, and hug him and whisper into his ear some story that won't mean she had been hurt, that she had wanted to hurt him.

He thinks he sees his wife everywhere. His heart pulses, sure that a thin figure in the distance is Helle; he runs into a café, certain that a half-glimpsed face in the window is hers. They never are. He is stuck, he is suspended. Under the strain of his hope, his daily walks through the city have become unbearable.

The night before she vanished, Helle had woken him. It was very late and her hands were cold on his chest, the smell of winter rain in the folds of her clothes. Her hair was wet against her forehead and cheeks, her face in the darkness unreadable. She had shrugged off her raincoat and boots in the middle of the floor, and he was groggy when he woke at the cold shock of her. He saw the rug getting damp with her wet clothes and, irritated, almost pushed her away.

But her hands moved down, unbuttoning his pajama top, bending her body toward his so she lay against his skin, and he put his arms around her to stop her from shivering.

What's wrong? he said, but she didn't answer. She peeled him out of his clothes, pajama top, bottoms, socks, boxers, then pulled off her own clothes violently and came back under the covers where it was warm. Her cold body, knobby and terrible against his.

Helle? he said.

She didn't answer. Now her mouth was at his chest, moving across it, biting, not hard. The door was cracked open and there was a light still burning in the kitchen, and he could see that her makeup had washed off in the rain. Without it, her face was ravaged, the hard life she'd lived before Bit, her twenty lost years, imprinted on the skin.

You're more beautiful to me now than when you were perfect, he'd said once, kissing her shoulder when she cried at her reflection in the mirror. She'd turned away, disbelieving, but he'd meant it. Her life was written in her face. There, at least, she could be read.

His love for her sometimes felt enormous in him, a solid thing made of spun wool, soft and deep. Even in his irritation, this love warmed him, returned her to him.

Her mouth moved down, then farther. He touched the top of her head, her fragile skull under wet hair, pulled her up gently. He wanted slowness, warmth, kissing. But she wouldn't. She grasped him, though he wasn't quite ready; she wasn't either, she was dry, still cold. But she moved just slightly, sitting there above him, and after a few minutes he took the bones of her hips and pulled himself in until he'd fully stirred. She pressed down again, her body against his chest, and at last her mouth found his. He imagined the quiet street outside shining in the lights, the millions of souls warm and listening to the rain in their beds. He couldn't stop looking at the side of her face, her eyes closed, the small shell of her ear, the scar in her nostril where the stud had been, her thin pale lower lip in her teeth. He was close but held off, until at last she whispered, Go. I can't come.

He wonders now, the wine bottle empty on the table, if he hadn't heard all of what she'd said. If he'd missed the most essential word. Again and again, he has replayed it, trying to hear deeper, to find the moment that foretold the future.

Go, she said; and did or didn't say, I can't come.

Go, she said; and did or didn't say, I can't come back.

In the morning, Grete dresses herself: leopard leggings, frilly pink dress, green rubber boots with googly eyes that spin and spin. She considers wearing her ladybug earmuffs, turning her head this way and that in the long mirror on the door and pursing her lips. She decides, instead, on one of Helle's long strands of purple beads, looping it over and over so she looks like a Padaung woman. Sharon opens the door with a cup of coffee in her hand and whistles. What a fashion sense, she says. Watch out, world, here comes Grete!

Grete hops on her toes toward the door and mashes her face into Sharon's thighs.

Sharon's son, Frankie, comes out. He is an owlish boy, half crushed under his enormous backpack. He hands Bit one of his shoes and says, It came off. When Bit kneels to put the shoe back on, Sharon smoothes down Grete's fine white hair, and Bit sees with a pang that he'd forgotten again to brush it this morning. Grete is a dandelion gone to spore.

Sharon takes an elastic from her own short hair and pulls Grete's back into a ponytail. She smiles at Bit, the skin by her eyes crinkling, and she's no longer the rumpled middle-aged mother he sees every day; she is pretty. No harm done, she says.

When Bit stands, Sharon hands him the coffee and kisses both kids on the forehead. See you this afternoon, she says. Be good.

I *am* good, Frankie says in a hurt little voice.

I'm bad! says Grete and gives a wicked laugh.

They go off, Grete holding Bit's hand, Frankie clutching Grete's, into the streaming tides of people. Bit's own Kid Herd of two. In the morning crush, the children are swallowed by legs and rears, smashed with purses and briefcases. In a marl at a stoplight, Bit bends and lifts them in both arms. The children lean their heads on his shoulders and breathe into his jawbone. Their school is squat and brick, shielded by scraggly plane trees that Grete hugs solemnly, one by one, before they go inside.

The teacher is a plump woman so tender-looking that she seems as if her skin would bruise if she were yelled at. She looks at Bit and gives a little tremulous cry. Oh, my, she says. Are you okay? Are you getting your sleep? Are you eating? Oh, you don't look so good.

I'm fine, I'm fine, he says, and *fine, fine* repeats in his head as he escapes back into the chill. Around him, a spin of bodies in dark coats, tapping thumbs on pads, pressing phones to heads, settling buds into ear canals, projecting an invisible shield of music as they move through the crowd, digital companionship warmer than the bodies around them. Every soul on the street is sunk within its body. Sometimes Bit imagines that he, alone, bears witness to the world.

It amazes Bit how well he can teach with a fraction of his attention. Better, perhaps, than when he is fully invested in what he's doing. These children of blog and text go uneasy near focus. They clam up. He is more relaxed when he can't give a damn, and they are too. They learn.

In the red glow of the darkroom, skinny, odd-looking Sylvie tongs paper from one bath to another. Bit stands beside her. Her skin is marked with raised moles, and she smells like powder, coffee, honey shampoo. She looks up at him. I love this, she says. The darkroom. I didn't think I would. Digital's just so much easier, you know?

I know, he says. That's why I don't do it.

Sylvie gives a private smile. That's your reputation, Professor Stone, she says. Nobody says you're *easy*.

He is startled; did he mishear? There are too many ways to read what she said, three at least, and Sylvie always seems to speak in layers.

He backs away through the rubber curtain, and into the bright room where the water bubblers gurgle. He sits on the table and lets his students slowly flock to where he is. How sweet they are; the boys are inches taller than Bit but sit in the chairs to reestablish Bit's eminence. The girls play with their hair, watch him from the corners of their eyes. They know his story somehow: since Helle vanished, he has become more handsome than ever to these susceptible young women, the weight of his tragedy transforming his soft features into something noble, suffering. He feels himself flush and speaks to shake his embarrassment.

All right, my friends, he says. Out with

your notebooks. This one is the toughest yet.

Most weekends he gives his classes a mission. Make a camera obscura in your room and draw what you see. Photograph strangers on the subway without letting them know what you're doing. Stand in the pitch-black film closet and roll twenty rolls of film, blind. When you come out, write down everything you've thought of in there without self-editing.

His job is officially to teach the lost art of the darkroom; analog studies in the Photography Department. Or what used to be called simply Photography, all that chemistry and film, most recently downgraded from a requirement. *Digital is just so much easier.* It has been years since he taught an advanced course, the wet-plate, the large format. For most of his students, his classes are way stations into a hobby. But his job, as he understands it, is to help his students *see:* to make them pay attention, slow down and appreciate what they're doing. This is something they can use in life.

This weekend, he says to the eight faces arrayed at the table, you will go on a digital fast. He catches himself: he's almost said *yoga,* vestige of Arcadia. Doubleplusgood duckspeak he sometimes calls the old language, laughing, when it comes out despite his censor. I was raised in a commune, he'll say, and he'll feel a bit treasonous and tell some of the funnier or sadder stories; the summer they all got hepatitis from eating the watercress in the stream near the Family Quonset loo; what happened to baby Felipe, whose white crease in the fat brown neck remains indelible in Bit's memory, even thirty-five years later.

What's a digital fast? says Sylvie. There is a designated speaker in every class, and she is it for this one. Awkward girl, overeager. He has to be extra gentle with her. Her eyes fill with tears after a curt word.

No cell phones, Bit says. No computers, no MP3s, no GPS, no social networking, no e-mail, no whatever else it is that you do and frankly I don't understand. If you have other coursework, try to do it all tonight or put it off until Sunday night, if you can. Let's see how long you can resist the siren song of the outside world. Have a response paper to your digital fast for me on Monday. One page. Written by hand, of course.

Some make faces; others, the hipsters, smile. They love being throwbacks. They wear the jeans and teeshirts and sneakers and sunglasses he wore when he came to the city so many years ago from Arcadia.

He reminds himself that the hippies seemed just as childish in their own time.

Sylvie calls out as she stands and gathers her things, No problem. Smiling, her bone bracelets dully clinking on her wrists, Sylvie sings out, Easy, easy, easy.

When he woke that first morning without Helle in bed beside him, he was almost calm. He made excuses in his head: she had gone out on a long walk in the afternoon and visited an old friend, stayed too late to come home. Once in a while, she'd do this. Regina and Ollie owned a cupcake emporium in the city and a frilly apartment by the river where Helle had her own key. Maybe she was housesitting their cats and forgot to tell Bit. Or maybe she went up to Jincy's in the suburbs, Jin just having given birth to her twins; and Helle forgot to tell Bit. He didn't want to push beyond this thought for what followed; the drugs again, scourge of Helle's twenties, the desperation, the needle marks between the toes.

To avoid the apartment, Bit took Grete to the children's museum all day. The two of them ate an early dinner out. It was passive-aggressive, Bit could admit. He'd wanted Helle to come home to a cold apartment and worry about where they were, the same way he had barely contained his panic, a tightness in his chest, all day. It was dark outside when he and Grete came home; but the apartment, also, was dark.

By night, he grew worried. Grete finally fell asleep after calling out Mommy! for an hour. Bit sat at the heavy old rotary phone he would never replace for a cell and dialed their friends. Nobody had seen her. He called family. Erik, an engineer in California, was grumpy, still at work. Handy was having dinner with his fourth wife, Sunny, who told Bit that Handy was saving his voice for a concert, could she take a message, and hung up when Bit shouted, It's Handy's *daughter,* dammit, put him on the line. Astrid was at the Tennessee Midwifery School. Nobody had heard from Helle for a week.

Ike's number was still in the ancient pleather phone book: poor Ike, dead these twenty years, who, like his sister, had grown into beauty in his midteens. Who loved his new adult body, used it indiscriminately, with gorgeous Norwegian women who knitted him sweaters, men in the park at night. By the time he finally admitted he was sick, he had lesions. It didn't take much for him to die. A breath of cold air, pneumonia, one weekend in a hospital, and Bit arriving too late with flowers, finding a bed still warm under the imprint of Ike's body. Those were the years when Helle's family rarely knew where she was or how to get in touch with her. She didn't know to come to Ike's memorial. This broke her heart, even twenty years later, made her cry and cry when the shame of her life swallowed her down.

He called Leif, who answered coldly. Couldn't talk. In editing. Hadn't heard from his sister. Wait until morning then file a police report. Get back to him after Bit calls the cops. Earlier's better than later. Dial tone.

It was midnight when he called Hannah, who had just begun living apart from Abe. He'd watched, alarmed, as Hannah suddenly became a fury of a woman, a new Hannah, a shouting one. When his mother answered her phone, Bit heard the desert behind her, the coyote howl and insect hum; could almost feel the wall of heat rise up against him, almost see the grasping saguaros. She was teaching history at a university there, and was still so full of anger at Abe that she couldn't say his name. *Your father,* she called him. I haven't heard anything from Helle, she'd said that night. Call *your father.*

Although Bit was on Hannah's side

(always on Hannah's side; poor Abe), the richness of his mother's fury took him aback. Her rage seemed immoderate in light of Abe's sins. Bit could understand how she'd be upset: Abe had used their life savings to build a house in the Arcadia Sugarbush, throwing away all those years of scrimping, telling her they were poor again only when their new house was mostly built. Worse, Abe was officially squatting: Leif's corporation, Erewhon Illuminations, now rented the old Homeplace from Handy. Leif had been a puppeteer, then went into movies and, when he'd tired of shoving his hand up felted asses, had gone on to computer-generated films. His last one was a retelling of the old Scottish ballad "The Well of the World's End." It was nightmarish, shockingly beautiful. The landscape was pure Arcadia. The company's ranch in California had proved too small and Handy still held the title to Arcadia and always needed money, so Leif took over. What had been the Free People's was now a corporation's; sacrilege! The diaspora of Arcadia had rebelled. Squatters had descended, ponytailed men with tents so old the sides shivered apart in a small wind, women with rears gone soft as brioches. Most wandered home soon, but four stayed to build houses.

Midge dug into the hill on the side of the Sugarbush, a geothermally controlled cabin, her own Hobbit hole. Titus and Saucy Sally and their kids built a treehouse. Scott and Lisa, hiding their anarchic hearts under Brooks Brothers sweaters, built a Mission-style cabin overlooking the Pond. And Abe, old engineer, had poured his whole being into his house. He had become obsessed with what would happen in the end of the era of oil and went offgrid, solar everything, backup windmill; rainwater catchment system, backup well; ambient solar heating, backup woodstove; materials eighty percent salvaged. Even the insulation was shredded dollar bills from Fort Knox.

When Bit called his father the night after Helle disappeared, he imagined the dark lonely Sugarbush, the forest pressing in on the old man. Abe picked up, panicked. What's wrong? he said. When Bit explained, his father went silent. At last he said, Helle was so troubled, honey.

I know how troubled Helle *is,* snapped Bit. She's been fine for four years.

Abe said nothing. Bit hung up, hard.

Bit wanted to weep with frustration. He heard a mouselike noise and looked up to find Grete, pale in the door, her stuffed frog in her arms. I can't sleep, she said. Mommy needs to come.

Bit said, Can I try?

Grete said, No. It's Mommy.

Mommy's on a walk, said Bit. Why don't I tell you a story? And she was too tired to resist, and he sat with her then the way he has sat with her every night since that first one, waiting until her breath evened out into sleep, into the morning, wondering how in the world he was going to protect her now.

He reads Sylvie's paper about her digital fast three times before he puts it down. She has a tight, tiny script and uses the whole page. She describes how lonely she first felt when she put away her digital things, how cut off from the life she knew. She panicked a little, thinking about what would happen if her father had a heart attack or if a professor sent out an important e-mail, and to escape the anxiety, she went for a long walk. It was strange to walk outside without music in her ears. The city seemed so loud, and now that she could hear its regular noises, she could sense other things, too, the smell of the pretzels from the cart, the deep blue color in the folds of the steam from a grate. She sat for a long time in a park and watched the iridescent throats of pigeons. It seemed miraculous, this glorious color in such filthy birds. The people sped by, and she noticed how naked their faces were, as if they had become so used to nobody looking at them that they allowed themselves to be *seen* again. She was cold because she had watched for so long. To warm up she went to the Film Forum; they were playing movies from the forties. It was strange to be going into a theater on a bright cold day, and she kept itching to check her e-mail or text messages, feeling awkward because she was alone. But she bought a huge tub of popcorn and sat there, and after the first movie, began enjoying herself enormously. It was like taking a vacation from her life. Then a man sat down next to her. He was good-looking, salt-and-pepper. There was something about the almost-empty old theater with its velvet and gilding, the hot butter on her hands, the emotional sweep of the movies above, the man's handsome profile, his smell of soap and shaving cream, that seemed glamorous and filled her with tension. She stopped seeing the movie, waiting for the man beside her to touch her, not knowing if she was going to scream and run or if she was going to sink into the feeling, let herself lose her head. She doesn't say what happened. Only that when she was walking home, her knees still a little rubbery, in the thrilling cold darkness without even a phone for protection, she understood how alive people must have felt before you could reach anyone at any time. How it must have taken so much effort to connect with people. Back then, the past was more subjective, she imagines, because things weren't immediately logged online for everyone to see; the future was more distant because it had to be scrupulously planned. That meant that the present would have been a more intense experience. The last time life felt like that to her was when she was a child, and the nostalgia for that time almost swallowed her up.

Sylvie watches him when he distributes the papers, keeps her eyes on his face when he gives hers back. When she leaves, she says, Professor Stone? About my grade? The other students pour away, and he can hear their feet in the hall, their voices released, going louder on the stairwell up to the street level. He packs his things and opens the door for Sylvie, locking it behind himself when they're both in the hall.

You got an A-minus, Sylvie, he says.

I know, she says. I was hoping for an A.

He smiles, and she smiles back, friendly. She has a bright face that is always hungry; a puppy's, ready to be petted. He says, as kindly as he can, Sylvie, an A means perfect. I've never had a perfect student. Nobody is perfect.

He says this, yet there is a strange thrill in him, a sharpness, and he understands how very much he longs to find someone who will prove him wrong.

Well, says Sylvie, pushing the door into the bracing chill. In the sunlight, the dark moles on her face are even darker, her skin translucent. There's a blue branching at her temples. She stands, all awkward angles, one foot rubbing on the other. Her glance darts away, darts back to his chin. Try me, she says, quickly, under her breath.

Layer-speak. He waves and goes off. Three blocks later he is attacked by staircase wit. He should have said, he understands now, It's not for *me* to try.

Every few semesters, there is something like this: a shy girl who flushes when he stands near, a confident girl whose eyes go dewy with suggestion. Helle used to say it was because Bit was small and gentle and *emanated* care. They look at you and see a husband, she said and laughed.

I always thought it was because I'm overwhelmingly sexy, Bit said.

Oh, you're sexy, she said. But closer to the ground, which makes you more humble.

You're unthreatening.

Bit had felt the sting of this. Is that what you see? he said, at last.

Helle came close, then, and put her forehead against his, her eyes smiling. I see my best friend, she said. At the time, it was enough.

He is cleaning the darkroom at the school, wondering where his dreams went. They were not so very large; they were not too heavy to carry. One legacy of Arcadia is that his push for happiness was out of sync with the world's; his ambition was for safety, security, a life of enough food and shelter and money, books and love, the luxury of pursuing the truth by art. The luxury of looking deeply, of finding a direct path to empathy. It didn't seem unattainable. In the city, where there were a million talented artists, his quiet, slow pursuit was seen as a form of ambitionlessness. And even that push, after Helle, had vanished.

In a kind of anger, he grabs a developed photograph — a test run to figure out the kind of cropping needed — and writes on the back. He lists the solo shows he knows he should want, the fellowships, the competitions won, lists the galleries he should be courting, the prices he should be charging.

He envisions a new set of portraits, blown up so large the whole is swamped by the particulars: this follicle, this pose. He writes a step-by-step plan over the next year to get it all and locks the darkroom behind him, feeling powerful.

But the paper embarrasses him, the vulgar scrawl of it. Just as he's leaving the building, he folds it over and over and shoves it into his wallet. There it sits all day, a strange, bad weight. It falls out of his pocket that night as if telling him something he already knows, and he is relieved to shove it at last into the trash.

His women call him. Hannah from the desert every day; every few weeks, Pooh, Marilyn, Midge, Eden, Regina, Sweetie. Once a week, Astrid, breathless for news. He says, as always, that he has heard nothing from the police, nothing from the private detective. The detective is ferrety and lush of moustache, like an overgrown Hercule Poirot, a cliché of grooming that, absurdly, had put Bit at ease when he met the man. But Bit is starting to suspect the detective is doing nothing more than pocketing the thousand dollars a week that Bit can't afford. Astrid's voice always breaks a little on the phone.

Today, she says, Oh, my poor girl. She's dead, I can feel it.

A flare of anger in Bit, and he says, Astrid. She's out there. I believe that she's still alive.

A breath on the other end. Assent on the intake. Yes, she says slowly. Do believe. One of us must.

Immediately afterward, Jincy calls, her twins screaming behind her. For six months last year, Jincy wouldn't speak to Bit, after she'd taken Bit and Helle out to dinner and stuffed them like foie gras geese and had played nervously with her hair so that it spun up from her head in a wild frizz, until Helle had put down her fork and said, Okay, Jin, tell us what this is all about. Then Jincy looked at Bit and said in a great blurt that she was forty-two already and always thought she didn't want kids but now she wanted them, badly, and would like for Helle and Bit to agree to donate sperm, and, oh, my God, she actually said it. And she didn't mean to offend them. So consider it? And they said they would and soberly went home. Bit watched Helle get undressed that night in the dark, the slow peel of the black dress from her shoulders. Bare, they began to shake. He reached out to comfort her, only to find she was laughing. When she calmed, she said, You should do it. It's the right thing. Plus, everyone knows you should have married Jincy anyway. You'd be happier. She smiled wanly and pulled up the sheets and fell asleep. And so Bit told Jincy no, though it broke his heart; he said it was because the world was too terrifying these days with *one* child of his in it. But he knows he declined because of Helle's steadfast refusal to be jealous. When Jincy was pregnant with the twins, she rang the doorbell and came in with an armful of peonies and a chocolate cake, saying, Bygones, and that was the end of that.

He hangs up at the end of the call and is about to go back to the mural on Grete's wall — he is painting in Titus, a giant, at the Gatehouse — when the phone rings and it is Hannah.

Nothing? she says.

No, he says. He imagines his mother. She has lost a great deal of weight: she looks like one of those lean, browned outdoorsy women who hike all day, with their beautiful legs and sunshot hair. But her voice has grown progressively darker. He says, Are you okay, Hannah?

I guess, she says. I think I'm lonely. Drinking too much.

Now he hears the bourbon in the smoky rasp. How disappointing, when people succumb to what is expected of them. Then again, his wine bottle is already empty tonight. He says, Me too.

They sit together in companionable silence. When a garbage truck churns on the street below, Bit says, Hannah, is it worth being lonely just because you're proud? I mean. You have a choice.

Just because, Hannah says, chewing on her words. Just because I'm *proud.*

Well, Bit says. That's why you're not talking to Abe.

Please. I have better reasons than *pride,* she says.

There's more to the story? Bit says. He had assumed it was so simple: money, the universal wedge between people. He hadn't the energy to imagine more.

Isn't there always? Hannah says, and Bit understands that, whatever it is, her loyalty to Abe is still too strong to tell.

I miss her, he says, at last.

Oh, honey, says Hannah. And I miss your father, that old bastard on wheels.

Sharon opens the door raw-eyed, her brown hair puffed on her head like a mushroom cap. Grete and Frankie squeeze one another around the neck. Bit says, Bad night? and Sharon shrugs and says, Worse than average. I was served with d-i-v-o-r-c-e papers yesterday.

I'm sorry, Bit says, but he has to settle a twinge of envy; there is an endpoint to Sharon's grief, at least.

Yesterday, the girl Helle had been was everywhere. In photographs on the walls in the apartment, in the frail wrists of the barista who served him tea at the university café, in the magazine on the coffee table at his dentist's. These young starlets in Hollywood all seem to want to be who she had been: skinny within layers of clothing, with her clear white face, her vagueness. It is as if the idea of Helle he'd carried around with him for twenty-five years had bloomed external into the world.

He had barely survived his transition from Arcadia to the gritty Outside when he was fourteen. He was lonely. There were ugly urban trees, pigeons, piss caked on walls. He knew nobody and filled his time by walking for hours. The streets of Queens pinched crookedly into other streets; the parks, a mockery of countryside. He felt tender, unshelled. The warp of stories that had always blanketed him, his personal mythology, was invisible, so nobody knew him; no one knew he was the miracle baby, Little Bit of a Hippie, Abe and Hannah's boy; no one knew about Abe's fall and Hannah's legendary strength and the fable of his meeting Verda on a snowy night; they didn't know the traumas of baby Felipe and the Dartful Codger and Cockaigne Day; they didn't know anything at all. They took one look at his slight body and tried to put him with the seventh graders; when he showed them his calculus, history, biology, they reluctantly shelved him with the juniors, two years older than he. There he rested, perilously. The other kids were incomprehensible. They fistfought, snapped gum, played sports as bloody as miniature wars. They were cruel. They called Bit Dippie because he was a hippie-dippie; they called him Stinkass because at first he didn't dare to take more than two baths a week, even though water was free and soap abundant. When he came home from school, it was as if he were dragging a sack of lead.

Even the things he first found good soon made him feel hollow: Cheez Doodles, peanut butter, sodapop, Red Hots, which he ate until he was sick. The flickering sorts of lights they used in supermarkets and schools made even blinking feel like work. The streets were full of dogs, which he had always imagined to be good, peaceful creatures, but these dogs choked on leashes, left shit to rot on the concrete. Summer cooled into autumn, but beyond the softer light, a hint of cold, the season couldn't come into its own. There were no golds, no blazes, no woodsmoke. The sidewalks only grew sadder until a dirty ice emerged. Worst were the people. There was no care in what they did. The pipes burst one day on the corner, the men in orange came, slapped a patch on the concrete, and within a week, the pipes burst again. People argued with themselves in public and wore their faces savage. Everyone was pale, puffy, unhealthy. At first, he marveled at the grossness, the fatness of everyone, and then one day it struck him that it was not normal to be as brown and scrawny as Arcadians were: it was not normal to see your friends' ribs through their shirts, for men and women both to work bare-chested all day, equally topless, everything shining back at the sun. At night, the voices that came through the walls were canned, the many inflections of television, or the neighbors' raised in anger. There were no soft songs, no lullabies. In the hall, he saw a mother hit her baby with a fist.

Even inside the apartment things were bleak: gray linoleum, Goodwill furniture. His parents moved about, faces in grief thick as paint. A silence grew between them and formed into a solid the consistency of wet sponge. Hannah stood at the window, her long hands cupped around her tea until it went cold. Her eyes sagged with winter. When she returned home from work, an administrative job at a social services clinic, silently, they had dinner. They were on the sixth floor, and there was no elevator and Abe could not descend to the street without Hannah and Bit to carry him, so all day he circled the apartment in his new wheelchair bought by welfare. Around and around he went, a thousand times. His wheels chewed tracks into the carpet.

What Bit hated most in all the Outside world, hated with an irrational, puking hatred, was the goldfish in the pet store a street away, its endless dull slide around the glass. When he passed the store on his way to school, he crossed the street. He was afraid of himself, of how badly he wanted to smash his fist through the window, to cradle the fish in his bloody hands and carry it down to the river. There he would dip it to the surface and free it into the terrible cold water. It might have been swallowed in a second, a sudden jagged mouth out of the black. But at least that second it would feel on its body a living sweetness, a water that it hadn't dirtied with its own dying body.

His friends from Arcadia had scattered and he couldn't track them down. He didn't try for Outside friends. He did perfect work in school, so adults would leave him alone. Hannah and Abe wagged their lips at him, and he nodded and turned his back. He slept, later and longer, and when he wasn't sleeping, he was locked in the bathroom. He had liberated a red lightbulb from a photography store and stolen cash from Hannah for the chemicals, and only in the half-light of his improvised darkroom, watching the world emerge on a piece of white paper, did he feel his old self stirring. He could control this world. He could create tiny windows he could fit between his hands and study until he began to understand them.

The spring of his first year out of Arcadia tumbled into summer. Without school, he didn't get up at all. He refused to eat. He lost twenty pounds. When he stopped speaking, his parents, who had seen this before from him, took him for help.

The dreary corridors, the female doctor who held Bit's hand, the gelatin and canned fruit, the rings of sad people talking their demons out of themselves and into the air, a kind of spiritual siphoning. A fog of time,

Hannah crying at the window, clenched with guilt, once confessing to the doctor how she had given this sadness to Bit, it was all her fault. He watched, as if from far away. She visited every day, and clipped his fingernails, and combed his hair and told him stories, holding him on her lap as if he were a baby. Every morning he swallowed a pill, and slowly the chemicals settled into his system, built up there, a superconductor, pulling back the magnetic splinters of himself one by one. Eventually, they erected a barricade between his sadness and the world. He has swallowed the same pill every day since. He is afraid of what would happen if he didn't, the chemistry ebbing in the dark of his brain. Even on the drugs, he has had some long bad slides. In graduate school, anxiety swallowed him whole and he didn't come out of his apartment for a month; after the terrorist attacks on the city; a quiet slipping in the first few months after Helle left. He hasn't yet dug himself out of this last one.

After his very first episode of sadness, Bit returned to school and kept going until he graduated and went smoothly into college. His sophomore year at Cornell, when he was visiting Jincy at Smith, he heard that Helle had returned from Norway. Jincy was somehow the knot at the center of the net, the one who searched people out and stayed in touch with them. And over the years after the first sighting, it was Jincy who told him that Helle was modeling, mostly local stuff, JCPenney catalogs and ads. Then she'd gone out to Los Angeles. Then she'd gone to San Francisco. Then she was in rehab. Cole had become Bit's best friend again; they'd found each other at age twenty-four in a grocery store two blocks from where they both lived. Cole took over the narrative: Helle was married. The marriage was annulled. She was in Miami. Then, for a long time, nobody knew where she was.

Suddenly, Bit was thirty-five. Time, he often thinks, goes like that. He had grown tired of poverty, of scrambling for galleries' attention, the few solo shows not fulfilling enough, anymore. He had gone back to school for his MFA, had gotten an assistant professor position in the university.

Then one drizzly day in spring, Cole called Bit up, saying that Helle was coming to town. She was going to stay with Sweetie, who had married wealth and had a cavernous apartment on the park. Sweetie had invited her sons for dinner, but Cole and Dyllie hated one another because Dyllie, after years of editorials, had been hired as a commentator on a far-right cable news show.

A young, handsome, bowtied black man with an irrational hatred for all things liberal and hippie, said Cole on the phone. He's the neocon wet dream.

Dear God, said Bit, though all he was thinking was *Helle, Helle, Helle,* the girl with the vulnerable white face, the stud flashing in her nose.

Cole was laughing. He said, Sweetie always says, *Lord knows, kiddos, that I named you the right way, Cole black and Dyllie white, but fate somehow dipped you in the wrong tie-dye.* Of course, that makes Dylan scream Racist!, which he does only when convenient. So what I'm saying is that you have to come to the dinner, if just to keep the peace between us. You're so inoffensive.

Bit would have given his right arm to see Helle again, but he had a show opening that night. The Chemical Quatrain, the gallery called it. There was a woman who took huge closeups of the sexual organs of wildflowers; a man who trucked in double negatives and found the ghost of himself in the shadows of buildings; a woman who staged savage little scenes with naked children. Bit and his large-scale portraits.

No problem, said Cole. We'll come to the

show first, then all go to Sweetie's after.

But Bit never made it to Sweetie's that night. The brothers were bickering about parking, and Helle had given up; she'd opened the car door in traffic and run inside to get away from them. She shook the rain off her cropped hair, her earrings jangling. Even from afar Bit saw that life had ridden her hard. The sight of her drooping skin, her painted-on eyebrows, broke him. She was stringy and sad, but somehow turned heads as she walked, as she'd always done. He held his breath watching her. Then she saw him in the corner with the wine, and her false smile fell, and she walked very fast right to him. She collapsed onto his shoulder, her skin's deep smell still the same under all the orange and clove of her perfume, her body in his arms the same, his own body's movement toward hers the same. There in the chic gloss of the gallery, the years peeled off of him and all the old stories hummed, taut, between them, electric lines.

Take me home, she said into his neck. So he took her, darting out into the night, before the Fox brothers even parked, before they entered the gallery and saw their own handsome adult Outside faces juxtaposed with their achingly tender and open Arcadia faces, shelled and unshelled, among the dozens of portraits of Arcadia that Bit had hung that night. What they found most moving, they told him later, were the blanks between the frames, the leaps that happened invisibly between the *then* and the *now.*

A brutal November morning, and Bit is walking through protesters in Union Square. Cold enough to make your balls vanish, he thinks, and remembers his hungry year in France after college, panting for the crumbs of insight strewn by the great photographer he'd traveled half the world to be near. Bit was willing to do anything: sweep the atelier, make excuses to the photographer's wife when the photographer was with his mistress, print the contact sheets, do the enlargements alone. He was freezing and starving, wretchedly poor. He saw himself in the shop windows and was surprised at the small skinny urchin he looked like, something out of Hugo, a Gavroche nightly nibbled by the rats in the belly of the steel elephant. He was in the market searching for bruised fruit to bargain down to centimes when one old woman, peasant-fat, with buckteeth, beckoned him over. *Mon pauvre,* she said, eyes full of love. She was someone's mother. She made a basket out of Bit's hands and filled them with gorgeous purple figs, a delicate vegetable frost on them. *Couilles du pape,* she said with a wink, and he grins now, remembering. Pope's balls: tiny, cold, purple.

He is still smiling at the thought, he knows, because the protesters smile back when they see him. Their faces are painted in white, and they are wearing white robes. He takes a picture, then ten. He looks over one of their leaflets, printed on paper the color of a rosy cheek. They are protesting Guantánamo, that limbo of terrorists. They protest the torture, the lack of due process. Well and good; he is on their side.

But his eye falls on a phrase that sends a white bolt through him. *Ghost detainee: a person taken into detention anonymously so their families don't know what has happened.*

For a moment, the winged thing in him is relief. *This* is where Helle went, he thinks wildly; a mix-up, Helle saying something foolish in public as she always does at parties; *Jesus, if I had a terminal disease, I'd strap a bomb to me and get rid of the Dick and the Bush in one blow.* Or, looking at a television where women weep and ululate by a destroyed market: *Fuck, what are we doing to that poor fucking country, no wonder they want to murder us all.* Someone told on

Helle, he thinks, a file was opened. He sees her go out of the apartment for a walk, sees a van pull up, a burlap sack on the head, a swallowing; she in an orange jumpsuit at a stainless-steel table, the Feds not knowing how harmless she is, how damaged, how deeply Grete needs her.

Bit lets the flyer drop into a rubbish bin. He is staggered; he has to sit. For a moment he felt relief at the idea of Helle being an enemy of the state, that she hadn't been abducted, sold into slavery, raped, murdered; that she hadn't fallen off the wagon and passed out in some ugly motel room, the needle in her vein under the rubber thong. Worse than those awful possibilities is the thought that she walked away in health and sanity. And what hurts him most is the gleam of peace he'd had: he would rather imagine his wife tortured in a secret cell than imagine that she chose to not love them anymore.

At morning drop-off, Bit stands watching Grete until long after all the other parents are gone. The aide has a face as lucid as a dormer window under the brown eaves of her hair, and she takes his elbow and deposits him gently into the hall. He blinks. There are the distant voices of children, the smell of their warm bodies, the sun in its pour over the honey-colored hallway, but something cold grips the back of his neck and refuses to let him move.

Look, he commands himself. Look hard. There is a piece of paper in the middle of the floor. He looks until it becomes terrifyingly strange. The branched folds across the surface, the incisor dents on one corner, the way the paper holds pores like skin, the feathery scrawl of pencil drawn across it, the way the corner shifts ever so gently in some tiny invisible wind, rocking and rocking into its own small shadow beneath, how the light from the windows condenses in the white until the paper holds a power beyond that of any other object, merely because it has been seen.

He remembers the lists of beautiful things that he used to make when he was little, and how he would say the litany quietly to his mother to try to pry her from her sad bed. He gathers a list again: this slice of late afternoon light across the subway tiles on the wall, the tree outside full of plastic bags white-bellied in the wind, Grete's tiny spoon in her hand this morning, the gerbil smell of Grete's breath, Grete running away from him at the playground, becoming a peapod, a spot, a dot. Again and again, all good things circle back to his breathtaking Grete. She breaks the spell. He can move again.

Hannah flies up for the week of Thanksgiving. Abe is coming also, Titus having agreed to drive him down on the morning of the feast. Abe is a secret. Bit hasn't told his mother yet. He doesn't think he'll have the courage to do so until the doorbell rings.

In the airport, as she comes into baggage claim, Hannah's face seems old and worn. Her hair has gone a heathered gray, the one long braid of it snaking around her upper arm. Her duffel is heavy. She studies the ground. Her lips are moving almost angrily, and Bit can't believe his mother is the kind of woman who, in her loneliness, would begin talking to herself. He imagines a slippery slope; a roil of cats, a trashcan full of bottles, Hannah as bag lady. He scans behind her for Abe without thinking. He hasn't seen his parents apart since he was little.

Then Grete bounces and shouts, and Hannah looks up, and when she sees Grete, her face is young again, and she is the great golden Hannah, dropping to her knee to hug her granddaughter. The part in her hair has the same warm sourdough smell when he kisses it. His head swims; he feels awakened.

They have a luxury of time together, almost too much. Grete clings to her Grannah, squeezes her, leads her from toy to toy and store to store, plants long slow kisses on her mouth. They are so absorbed in one another that Bit feels a flush of jealousy and laughs at himself: which one is he jealous of? Whose attention does he miss most?

At the old-fashioned ice cream parlor, as Hannah and Grete whisper and feed spoonfuls of frosty sugar to one another, he has an idea. Hannah, he says, and she looks up, her face rosy. Would you mind watching Grete all day tomorrow? I'm thinking I want to take the train to Philadelphia.

She fumbles in her purse and hands Grete two worn dollar bills. Monkey, she says, your Grannah desperately needs a chocolate chip cookie. Grete skips off: ordering at counters is her favorite thing to do.

Hannah looks at Bit. You're going to see Ilya? she says.

What? he says. You think it's a bad idea.

It's just. What are you hoping to find?

Maybe she went to him, he says. Maybe she chose him. It'd be bad, but not as bad as not knowing.

You didn't call him when she first vanished? You don't think the detective would have dug her up, if she were there? She reaches her hands toward his, and he is shocked at the feel of them; bird-boned, tissue-skinned.

I did call him. I don't know about the detective. But I didn't go look, myself.

Hannah blows a graying wisp from her eyes and says, What, you think Ilya lied?

Bit says, softly, as Grete begins to speed back with a cookie raised high, I would have, if I were him.

Hannah plays with a red-and-white straw, thinking. Grete climbs up into her lap, and Hannah says, All right. Maybe not finding her there will give you something. Closure. You can live again.

Maybe, Bit says. I think I have to try.

Hannah pulls Grete to her, wrapping her long arms around Bit's daughter, nestled and calm. Two versions of the same girl, peeping at him.

My potbellied Orpheus, Hannah says, theatrically, toward the light fixture that just came on overhead with a warm sizzle. My Orpheus descending into the underworld, whistling his gentle tune.

Grete, who couldn't possibly understand, hears the laugh in her Grannah's voice and guffaws, showing her tiny crooked teeth.

▪ ▪ ▪ ▪

Bit takes the predawn train and walks through the awakening city. He likes Philadelphia, the no-nonsense hardness of the place. The day is already crisp and bright. It takes much longer than he thought it would to get to Ilya's; he has to walk a bike path by the Schuylkill for miles to get there. The water ruffles under the wind bounding off it, blasts him with cold, whistles merrily into his ears. Sculls dart elegantly by, eights like crawling monsters muscle their way up the river. At last, he sees again the church where the schoolchildren mass in their uniforms, waiting for school. He'd come here once before, with Helle, when she took her things away from Ilya's house and home to Bit's. He stands in front of the brick house for a few minutes, unwilling, then knocks. The door opens.

For a moment, Bit feels like he is staring in a mirror that reflects his own future. It isn't good. A small man, dark-haired, jaw like an andiron; but his once-handsome face is clotted, like milk left out for days. Ilya, Helle's previous husband, reaches out a white hand and guides Bit in.

It is cold in the apartment and smells

feral, and there are so many beer bottles and takeout boxes that Bit knows immediately Helle is not here. She cannot abide a mess.

They stand in the glum kitchen, and Ilya says in what Bit thinks is a Russian accent, Tell me. So. She is dead.

She is? Bit says.

I don't know, Ilya says. I thought that is what you have come to say.

No, Bit says. May I sit?

Yes, yes, yes, yes, Ilya says, clearing a chair of newspapers. I am sorry I did not ask first. I believed you were the bearing of bad news.

No news, Bit says. I wanted to see you.

No news *is* bad news, Ilya says and smiles, showing briefly his brown teeth, the recessed gums. He sits also and fiddles with a cigarette and draws on it, pulling his yellow skin against his bones. When he breathes out, his face is soft again.

And so you have come to ask if Helle is here or if I have seen her. I can only say, No. To my greatest sorrow, as you understand.

Bit does understand. Helle had come to Bit just after her marriage with Ilya had dissolved. He is a violinist with the orchestra and a troubled man. Helle had told Bit about the rages, the furniture splintered on the walls, the time he held her by the throat over the upstairs banister. They had met during Helle's last time in rehab, the time in her early thirties when she spent a whole year there. She had left Ilya when he grew so sad he tried to stab himself in the heart. He only grew sadder when he woke in the hospital to find her gone. It took him two years to emerge from the hospital and play his instrument again. By then, Helle was with Bit, and Grete was already one.

I should be happy if she were to come to me, Ilya says, now with great effort. But, alas, she will not. I am going home.

Home? Bit says, looking up. Russia?

Odessa, Ilya says gently. I am dying, and would like to die around my own. And this country has lost what has made it magic, of course. The exuberance, you know. Things, I am afraid, are soon to fall apart. The center cannot hold, all that. As it is, it is no different from Ukraine. So, to go back, in the end, from whence I come. There is a certain lovely symmetry, yes?

Bit isn't sure what to say. A bell chimes down the hill and Bit loses count. He says at last, I am sorry you're sick. I know we're not friends, but it makes me very sad to hear that.

Oh, no, I am dying, Ilya says. Not sick. I

am born dying. But I am not so unusual. There are many like me in the world. And you, why should you say that we are not friends? You and I are not enemies. Quite the contrary. Brothers-in-arms, the walking wounded. A connection to Helle. We are not so different.

He looks at Bit for a long moment, then looks away. However, if you ask me, and it does strike me that you have *not,* you might stop looking for her.

Why? Bit says.

I do not think she is alive. I have had a feeling for some time. I am sorry if this hurts you.

Well, I feel strongly that she is, Bit says.

Yes, says Ilya, we are similar in many things, it is true, but we are not the same. You have idealism still.

They sit for a very long time in the sour kitchen. There is a plastic clock on the wall that ticks and ticks and ticks.

Would you like to have my house? Ilya says suddenly.

Oh, Bit says. He imagines Grete here, space, peace, privacy, going to the school at the bottom of the hill. She could have a whole playroom: he could have a darkroom. A quieter pace, the river down the hill murmuring in their dreams at night. But he wouldn't have his job, his friends.

The house is beautiful, he says, but our lives are in the city and I have no money.

Ilya flicks his delicate violinist's fingers. No matter, he says. I do not need money where I am going.

Ukraine? Bit says, and Ilya laughs and puts out his fourth cigarette in the short time they have sat together.

I give you it. The house. You can sell, do whatever with it, I don't care. On one condition, he says and seems almost hysterical with the idea in his head. He leaps up and begins to pace. His hands, loose in the room, seem like spiders, too big for his small body.

What would that be? Bit says, feeling a little sick.

You give me a photograph of the little girl. Helle's daughter. Your Margrete.

With this, Ilya laughs and laughs, a warm laugh full of a strange dark joy.

Bit takes a moment to think. There is no harm in showing the picture. Bit would have sent photos regularly had he known Ilya wanted them. Yet somewhere within him a small beastie protests, urgently opposed. He waits, trying to understand why.

When Ilya's smile seems about to break, Bit pulls his wallet from his pocket and takes out the most recent photograph he'd developed of his daughter, Grete holding a jack-o'-lantern, feet sturdy, her smile as broad as the pumpkin's. There is Abe's calm confidence in her gaze, Hannah's lush lips.

Ilya takes the photo and stares at Grete for a long time. Bit squirms. He is just about to ask for it back, but then Ilya looks up and there are tears in his eyes. He smiles, but there is something of the crushed insect to his mouth. He shakes Bit's hand and Bit squeezes back too hard, and belatedly remembers the tender violinist's bones. Ilya winces, holding his hand to his chest.

I'm sorry, Bit says.

Ah. I won't be needing the hand either, Ilya says. So. We have a deal. He shows Bit out, patting him gently on the shoulder.

Have a good trip home, Bit says. Yes, Ilya says, slowly. Yes, I think it will be good. And with a wink, he shuts the door.

Bit comes home on the clacketing train. There is a woman at the end of the car, facing him, whom he had barely noticed when he first got on, but who becomes more beautiful the more he looks at her. She has long wing-black hair and heavy brows and the kind of nose that reminds Bit of Greek statuary. Her earrings catch the glint from her overhead reading lamp, and gold coins of light dance on her jawbones. He would capture her in collodion, with its beautiful imperfections, its long, slow stare. Her hands are quick and nervous when she turns the pages of her book, and her face so sensitive and mobile that it is almost as if he is reading along with her: here a beautiful moment, here a tense one, here a release into a laugh, here a love scene. She bites her lip, and her face fills with a gladness that makes Bit know how she would be in bed, giving, soft, bird cries rising up from her throat. He could love this woman, he knows. There is nothing between them but an aisle and some seats and a quantity of air to move through; nothing to keep him from sitting down and her shy smile lifting from the book.

Hello, he would say. Hello, she would say. And the rest of his life could begin.

There is nothing keeping him, that is, but Helle. Her invisible hands are fetters, her invisible eyes watching. Her parsnip white body that he cannot stop believing is, just now, waiting for him at home, in the small close apartment, dozing until he slips back into the sheets they bought together those very few years ago.

The woman stands at an anonymous stop

and moves to the door. She goes out to the platform and the train begins moving again. One blip in the window, shining with street light, and there goes the woman, forever gone to him.

In the morning after their first night back together in over twenty years, he ran out for Nutella sandwiches and coffee, and found Helle crying great ripping sobs when he came back. It took hours for her to say, I've done so many bad things in my life. I don't deserve you.

The city was toxic to her, full of temptation and fear. He'd had no money. He was assisting photography shoots and selling only a few pieces a year, and his salary at the university was laughable. His apartment was above a Chinese restaurant; he thought his heart palpitations were coming from the MSG aerosoled into the air. But he borrowed from Cole, from Sweetie, from Regina and Ollie, and rented a little stone farmhouse in the country for a year.

If asked what time in his adult life was nearly as round and full as his childhood, nearly perfect, Bit would have said this year in the drafty old farmhouse. Every day waking to Helle in tattered pajamas and woolen socks, at the kitchen table, a cup of tea steaming in her hands. Those months of lying in the grass, of walks through the hills, of wanders through damp, chill barns overladen with antiques. Helle could spend an entire afternoon watching a swallow build its nest in the eaves. They drove all the way to Vermont for the farmers' markets. The spring eased into summer, into fall. Helle let her hair grow out, gained weight so she looked flushed, not skeletal, and, to her delight, grew breasts for the first time. By October, she was showing Grete.

They had the luxury of time. They spent hours talking, and Bit would describe the life he longed for their baby to have, what kind of a world they would build for her. One night, watching the long angle of Helle under the tented sheet, he described a tight, beautiful community, filled with people he loved like family, living closely and relying on one another, a world with music and stories and thought and joy, of earthy happiness. He realized as he spoke that it sounded like Arcadia and laughed as he said so.

Helle's voice, so distant, when she said: You're not remembering right. Your memory's doing some kind of crazy gymnastic routine to get *happy* out of our childhood.

What? Bit said, feeling a creeping sickness in him.

Oh, Bit. I can't believe you don't remember. It was cold, Helle said. We were never warm. We never had enough to eat. We never had enough clothes. I had to wake up every single night to someone fucking someone in the Pink Piper. Everywhere I was smelled like spunk. Handy let me drink the acid Slap-Apple when I was like five. What kind of hallucinations does a five-year-old have? For two months, I saw flames coming out of my mother's mouth every time she talked. We were like guests at the Mad Hatter's table, but didn't even know the world was flipped around.

Helle turned to him, her belly swollen. Her eyes were red at the rims. She said, I'm dying of boredom, Bit. I want Thai food. I want *life.* This was good for a little while, this isolation, the little house in the middle of nowhere. But two people isn't enough, Bit. It's not enough. Let's go back to the city. Please, please.

He didn't say, Not enough for what? He didn't say, Do you think you're ready for that? He said, All right, and called the landlord and began to pack.

Amenable Bit, good-hearted Bit, gentle and generous Bit. He hates that man.

Wishes he'd had any kind of backbone, the guts to say No. If he had, she would still be here. If he were more commanding, he would not be a person people would leave.

The black-and-white darkroom is in the basement of the arts building, which has long shadowy hallways and furnaces that clank and murmur. When he is alone here at night, the wood floors release the pressure built up over the day in sharp cracks that sound like footsteps. The only time he can use the darkroom for his own work is during the holidays, like this Thanksgiving week, when his students are all home, getting drunk, seeing their high school sweethearts in bars.

Hannah and Grete are at a play for children tonight, dressed like glamour queens, with sparkle on their cheekbones. Bit will use his time as well as he can. He had felt the old flame in himself. The tingle in the fingertips. He is eager to begin. He comes in whistling; someone has left the safelight burning, he sees with dismay, and takes off his coat and rolls his sleeves. When he looks up, he sees that the dark heap by the bank of enlargers is a person, watching him.

Hello, Professor Stone, says Sylvie.

A claustrophobic feeling thickens in the

room. Bit frowns and says, Sylvie. What are you doing here?

I'm passionate about my art, she says, and she laughs.

Bit wavers. What is it about this girl that bothers him so much? He is half ready to get to work, start developing his film, damn the impropriety, when she speaks.

Actually, she says, I'm getting away from my family. Everyone is drunk and fighting. My dad is off somewhere doing work, per usual. We're such a mess. Her voice throbs a little.

Sorry to hear that, he says. Families are tough.

You getting away from your family too? she says.

No. Holidays are when I get my own work done here. I can only work alone.

She smiles, her cheeks dimpling in the dim red light. But with me here, she says, you're not alone.

Exactly, he says. He puts his coat on again. Happy Thanksgiving, he says and goes out the door, and even though Sylvie calls out, Wait, I'm sorry, he doesn't stop.

He is irritated, irrationally angry. To calm down, he stops on the way home at an all-night diner where he has a linoleum table and a pot of coffee to himself. When people come in, he tries to guess who they are. Tonight it is too cold to tell. The insomniacs could be whores, could be drunken revelers, could be wealthy divorcees hungering for a hand on their skin. They sit here in the darkness, trusting. That the coffee will be hot and unpoisoned. That no raging madman will come in with a gun or a bomb.

It leaves him breathless at times, how much faith people put in one another. So fragile, the social contract: we will all stand by the rules, move with care and gentleness, invest in the infrastructure, agree with the penalties of failure. That this man driving his truck down the street won't, on a whim, angle into the plate glass and end things. That the president won't let his hand hover over the red button and, in moment of rage or weakness, explode the world. The invisible tissue of civilization: so thin, so easily rendable. It's a miracle that it exists at all.

He imagines snapping his fingers, making all the people in the diner stand, at once, and become their better selves. The woman with the cragged oak-bark face throws off her hood and shakes her hair and her age drops off of her like bandages. The man with a monk's tonsure, muttering to himself, leaps onto a table and strikes music from the air. Out of the bowels of the kitchen the weary cooks, small brown people, cartwheel and break-dance, spinning like upended beetles on the ground and their faces crack into glee and they are suddenly lovely to look at, and the dozen customers start up all at once into loud song, voices broken and beautiful. The song rises and infiltrates the city and wakes the inhabitants, one by one, from their own dark dreams, and all across the island, people sit up in bed and listen to it lap around them, an ocean of kindness, filling them, making them forget all the evil leaching out of the world for a very long moment, making them forget everything but the song.

He laughs to himself and the vision dissolves. There is lassitude, the door opening to the cold air and single bundled bodies coming in. The silent waitress ministers to those who sit down. The night draws into morning. Here they are forever, sitting at their tables, separate, alone.

It is Thanksgiving Day.

Grete is napping. The Tofurky roasts among the root vegetables, and Hannah has just sat down beside Bit at the kitchen table, taken a long breath, dived in. She is saying, The trouble is, Bit, that you can't start to live your life again until you make yourself let go — But the doorbell interrupts her.

Grocery delivery, Bit says, though he knows it isn't. He feels a little ill. You can give me the business after I tip the man.

All right, she says, disgustedly. She was early at the booze, is on her third tumbler of bourbon already.

Bit buzzes without answering and holds open the door. The elevator pings and the doors part to Abe's beaming face. He is the same, always. His face has as few wrinkles as Bit's, and his shoulders and arms are vast from wheelchair racing. He gives Bit a kiss on the cheek, and here is the old scour of beard against Bit's skin. Abe gestures at the bottle of Pappy Van Winkle bourbon on his lap, Hannah's favorite, and winks.

Just what we need, Bit says loudly. You can put the groceries down on the kitchen table.

Hannah is rehearsing her interrupted argument with Bit when Abe wheels in. She goes very still. He pushes himself to her. They are the same height, sitting, and he takes her hand. She lets him.

Oh, Abe, she says, after a while. She can't keep the happiness from her face.

I know, he says. I'm an asshole.

Yes, she says.

But you love me.

Unfortunately, she says.

Haven't I been punished enough?

Hannah wipes her eyes, still smiling. The problem is, she says, I'm really only punishing myself.

So you think, says Abe. I can't live without you, my Hannah.

Well, that was my plan, she says. I wanted to kill you.

I know, he says. But wait until you see the house. Honestly, it's a thing of beauty.

Was it worth it? she says, sour again.

Not a single day of our separation, he says. Not a moment. But if you come back to me, I can have both. The answer, then, would be a solid maybe.

She looks at Abe, her face drawn with exhaustion. Bit is wrenched for a moment out of his own sorrow. He sees now what he should have been attentive to all this time: the terrible hollowness of Hannah's days. How her body at night would reach for the warmth of Abe beside her, as it had lain there for forty years, only to find a cold sheet; the dry, dusty feel of her anger, how stuffed she was with it, how bitter it tasted on the back of her tongue.

She scowls. Abe smiles and touches her nose with the tip of his finger.

Oh, all right, she says at last. I thought I'd

make you beg more, but who cares. We're not getting any younger. She looks at Bit significantly and says, You only have so many days in your life to try to be happy.

She turns back to Abe and says, Give me a few more weeks until the semester is over and I'll drive back home to you. You irresponsible, irritating, lying old man.

Abe smiles and leans to kiss her, but she's not ready for that and pulls away. God. You always get what you want, she says.

Although his voice is apologetic, Abe says quietly, I do.

They eat at four, when the city is so quiet it could be a village. It is dark enough that the thousands of windows Bit can see from his apartment have begun to glow.

This is nice, says Abe, looking out the window at the flicks of falling snow. I always thought it was odd, you living in the city when you were born and raised on a commune in the middle of nowhere. Having to deal with all the pollution and stink and poverty and rats and junk. But days like this, I get it. It's almost sweet, today. Or, at least, palatable.

Bit tried to live in the country, Hannah reminds Abe. For a little while.

It startles Bit to hear Hannah imply that

it hadn't worked out. Grete, who is chasing a Brussels sprout across her plate with her fork, was the result of that year. How could it have gone better? He thinks of Helle holding Grete for the first time. He had longed for the old way of childbirth, naked behind Helle, helping her rushes, smoothing back her hair, but she had been adamant: No way in hell we're doing that dirty hippie shit, she'd said, and had scheduled the cesarean. Bit stayed planted at Helle's head during the surgery in a fug of grief. In the end, though, it didn't matter. The nurse hustled Grete away and brought her back clean, her face red and round with skin as ravaged as her mother's, Helle's as raw as the baby's, a perfect match, a dovetail of need. At home, Helle's hunger for her baby surprised Bit. He thought he would be the caretaker, the one who would get up, who would change, who would sing. It was Helle, though, who took over, and he knew the love she had for Grete for what it was: a seamless accord between souls. He tried not to be jealous that neither of the souls was his.

The loss cudgels into him again. His fork full of mashed potatoes is heavy in his hand. He'll never understand how anyone would walk away from the tiny perfect place between Helle and Grete. He doesn't believe anyone could.

His parents speak to each other; Hannah dabs cranberry sauce from Grete's cheek. Bit can only look into the soft sift in the windows where he sees what his parents can't; not knowing the whole, they can't understand the lack. He, Bit, had let a coffee go cold in his hands, as he listened to the radio announcer describe how the two planes had flung themselves into the buildings there. Nearly two decades earlier, when he and his parents came into the city, he had named the buildings after Hannah and Astrid, playing with the way everyone in Arcadia had called the women the Twin Towers for their height and blondness; no matter that the buildings themselves grated on his sense of beauty, too awkward in their ambition. He'd grown accustomed to their silhouettes on the skyline. He gave them characteristics shared with their namesakes: Astrid colder, Hannah's antenna the crown he'd always imagined for his mother. Almost twenty years after he first saw them, the one called Astrid collapsed in a skirt of dust. After that, the one called Hannah. He turned off the radio and felt the sadness well blackly up, and there was no way to tamp it down. It was absurd; thousands had died; his personal loss was a hole in the sky.

But he couldn't help it. He knew enough to get out, on foot, to go to Jincy's neatnik house in the suburbs, to let her care for him.

The city, he'd thought at first, would do all right: there was hurt but a terrible rage to temper it. He was wrong. Even now, years later, it hasn't quite rebounded. It winces and holds itself more closely. Even before the global downturn it seemed to Bit as if people were making do with their second-best coats, withholding their fullest joy. On the days that he swings through the city on his walks and watches his fellow creatures move with tight, clipped steps, he can almost grasp what they lost. It wasn't what they believed; it wasn't real estate or lives. It was the story they had told about themselves from the moment the Dutch had decanted from their ships onto the oyster-strewn island and traded land for guilders: that this place filled with water and wildlife was special, rare, equitable. That it could embrace everyone who came here, that there would be room and a chance to thrive, glamour and beauty. That this equality of purpose would keep them safe.

It isn't important if the story was ever true. Bit manipulates images: he knows stories don't need to be factual to be vital. He understands, with a feeling inside him like a wind whipping through a room, that when we lose the stories we have believed about ourselves, we are losing more than stories, we are losing ourselves.

Bit surprises himself by interrupting what Abe has been saying, something about curmudgeonly old Titus winning a thousand bucks from a lottery ticket. His voice is loud and fast with an urgency that startles Grete out of her dreamy play.

Abe, he says, it wasn't the country that was so beautiful about the whole Arcadian experiment, don't you see? It was the people, the interconnection, everyone relying on everyone else, the closeness. The villages are all dying now, small-town America is dying, and the only place where the same feeling exists now is here, in the city, millions of people all breathing the same air. This, here, now, is more utopia than utopia, more than your pretty little house out in the middle of the forest with only woodchucks for neighbors. Can't you see? All of we kids are here, almost all of the kids from Arcadia, are here in the city. We've gone urban because we're all looking for what we lost. This is the only place that approximates it. The closeness. The connection. Do you understand? It doesn't exist anymore anywhere else.

He feels himself close to tears. The others stare at him. Grete puts down her fork and slides off her chair and climbs into Bit's lap and pats his cheeks with her starfish hand. His parents send looks across the table to one another, as if to say, He's finally going off the rails.

I'm not going off the rails, he says.

We never said you were, they say at once, and smile at each other. Jinx, says Hannah. You owe me a sodapop, says Abe, and they laugh in relief that they have deflected Bit, at least for now, at least a little.

Classes are like shoals of fish, Bit thinks at this week's photography critique: something hungry gets into them and they surpass their natural speed. Sylvie's group has begun to astound him. Their subjects are adult, deeply thought, riskier than undergraduates usually work (one boy takes photos of his little cousins in the bathtub, flirting with the line between art and child pornography; one girl takes a series of hands disappearing into the folds of fabric, silks and burlaps and muslins and cotton wool, gorgeously sensuous). There is a strange heat in the room whenever he enters it. And Sylvie of the shredded teeshirts, the knee-high boots, Sylvie whose face is so naked and pleading, smiles and praises when praise is due, and when it isn't, she looks at Bit and holds her tongue and seems to be saying, Go on, please. I'm waiting.

It is a year to the day that Helle went missing. Bit hires a babysitter and takes Sharon from downstairs to dinner.

Are you sure? she said this morning, handing him the coffee, trying to keep from looking too pleased. This could ruin everything, you know. She passed her hand through her short black hair, blinked her dark eyelashes prettily.

I'm sure, he said and carried her smile with him through the day.

They go to the Italian place down the way. The food isn't wonderful, but it is fine: Chianti out of straw-trousered bottles, fettuccine Alfredo, cannoli. It feels odd, good, to walk with a woman who is smaller than he is, even in heels. Sharon looks surprisingly beautiful tonight in her neat blue dress, sleeveless to show off her sharp shoulders, her face carefully outlined with makeup. She smiles a lot. Only her hands are nervous, patting the menu, straightening the silverware, plate, votive again and again.

They talk about the children, about their

exes, about the weather. They relax. Now they're on the subject of books. Without other media, never a television, never a computer, books have always made up much of Bit's life. Sharon leans forward, her brownish lipstick worn off at the center of her lips. Her eyes kindle. She begins talking about Ayn Rand.

She changed my life, she says breathlessly. Howard Roark! Dominique Francon! Ayn is the greatest philosopher of the twentieth century. Objectivism. I read *Atlas Shrugged* in college and thought, Oh, my God, everything's coming into focus, finally. You know what I mean?

Bit listens, trying to make his face neutral. And talks, in turn, about George Eliot, whom Sharon had never heard of. *If we had a keen vision and feeling of all ordinary human life,* he quotes, *it would be like hearing the grass grow and the squirrel's heart beat, and we should die of that roar which lies on the other side of silence.*

Sharon takes a long slow sip of wine. I don't get it, she says finally.

They go back to Sharon's apartment. Frankie and Grete are asleep upstairs at Bit's, with the babysitter. Sharon's place has the same floor plan as Bit's, and it is almost as bare as his, as if she, too, had been reared in a bread truck the size of a closet. But Bit's has color and comfort and heat, and Sharon's is white and very cold. Sorry it's so chilly, she calls from the bathroom. When Frankie's not here, I turn down the thermostat. Saving pennies. Times are tight.

When she comes back, she sits next to Bit and without much ado presents her mouth to be kissed. She is a good kisser, involved and slow. Her belly is slightly springy to the touch, but warm.

Bit extracts himself. I'm sorry, he says.

Oh. Me too, she says glumly. She bites her cuticles. I'm not beautiful like your ex.

No, he says, and when she looks startled, he says, Oh, yes you are. I meant, no, that's not it. It just doesn't feel right to me.

They hold hands and listen to the clock on the mantel ticking. They can hear the babysitter upstairs, the movie playing on her laptop.

He says, I think it was the Ayn Rand.

Sharon laughs and laughs, and when she stops, she squeezes his forearm. Oh, I always seem to have a hopeless crush on you handsome bleeding-heart liberals. I need to find me a nice old conservative.

Good luck in this city, he says, standing. If you want, I'll carry Frankie down.

Well. Could you let him sleep? she says. If

you don't mind watching the kids, I'll call a friend and go out on the town. The night's still young. And so are we.

You are, he says.

You will be young again someday, too. If you let yourself, she says, and she gives him a sisterly kiss on the cheek. Now scram. I have to get on my dancing duds. He climbs the stairs and imagines Sharon in some flashing club, closing her eyes to the music, something throwbacky, full of synth and falsetto, and wishes that she could have been different than she was, a thinker; or, better, that he could have relaxed his personal code and pretended to be a different man than he is, even for the space of one night.

He goes to his last classes of the semester and collects the portfolios. His students, suddenly beautiful and dear to him, thank and touch him as they file out the door. Claps on the shoulder, hugs, handshakes. Their warmth surprises him. He thinks of himself as strict, not the kind of professor to whom anyone would feel close.

Free, he spends an hour wandering. He feels the urge to look for something, but needs nothing; he goes into and out of stores, buys a cookie and a toothbrush and a penguin for the bathtub for Grete.

Finally, he sits in the train station, watching the people go back and forth.

Once, when he was on a shoot in Europe, he went off for a few days at the end to travel. In a Swiss station filled with honey wood and clerestory light, he saw a woman on a bench, weeping. She was enormous; pieces of her hung over the armrests and into the surrounding seats. She wore a smock printed with faded blue puppies and Chinese slippers with spangles, and her feet looked like baked potatoes split out of their skins. But her hair was upswept elaborately as if she were about to attend the opera, and the hands she held in prayer before her mouth were small as finches.

Bit stood, frozen in the current of people, watching her. Not a soul stopped to ask what was wrong. He moved in indignation toward the crying woman; the crowd parted. When he was very close, he saw the broad straw hat upended and the sign propped on the woman's belly: *Weeping Woman,* it said in four languages: *Femme Sanglotante; Donna Piangente; Weinende Frau.* The clock struck a ponderous hour. The pigeons in the rafters lifted and settled. The weeping woman turned off her sobs like water from a faucet and gathered her sign and hat. In a blink, the great mass of her dissolved into the crowd, and Bit was alone again.

Remembering this, he feels the old, hot prickle in his eyes. He thinks, Yes. But it vanishes. His angry heart calls for his attention, a fist on the door of his ribcage, beating.

Over squash ravioli and the tender new vegetables from the farmers' market, Bit says to Grete: The sharpness of radishes on the middle of the tongue. A hot shower after a cold day. Feeling how strong you are when you squeeze my neck. A spritz of lemon in my water.

Grete has stopped eating. She is staring at her father.

The taste of an icicle, he says. The feeling of floating in a pond. A chocolate Kiss in its little foil wrapper. He smiles.

Grete says, slowly, Pumpkin pie? And when a puppy licks you on the mouth?

When a cashier's hand touches yours when they hand back change, Bit says.

The way Hannah smells, says Grete. Abe's funny little knock knees. Pom-poms!

And his daughter is off, so excited she is standing on her chair, invoking the tiny domestic gods of grape cough syrup and Japanese beetles and the cedar bed in the preschool's hamster cage. Bit thinks of Helle, the long, dark path she had been for him and how the light at the end of it was this plump blondie just now spraying pesto on the floor.

Sylvie comes into his office without knocking, and locks the door behind her. He sits back. He should be grading portfolios but, with astounding inappropriateness, has been reading Duras's *The Lover* again. It was Helle's favorite book. He puts the book under his files, but Sylvie teases it out. She leans on the desk beside him, her legs long and pale and bony, and he thinks of the chill outside, the sleet coming down and the sludge coating the sidewalks, the goosebumps she would wear on her skin. She reads, making a moue with her lips. Her hair seems excessively clean. If someone drew lines between the moles on her face, there would be the Big Dipper on her cheek and chin. He waits. She puts the book down, bracelets clinking.

You know, she says. After you've graded my portfolio, you're no longer my professor.

I've graded it, he says. A-minus.

When she looks hurt, he sits back. What is it about this girl that makes her so easily wounded? How easy it would be to take his anger out, to crush something good in her. There is a piece of him that is sorry she isn't five years older, that would find her a fascinating woman when she's been more toughened by time. Something in her could soothe him.

Well, she says. As I said, you're not easy.

Right now I'm distinctly uneasy, he says, trying to lighten things.

She slides a foot between his. Good, she says and leans forward, her mouth coming close. He can smell the cinnamon on her breath and, deeper, the coffee.

Oh, honey, he says. No. You're lovely, but no.

Why? she says. I'm of age. You're not my professor.

I'm not that kind of man, he says. And you remind me of someone.

Who? she says.

Me, he wants to say. He smiles at her.

My wife, he says. When she was a little younger than you.

She leans back, chewing her lip, thinking this over. She looks as if she's going to mention Helle's disappearance, and he is grateful when she retracts the thought. She says, I don't think I mind. She flushes when she holds the book up. To be a mistress. Fine with me.

I mind, he says.

I don't get it, she says, her eyes shining. It doesn't have to *mean* anything.

He takes her hands in his and leads her to the hall. He kisses both of her moist and shaking palms. The smell there, photographic chemistry, touches him.

All the more reason to refrain, he says and shuts the door.

Spring a stirring of the world's optimism. Inside him, too, a tendril grows. He sees women every day in their too-early espadrilles and hopeful light coats. Soon, soon, he will approach one over the protestations of his shy heart and begin a conversation. You should always wear flowers, he'll say to one, pretty in a floral blouse. Or, if that's too embarrassing, maybe a simple Hello, like a window thrust open.

There is a whiteout, then a thaw. Hannah returns to Abe in their little Green house in the woods, telling everyone, My husband couldn't live without me, though Bit knows it was mutual. The desert's broad heavens, full of vultures, were sucking her dry.

In the mail one day, a shattering surprise: a letter from a lawyer, a clipping of an obituary, Ilya, so young and so beautiful in the picture, his face soft with hope.

Bit goes in to see the lawyer and emerges with a bouquet of papers and a key.

At home, he goes over and over what had happened and only ends up more confused. The house in Philadelphia is more than enough, but there also is a small amount of money. Bit's head swims for days.

He and Grete run through the old brick house on the weekend that they sell it. The cleaners have been in, and the place no longer stinks of cigarettes and sorrow. For a moment, he can see their lives in Philadelphia spinning out before them, a parallel existence, bright and good in this house with its original hardware and picture rails. He has a great urge to call the Realtor, to throw everything up, to move to this smaller city, this slower one.

He knows he won't. If they moved, Helle wouldn't be able to find her way back to them. He opens a door to the garden, and the winter light and cold air pour in. Sun falls onto the old floorboards, and his daughter spins and spins and spins into the light, out of it, into it again, her red skirt flaring, ablaze.

Newly flush, he says to Grete, Where do you

want to go for vacation? He knows she will say Grannah and Grumpy's. Arcadia.

But she surprises him. She considers her toes. At last she says, Greece, shyly, watching him from under her brow.

He carries his bemusement with him for an hour, and when he understands, he is on the subway among all the pressing anonymous bodies. Helle. The story, Hellespont. In his daughter's mind, Helle is infinitely falling from the back of the golden ram and through the air, a coin tossed, winking and cheery, into the water below.

They can wound, stories, they can blister. He had begun one that night he fell in love with Helle again in the gallery. It went like this: a vast expanse of time unrolling before them, he waking to Helle's sour breath and rumpled hair every morning, making one Grete or even two, Helle's and Bit's bodies aging over endless mugs of coffee, endless dinners, the days shortening as they grow old, the pair at last helping each other gently into death. He lost this story the night she left. Now time stretches just as vast, but he doesn't know what he should do. He doesn't know what magic words are necessary to get their story back, to return her from her chosen darkness.

■ ■ ■ ■

Up near the stone farmhouse during their year away from everything, there was a little river that cupped a spit of land that they could walk out onto. After heavy rains, the river overran the bank so that the spit became an island. Out there was the frantic smell of spring, all mud and buds, the broad slow swoop of clouds. The wind was rougher, without the trees to moderate it.

Helle and Bit would wade out with a picnic and lie in the sun and swim in the frigid river.

There was a moment on that island that lives in him when he rises in the morning, when he showers, when he walks, when, as now, he wakes to the devastating night.

Over and over, he sees Helle pulling herself up out of the river, hair sleeked, water coursing in glad drops over her skin, a flush from the cold across the whole white stretch of her. The chill sun loves her, touches her, plays prisms on the fine hair on her arms.

Are you happy? he says, inches from Helle's mouth.

I'm so happy, she whispers. Her cold

breath, her cold skin. Her cold lips upon his.

Bit has stopped looking for Helle. He never stops looking.

There is a hole in his life where Helle had been, a vacuum. Yet, for years afterward, Bit finds her. For a glimmering breath, he finds an astonishment of Helle that crumbles into dust when he looks harder and she is gone again.

He finds her at home, in her bed, where she had been all this time, waiting for him: white sheet undraped from her chest, bare nipple in the daylight. Where have you been? she says, voice humid with sleep. I've been waiting for you.

He finds her in a graduate student bar. He is buying his MFAs a round of beer. Her hair is hennaed; she wears black leather and walks past him, her face a blade, and out the back door.

He finds her one night as he shuts the window against a storm and a woman in a clear plastic trench coat runs across the street, the knobs of her spine vivid under her silk blouse, her white hair plastered to her cheeks; and when he runs out into the torrent to chase her, she is gone, and the bum on the vent insists there was nobody there at all.

He finds her in the hospital in Thailand, after he brushes up against a stonefish on a dive and goes into toxic shock, and dies there on the table, and is being restarted; just after the electric pulse, he sees, above the doctors' heads, Helle's face silhouetted against the light, a halo, a spherical aberration; and then she moves and her face shifts into that of a nurse, pale and old and thin and smiling gratefully at him for being alive.

Mostly, he finds her in his daughter. He carries Grete from a child's party to her room, and pulls up the coverlet, and when he turns out the light and closes the door and waits there, resting his head against the wood, he knows Helle is there, inside, sleeping. She is in Grete's face as she grows. Her fat melts away and her mother's cheekbones emerge and those same gold-flecked eyes grow complex; Helle is in Grete's voice as she looks at him and puts her head on his shoulder and says, Oh, Dad, why are you crying? His daughter, a gentle girl with plenty of Bit in her also, laughs up at him, saying, You're always crying, Dad. Why are you always crying?

Garden of Earthly Delights

At the end of a sunset party in an apartment overlooking the city, when the Sibelius has given way to the ambient Icelandic rock of their late youth, when the goat cheese canapés and stuffed mushrooms have cooled to the sticky consistency of kindergarten paste and everyone has had enough of the sour local wine from the city's rooftop vineyards to be mildly drunk, Bit finds that something in the air subtly shifts; a certain hilarity effervesces out of the partygoers and they pair themselves into odd couples, draped on the sofas or leaning against the doors, sharing the deeper secrets of their lives.

A woman stands before Bit, tall, her sparse eyebrows filled in with what looks like ash. Oh, I loved him, she says, her face gleaming with the beauty she must have had in her twenties. He lived in Venice. He was married. We met on a vaporetto. Her lips go soft, remembering.

Bit bites back what rises to his tongue: poor half-drowned Venice with its overwhelmed pumps. Poor Micronesia, poor Tuvalu, lost Atlantises. Instead, he nods. The woman's face sags into the present. She winces and kisses his cheek and disappears into the crowd for more wine.

Bit presses his back against the glass wall to watch the party. His friends are lit in orange from the sun going down over the river. Dylan raises his wineglass to Bit across the room, and the liquid slides red against the curve, catching the light. Pooh, whose apartment this is, laughs so hard she has to put her drink down on a side table and dab at the corners of her eyes with her tiny white hands. Cole touches the chandelier with a finger, frowning thoughtfully. A half a century of life has creased his friends' faces with wrinkles and made their bodies go soft around the middle, yet there lives a sympathy so deep in their marrow that a single word spoken by a stranger can spark the same light in each. A woman calling out . . . *trip?;* and they think *Trippies,* skinny Kaptain Amerika in his flag sarong. Someone saying the word *pure;* and before them rises a phantom silver Sugarbush, sap ringing musically into tin pans.

He thinks of the rotten parachute they played with as kids in Arcadia: they hurtle through life aging unimaginably fast, but each grasps a silken edge of memory that billows between them and softens the long fall.

For a breath, Bit can hardly bear the love he has for his friends. He goes out onto the balcony in the cold blast of air and watches the people move, perfect and tiny, on the street below. He imagines them all young, the men shouldering down the street, holding their excitement for the evening in their guts, the women with their high heels tapping codes. He thinks of Grete earlier, heading out to be with her friends, pausing in the dim hall of the brownstone to check her makeup in the pier glass, to touch her pink braids, to smile at herself as she turns toward the door. Contentment rises like a warm wave and dissolves just as it breaks over him.

He walks home through the quiet city until the party's buzz clears from his head. He finds himself looking for stars he knows he won't see. It is after midnight, and Grete still isn't home. The brownstone folds itself around him. The long windows are open, and a cold spring gust comes in. To stave off bad images of his daughter lost somewhere in the city, he tries to read poetry, an anthology of 2018's selected best. Poetry is what he turns to these days, finding in its fragmentation the proper echo of the disintegrating world. But tonight, in the strange slackness that arose in him after the party, he can't concentrate on words.

He reaches for Grete's e-reader, turns to the news for company. But there is a *viral epidemic in Indonesia,* the grave blond newscaster says, *a sudden airborne event.* Bit turns it off.

The monster is peering in the window. The ice caps have melted, the glaciers are nearly gone; the interiors of the continents becoming unlivable, the coasts so storm-battered people are fleeing by the millions. New Orleans and the Florida Keys are being abandoned. The hot land-bound places are being given up for lost; Phoenix and Denver becoming ghost towns. Every day, refugees show up in the city. A family takes shelter in the lee of Bit's front steps, parents with two small children, silent and watchful. They arrive after the lights are off in the brownstone and are gone by morning, their only trace the wet concrete from their hose baths. He leaves food for them in a cooler. It is all he can do. As ever, his kind is frozen by the magnitude of the problem; the intentionally ignorant still deny that there is a problem. Bit spends little of his salary, saving for the future, when, he knows, the well off will survive. Abe took a month last year to outfit the basement with food and water and gear. There is a gun waiting for Bit down there, and at times like these, Bit can feel the weight of the Ruger in his hands, a comforting counterweight against the eventual.

During the bad nights, when deep sadness threatens to descend again, although he is ashamed at his selfishness, he pleads: Let Grete survive. Just let Grete make it.

On the street, a trickle of rats moves silver in the moonlight. The clock chimes two. Someone is singing a song that filters to him through plaster and lath and brick. At last, Grete's steps come, uneven on the pavement. She looms into view, disappears in the cup of shadow between streetlights. That skirt so shameless, that top held on by strings, that face moonlike in its cake of makeup. His relief ebbs as she climbs the steps and is replaced with a low anger. She is only fourteen. He opens the door to find that she is already crying.

Baby? he says. What happened? She buries her head in his shoulder, and he feels her knobby back. She smells like vodka and smoke and sweat.

I *hate* girls, she says into his shoulder.

Oh, Bit says. He closes the door. You're two hours past your curfew.

Shut up, Dad, she says. Can't you *see* I'm so, so sad? I *hate* my life.

She's just warming up. She needs to take it out on somebody. He is suddenly too tired for this same yelling Grete, again. She launches into the old refrains: he's too wishy-washy, they're poor, if only he *tried* a little harder he wouldn't be so embarrassing, he wouldn't be so *lonely,* he's not *totally* repellent even if he is a shrimp.

The antique telephone rings on its stand. He still doesn't have a cell, loving the anchor of the landline, and to escape from his daughter, he picks up the receiver. A mistake; Grete shouts louder. But she goes silent when she sees his face.

Mr. Stone? the voice in the receiver says again. Do you understand what I'm saying?

Oh, he says, lost. Through the wavery glass of the transom above the door, the streetlight repeats in a stuttering arc.

We'll be there, he says and hangs up.

Dad? says Grete in a small voice. His daughter has turned stranger in the dim hallway.

Dad? Is it Grannah and Grumpy? she says. Please say something. Please.

He is unable, just yet, to speak. He reaches out a hand, and the feel of her cheek under his fingertips returns the words to him. Pack your bags, he says as kindly as he can manage, and he moves his body, thick and strange as if stuffed with clay, up the stairs.

Bit sits in the darkened room. The hospital churns around them; behind the closed curtains another dawn spreads across the landscape. A lump of Hannah is in the bed, a lump of Grete on a cot below. And bigger than the room itself, bigger than the hospital, bigger than the morning coming creeping toward them, Abe's absence, biggest of all.

The scene plays over and over in his head as it has all night, in obsessive detail, repeating itself beyond his invention until it becomes truth. He sees his parents as they must have been a year ago, just after Hannah's diagnosis. They would have been in the hospital courtyard, Hannah on a bench, Abe in his wheelchair beside her. A spring-like day during the warm February of last year. There would have been neglected perennial beds with volunteer tulips crowning above the winter weeds. Plastic bags shushing as they slid along the wall. A comically fat bird, a Tartuffe of a finch, jerking upon a cherry branch.

Hannah stuck out her tongue. It was grayish and twitched as if there were tiny creatures inside trying to tunnel their way out.

Fasciculations, she said. Some of my lovelier symptoms. With her good hand, she squeezed Abe's knee.

ALS, said Abe. I'll be damned.

Apparently, Hannah said, I'm the damned one. He made a choking sound and she said, I'm sixty-eight, baby. Hardly too young to die.

Between them, like an unacknowledged child, their year of changes noticed but not remarked upon. Hannah had thought she was just getting old, swiftly declining. She could no longer open jars or tweeze the coarse black bristles from her chin. A hollow developed between her thumb and index finger. She tripped, mowing the patchy grass around their house, and cut her head on the blades of the motorless mower. Abe found her half-laughing on the lawn, her face streaked in blood. She choked on her tea. Words became strange in her mouth. Life was effortful.

She didn't think to go to the doctor until late February, when she could no longer shovel the first and last snow of the year from the walk. This woman, who had mixed concrete by hand and kneaded dough for hundreds, who had picked her husband up out of a bath for over forty years. This strong woman, defeated by two inches of powder.

The sun warmed the skin of their scalps. A woman's voice floated to them over the air. What are we going to do? Abe said.

We're not telling Bit and Grete, said Hannah. I can't be a burden.

All right, Abe said.

We'll take all our baths together from now on, said Hannah. You wash me, and I'll wash you. She brazened a smile.

I'll build us a waterslide so that we can get in, Abe said, wiping his eyes.

The breeze picked up and blew lovingly against them. The finch chattered away.

When I twitch, Hannah said, laughing, it'll feel like a Jacuzzi.

The details that Bit has concocted seem important: the bird, the tulips, the dialogue he worked out these last hours for accuracy. With details, he builds a barricade against the hopelessness, the rush of the hospital beyond. In the weak light from the crack under the door, he sees Grete's face in its nest of pink braids. Only in sleep is she so still, his restless, skinny girl. He is old and lives on a single plane of existence where Grete is the primary object; she is young and comfortable on many planes, some he can't fully guess at, lives at school, lives with her friends, digital lives. He crawls to the ground beside her to watch her breathe. When he wakes, the room is dark but the doctor is standing above him, her face obscured, her hand beckoning him outside.

There are too many people moving in the harsh light of the hall. The doctor hands him a coffee still boiling in its cup. Her sharp features look rested, though she was here to meet Bit and Grete when they came late in the night. When she speaks, she shows her huge white teeth. They make Bit think of ice cubes; when she met them at intake, he had longed, absurdly, to lick them. She hugs him, and she smells like powdered violets, such an antique smell for one so young. It unsettles him. Try as he might, he can't remember this lovely woman's name.

If you want to talk . . . , she says, her voice fading.

I wouldn't even know where to start, he says. He hears his anger only when she takes a step back. It is new in him, and not unpleasant. I'm sorry, he says. It's so much to understand.

Will you sit? she says. He drops onto the chair beside her. Around them, people in blue and pink scrubs move with quick steps toward other people's disasters. Some wear masks, wary of the new Indonesian virus, even so far away. She says, Tell me.

I have too many questions, he says. Why they didn't tell us that Hannah was sick. For a full year they hid it. Why is she not on any medication, why did they let the disease go unchecked. Why the fuck they decided to kill themselves, instead of dealing with it like a family.

These are things you'll have to ask your mother, the doctor says.

If she ever wakes up again, he says, I will.

Oh, Mr. Stone, she says, gently. A nerve has begun to twitch beneath her eye, and she hides it with a hand. Your mother was awake even when the Amish woman found her. Hannah just doesn't want to open her eyes right now.

Bit touches his knees with his forehead and breathes. He has to restrain himself from rushing into Hannah's room and shaking her. Gently, the doctor's cold hand falls on his neck and steadies him.

■ ■ ■ ■

In time, the doctor's hand warms and it becomes only another weight on him. There's a white flutter under his leg as she gives him the note in Abe's beautiful script. Bit reads and rereads the note. His parents felt blessed to be able to go together, as they had lived together their whole lives, since they were romantic children. The doctor begins to talk of what his parents did. Such elegant phrasing she has, so empty of emotion or blame. He wonders if they teach such detachment in medical school. He holds himself still, so that some might seep into him from her skin.

Between the doctor's sentences and those in the note, Bit finds the time to hang his own lines of grief. He can see the moment when it became too hard for his parents to take care of one another: how Hannah might have dropped something that Abe couldn't pick up. Then, just after supper, Abe would have closed his book and wheeled himself to Hannah, opening his palm to show her the pill case. They would have put the house in order, leaving the spoilable food out on the porch for the skunks and raccoons and starving deer, cleaning the compost toilet, writing this note. How they dressed in clean clothes and lay down on their bed. How they split the pills evenly and chased them down with the same glass of cold water. Warm, they held each other and waited for everything to fade, to float away. Abe succeeded. Hannah failed. She returned to Bit.

He crumples Abe's note, puts it in his pocket. He stands in the middle of one of the doctor's sentences and walks down the long hall. He doesn't want to be rude, especially to this lovely doctor with her twitch, but he longs only for a blank room and the clean cold of solitude.

It is noon, somehow. Grete has buried her face in her e-reader all morning. Bit feels suffocated between his furiously silent women. At last, he and Grete go to the cafeteria for sandwiches and discover flaccid rolls with morose greenhouse lettuce. Only a few years ago, crisp heads of iceberg had rolled abundantly up from Mexico. Such a small thing, signaling such change.

They have paid and are sitting down when Abe's death cracks the ground beneath Bit. He would fall in, but for the glimpse he has of Grete's long hands on the bread, the black chipped polish on the bitten nails.

What? Grete says, looking at him. Dad, what?

The world merges, colors trembling. He feels Grete's touch on his cheek. Abe, he says.

Oh, says Grete, and there is a shift in her, too. She pulls her chair as close as she can. Together, they close their eyes against the others, the sad food, the sapping cafeteria light.

If Abe were here, Bit might throttle him dead again: what appears to be sorrow is rage. Abe was bedrock; Abe was his world's gravity; since Bit could remember, his father was his one sure thing.

Hannah's room fills with dried wildflowers. The local florist is resourceful, faced with the exorbitance of imported goods. But the dusting of pollen makes Grete's face puff up, and even Hannah stifles sneezes in her bed.

Jincy and the boys arrive, and Grete runs downstairs to meet them. Alone for a minute, Bit goes to his mother's side. He crouches before her, inches from her face, his eyes watering from her rancid breath. I know you're awake, he says. Open your eyes.

Slowly, one eye opens in its nest of wrinkles. Hannah blinks. Almost so softly that he can't hear her, she says, I would prefer not to.

He gasps. He laughs. But the fury quickly settles upon him again. You're no fucking Bartleby, he says. Her open eye narrows at him.

Jincy and the twins run in, and Bit is engulfed in boy-smells, the funk of filthy hands and breath. Look at this! Oscar says, opening his hand to show the delicate cog of an antique watch. I found it in the playground at school and saved it for you. Isaac had brought nothing, but not to be outdone, says, Look at this! and does a handstand in the middle of Hannah's hospital floor. *Look at this!,* the twins say. *See me!* Jincy has never had a husband or long-term boyfriend: Bit is all there is. When the twins stay over, they start the night cuddling with Grete in her bed, but the morning finds them curled together on Bit's bedroom floor, faithful as dogs.

Bit pulls the boys to him, where they rest, bony creatures. He looks at Jincy in the door. Unlike the rest of the world, whose good looks slowly and gradually declined into gray hair and wrinkles, her attractiveness has remained stable. What was mousy for a teenager has held steady and turned her striking for a fifty-three-year-old. The spirals of her hair are threaded with grays, and her face is rosy and unlined. She is pleased and bashful under Bit's admiration. She leans over Hannah and kisses her, brushes her hair from the temple, whispers something. Though Bit strains to hear, he can't make out a word of what she says.

Grief as a low-grade fever. His sadness is a hive at the back of his head: he moves slowly to keep from being stung. Things bunch together, smooth endlessly out. Astrid arrives; Grete leaps from the chair outside Hannah's door, shouting Mormor Astrid, I *so* hoped you'd come! Doctors huddle around Astrid; Astrid marches into Hannah's room and orders her to sit. A well of surprise in Bit as Hannah painfully pushes herself up. The old friends gaze at one another from across the room, and the way they had been once upon a time washes over him: tall and young in Ersatz Quad, honey and white, Bit tiny, gazing up at their indecipherable stretch.

The car ride back to Arcadia takes a century. The radio reports a thousand dead in Java, sudden sickness, quarantine. Bit turns it off, but Astrid turns it on again, snapping, Ignorance is no help to anyone. He blocks out what he can, the way the disease sets in suddenly, twelve hours and people are dead, a doctor calling it SARS-like, avian flu–like, nobody knows the vectors yet. At last Astrid consents to classical music. Bit is sure that he'll be bearded and bleary as a hermit when he looks in the rearview mirror, but his eyes shine, his cheeks are flushed. He can still feel the doctor's small bones under his hug; her violet scent hangs in the air. Call me as often as you like, she'd murmured. Here's my number. A last flash of white teeth, and he wanted to carry her away with him.

In the calm of the Sugarbush, the sun is tinted green and the birds bugle in the treetops. Bit has to tell himself to not be angry at them. They couldn't possibly know.

Home is the same. In the pantry, the same rows of glass jars are full of the same beans and grains. The workshed, all tools ranged at knee level for Abe. The path into the Sugarbush, half-choked with weeds. The firewood snaked optimistically around the house, a fortress, a windbreak, an embrace. The heap of the hills purple in the dawn. The way the darkness moves like a creature in the night woods. The woods themselves, tens of thousands of acres that Leif had reclaimed from abandoned farms long before land was valuable again. Abe's same favorite plate left on the top of the stack. The same double depressions that his parents' bodies have carved over the years in their mattress.

Hannah's silence, lifelong, the same.

It would be so easy for him to fall asleep here, to succumb to bed, but Grete is beside him, her eyes narrowed with disgust. Snap out of it, Dad, she says. He breathes and lets home wash and wash over him and busies his hands with tasks — scrubbing the reclaimed floorboards until they shine, baking cakes, making beds — taking solace in the stupid brute motion of his body, letting it lead him through the hours.

Moments, somehow, hatch a week. Now the memorial service. So many people have come. He is dizzied, can hardly see.

The sun is too high, the wind too strong, the Pond smashing against the bank. People feel the need to touch him. Bit is a short man, but they remember him tiny: they pat the crown of his head, and he resists the urge to crush their hands. Hannah's arm in his twitches. Someone he should recognize in a navy robe is saying an incantation. People say things about Abe: he was the secret strength of Arcadia, he performed a miracle by renovating Arcadia House in three short months, he kept the community going for another decade. And the organizing he did in his old age, the marches on Washington, the impassioned fundraising letters alighting in their mailboxes like stern gray birds of peace. Abe was true to what he believed. Abe, the unswerving one.

Some of the original Circenses Singers, old and flabby, sway under their newest puppets. Their voices are cracked with age, more powerful for loss of pitch. Bit is moved from numbness to hurt. This, he thinks, is what transported means.

He looks up the hill to Arcadia House. Erewhon Illuminations abandoned it after Leif disappeared, and Astrid has left it vacant for two years. Ivy is choking the windows on the west side. There are saplings in the gutters. Pigeons sit heaped on the roofline, buttoning house to sky.

Bit and Grete and Hannah are given an urn. They uncap it. A black smoke of Abe pours into the wind over the Pond. A gray film settles like grease on the water, the harder pieces of Abe falling down to be nibbled by minnows. To wash, molecule by molecule, into the water itself, to be drunk by deer and bears and the muskrats just now watching this strange congregation of humans from the dark safety of their burrows.

Afterward, the mourners mingle in the downstairs of Arcadia House and someone puts Handy, raspy and young, on the sound system. Hannah is an empty flour sack, heaped on a chair in the corner. Through the music, Bit hears angry whispers about the changes Leif made to the old Homeplace, the downstairs wing of bedrooms now opened into a great hall where cubicles had formed a labyrinth. If the Old Arcadians saw the glossy gutted upstairs, Bit thinks, anarchy would spark again in their tired hearts. Poor Leif; he was one who never minded change. For a moment, Bit's eyes sting for the eccentric who lost himself in a super-high-altitude balloon three years ago. He stares through a window at the graying sky and imagines Leif still there, frozen and peaceful in the balloon's cabin, his eyelashes iced, his smile on his blue lips, his body scuttling in the wind at the edge of space.

They come to him, the people he loved when he was a child. But they have gone grotesque. Erik is fatty as a doughnut, spinach stuck in his teeth, an engineer, the sole surviving child of Astrid and Handy because he made boredom his lifeboat. Midge is a bald crone, so tiny that Bit must bend to her: this is the last time she will come here from Florida, she whispers through the green mask she wears against disease. She is too old to suffer the train ride. Tarzan is now entirely crafted of leather, the same suede brown from pate to hands. Simon has a toupee that had lost a corner of adhesiveness in the elements; when he kneels before Hannah, kissing her hands, his hair is like the black lid of a pot canted to check the boil within. Scott and Lisa shine with money. Regina and Ollie are baked by Bermuda sun into the perfect gold of their own cupcakes. Dorotka, blind now, has a rattail braided at the nape of her mullet that her lover tugs affectionately like the leash of a small dog.

The small, thin doctor from the hospital has come, and when she nears, Bit is glad. She is a new person: there is no weight of memory to her. There are cracks in the brown skin around her eyes. She kisses him on the cheek and disappears.

We feel so terrible for you, Little Bit, people whisper.

We loved your father so much, they whisper.

If there is anything we can do, they whisper.

They whisper, whisper, whisper. All whisper, save for D'Angelo, who shouts in his new voice of a Pentecostal reverend, God bless that old skinny bastard, Abe!, as tears course down his face, unlined and baby-soft, miraculously unchanged.

Most leave soon. They have work, family, trains to catch. Dylan and Cole and Jincy and their broods are the last to go: they have rented a bus together to save on gas. Only when Bit walks into the humid Green house of the courtyard, which Leif had enclosed entirely in glass a few years back, does he see the Amish. The courtyard is a strange place now, the air heavy and damp. A stream trickles, hidden by the ferns and mosses and overhanging mist. The dark bodies of the Amish have gone vague in the fog; from where Bit stands, they could be Puritans just stepping off the boat into the New World, fearful and awed to have earth beneath their feet again.

He doesn't want these people here. They are too close to a kind of God he has never been able to believe in, a flesh-eating, stern-browed, whipping-post kind.

One of the bodies separates from the

group, comes closer, then clear. When she approaches, her little face is a white saucer, features like berries bunched neatly in the center: blueberry eyes, cherry nose, strawberry mouth. She reaches for Bit's arm, and he understands, as the woman's face breaks apart, that she was the one to find his parents in their awful half-success.

She says nothing, just squeezes his bicep again and again. He bears it. He looks up through the vast branches of the oak tree, his old friend. Through the soiled glass above, a black cloud has gathered. The first drops bullet overhead. He can feel, just now, what it's like for the poor ancient oak, sleeping under glass. No more burn of sun on its leaves. No scour of winter, no smash of storm, no relief when its own dead weight falls away.

Bit goes for a walk to be alone. The rain has stopped, but wet grasses cling to his ankles, leaves shiver rain onto his head. The Sheep's Meadow is gone, replaced by a low sweep of birch trees pale as girls in the dusk. There's a feeling of captured movement, a slight tilting down the hill as if in a breath they will regain their human shapes and stumble back into a run. Where the ground lips into the forest, there's a small opening,

Handy's spot, and Bit can see Handy as he'd been a lifetime ago, cross-legged, hair bound by a strip of Naugahyde, face beatific and froggish.

Bit sits where Handy had sat so often. Instead of grace, however, he feels the damp ground seep into his pants. Well, he says aloud. Let it.

The sky fades from gray to inky blue. The moon, bright arbiter, waits for him.

In one hand, Bit holds his life: his students, faces cracked with interest; the brownstone; the dates with lovely women who keep his attention for a night, a week, a month, until they drift away; the parties, the gallery openings, the brunches with Grete in the park. The civilization of the city. His calm, unruffled life, his books, his friends. In this hand, his sick mother would move to a hospital in the city, where Bit and Grete could visit her every day, bringing flowers, ice chips, news. If there is quarantine, if the disease arrives, he has water tanks, he has food, he has Abe's gun in the safe in the basement. They could wait it out.

In the other hand, he holds Hannah's death in Arcadia, the place where his parents were so happy. Where he was so happy as a child. (Or was he? Best to distrust this retrospective radiance: gold dust settles over memory and makes it shine.) In this hand, Bit stays in Arcadia with his mother, cuts the gnarled toenails, washes her skin, remembers her medicines, feels daily the bone-aching worry of it all. He remembers the births he assisted when he was young, brushing the sweaty hair from the women's foreheads and rubbing their swollen flesh. Here, he would be a midwife to his mother's decay, Grete beside him, watching it all.

The latter is the heavy hand, the difficult one. It involves action. He has gotten used to sitting quietly aside, to watching. He palpates his anger like the edges of a wound. Does Hannah deserve such care after what she tried to do? What would her decline do to Grete, his daughter of the city, who has barely seen death, only a speckle of flies on the sill, a rat in a trap?

He wishes for a sign, but the night pulls its drawstring tighter and the wind hushes the trees to sleep. Two choices. To float as he has done since he was young. Or to dive in, to swim.

It is night. Funeral pies are on the counter. The four of them sit around the table in the Green house. Bit tries to take his mother's bad hand, which shocks him with its lightness and coolness, but she snatches it from him with her good one. In the low glow of the kitchen chandelier, his mother's face looks carved from soap.

Astrid waits beyond the point of comfort to speak. Ever majestic, she is now blinding in her authority. The midwives whom Bit knows in the city speak of her with reverence; it wouldn't surprise him if somewhere in the world there were shrines with her picture, the way Arcadia had been stippled with colorful altars to Gandhi, Marx, the Dalai Lama. Astrid had her bad teeth pulled in her fifties, and the dentures finish her face the way woodwork finishes a room. She wears long, loose clothes in earth tones that she manages to make elegant. Helle would have been like her mother, if his wife had chosen to share her old age with Bit. But when Grete sits beside her mormor, leaning against her warmth, he sees how his daughter is a second Astrid, leavened with Hannah's honey. It brushes him, the good feeling that he is sitting in a fold of time.

I wish you could stay, Astrid, he says, surprising himself.

The old Astrid looks at him, her face soft. She shrugs, says, Handy.

Handy is demented. He thinks at night that he's in Korea, shouts things like *Off to the Repo Depot for you, soldier!* and *Ash and trash!* Everything after his early twenties has been expunged: Arcadia a golden hope perpetually growing in him, his experiments with the doors of perception only glimpses down a long corridor. After his fourth wife left him, only Astrid visits every day. Fat Erik comes three times a year. Old-people garage, Astrid calls the nursing home. But there is a pool, gourmet buffet spreads; it is its own perfect place, in its way.

Into the silence, Hannah speaks. Her hair is still soft around her face, though white. The black dress bags on her, the pearls as sallow as her skin. The only thing I wanted, she says, was to not be a burden. Quick and painless, how I wanted to go.

But the Universe called you back, Astrid says.

For no reason, Hannah says.

You find the reason, Astrid snaps. Finish with the self-pity, and move on.

Bit is so surprised he laughs. Grete begins to cry: So mean, Mormor, she whispers. Astrid ignores them. First, I have hired a nurse, she announces. She is beginning tomorrow. Luisa, her name, a fine lady. When more help is needed, we will hire more help. Second, she says, Ridley, you must talk today to your department and take the rest of the semester off. Third, I have talked to Grete's school in the city and the school up here. All is settled. She may start on Monday.

Wait. No, says Grete. I have a *life.* I can't be here. I have college prep tomorrow. Right, Dad? We have to go home.

Oh, yes, says Astrid. Your father has decided. I'm surprised he hasn't told you.

I wanted to, he says, ducking from his daughter's glare. But you were out for a run.

No, Grete shouts. I will *not.*

The strange new anger rouses itself in Bit, and he hears himself saying in a tight voice, Grete, outside, now. His daughter shuts her mouth. They walk through the ferns into the Sugarbush, Grete's face blanketed with darkness. Dad, she says, turning on him at last. Isn't this already traumatic enough for me?

Since when, Bit says, has this been about you?

I don't have to be here. You could be here and I could go home and stay with Matilda. Or Charlotte. Or Harper, you love Harper, she's a total nerd.

I'm going to need your help, he says.

She looks trapped. But what about my stuff? she says.

I'm heading home tonight, he says. Make a list. I'll be back when you wake up.

What about school? I'm not going to any shitkicker school. They *can't* be as advanced as we are. I'm doing precalc. I'll be *bored.*

It's only the rest of the semester, baby. Probably.

I can't. I can't, Dad, Grete says, her voice sharp. I can't be in the house. She smells like she's rotting or something. I can't be where Grumpy fucking killed himself, Dad, I can't do it. You can't *make* me. I'll run away.

She sees the way he winces. Like Mom, she says, watching him. I'll run away.

Bit turns. He can hardly see the ground. How did I raise such a selfish child, he says, so quietly he's not sure she heard him. But when he walks into his parents' house, he can hear her sobbing, then the heavy front door of Titus and Sally's treehouse slamming over and over again.

When the others have gone to sleep, Bit takes Hannah's ancient car. For the first hour of the drive, he loves the violence of the wind through the open window, how it chases off his cloud of dread, but when it gets too cold, he rolls up the window and turns on the radio. Classic rock, apparently, is the music he loved in his twenties. He finds himself singing along in a voice raspy with disuse. The announcer comes on, then three chords that make Bit laugh with surprise: a funk-flavored song, Cole's one big hit. He'd struggled for so long, had so many bands, and this success out of nowhere had shattered him. He stopped playing music and bought a nightclub. Now he writes monographs on Palestrina, of all things.

At the end of the song, Bit turns off the radio to savor the pleasure of Cole's young voice. The lights of the city rise in the windshield. He pushes through the flashing streets. There are fewer pedestrians out now that the disease is rushing toward them, and on most faces there are masks like glowing muzzles. He drives into his poorly lit neighborhood. When he steps from the car, he hears the deep, low hum of the city, both growl and digestion. He only ever notices this sound after returning from the quiet of the country.

Inside, the house is cool and there is the sweet rot of garbage he'd forgotten to take out when they left. He does the dishes, pays the bills, redirects mail, turns off the water, sets the lights to turn on randomly at night, makes sure everything is secure.

He takes a cooler of food outside for the family beside the steps. They are under a tarp, in two connected sleeping bags. The heads of the parents curl over the children, two small lumps close together. He watches them for some time and wishes he had the courage to rouse the father, tell him quietly that Grete and he will be gone for some time, to apologize for not leaving food every day now. But he can't take the risk they'd try to break into the house, to squat there: squatting laws being what they are, it'd take months to get them out. He creeps away, unsettled.

He spends only a few minutes packing for himself. In Grete's room he gathers everything he thinks she'll need: the clothes he remembers her wearing recently, the shoes, the photograph he'd taken of her and her mother when Grete was a toddler, forehead to forehead like conspirators. How alike they'd been, two sections of one soul. He takes the stuffed frog from when she was little, knowing she'll need it. She looks like an adult now, but there is still a sliver of girl in her that Bit would fight to protect: the uncertainty that steals over her when she's talking about boys, the delight on her face when he buys her anything pink. The moments when the e-reader has fallen from her hands and she gazes out the window, biting the corners of her long pale mouth, dreamy as her mother.

He has been staring for a while at a yellow raincoat when he sees that its big pocket is bulging. He reaches in. When he opens his hand, he finds his own Zippo lighter from so long ago, rolling papers, a huge bag of weed. Something catches like a fish bone in Bit's throat. It doesn't dislodge again until he's a half hour away from Arcadia, the sunrise burning in the rearview mirror. He steers down a long straight road with his knees and rolls a hasty joint and smokes it. When his head swims, he tosses the inch-long roach and the rest of the weed out the window in the direction of a maple thick with crows. A mile later, he goes hysterical at the thought of stoned birds, their wings failing them as they drop lazily from the sky.

The dawn echoes its quiet in Bit's city-dinned ears. He is making pancakes to wake up Grete and can't resist gobbling the first four down. Astrid marks Hannah's medication bottles, and they're drinking orange juice from powder. It is all they can get anymore, after the citrus blight. He misses pulp and the acid burn of real juice in the throat.

Honeybees, Astrid says out of nowhere.

Honeybees? Bit says. He wonders if this is a rational thought that his pot-slowed brain just can't digest.

Passenger pigeon, she says. American bullfrog. I am trying to discover what we are, Arcadians. Going extinct. So many of us dead, dying, gone.

We are the dodo, Bit says and laughs. Abe's shadow moves, brief and cold, over the room.

I'll say honeybees, says Astrid. You remember before the die-off? Their funny fuzzy bodies. Always, they seemed to me, the symbol of happiness.

I remember, says Bit. But it's not just Arcadians dying off. It'll be all of us soon enough.

Astrid frowns at the bottle in her hand. That sickness hasn't reached us yet, she says. It will be contained. It always is.

I don't mean the sickness, he says. That's just a symptom. Too many people, too little land, the oceans polluted, animals dying. It makes me think we don't *deserve* to be saved.

She puts down the medicine and spears him with her icy blue stare. If this is what you think, she says, I don't know who you are anymore, Ridley Stone.

He opens his mouth, but finds no words

there. In any case, he can say nothing for the bald eagles, the bullfrogs, the honeybees, just now filling up his throat.

The house is quiet, save for the gentle ticking of solar panels on the roof. Hannah has disappeared into her room; Astrid has driven her rented car to the airport, promising to return when she's needed, damn the fortune it takes to fly these days; Grete has gone for a furious run.

After so many days full of people, it feels good to Bit to have this solitude. He wanders into Hannah and Abe's little office. It is shining, even the drafting table Abe had used as a desk. Abe kept some of Bit's earliest photos on a shelf: Verda's face, reflected again and again in a heap of tarnished silver; Helle standing on the boulder by the Pond, reflecting into two long girls joined at the ankle; Hannah, gorgeous and young and slender on Abe's lap, both beaming as they hurtle down Arcadia House hill as fast as Abe's wheelchair could take them.

He reaches out with his finger and brushes Hannah's cheek. He can't believe what babies they were. The reaction seems to well up all the time now. A few months ago, walking through the city, in the window of an old record store he looked up to see a huge poster of Janis Joplin with round glasses and feathers in her hair, and almost wept at how just-hatched she'd looked. Now, nestled behind his photos, he finds his first Leica, the one his Kentucky grandmother had sent him. He picks it up, marveling at its lightness. Since he begrudgingly began to use digital cameras, a few years back, began doing more commercial work and less of his own art, his own analog gear has sat neglected on its shelf. He has grown accustomed to the ease of digital life.

He rummages in Abe's drawers and finds a shoebox of color film. He feels a dizzying upsweep of possibility: the rolls could be thirty years old and useless, true, but the distortion of age could make for the unexpected, the sublime: the emulsion cracked or melted, the plastic fragile and easily rent, the effects unreplicable. In his mind, the images unfold atop one another like layers of translucent tissue: ripples of off-white and red, a watercolor cloud composed from the silhouette of a tree, a bubbled landscape of grasses.

He wants to sing. How perverse, the possibility of beauty, unearthed when he least expected it. That there could be such surprises left in the world. He goes out into the sunlight, something softening and settling within him.

The winter before Leif disappeared was the last time Bit had walked out into the forest. He was usually in Arcadia briefly, to drop Grete off for a month in the summer or to spend a night during a holiday. That time, they had all taken a walk together on the twenty miles of trails that Erewhon kept up. His parents were hale, Astrid and Handy were there, Leif even let them see him smile. Bit pushed Abe easily over the frozen ground, his father turning around once in a while to beam at him, his grizzled beard full of ice. Every so often, employees would whip by, snowshoeing or running or in the sleek black uniforms of cross-country skiers, gliding over the hills like tall skinny birds. Grete was a little girl still, her long legs gawky as a fawn's. She tried to pack the powder into snowballs and heave them into their faces. Their breath wreathed their heads, the crows shimmered so black they were green. It was just an average afternoon in the winter's dim at the end of a forgotten year, but that day, everyone was happy.

Now the Pond is forlorn, with its lifeguard chair overturned on imported sand. A kickbuoy between two rocks makes a sad thumping sound in the wind-driven waves. Bit thinks of another man at another pond, long ago; the way Thoreau saw the moon looming over fresh-plowed fields and knew the earth was worthy to inhabit.

Bit is not so sure. Besides, there are no fields here. In what he remembers as the sunflower patch, he finds thirty-year-old trees, more enormous than the trees of his youth, greener, casting deeper shadows: all the extra carbon in the air. He follows a strange metallic scrape off into the brambles and, after some effort, locates Simon's sculpture for Hannah in a wild raspberry bush. Swords into plowshares, the painful earnestness of the thing. Oh, he thinks, helpless before the squat sculpture. This could be a poster illustrating the early eighties. It is iconic, almost already in silkscreen.

He laughs, and the forest, which he has missed to his marrow, laughs back at him. He feels everything, the birds swinging on the currents of air, the early ferns uncurling, the creatures hunched somewhere, watching him. Faster, almost running, he goes through the woods that were once cornfields. These he remembers as sorghum, the Naturists bending in their sun-bronzed flesh to weed. He emerges onto the edge of the tennis court Leif put in, plunked in the middle of what had been the soy patch. Already, tiny trees have sunk roots into the clay. They stand, brave and budding on the fault line, like a small child's prank.

Back into the woods, toward what he vaguely remembers to be the waterfall, the trail grows narrower, more overgrown. Hannah, when she could still walk, probably didn't make it this far to trample down the weeds. Two years of growth have almost swallowed the path. The day dims into twilight. He catches spiderwebs with his cheeks.

He comes into a natural clearing, and a shriek startles his heart to flapping.

Grete stands at the far side, clutching a stick like a baseball bat, her face paper white.

Dad, she says in a wobbly voice. Oh, I'm so glad it's you.

Lost? he says. He tries not to smile. What luck to find his daughter the one time he wasn't looking for her.

She shrugs. Kind of, she says. But mostly I thought you were a bear.

He takes a photo of her as she picks toward him over the grasses in the last slant of sun. She stops when she is near. She stinks of sweat, has scratches on her face and brambles in her many pink braids, and her face is raw as if she's been crying. She must have been out here for hours. They are miles from the Sugarbush. On her own, she wouldn't have been back until deep in the night, if not the morning.

It's this way, he says, gesturing into the throat of the woods.

Okay, she says. She starts, but stops and turns to him. I just. I'm sorry.

I know, he says.

I'm scared, she says. I don't want to watch Grannah die.

Me neither, he says, pulling her toward him.

Grete's teeth clatter. It is colder up here, away from the city; although it's still late winter, he remembers summer nights so long ago, filled with exactly this fresh dampness, as if exhaled from underground. They come out into the Sugarbush when it's dark, and the moon fills the tree limbs with a shifting, breathing light. The other houses sit in darkness, ownerless: Midge in Boca Raton for the rest of her days, Titus and Sally having died in a terrible car accident years ago, Scott and Lisa with too many houses to care much about the cottage they'd built in protest of Erewhon twelve years ago.

Bit and his daughter stand out on the porch of the Green house, unwilling to breathe the bad spores of Hannah's sadness into their lungs.

Up the drive, however, come headlights. The car stops and the engine shuts off. A woman emerges, saying, Stone? This is Stone house?

Nurse Luisa? Bit says, remembering the name Astrid had mentioned yesterday. He flicks on the porch light and sees a very small woman shuffling up the steps. Her face is cracked with a broad grin; she wears a child's pink backpack high like an extra hump on her shoulders. I lost for half hour! she says. So glad I find you!

The nurse surprises Grete with a hug. When she turns to Bit, she squeezes him fiercely around the middle and says, I come to make things easier. Now. Have anyone eaten dinner?

No, Bit says, and Luisa clucks. In you go, she says. Make the dinner.

Oh, he says. It's been a long day. Nobody's very hungry, I think, Luisa.

She beams up into Bit's face and says, Times like this? Schedules are lifeboat. Make the dinner, make the breakfast, make the bed. It will help to be strict with yourself.

He likes this bossy Luisa, this plain brown woman, a stranger but familiar as an aunt. She pats his arm and gives him a little push inside.

He brings his mother a bowl of soup. She doesn't open her eyes but accepts half the bowl in spoonfuls. How like a baby bird, he thinks, seeing her open her mouth, her eyes swollen shut, the skin so thin against the bones of her skull. Or, simply, a baby: tiny Grete gazing at him solemnly over a spoon full of pureed peas.

He goes to the closet to find Hannah another blanket. The night is cold, and the window was left open too long for the house to have retained its warmth. When he opens the door, Abe's smell rises to Bit from the clothes: that clean sweat of him, the metal of him. The lingering last ghost of his father sideswipes him. He knows it's absurd, but he closes the door to save a little of his father for later.

All weekend, Hannah won't get out of bed save to drag herself to the bathroom. She sips at the soup Bit makes and only nibbles at the toast. Luisa comes at nine every night and leaves at five, and though it isn't her job to clean, the house is scoured when he wakes in the morning.

Hannah still won't talk to him, not a word.

On Monday morning, Grete is eating the

last of the granola in the jar. Her face is so carefully made up that Bit stares at her. She touches her cheek and frowns. War paint, she says.

You're going to blow these country kids' minds, Bit says.

What if I don't? she says.

Then they're brain-dead, he says. Then they don't have minds to blow.

She sighs and washes out the bowl. What are we going to do about Hannah? she says. She needs to get up. There's no point in us being here if she doesn't make any effort to be human.

If she hasn't gotten out of bed by tonight, we'll get her up ourselves, he says.

Okay, Grete says. She shoulders her backpack and says, with Hannah's old wryness, Goody. That'll give me something to look forward to while I'm getting wedgied.

They drive in silence to the school, and he gently takes her hand when she begins to chew her nails to the quick. In the drop-off area of the squat brick high school, Bit sits with Grete, gazing at the flickering clumps of students.

Boys, Grete says, frowning. They watch the boys buffooning around, and Grete says, I think I'm already starting to miss the all-girls' pedagogical model.

Bit laughs. I'm having bad flashbacks of my first day in real school, he confesses. If I can give you any advice, it's to smile and be cool.

Smile and be cool, she mocks him. She squeezes his hand. Then she squares her shoulders like a diver at the end of the board and steps gracefully out. A sudden magnet, his tall, bony daughter with her pink hair in this sea of sweatpants and hunting camouflage. Even in his car, Bit can feel the weight of the attention upon her. He has to pull away to stop himself from leaping out after Grete and dragging her safely home.

He sits in the dark room with Hannah. All day, he tries to feed her soft fresh bread he's baked and reads her *Tristram Shandy* to make her laugh; she refuses both. Her breathing is labored. Radio, she commands, and he listens with her to a radical homemaking show (how to make dandelion wine; how to set your own broken bones) and, for as long as he can stay in his seat, to the news. They're now calling the pandemic SARI, for severe acute respiratory infection. Oops, says Bit. Sorry! But Hannah doesn't laugh.

Over seven thousand people are dead; the disease has spread to Hong Kong, Singapore, mainland China, San Francisco, Adelaide in Australia. The Centers for Disease Control, gutted by low federal taxes, have sent out a strongly worded warning for people to avoid hospitals and flights, and nobody is doing much more. Bit stands, agitated. Although it's early to pick up Grete, he lets himself be chased from the house by the news. First, he'll stop in town to pick up vegetables and coffee and tofu and rice milk. Muffin's mothers still run the natural-foods store in town, and they fall upon Bit when he comes in. He finds himself squashed in a middle-aged lesbian sandwich smelling of herbal cough drops and celery. Cheryl and Diana cry, now, as they hadn't cried at Abe's memorial service.

Abe was the most practical man, says Cheryl. Infuriating as hell, but *always* got his way.

He was the last person in the world I thought would do what he did, Diana says. We always thought Hannah . . . And she trails off, stricken, bulging her eyes at her wife.

That's why Abe succeeded and Hannah didn't, Bit says when the surge of pain has faded.

They show him pictures of Muffin's children, all eight owlish in glasses, shirts buttoned up to their throats. Missionaries, Cheryl says with a snort. With two old heathens like us, it makes you wonder where all that religion came from.

Before Bit leaves, Diana hugs him and whispers in his ear, You'll get your mother out of it. You always do.

Then she holds up a carrot from their garden. It is an odd, mutant thing that looks like two human bodies twined in coitus. Show Hannah this, she says. Our Kama Sutra carrot. We've been saving it for a special occasion. Alone in the car again, holding the lewd thing in his hand, Bit hears the ladies' jollity ring in his ears and it makes him glad.

When Grete comes out of the school, he is so flushed with relief his hands tremble. She walks slowly, but her chin is dangerously high. She gets in the car and won't speak.

Halfway home, desperate, he says, At least you have all your limbs, and she says a brief Ha! Then she says, Let's just call it an interesting sociological experiment; and she won't say any more.

Bit can barely park before Grete leaps from the car. She marches into Hannah's room and throws open the curtains. That's it, she says. That's enough. She disappears into the bathroom and begins running the water in the tub.

Bit picks his mother up. He expects her to be light, but she is dense and he almost drops her. With great effort, he carries her into the bathroom. Whoa, he says. Grete has loaded the water with so much bubble-bath that the foam is already a foot high.

What? she says. She smells bad. No offense, Grannah, but you stink.

You stink, whispers Hannah. She is crying. Both of you. You stink.

Together, Bit and his daughter unzip the dress and pull it down over Hannah's arms and belly. They peel off the support garments unseen in the world for ten years: a bra pointy as a pair of missiles, sad orangey hose, a potato sack for underwear. They help her into the tub, bending her stiff limbs. She is still wearing the pearl necklace that Abe gave her on their thirty-fifth wedding anniversary. She was almost angry with him that night, saying it was wasteful, asking if she was the kind of woman who'd wear pearls. Everyone at the table had suppressed a grin. With the pearls around her neck, the shadow Hannah became visible, the debutante who lived in the old hippie. Had she fallen in love with a different kind of man, Hannah would now be hosting Derby parties, getting tipsy on juleps and wondering why the world felt so hollow under her well-gilded knuckles.

Bit tries not to see what he has already seen, that her right leg and arm have atrophied and twisted. The left arm is going that way, also. There is a strange gray tone to her skin.

Hannah hides her face in the bubbles. Grete builds devil horns on her head. And Bit takes the warm washcloth and slides it along his mother's body to scrub away the stink of her mourning. When he is cleaning her feet, Hannah lifts her face and it is featureless as an Amish doll under the scrim of soap. Grete gently clears her eyes and mouth of the suds. Bad girl, she leaves the horns.

Clean, now, Hannah is at the table. Her hair is dried and braided, and she is in an ancient sweatsuit so soft it felt like her own skin when Bit put it on her. She manages an avocado–soy cheese melt and some chai. Bit puts on an old record, and while Joan Baez warbles through the house, Grete escapes for another run in the dusk. When her footsteps have gone, Hannah turns on Bit. This is cruel, she says. Her tongue is thick in her mouth, her muscles spasming in her chin. She says, Selfish of you to make me go through this.

Selfish, he repeats, very softly. A daddy longlegs skirts the edge of sun on the linoleum.

When he responds, much later, it is toward the kitchen window. The world held in a frame calms him: the sparrows darting over the green fields, the last flush of Arcadia House through the maple trunks. That small square is all he can take, just now.

When I was little, he says. When you'd grow sad and tired and sleep all the time in the winter, I used to watch you just lying there. In the summer, you were so loud and golden and happy, and suddenly one day you'd just go away. You'd become this pale changeling in place of my mother. It was so cold in the Bread Truck. Unless Abe came home early, I didn't eat anything from breakfast to dinner. Sometimes I tried to kiss you out of it, but I never was enough, I could never get you to wake up. Deep down, I was sure it was my fault.

It wasn't your fault, she snaps. And it wasn't my fault, if you're trying to say that *I* was being selfish. It was brain chemistry. You of all people know this, Bit.

He looks at her. Her jaw is set: she is fighting hard. In the window, the world is blue.

All those times, you took yourself away, he says. All I wanted was for you to come back.

He watches her try to pick the crumbs from the table with the fleshy pad of her palm. She gives up, and her hand curls beside the porcelain.

But I did, she says. Come back. This time too. You weren't there, you didn't see it. There was a sea. It was very warm. I was holding Abe. Then the waves worked their way in between us and he drifted out. I tried to swim for him, but he was gone. I came back.

They hear Grete on the porch, stomping the mud from her running shoes. She is singing something in the off-pitch voice Helle gave her. In the dim at the kitchen table, Bit and Hannah both wince.

I'm too tired, Hannah says, under her breath. I'm too tired, Bit.

If not for me, Bit says quick and low, for Grete.

His daughter is a silhouette in the screen. Hannah reaches out and touches Bit's cheek with her good hand. Grete runs in. She drops onto Hannah's plate what Bit sees is a handful of wild narcissus, ripped from the ground, bulbs and all. Grannah, she shouts, her cheeks pink with delight. Flowers! In February!

Hannah smiles. It is a dry, unconvincing smile, but she takes a tiny pale bloom from the clump and puts it on the back of Bit's hand. For you, she says. Then Hannah asks Grete about her day and Grete's face lights up lovely under her grandmother's attention, and Bit leaves the flower where it is until his hand jerks in revolt.

They take walks. Twice a day, they go out, and Hannah stumbles against Bit; at first, she can only make it to Midge's before she collapses into the weather-beaten lawn chair in front of the cave-house. She peers at her feet and says, Come on, you old clodhoppers, and heaves herself up and painfully presses on. She insists on showering alone. She dresses herself; it takes an hour. She swallows her antidepressants, pain relievers, laxatives, one by one, choking them down with a look of dour satisfaction. She goes to the bathroom; it takes a half an hour, and she comes out trailing toilet paper on her shoe. Fierce, now, she is grabbing what she can to her. Soon enough, you'll help, she tells Bit. Soon enough.

Alone at night in the stark room where he

sleeps, Bit dreams of the city. It is depopulated, shining with wet. The streets are long and gray, and the shop windows are so glorious they fill him with wonder: the mannequins are luminous, at the near cusp of human, their clothes made of cut paper, a pane of glass away from dissolving in the rain. As he walks, he hears noises behind him drawing nearer: the click of nails, indrawn breath, the slide of something heavy against a wall. But when he turns, there is always the street stretching behind him into the dark and nothing moves, and he is alone and not alone, and frozen in horror.

Grete goes to school. Already thin, she grows skinny. For a week, he presses his ear to her door as she sobs into a pillow. She is always on Hannah's telephone, her cell not working in these wilds. Her friends must grow tired of her sadness, though, and Grete begins leaving more messages than talking. When they ignore her for days at a time, he wishes he could march them all off a gangplank. Pirate Bit with the baby face; just wound his daughter and see how savage he can be.

The doctor calls, and her smooth voice calms Bit for hours afterward.

Cheryl and Diana visit; the ladies Hannah

volunteered with at the library visit; Hannah's many friends from town visit. Jincy and the boys come up for an afternoon. They play in Titus's treehouse, and when they come out their faces are swollen and red. At dinner, the twins cling to Hannah, kissing her cheeks over and over until Jincy calls them off. Let the woman eat, she says, and they all watch breathlessly as Hannah maneuvers a cherry tomato to the side of her mouth, slides it along her lips, finally gets it in.

Goal, she says, to make the boys laugh.

When Jincy says goodbye, she whispers, This'll be the last time for a while. My friend at the *Times* says it'll be a matter of days before we're all on quarantine. She kisses him on the nose and says, I'm not surprised you found the safest place to be when the shit hits the fan.

Stay here, he says. Be safe. But she shakes her head sadly. Our life is elsewhere.

In the afternoon, when Bit and his daughter are in town at the pharmacy, Grete begs for a twenty and buys something that she hides in her backpack. When she comes out to dinner, her hair has changed to an inky black, blue swoops of dye still on the pale skin of her forehead. She stares at Hannah and Bit, daring them to say something.

Hannah puts down her forkful of pasta. Black, she says thoughtfully. It sets off your beautiful green-gold eyes, Grete. Grete scowls, pleased. Hannah negotiates the fork almost into her mouth, missing, and all three watch the linguine slowly unthread itself from the tines and slide back onto the plate. Meals these days have become thrillers. Here, Grannah, Grete says and twists her fork into the slippery noodles, and Bit watches, fighting to stay in his seat, as his daughter feeds his mother bite by careful bite.

Grete gazes out the window with the smell of bad Chinese takeout tendriling toward them from the backseat and says, In gym today we had to run a mile. And I beat everyone, even the boys. She says it indifferently but doesn't exhale, waiting for him to speak.

I was fast when I was your age, too, he says.

She gazes at her fingernails, says, It's dumb, but the coach wants me to run Varsity.

Bit says, How exciting.

She turns to him. But Dad, it means that you're the only one all day long with Grannah. It's too much, two extra hours every day. You look *awful* already.

Thanks, he says. Punk.

I mean it, she says. I think I have to say no.

You'll have to say yes. It would make me happy to watch you run, Bit says. It would make Hannah happy to see you use those healthy young legs of yours. He imagines his mother stuck in her renegade body, watching Grete whipping around a track. It could be painful, the juxtaposition between her imprisonment and Grete's freedom. But he says, She'll live through you, and hopes it is true when Grete turns away to hide her smile against the window, her tattletale arms pricked with goosebumps.

Bit is woken by a rasp. It is Luisa's night off, and at first he thinks it's the wind against the screen. He sits, heart thrumming in his ears. The sound is coming from the room next door. He hurries over the rough planks into Hannah's room. Even in the shadows, he can see she's rigid with terror; when he turns on the light, her face is bluish. He pulls her to sitting, and supports her body as she gasps deeper, calming, quieting. He puts pillows behind her back and props her against the headboard.

Oh, Bit, she says. Can't sit up. No air.

Scary, he says.

Stupid, she spits. Her fear has disintegrated into fury, he sees. She says, Wasted your potential, Bit. All your life tried to make people whole. What you could have done. If you didn't have to *nurse* everyone. Helle, Grete, me. Students. You could have been an *artist.*

He says, very quietly, I am an artist.

She flicks her good hand at him but says no more. When her eyelids grow heavy and her head nods forward, he goes to the kitchen and finds the number that the lovely doctor at the hospital had scrawled on a napkin and pressed into his hand. He feels sick to call her so late; his heart beats in his throat. But she answers on the first ring. She is calm and clear, and there is only the smallest touch of sleep in her voice. He imagines her bedroom, spare and neat, imagines the straps of a chemise slipping from her shoulders. I'm so glad you called, she says warmly and makes sympathetic noises as he talks.

He looks at Hannah sleeping in the light of her bedside lamp. He feels how, out in the night, his sadness is prowling, watching the one lit window in the Green house, biding its time.

It's like she's slowly turning into a lump

of clay, he says. A piece of rock.

Well, the doctor says and hesitates. He can hear a whine in the background, and Bit feels ashamed, thinking it's a newborn — what a pervert he is! of course, she has a family! — but she says, Down, Otto, and he smiles to know it's a dog. She says, Your mother's not yet made out of stone. Not yet.

He is too tired to sleep, and sits under an old comforter on a rocking chair on the porch, watching the dawn slip in. He can't remember the last time he quietly watched this drama unfold; what could possibly seem so important that it kept him from doing this? When did he become a person who stopped *noticing?* First the moon dims, and in the east there's a slit in the belly of the sky. A trickle of light pours over the hills, over the Amish farms, over the country roads, over the limit of Arcadia, the miles and miles of forest, startling the songbirds and lighting the dew from within. He thinks of Linnaeus's flower clock blooming the hours, chicory to dandelion to water lily to pimpernel, a gentler way to live time. In a breath, the day is full upon him. Hannah is calling him weakly from her bed, and in her voice he can hear the apology he wasn't expecting he'd so badly need.

■ ■ ■ ■

The doctor's car is mud-spattered when she pulls up. Through the windshield, they grin at one another, and neither stops smiling when she gets out. They hug: her thinness beneath his arms, her cold hands. His mother is in a slice of sun on the porch. Hannah's eyes flick, amused, from Bit's face to the doctor's and back, when the doctor does her exam.

But the more questions Hannah answers, the more serious the doctor looks, until she makes Hannah breathe into a machine. A spirometer, she explains. To measure forced vital capacity. When Hannah does the test again lying down, the doctor's face turns grim. Without her permanent smile, she seems older than he thought: early thirties, not late twenties. Ms. Stone, she says, severely. Are you still against treatment? Riluzole, stem-cell therapies?

Ameliorative, yes, Hannah says. Palliative, she says, and pauses. Then she says, Hell, bring on the morphine.

The doctor relaxes. Good, she says. Martyrdom is overrated.

Hannah laughs aloud, the first clear Hannah laugh Bit has heard for so long. For some, she says. For my son, it's as natural as breathing.

This time, the critique is infused with warmth. In Bit, though, a flash of bitterness like a bird winging away. Unfair, he says. She winks, and he can almost hear her say *Not untrue.*

Speaking of breathing, the doctor says and clips off to her car. She is so small and tidy; he thinks of a lithe brown cat. He avoids Hannah's knowing grin. The doctor returns, bearing a pamphlet. I'm going to have you fitted for a BiPAP, she says to Hannah, so you can breathe better while you sleep. You almost scared your son to death last night.

She is finished with the exam but seems loath to go and Hannah asks about the pandemic. The doctor shrugs. SARI, she says. What a name. Makes you wonder who's in charge. She sits on the steps and talks about quarantine, online tracking of the disease, precautions. I wear a mask in the hospital now, she admits. Everyone does. Mostly, it seems to be killing the immune-compromised, newborns and the old and the sick. Some healthy adults. But the onset is sudden, within an hour or two. I came here straight from my house without seeing anyone on the way. When she smiles, small parentheses go white around her mouth.

She touches Hannah's hand. If I ever suspect I could be carrying it, of course I won't come out. I wouldn't risk your health.

If you have it, Hannah jokes, come straight here. Save us all some time.

Bit studies the pamphlet in his hands. Death by pandemic and death by ALS: severe pneumonia in both cases, Hannah drowning in the sea of her own lungs. But between slowly being mired in her body and a half-day drowning, she may be right. Quicker might be better.

He hears a clip-clop down the drive and looks up. An Amish buggy among the maples. Hannah peers, shields her eyes with her hand. What a day, she says.

The buggy comes to a halt, and the saucer-faced woman from Abe's memorial service climbs down from her bench and ties the horse to a tree. Glory, Hannah calls out, and at first, Bit thinks it's an expostulation, but the woman gives a wave. She comes up the porch steps, a pie wrapped in a dish-towel still steaming in her hands. She places the pie gently on Hannah's lap. Her eyes are sad, though, and skitter off Hannah's face.

Hannah reaches with her good hand and grasps the woman's wrist. She says, gazing up at her Amish friend, You young people, take a walk up to Arcadia House until lunch. It seems I need to do a little work at redemption here.

Indeed, the little Amish woman says in a low and guttural voice. You do.

The sun is hot on Bit's shoulders. The doctor's fine, tiny sandals are caked with mud, and Bit wants to take them in his hands and beat them clean on the grass. There is dirt worked into the cleavage between her toes. His own are irritated in sympathy, but she doesn't seem to mind. Bit and the doctor walk up the ancient slate steps. They don't talk until they are standing on the porch, gazing at the gnarled apples on the Terraces below. Leif had planted saplings on the lowest level, replacing the trees so antique they no longer fruited, but the young trees were chewed to nubs by starved deer, and now the Terraces are scribbled with brush.

The doctor tucks a wisp of hair behind her ear, her hands shaking a little, and a warmth starts in Bit's stomach and spreads. This place, she says. My uncle said that for a while after the commune broke up, high school kids came up here to fool around. There was this story about these two kids who looked up in the middle of getting it on to find a scary huge hippie with an ax glowering at them.

That would be Titus, Bit says, stinging at the thought of his old friend.

Then, of course, the film company came, the doctor says. We used to take field trips out in elementary school. All the other kids on the planet wanted to be rap stars and marine biologists, but we wanted to be animators. Everyone had a crush on that blond CEO. I used to dream I was married to him and rode around on horses out here all day long.

That was Leif, Bit says. His sister was my wife.

Oh. Her eyes scan his face, and he can see her decide not to ask about the *was,* or about the *wife.* She says, It was pretty traumatic for Summerton when the company left the area. We were just getting a downtown back, then it died again like every other town around here. I had a clinic for a little while, but it closed and I had to move to Rochester.

It was in Leif's will for the company to stay here, Bit said. But you know stockholders.

What ever happened to him? she says. Nobody in town really knew. You should have heard the stories. He was eaten by a bear, he was extradited by Homeland Security. It was nuts.

The truth is weirder. He was lost in a high-altitude balloon, Bit says. That family has a genius for disappearing. He looks at her profile, the teeth caught on her lower lip, the crow's-feet as she squints out toward the hills. My wife disappeared, too, he says. Eleven years ago. She went for a walk and never came back.

I'm sorry, she says. He notices a short yellow hair curled on her breast and stops his hand from reaching for it. She flushes, then picks it off. My dog, she says. I thought he'd be good protection for a woman living alone, but he's scared of everything. Lightning, strangers, ice, the dark.

I've never had a pet, Bit says. We were never allowed to have dogs here when I was a kid. We considered it animal slavery.

Otto thinks I'm the slave, she says. I pick up *his* poop, after all.

They watch a little red fox come out at the edge of the forest, crouch, pounce, and carry off something gray in his mouth. The doctor's small hand touches his arm.

Bit, she begins, too solemnly, and something seizes in Bit: she is going to say it, the things he knows deeply but can't stand to hear: his mother is going rapidly; she'll be in a wheelchair within a month; it is only her stubbornness that has kept her from one so far; instead of going with the slowness he's been fearing, she'll go with dreadful speed. If he hears the words, he thinks, it will come true. He has to fight himself to answer. What's that, Dr. Ellis? he says, at last.

Ellis is my first name, she says and tries and fails to not laugh. Ellis Keefe. I didn't want to correct you in the hospital. All I was going to say is that I can see why you love this place; and she gestures toward the forest that spreads all the way to the hills in the distance. In the motion, Bit sees what Arcadia had been, populous and full of song. Now it feels empty. Without people, land is only land.

That's it? he says. I thought you were going to say that Hannah's disease is progressing faster than expected.

She peers at him sideways, her mouth twisted.

Oh, he says.

I can manage to come up a couple times a week, if you want, she says. I love it out here.

We'd be thrilled to see you as often as you can make it, he says.

She turns her head to look at him. He is acutely aware of the fact of her, solid and real, her gentle gravity, her breath on his cheeks. I would like to see you too, she says, then shyly looks away.

In a small clearing where the Sheep's Meadow used to sprawl, Hannah is on a blanket, eating Glory's applesauce. Bit takes a photo and she preens. It is a new compulsion of his to snatch Hannah's face with the camera whenever she's not looking. Words have thickened past the point of clarity in her mouth, but he thinks she says, Surely, you've shot lovelier cover models.

Never, he says. You're by far the loveliest. She beams as well as she can, posing.

Soon she is tired; she wants to go home. She struggles and waves him back. A slow one-armed push up onto her knees, a wobbly stand. Hannah stretches as he packs up their lunch. She takes one step onto the path, and he raises the camera to his face. Then she falls out of the frame, and he looks into the world to find her crumpled on the ground.

Hannah, he says.

I know, she says. I know. He half-carries her home.

Grete comes in, wearing her track sweatshirt, smelling of perspiration. She sees her grandmother in Abe's old wheelchair and says nothing. But in the night, Grete and Luisa conspire. And when dawn brightens the window, it lights up the wheelchair, where a pillow sits, repurposed from one of Abe's ancient cashmere sweaters; the wheels sparkle with glitter nail polish; there are pom-poms on the handles. A queen of hearts is lodged in a wheel, and it whirs when Hannah moves. So you can't sneak up on us, says Grete. Hannah gives a wheel a spin with the knuckle of her better hand; she laughs until she cries and cries until she laughs again.

These days, the house is oddly full of Hannah's laughter. She laughs about everything: the way she can no longer speak, a funny story on the radio, when Grete in her eagerness trips on her own shoes; when she and Grete drink cocoa from the beautiful bone china cups of her grandmother and Hannah's hand goes rogue and shatters one.

Are you happier now? Bit says, alarmed by this excessive laughter.

No, she garbles, I'm petrified! And this, too, cracks her up.

The track is recycled tires, and when the wind rises and blows across it, Bit smells highway, the American longing to go. All he wants to do is stay. In this place, in this bright day, the children flitting in their uniforms like vivid butterflies, Hannah's jerking smile. He tucks the blanket around her legs, more in protest against the wheelchair than against any chill. It is a miracle they are even here at the track meet: at the eleventh hour, the school superintendent saw how distant SARI was from them and grudgingly gave permission.

Hannah's neck is weak today, and she rests her head upon Bit's palm. Her skull is heavy and overly warm. I'm happy to be here, she says thickly.

He watches the boys, the brutes hurling shotputs like marbles. A girl spins a discus, and the meat of her arm ripples as she throws. The children go blazing by, and their parents dance and shriek. How it would feel, Bit thinks, to be young again, to lift through the air on a pole, to fly over the sand and land in a great explosion. He loves the good sediment of time, wouldn't trade anything to have to go through that adolescent pain all over again. But, for a moment, he longs to be one of these runners, these leapers, these fliers; to be one of the lovers standing there, that boy holding the willowy girl, so easily able to forget the world because a pretty young person longs to press close to him.

It is time for the one-mile. Grete sends a nervous smile their way, her black wisps blowing under the folded green bandanna. Bit can hardly bear to watch the runners assemble on the line. The gun pops. There's a blur of sharp elbows. Within a hundred yards, the pack thins out. The slenderest pull away, Grete's legs longer than the two in front of her, turning over more slowly. The runners pass for the first time in a patter that Bit can feel inside himself. They dissolve behind the high jump; they reemerge. The second girl falters, falls behind. Now the race is between Grete and the leader. The track goes quiet. People watch the two in front spin by again, dragging the slower girls like a lengthening train.

Come on, Grete, Bit groans, but Hannah says something that sounds like, Smart. Waiting.

Around again. When they pass, there is a sheen of sweat on the face of the lead girl; Grete is dry and watchful.

Voices begin to build. Around the last curve, one hundred meters left to go. On the straightaway, Grete moves even with the leader, easy, and her legs seem to blur. Side by side, the girls bear down into the sprint, and everyone is screaming. Bit himself is urging Grete forward with his voice, hopping up and down, frenzied, washed with a strange relief in this senseless shouting. The girls chest forward over the last ten meters, strong as horses. They tick down to a walk, nearly falling on their wobbly legs. It is impossible for Bit to say who won.

Now they wait, Grete in a swarm of petting hands, as the other girls trickle in. An official puffs over and confers with the coaches, then turns to the two leaders. He murmurs something.

Grete screams, Fuck! and throws her bandanna and stomps away.

Bit has to wait for the downswoop of his heart to steady. Apparently, he says, my daughter is a poor loser.

But Hannah's face reflects back the sun. Got my devil in her, she says.

Bit leans closer. You were a poor sport? he says, knowing it's true, even as he says it.

No. Fast, says Hannah. Together, they watch Grete composing herself at the fence. Fast, fast, fast, Hannah says, and she pats her wasted legs with her good hand, as if to praise them for everything they had once so easily done.

Bit is in the dawn in the forest, breathing the scent of water, all fish and sweet leaf rot, when the sun grows through the treetops and touches him where he stands, camera forgotten. He is so still the doe doesn't see him and bends her elegant head to drink at the stream. There is a flash of red: a fox, startled, running fast and looking backward; it careens into the doe's haunch and bounces back on its rear. The creatures gaze at one another, appalled. Bit guffaws, and the animals disappear in a blur. Alone now, Bit can't catch his breath, and he laughs so hard that he goes dizzy. Something breaks in him, and the breaking, at last, feels good.

Grete has one friend. Her name is Yoko, and she has a sweet cupcake face, a trill of a laugh. She is a Japanese exchange student in this wee country place; now that Grete has come to school, Yoko is always at the house. She was supposed to go home but can't: Japan is under quarantine, ten thousand dead already, the photographs of the streets swept of people, and those who can afford it wearing oxygen tanks. Yoko's host parents in Summerton are dim, strict Christians who make her play the organ for hymn hour at night while they sing. When they pick her up at the Green house, they honk impatiently and never come in. Behind Grete's door, there are sobs and Grete's gentle soothing. When they emerge, both puffy-faced, Grete and Yoko bake cookies, watch movies, build panoramas of classic short stories for English class. A man and a woman at a little table; the hills in the distance, white elephants. A heart below the floorboards, and curled within it, the text of the story on a strip of paper that scrolls out; a tale-tell heart. A brain like a phrenological illustration, a bullet passing through it, the sections each filled with a tiny image of bliss.

Bit studies the last project for hours. During his white nights, he holds the shoebox in his hands and looks at the delicate drawings of happiness in the lobes. If he holds it long enough, his own scenes swim up. The long stretch of Helle under a white sheet, Cole's adolescent face the first time he heard *Houses of the Holy,* a sea urchin in a tidepool on a trip Grete and he took to the shore, spiny as a horse chestnut on her fat pink palm.

Hannah can't be understood. She must take Grete's e-reader and pluck out the words with her two fingers that work. She barks with frustration; she weeps over nothing. At supper, which Bit cooks — peas and grilled tofu, soy cheese enchiladas, the old Arcadia standards he has been cooking for thirty years now — the conversation between Yoko and Hannah is a surreal play.

Hannah: Gwabway eel o aampee en ooah eewa, Oko.

Yoko: Sofunneee, Glannah! Ha-ha-ha!

They fall into stitches, and Grete and Bit look on, bewildered. They share a glance, shut out of the delight in the air; for a breath, envious of the inarticulate.

In the full blow of April, Arcadia seems even emptier of people. The strong wind rises against the trees so they bend like girls washing their hair; it rattles the Arcadia House windows. Wandering through the upstairs rooms one day, Bit finds a raccoon in Leif's vast bathtub, spinning a bar of soap around and around in its humanoid hands.

If he listens closely, over the wind against the screens and a distant plane above, he can almost hear the Arcadia he knew, the strum of Handy's guitar somewhere in the thickness of the house, the women in the Eatery kitchen, laughing as they cook. His own young voice, urgent and high. Although he almost hurts his ears, straining, he can't understand what the once-upon-a-time Bit is saying to the current version of himself or to the one who will stand here in the future, a man changed as the house is changed, worn a little more by time and loss, gradually dragged down by gravity. If he is so lucky. If they are all so lucky. The schools on the West Coast have been closed; the airports are bare. Dogs trot down the middle of L.A.'s freeways. In Summerton, the mail carriers wear gloves and masks, and in all the stores, there are great tippy stacks of wind-up radios and soup and bottled water. But in Arcadia, with their well and garden and basement full of food, they are an island. They could wait as the disease washed again and again over the world and emerge when it was safe again.

What relief there would be in starting anew; what hope there would be in doing better. The old story, Noah's, the first step into the world scrubbed clean.

The raccoon is watching him, holding out his uncanny black hand, the sliver of soap catching the light from the window. Bit reaches slowly and takes it. Though the creature surrenders the soap, it curls its black lips and reveals its teeth, and Bit can't tell whether it is smiling or showing its fear.

Ellis steps through the ferns and onto the rock beside Bit. A Saturday and Grete is Hannah-sitting. After the examination — Hannah losing function and weight in shocking numbers — Ellis looked scared. In the hallway Bit said: Tell me on our hike.

A date? Perhaps. They had arranged it on her last visit. He wanted to show her the waterfall, the spring-fat waters coming down, a white sheet fading into the wind. But they are here and it is only a strip of ribbon. He looks at the ghost of the waterfall and feels ill.

It's beautiful, Ellis says.

No it's not, Bit snaps at her. She frowns back at him, and he says, Sorry. It's just less than it should be. When I was a kid, it *roared.* We could hear it a mile away. He laughs in embarrassment at his swoop of sadness and says, Everyone in my house seems to have inappropriate emotional reactions these days.

Ellis presses his arm. Understandable. Grete's fourteen. You're bearing the weight of your mother's sickness. And Hannah's bulbar paralysis is causing her to react wildly.

Oh, says Bit. I just thought my mother was happier.

Ellis sits and pulls out the sandwiches she'd brought. Chicken or egg, she says.

I'm so sorry, Bit says, dismayed. I've been vegan my whole life.

Ellis gives a beautiful guffaw that echoes

against the cliff. I meant, she says, who knows what came first. Hannah truly could be happier. She has her two loves near her; she's on massive antidepressants. It's spring, and you make sure she sits in the sun for hours every day. And maybe all that crazy laughter in itself is making her happier, sparking some kind of neural pathway in her brain. Whatever the case, treat it as a gift.

A gift, Bit says, sitting. A gift would be lunch. What are the sandwiches?

Peanut butter and jelly, she says. I can't cook.

My favorite, he says and cuts an apple for them to share.

Ellis stretches her bare feet into the little pool. She smiles at him, chewing. Listen, she says. This is probably not what you want to hear. But do know it'll get worse before it gets better.

Your cooking? Bit says.

Ellis doesn't smile. Her eyes, in the sun, are the deep blue of dusk. She rests her side against his, and he can feel her waiting for him to either lean in or shift away. I know it will, he says, leaning in.

In the kitchen window, there appears a lady in a bedazzled purple mask. In the kitchen,

Hannah says, Shit, and wheels into her room. The lady goes to the back of her car and heaves at something in the trunk. When Bit comes into the bright dust to help, she gives a squeal. Oh, thanks, she calls out. I'm helpless!

She's one of the Library Ladies; such creatures everywhere have blue marshmallows for hair. Bit carries the box into the house, and she fills a glass with water and drinks it down. In the pink circle where the mask had been, the moist skin of her cheeks has collected dust; the wrinkles fanning from her lips are making their own mud. I'll just leave it off, she declares. You are hermits out here, no way you got the SARI. Your mom around?

She's taking a nap, Bit says.

We passed a hat, the lady says, patting at herself with a tissue. All around town. Your mom's beloved, you know. And we bought her a computer.

Oh, Bit says, at a loss. Gently, he says, But she already has a computer.

The lady says, Not like this one, she doesn't. Then she cocks her head to the side and says: Are you well? You don't look well. Are you sleeping? Are you eating? Who's taking care of you? Do you have a girlfriend? I know a lovely young woman. Pretty hair.

What do you call it? Auburn. Are you sure? Take her number. And Bit is left holding a scrap of paper, which he tosses as soon as the lady is gone.

For an hour or so, Bit gazes at the booklet. Such fine calibrations; such delicate technology! This computer can track the weightless touch of a glance on a holographic keyboard. The booklet says that those who are proficient can do more than twenty words a minute. Bit thinks of what Ellis said on the hike back from the waterfall: Hannah could have a month, maybe more. He does the math. If she were to start now and not stop, she could write another of the short popular histories she'd written when she was a professor. Or one long essay. It is no time at all.

Bit struggles with the setup until Grete comes home from the morning practice. Grete, child of the Digital Age, struggles until lunch. They are eating their salads, gazing at the screen and nest of wires, when Glory says from the door, I see you need help.

Grete snorts. Glory's woolen dress emits a damp heat, and she has a straw of hay in her bonnet. They hadn't heard her horse on the path; the maples are swarmed with raucous magpies.

Oh, Bit says. It's. Well. A computer, Glory.

Glory says, I know. I was in IT for five years.

Grete whispers, Is this a joke?

No, Glory says, bending down and fiddling.

They finish their food but stay, fascinated by Glory's rough hands among the wires. Why'd you leave the world, Glory? Bit says. Why did you come back?

She stands and shrugs. It is lonely, she says. Five years, I was lonely. Then I realized that I was not happy, and would do anything to be taken in and loved. It seems a give-and-take, you know? Freedom or community, community or freedom. One must decide the way one wants to live. I chose community.

Why can't you have both? says Grete, frowning. I think you could have both.

You want both, Glory says, you are destined to fail. She looks at Bit. I remember when your people were here, it was the big debate among my family. What to do? We watched with horror! Naked people, drugs, loud music! You were like babies, you could do nothing. You didn't know how to plow a field. But we couldn't let you starve. Eventually, we had a meeting and agreed to help enough to feed you, but let you disintegrate on your own. And when you did, there were some of us who felt very smart. Too much freedom, it rots things in communities, quick. That was the problem with your Arcadia.

Bit thinks of the poverty of the last years of his childhood, the kidlets with scrawny limbs and terrible teeth, the drugs, the cash going to relief efforts, to the Midwifery School, to the Trippies and Runaways. He thinks of easygoing Handy, and his pride that started the rift.

Well, says Bit slowly. I guess that's as good an interpretation as any.

Yeah, but it's not like you Amish are perfect, Grete says. You're human, too. I mean, even you guys get sick. What happens if you get SARI? I bet your community would suffer.

There are always diseases, Glory says. You're too young to remember measles, chicken pox, polio. Spanish influenza killed millions in 1918, and nobody ever hears about it. We have survived other things.

Glory nods toward the cookies she brought. Now. Eat your dessert, she says. Allow me to concentrate, thank you. In fifteen minutes, Glory has the computer running. She settles Hannah before it. They wait as Hannah figures out the mechanism that makes it work.

Bit finds himself holding his breath, urging the computer inside his head, making deals. If you let my mother speak, he thinks, I will repudiate my repudiation of technology.

A smooth, light voice rises and startles them, a voice unlike Hannah's. Only after it has passed does Bit understand what it said into the dimness of the house: Glory be.

They hear from Cheryl and Diana, who come, sobbing. Muffin and her family are missing in Madagascar, and all the news they can get are pictures of bodies lining the street. As they are leaving, the ladies remember another sorrow and tell how Pooh's two-year-old granddaughter in Seattle has died in the night, and the family is in lockdown and can't travel to mourn together. The news touches the bone.

Ellis has watched silently, great-eyed, from a chair in the corner through their visit. When he passes her in the hall, she stops him, and takes his head, and gently leans it against her shoulder. He stays there until Grete comes from her bedroom, sees them, and shuts her door again.

In these quiet days, the house is full of slanted light and music from the ancient turntable. Hannah only ever wants Bach. Bit spoons a dollop of chocolate pie into his mother's mouth. It is hard for her to swallow, impossible for her to chew. To keep her from losing too much weight, they spend most of their days making her eat.

Hannah glances over at her new computer and eyes out some words. Benefit one to sickness, the sultry computer voice says. I can taste as vividly as when I was a child.

What's benefit two? Bit says.

He sees Hannah's eyes return to the keyboard. Benefit two . . . , the voice says, and there's a long pause. He goes to the sink to do the dishes, and when he returns, he peers at the screen, thinking that perhaps Hannah forgot to make the voice speak. But there is only Benefit two . . . trailing into nothing.

At last, he gets her joke.

Ellis comes every other day, mostly in the evenings after she's showered and had dinner and waited for illness to sneak upon her. Bit and she sit together for hours over tea in the kitchen, eating Glory's pies, while Luisa and Hannah murmur in Hannah's room and Grete sleeps the sleep of the young. Ellis tells him, piece by piece, about herself. The good little girl, beloved only child of older parents, piano-playing, churchgoing. Summerton was larger then. There was a Farm and Home store, a Newberry's, a Kmart, a smattering of hippie boutiques from defectors of Arcadia. She went straight to college at seventeen, to medical school at twenty-one. She wanted to fix people. She saw how her mother came back from the rheumatologist's glowing, her hands having been gently held for an hour, the power of touch. But her parents both died when she was in residency. She was very alone. She was engaged three times (she blushes). She called it off every time, a few months before the wedding. They were nice guys, she says. She didn't love them.

Bit folds her small brown hand into his. Her nostrils go red and her eyelids do too and there's something of the bunny about her as she wipes her cheeks on her shoulders. I'm not sure, she whispers, I'm capable of loving anybody.

Ellis, Bit says. Oh, honey, of course you are.

He lifts her knuckles to his mouth and kisses them, tasting the bitter almond of her skin. She stands suddenly, and says a hurried goodbye, and drives off, and all the next day Bit is afraid he's scared her away. But she comes again at nine that night, and when she enters the house, the cool air in her clothes, she kisses him gravely on both cheeks, next to his lips, and leans her head against his chest and keeps it there for a long moment, just resting.

Then she says, I have a surprise, and goes out to her car, and a huge yellow Lab comes bounding out, a streak of sunlight in the night-darkened house. He rests his muzzle in Hannah's lap and Luisa chases him from the kitchen with a broom and he wrestles with Grete until they both pant. Can Otto stay here? says Grete, grabbing the leonine head and shaking it until the dog nips gently at her wrist. Ellis grins at Bit. Not just yet, she says. Maybe soon.

Possibility, so strange in this house of sickness, washes over him. Soon, he agrees.

When Ellis drives away, a door seems to close behind her. In Mexico City, the morgues are full and the dead are stacked in the warehouse of a toy company. On Grete's e-reader, the images rise: babies in their canvas shrouds, stacked under drifts of dolls with unblinking eyes. The image haunts Bit at night and makes him sit at the window to watch the comforting dark until his vision goes blurry with sleep.

Bit can hardly catch his daughter alone. She

comes in at ten. He lifts himself, his body a heavy sack, and meets Grete at the kitchen sink.

Hey, Dad, she whispers. They can hear Hannah in her room, barking No! at Luisa, the last word she can say. Luisa always responds in her soft, kind voice. Grete's track sweatshirt smells of the woodsmoke of some bonfire. On her breath, there is whiskey.

Oh, Grete, Bit says.

Don't worry, she says.

I do, he says. The quarantine. Plus you're fourteen. And you have the genes. I mean, your mother started a little younger than you —

Dad, she interrupts him. In the dim kitchen, she laughs. Listen.

Whippet-thin, she leans on the sink. She talks about running. About how she pushes until the pain builds so high in her limbs that it breaks into bliss, how she is a raw nerve here, at home, but when she runs she's let loose from anxiety, how it threads itself all the way through her bones until she feels relief kindle in her, a kind of happiness.

I would do nothing to threaten that feeling, she says. Nothing.

He must seem dubious because she looks

at him for a moment, holding something in. You're a lot like Grumpy, you know, she says. You always have to take care of everyone else, and don't let anyone take care of you. It's kind of aggressive.

Aggressive? he says, startled. Me?

All I'm saying is, if you won't let me take care of you, at least take care of yourself. She turns away and closes herself in her room.

In the morning, Bit hears her stir and rolls out of his bed in his running clothes. It is the kind of dawn that seems to seep out of the trees' vibrant green. Grete comes onto the porch where he's stretching and says a small Oh!

How far are we going? he says.

Until you drop, old man, she says and vanishes with impossible lightness into the waking forest. It is all he can do to follow on the path where she's gone, the underbrush still shaking with her passage, each of his steps becoming its own reward, the day its own glory, his lungs' bursting a good pain and his daughter falling back, at last, in kindness to him.

Hannah makes a wordless bray when Grete goes out the door. Grete waits, impatient, for the computer voice to flute out: You, my darling, are not wearing underwear.

Grete flushes and mutters, Grannah, Jesus. I forgot to do my laundry, not that it's any of your business.

Hannah snorts, and the voice says, I can *see* your business. Hussy.

May Day, and he looks for nymphs dancing ribbons around poles but finds only the same sear that once afflicted August in his youth. The radio is an insect abuzz in the house, reporting heat-related deaths in the cities, five hundred thousand dead of SARI, general quarantine, hospital only for traumatic cases, airlines shut down. He flicks the box quiet before the personal stories begin. He can only bear tragedy if it's abstract.

Glory comes in the mornings and fills the air with the warmth of baking pies. They cover most of Hannah's newest smells: the ointments for her sores, the sickly whiff of her breath, the house-filling stink when she can manage to void her bowels.

Luisa lives with them on a cot in Hannah's room; it is safer for her here, in exile. The hospital is in crisis mode, but everyone is afraid of SARI and nobody but the sickest come in, so the doctors and nurses spend their days playing cards and watching television until the director announces voluntary suspensions of noncritical staff. Ellis chooses this option and comes every morning; she naps beside Bit, atop the covers, when it's Grete's turn to watch Hannah. Grete's school is closed. Yoko and Grete talk on the e-reader a hundred times a day. At night, the family eats the vegetables Hannah once canned, tasting the sun of other summers in them.

Sometimes Hannah seems so distant; he thinks she's trying to pray. It makes sense, in the light of her decline. Bit also tries to pray when he is unable to sleep, but he keeps his eyes open, because when they are closed he sees God in the form of Handy, who is most definitely not God. He turns toward the window, the cold coin of the moon, and tells it stories about his day, to pull the shapeless mass of his time into some saving form.

At last, Bit comes to Hannah when her face is peaceful, and he asks her what she is doing. The voice says, Practicing.

What? he says, and her proxy voice swims out beautiful and smooth: Make tofu. Baste. Play Chopin. Launder. Shell peas. Curry horse. Bake scones. Fuck. Knead bread. Swim.

He sits in the rocking chair beside her.

The women's noises fill the house at his back. He will make raspberry jam in his head, he decides; he hasn't done any preserving since he was a boy. He closes his eyes. At first he forgets steps, has to backtrack to squeeze the lemons, clean the berries, measure out the sugar, pluck the glass jars from the boiling water. But when he relaxes, things go vibrant. He feels the furry warmth of fresh raspberries in his fingers, and the smell rises up, sweet and tingling, made even brighter by memory.

The sun and wind pour into the sheets on the line. There are bodies in the billowing, forms created and lost in a breath. He takes photo after photo with his ruined film, to hold them there.

This is what, long ago, made him fall in love with photography: the paying of attention, the capturing of time. He'd forgotten exactly this.

He walks in, arms full of laundry, to find Grete shouting for him. He drops the clothing onto the kitchen counter, and socks roll across the tiles. He finds his daughter standing in the bathtub, Hannah leaning against the sink, her face gray, choking.

She knocks me back, Grete says. I try to help, she knocks me away.

Bit is also pummeled by Hannah's sharp elbows but leans in. Her mucus is too heavy for her, impossible to swallow. Bit takes a washcloth, seizes Hannah's head, and scrapes off the back of her tongue. She gasps: the color slowly flows back into her face. Tears roll down her cheeks and drip off. Bit cradles her head in his arms. When she is calm again, he wheels her into the kitchen to her computer. Into the heat of the afternoon, the voice at last comes: My body, she wisecracks, wants to kill me.

During the rainstorm, the wind in the trees sounds like panting. Bit remembers what Titus used to call his own spells of sadness: *the old black dog.* How appropriate: fanged and servile, neither wild nor human, but an odd by-product of civilization, hungry and slinking near. He can almost see the dog out in the wild rattling rainstorm, skulking in the blacker shadows among the trees. He can almost feel the softness of its pelt under his hand.

Grete has filled six of Hannah's skin-thin teacups with water and daisies. They shine in the dawn. These days, they use the antique lace tablecloth and the silver service at every meal. It comforts Hannah to handle things her own mother and grandmother touched.

While Luisa changes the bedsheets, Bit and Hannah are alone.

Hannah peers urgently at the computer. When the voice comes on, it says with gentle calm, My little Bit. Will you forgive me?

Bit's silence, born of surprise, stretches. Forgive what, exactly? Which of her many failures is she speaking of?

He stares at the claw of her hand until he somehow knows she means Arcadia, their common wound, how she had pushed toward perfection but, tiring, turned away. It is true that most of the children of Arcadia rebelled. Dylan went neocon, Cole became punk, Jincy searched for suburbia, Leif turned antiseptic and inward. It's the ancient story: the deliberate rejection of what gave birth to the youth and created the man. In the quiet of the house, Luisa's shoes squeak around the bed, the mockingbird begins a rill.

Bit feels it start to swell in him. The love, which he had turned from, breathes, blinks, swallows. A creature, stirred back to life. He *can't* be separate. It is impossible. He is part of the whole.

He looks at his brittle mother and says,

There is nothing to forgive.

Within the rebellious clay of her flesh, Hannah kindles, becomes so unbearably brilliant that it hurts Bit to look at her. Still, he keeps his eyes on her. He looks.

Hannah had once been vaster than Arcadia itself, her body so big it enveloped him, the warmth of her, the bread of her, so great that the sun had risen and set in her. Dwindling, she is a burlap sack and bundle of sticks; she is frayed muscles, weeping sores.

He carries her into the Pond. She dabbles her hands and legs, pretending to swim. They hear Grete's fast footsteps as she runs up. She wades in, still in her clothes, the jeans and boat shoes, the pretty top. She goes underwater and comes up next to them, her hair plastered and eyeliner streaming in black slips down her cheeks. She says, Let me, and carries Hannah away through the water toward Helle's rock. When she turns around, she is singing the song that Bit used to sing to her, the summers they spent up in Arcadia, when she was little and frightened of the thick water of the Pond . . . *swimming all day, In the ocean so wide, Now it's time to rest, And float with the tide, Hey ho, little fish don't cry,* she sings.

Luisa is calm but pushes through the countryside at such speeds that Bit is afraid of the trees rushing by in the darkness. Bit holds his choking mother. They are in the ER. In a moment, the doctor in his green scrubs brandishes a scalpel and Hannah has a hole in her throat. Cotton descends upon Bit's mind. For a long, good time, there is blankness.

They wheel Hannah out again. There is a ventilator attached to her. She is weeping. I didn't want this, she will say at home, clawing at the tubes; but it's clear, even now, what she means. Luisa says something: *refused to talk about advance directives. Hannah.* Bit finds himself in the car, going home.

He can administer enemas, hold his mother one-armed over the toilet, wipe her bottom. He can brush the shine into her long whitening hair and file her toenails and rub the muscles that cramp until she gasps with relief. He can spend all his patience from dawn to dusk spooning soup into her mouth which she chokes on more often than not. Even in the hospital, when they asked her about a feeding tube, she had been so agitated they understood her No. He can watch her waste away. To make peace with the problems of her flesh is not hard for him. But something deep in him resists the raw wound in her throat, the way it smells of death.

He watches his hand clean it, anyway. He has locked himself away so that his days are lived by a shred of himself. The rest of him waits somewhere on the outskirts, watching for the end.

But Hannah studies the part of Bit that remains. She is expanding while he is retracting. She is a cup. She overbrims with love.

Hannah cannot swallow her food. She chokes and lets it dribble from her mouth. Bit remembers a story, somewhere, of a woman bricked into a wall. This is his mother, interred alive.

Ellis kneels at Hannah's side. She isn't sleeping, either: she is pale, her face drawn in the sun. Bit hears among the murmurs, *starvation . . . feeding tube.*

No, the computer voice says cheerily. I am glad to have had these months. It was right. But I am almost done. Let me starve.

Ellis lays her brown cheek on Hannah's hand. You're right. It's a gentler way to go, Hannah, she murmurs. We'll give you opioids and keep you comfortable. As long as you're still happy with this decision.

Hannah's eyes dart at Bit. The computer sings out, I am happy, now, to go.

The women tighten, a knot, around Bit's small family. Luisa and Grete, always; Glory every afternoon. This morning, thumbing their noses at the quarantine, Cheryl and Diana, the Library Ladies. Grete is gone for hours on her runs. When Ellis arrived the night before, she held her soft cheek on his, and he could feel the pulse of her, the promise. Such terrible timing, to find what he had been hoping for, now. She had put her things in his closet, and slipped into his sheets, her body cool as a salve. When he rose to get a glass of water, he'd heard Grete in her room whispering into Otto's patient ruff.

Before lunch, Astrid, alerted by Grete, sweeps in. Bit doesn't see her at first, but he feels the house fill with her cold blue flame. Then she is cupping his cheeks in her callused hands. She kisses him on the forehead, and he wears the kiss for the rest of the day like a badge.

Cooking, tending, cleaning: omnipresent like flies, the hands of women.

When it is overmuch, he goes to the Pond and submerges himself in the too-warm water. The weeds grab and slide against him. A hawk watches him from a branch, a blue jay in its talons. When Bit proves innocuous, the hawk bends its head to the bird and down confettis onto the surface of the water. Small blue feathers stick to Bit's skin when he climbs out.

On his walk back, he sees a man sitting on Scott and Lisa's porch. Even from a distance, Bit can see the man is Amish: full-clothed in the heat, suspenders black against a white shirt. Bit approaches warily. The man stands and nods, and his beard wags. He's fair-haired with rosy cheeks and shoulders so square they could be hewn from oak. Bit had seen him on Glory's arm at Abe's service; her husband. When Bit nears, the man's eyes begin to twinkle. He makes a little pinching motion with his fingers and brings it to his lips. If Bit didn't know better, he would say that it was the universal sign of a toke.

I'm sorry? he says.

Amos, the man says, pointing at his chest. He makes the sign again, then a motion that could only mean waterfall. And it returns to Bit like a slap, the day at the end of Arcadia, Ike and Cole and he in the waterfall, the two Amish boys stepping out of the twilit woods, the crouching around the campfire, the joint. This must be one of those boys.

Bit gapes in astonishment. The man looks around and winks. Then he makes the toke sign again. One minute, Bit says. He walks through the back door and rummages in Abe's office until he finds the tennis ball he knows would be there.

When he comes out again, the man is looking squirrelly, but he beams when Bit presses on the side of the ball and the invisible cut in it mouths open and a little bag of weed falls out. Bit rolls one, and they smoke. It feels so good to stand with another man in compassionate silence. Amos goes heavy-lidded and says, Glory. They walk back together toward the Green house. When Glory comes out, tucking her loose hair under her bonnet, Bit and Amos are petting the horse, chuckling at nothing.

She sniffs and frowns at Bit with her bunched-berry features. She says, What have you done with my husband?

Bit only says, thoughtfully, I would like to eat the world; and his new friend Amos chuckles alongside him.

In the dusk, Grete arrives home, scratched and sunburnt, her arms speckled with bites. The house is packed. Ellis is giving Hannah a manicure; she grins up at Bit, and he blows her a kiss from the door. Grete leans toward Bit and mutters, Why are there old ladies all over the place?

He puts another biscuit in his mouth to keep from answering.

Hannah hears Grete, though, and the computer voice rises sweetly, saying: It's an infestation.

Wasting Hannah, faster and faster. Her belly, distended. Her face shrinking to settle among its bones, her flesh mottled. Bit tries to not shudder upon seeing her. Grete can't be in the room without closing her eyes to her grandmother.

So strange, however: with her body leaving, her soul is rising to the surface. There is fire there, he sees. An ecstasy. He hurts with recognition: where has he seen this before? The answer comes to him in the night. In his knowledge-drunk youth in the college library, the lonely section of art books, the giving spread of them, the lustful dizzied colors. The faces of the saints. Girls: Catherine of Siena, Saint Veronica, Columba of Rieti. *Anorexia mirabilis,* the body emptying of corporeal want and filling with the wine of God.

Bit buries his face among his father's

sweaters, yearning for Abe to emerge, to make it all better, to take over.

He comes out of the closet. Luisa moves about in the kitchen. Hannah's room is black and he and Hannah are there alone. Through the thick air, the smooth voice says softly, Don't be afraid, Bit. I'm not afraid.

He fills an entire roll watching the afternoon light slant across his mother's wasted face, watching her hands curled like snails on the dough of her belly.

He will develop these later in the pitch-black silence of a color darkroom; in the light, he will hold his mother in his hands again, fractured and grainy, her ruined body perfected by the ruined film.

Astrid sits behind Hannah, smoothing her hair. They used to be sisterly; now, the gulf is vast. Astrid flesh, Hannah bone. They remove the ventilator. Hannah's eyelids are the purple of a bruise. She doesn't wake. Her body is clenching back to its original form. She is a wisp, she would be gone in a slight wind.

Insomniac, he comes into the living room and finds Ellis in the recliner. She wakes to him watching her. She begins to say something, but he puts his hand over her mouth and holds it there, feeling the warm movement of her lips, her big teeth, her breath. She stands, and makes him dizzy with her perfume. He leads her out, into the night, over the ground that cracks with branches. The door of Midge's house, dug into the hillside, opens under his palm. A fury fills him, and he leads her into the farthest bedroom, the windowless one, the pure blankness of earth there. He presses her against the cold concrete wall; she gasps; he pulls her skirt roughly over her hips and finds the welcome of her. They slip to a low bed. The darkness in him comes alive, angry. When he is done, he lifts himself so he is light on her bones and her shallow breath can deepen. He feels the clammy sheets on his legs, her mouth sliding gently on his wet cheeks, the fist clenched in his chest loosening.

Despite the shame, it is good, this thing; in a world gone to shit, this between people should be preserved.

I'm sorry, he says.

Don't, she says. I'm not.

I'm an ass, he says. Her hands on his neck, shoulders, back. His ear is against the concrete. Ellis says, kindly, It's all right.

He says nothing, and she says at last, Listen. I love Hannah. But you know I'm not here right now because of her. Her eyelashes are damp on his cheekbone. It had to happen sometime.

He groans. I'll make it up to you, he says. His lips on the delicate, bitter folds of her ear. Her smile tightening along his jawbone. You will, she murmurs, her voice somewhere inside his skull.

It is the quiet hour. He can hear the tinkle of a wind chime forgotten up at Arcadia House.

Astrid looks at the clock. Luisa will be here soon, she says.

Bit holds his mother's frond of a hand.

Astrid moves to the table where the morphine sits. I'm giving her a large dose, she says. Enough to knock her out. She bends over Hannah, a willow.

She finishes and puts a palm on Bit's cheek. I'm not going to write this down, she says. The silence swells between them. You have to say you understand, she says.

I understand, he says. The words come from far away, years ago, the sun.

Astrid leaves. Luisa comes in. She flips through the log in the light of the pallid moon. Hm. Unlike Astrid to forget morphine, she says, but she is careful not to look at Bit.

He says nothing. He watches Luisa prepare the drug, find the catheter. He watches the slow slide in.

It doesn't take long. Asleep, Hannah folds further into herself.

There is a lightening, as if a weight has been removed from her chest.

And his mother is gone.

It is hot and windless and bright; the last flare of sunset, Hannah's time of day.

Many said their goodbyes to Hannah at Abe's services. This gathering is smaller. The stalwarts are here, the women. The Amish are here, mixed in. Ellis holds Bit's hand. Grete is pale and composed in the green dress Hannah had made her promise to wear. It brings out your eyes, Hannah had said. It makes Grete look like Hannah.

Astrid stands in the Pond, and the water draws slow dark swoops up the fabric of her white dress. She bends to a leaf, where she places a lit candle and pushes it off. The candle moves toward the center of the Pond in a length of ripples, then stops. Astrid sings, her voice cracked. *Swift to its close ebbs out life's little day; earth's joys grow dim; its glories pass away; change and decay in all around I see; O thou who changes not, abide with me.*

There is no wind. Grete wades out alone, tipping the basket. When Hannah's remains go into the Pond, they fall straight down. When the heavy pieces of her break the surface, the water heals itself. The rest of the ashes are lighter and float; they bloom in a slow flush across the surface.

Back inside the empty house, the black dog arrives. Bit opens his arms to it, tooth and claw. Outside, there are voices, people drinking juice and eating cake in the Sugarbush.

One week, Bit tells Grete. Give me one week. Then come get me.

Grete holds her sharp elbows and nods. She watches him go into his room.

All is still here, the walls full of comforting dimness. The bed is like two cupped hands, welcoming him in.

There is a landscape inside his head. Delicate hills, threading rivers of blood.

Unpeopled, this place would be nothing. Bit's people come at will. Abe, striding along, his toolbelt jingling. Grete, a fleet flash in the woods. Verda gathering from the shadows at the edge of the trees, the white dog her dapple. Titus, who reaches for Bit and swings him into the sky. Hannah, her hand stretching toward something, young, golden, round.

Everything he needs is here.

If he cannot be infinite — his love meeting its eventual exhaustion, his light its shadow — this is the nature of landscapes. The forest meets mountain, the sea the shore. Brain meets bone, meets skin, meets hair; meets air. Day would not be, without night.

Every limit, a wise woman once wrote, is a beginning as well as an ending.

Grete climbs behind him, holding him with her thin length. But she is made of flight and burrow, Helle and Hannah both, and leaves him to run when twilight falls.

Luisa comes in and, weeping, kisses him goodbye.

Jincy comes in, bringing the twins. They sleep against him, and Jincy sleeps in the chair, her face lined in the moonlight, mouth open, black as a cave.

Dylan comes in; Cole comes in; Bit's department chair comes in.

Ellis comes in, the hardcover book splayed in her hands like a bird poised for flight. She stays and stays. She whispers in his ear.

The night comes in, Grete comes in, Astrid comes in.

Glory comes in with muffins, saying

something over him in her guttural language, a prayer, perhaps.

In the window, the moon comes in.

On her e-reader, Grete holds Yoko, who was at last allowed to go home to Japan; the girl plays her violin but so poorly Grete snorts and turns her off.

Astrid comes in with avocados and mushroom soup.

Ellis comes in, puts his head on her lap, brushes his temples with her cool hands, murmurs.

Grete comes in; Grete comes in; Grete comes in. With a new song and a sun-warmed tomato, with applesauce and ice water, with a scrimshaw, brittle and yellow, Hannah's face endlessly carved in the bone. Grete, like water, like the world, will always let herself in.

The first thing is the tea. The stun of rosehip lets the ghosts enter, the cookies flavored with anise, the sighing cushion of the white dog, the close smoky cottage of his own story.

Next, the stars brief in a window between the maple branches. From under a rocking chair, a mouse. It prays into its pink hands, watching Bit, it smoothes its fat haunches like a housewife in a new dress. Bit laughs and the noise scares them both, and the mouse skitters off. Bit is lonely when it is gone.

Soon the page of a book can stay cohesive in the eyes; one sentence can lead to the next. He can crack a paragraph and eat it. Now a story. Now a novel, one full life enclosed in covers.

They are in the room when he wakes again.

It's been a week, Dad, Grete says, her voice tight with urgency.

Time to get up, says Ellis from the chair. She is rumpled; Otto sleeps under her feet.

Astrid, in the doorway, her own column of light.

Dad, says Grete. Please.

It is an effort like digging himself out from a mound of dirt. But he sits.

It is a cool morning. The spring has ended, Bit sees. Grete leaves her e-reader out for him to use, and he finds that the disease has tiptoed backward. Quarantine is over: three quarters of a million dead, only thirty thousand in the United States. Most deaths have been contained in a few areas, the city mostly. The president praises technology, the ability to track the disease and make decisions; he comes onto the e-reader, blue thumbprints under his eyes, and says, Without technology, the pandemic would have been a disaster of proportions never before seen on this planet. We must be grateful. Bit is.

Grete is rosy with health and tan from the sun. Home, she says, a flash of yearning in her face. He sees how the brownstone they bought ten years ago is to Grete what Arcadia is to him. Soon, they will leave the furniture where it sits in the Green house, the clothes neat in their closets. They will seal the windows against drafts and close the curtains. They will secure doors that have locks as afterthoughts: Titus's, Midge's, Scott and Lisa's, the Green house, quieted of its solar clicks. They will load the car. Ellis is coming for a week to help them resettle. There is little of Helle's in the brownstone: a chair, the same kitchen table, the same bed. He imagines thin brown Ellis filling those places, and is surprised to feel no pain.

He will miss this quiet full of noise: the nighthawks, the way the woods breathe, the things moving unsuspected through the dark. But he will take with him the canisters full of blasted images and have the pleasure of living them again. They are not nothing, the memories.

■ ■ ■ ■

The night before they go, he stays awake, watching the subtle seep and draw of the moon. In the dark, he scans Abe and Hannah's bookshelves until he finds what he's been looking for. The book is smaller than he remembered, the edges flaking like pastry dough under his fingers. But the color plates surprise him: they are so startling, so excessively beautiful. He hadn't remembered such beauty.

For hours in the sleeping house, he reads the old stories until they blend together. Then he puts down the book. When he turns out the light, the moon seizes its brightness again in the window. The stories themselves aren't what moves him now. They are sturdy wooden boxes, their worth less in what they are than in what they can be made to hold. What moves him are the shadowy people behind the stories, the workers weary from their days, gathering at night in front of a comforting bit of fire, the milk churned, the chickens sleeping, the babies lulled by rocking, the listeners' own bones allowed to rest, at last, in their chairs. The world then was no less terrifying than it is now, with our nightmares of bombs and disease and technological warfare. Anything held the ability to set off fear: a nail dropped in the hay, wolves circling at the edge of the woods, the newest baby in the tired womb. His heart, in the night-struck house of his parents, responds to those once-upon-a-time people, anonymous in the shadows, the faith it took them to come together and rest and listen through the gruesomeness, their patience for the ever after, happy or not.

Bit moves through the house, turning out the lights that Grete thoughtlessly left burning. And like that he lets the darkness in to take its place, where it belongs.

The early June woods simmer. When Bit and Grete lace up their boots, Ellis starts to put hers on, too, but something in Bit's face makes her sit back down on the porch steps with a book instead. Take Otto, she says. He'll dream of this walk when he's a city dog. Bit stays to look at the way the sun off the page shines on her face. I'll be here when you get back, she laughs into her book. Don't worry. In gratitude, he doubles back to kiss her on the soft part in her hair. By midmorning the birds grow heavy and watch the world with their beaks cracked, panting from the coolest clefts of the branches. Under such cheery light it is impossible to see the forest as he had so long ago when he was a lost child, grasping and bitter and ready to gobble him, the twigs turned fingernails, the roots sinuously rising from the ground to pull him in.

Grete tells him long, fantastical tales of the kids at the school. She had finished the year with a kind of shuddery relief: now she turns others grotesque to strip them of their terror. The girls are blades in female form; the boys lurch through the halls as rustic as bears. The teachers are gobbling amoebas, greedy for what they can't understand. Otto races back, his underbelly caked with mud, and squeezes his body between their legs, and races off again.

They come to the place Bit has avoided all these years and climb a storm-felled oak to find the path. Here is the island of trees between two snakes that once were knee-deep streams. Here is the house. The old walls are still standing. The roof has fallen in: a tree grows from the heart of Verda's cottage as if it were a vast stone planter. One window is breathtakingly intact. The cherries by the doorstep have spawned an orchard, and last year's pits gravel the ground. When Bit pushes open the door, it swings easily, true in its frame. Inside, the house is forest. The floor is dirt and skittering leaves; the beams have returned to mossy logs. They sit and unpack their lunch, the dog panting at their feet, and he tells his daughter of Verda.

Hm, is all she says.

He watches her, amazed. I'm not lying, he says.

I didn't say you were, she says. Just, how fantastic it seems. I mean, she was precisely the opposite of everything you were. A witch, magical. Old, self-sufficient, with a pet. You were tiny, overwhelmed with community, longing for a woman to take you in. It's interesting. She shrugs.

You think Verda was an imaginary friend, Bit says, laughing with dismay.

This place looks like it's been abandoned for centuries, Dad. But whatever. It doesn't matter. You found what you needed when you needed it, she says, and squeezes his knee.

She has more of a shell than he ever will. Already, she watches life from a good distance. This is a gift he has given her.

Peace, he knows, can be shattered in a million variations: great visions of the end, a rain of ash, a disease on the wind, a blast in the distance, the sun dying like a kerosene lamp clicked off. And in smaller ways: an overheard remark, his daughter's sour mood, his own body faltering. There's no use in anticipating the mode. He will wait for the hushed spaces in life, for Ellis's snore in the dark, for Grete's stealth kiss, for the warm light inside the gallery, his images on the wall broken beyond beauty into blisters and fragments, returning in the eye to beauty again. The voices of women at night on the street, laughing; he has always loved the voices of women. Pay attention, he thinks. Not to the grand gesture, but to the passing breath.

He sits. He lets the afternoon sink in. The sweetness of the soil rises to him. A squirrel scolds from high in a tree. The city is still far away, full of good people going home. In this moment that blooms and fades as it passes, he is enough, and all is well in the world.

ACKNOWLEDGMENTS

My gratitude goes to everyone who gave me shelter during the long development of *Arcadia:* to all at Hyperion, especially Barbara Jones, Elisabeth Dyssegaard, Claire McKean, and Ellen Archer; to Jason Arthur at William Heinemann and Stephanie Sweeney at Windmill in the UK; and to Mathilde Bach and Carine Chichereau at Editions Plon in France. To my dashing agent, Bill Clegg, for his honesty, patience, and kindness, and to his assistant, Shaun Dolan. To Erika Rix, who gave me her hours. To those who provided physical space for writing: the Groffs, the Kallmans, the Drummonds, the Peddies, the Herndons, the McKune-Parrishes, and Hannah Judy Gretz and Ragdale for the lovely fellowship. To the Bread Loaf Writers' Conference and the MFA program in creative writing at Queens University–Charlotte. To my readers: Sarah Groff, Steph Bedford, Kevin A. González,

Jaime Muehl, Ashley Warlick, James Willett, and Lucy Schaeffer. To my family, friends, and the authors of the many beloved books that made this novel richer: you are too numerous to list, but I thank you.

Above all, I am grateful for my household of boys: Clay, my bedrock, and my two sons. This book is for Beck, who taught me how great-hearted little boys can be.

The employees of Thorndike Press hope you have enjoyed this Large Print book. All our Thorndike, Wheeler, and Kennebec Large Print titles are designed for easy reading, and all our books are made to last. Other Thorndike Press Large Print books are available at your library, through selected bookstores, or directly from us.

For information about titles, please call:
(800) 223-1244

or visit our Web site at:
http://gale.cengage.com/thorndike

To share your comments, please write:
Publisher
Thorndike Press
10 Water St., Suite 310
Waterville, ME 04901